GLIMPSE

a novel by Lauren Somerton

 **FriesenPress**

Suite 300 - 990 Fort St
Victoria, BC, Canada, V8V 3K2
www.friesenpress.com

Copyright © 2014 by Lauren Somerton
First Edition — 2014

ISBN
978-1-4602-5426-4 (Hardcover)
978-1-4602-5427-1 (Paperback)
978-1-4602-5428-8 (eBook)

1. *Fiction, Science Fiction, General*

Distributed to the trade by The Ingram Book Company

For my mother,
Charmaine

Without your continued support and guidance
this book would never be.

June 15th

Emily closed her eyes, pinched the bridge of her nose, and took a deep breath. "These ones? You're absolutely sure?"

"Yes, of course, they look great on you. Plus, they match your dress perfectly," Amy replied.

Amy, Emily's younger sister, was getting married to Rick the next day, and the only thing she had left to do was to make sure her big sister looked perfect. Emily exhaled sharply, opened her eyes, and stared down at the most overpriced, uncomfortable shoes she had ever worn; the only pair that her sister approved of.

It was eight o'clock in Sierra Vista, Arizona, and it was hot; alarmingly hot. The shop was closing and Emily just decided to give in and get it over with. One day in those shoes couldn't hurt too much, if it made Amy happy. Especially when Amy kept mentioning how perfect the photos were going to be. Decided, Emily practically scraped the tight shoes off of her feet and threw them into the box as Amy had a quick look around the store. Now comfortable in her flip-flops, Emily grabbed the shoe box and walked to the counter, lightly placing the box down. The girl behind the counter seemed to come out of nowhere, and looked no older than fifteen. "And how will you be paying?" she asked, while placing the shoebox in an oversized bag.

"Visa." Emily gave a quick response, trying not to look at the total, as she signed her receipt.

Just as the girl passed over the plastic bag, Amy was by Emily's side. "All ready to go?" she asked, overly smug with the completion of her final task.

"Yes, please! I'm starving," Emily said with exaggeration, motioning for the door.

"God, you are so old sometimes." Amy rolled her eyes, laughing under her breath.

"Hey, I may be six years older than you, but twenty-seven isn't old. You know, I just hate shopping."

"To my great disappointment; yes, I know."

Amy planned on spending the night with Emily, getting ready at the house, while Emily's husband Mark stopped with Rick to do the same. Mark was honored to be one of Patrick's groomsmen, even though they were not the closest of friends. He knew it was more Amy's doing, but was still thankful.

* * *

Emily had met her husband on her first formal day at the Kindred Hospital of Tucson, Arizona. She had just finished her practicum and was ready to dive into the hectic world of a Unit Clerk, within the epilepsy clinic. That day, Mark had a lunch meeting with one of the other resident surgeons. Stopping by, he could tell Emily was slightly frazzled by the sudden intake of charts and requisitions. The phone would not stop, as she moved around her small desk.

Completely consumed by the task at hand, Emily walked into Mark, as he patiently waited at the opposite side of her desk. The sudden impact caused a number of loose pages to go awry, much to the dismay of her supervising manager, who had just returned from her own lunch break. Mark took pity on Emily, bending down and scooping up the near pages.

"I'm so sorry," Emily muttered, still not pulling her gaze from the pages on the ground.

As their hands reached for the same final page, a brush of electricity sparked as their skin touched. With a gasp, Emily's eyes locked with Mark's. It wasn't long before he would frequent her office in one circumstance or another. Every time he appeared, he loved to watch the cool, pink blush creep across her cheeks, as she grew flustered and tried to look away.

After a few weeks, Mark eventually couldn't stand another minute without seeing her. He spent one entire morning preoccupied with how he would approach her and finally ask her out. For all he knew, she wasn't even single, but he had noted the lack of a wedding band on her ring finger. Mustering what courage he could, Mark marched to her desk, an extra coffee in hand. After waiting patiently for her to end her current phone call, he practically thrust the coffee into her surprised hand.

"Have dinner with me?" His question was barely audible.

A wide smile spread across her features as she slowly stood, not breaking his gaze. "I'd love to."

Her blush returned, as he let out a sigh of relief. The rest was history.

* * *

Seven a.m. and the alarm buzzed offensively. Amy, who was accustomed to sleeping in the same bed as her sister on the nights she stayed over, just rolled over and covered her head with the soft pillow. After five loud beeps, Emily reached over and playfully squashed her sister while hitting the snooze button and turning off the alarm. Rolling back onto her side, she yanked the pillow out of the way, and began humming the wedding march at the top of her lungs. Amy just rolled over, eyes still closed, and smiled a bright smile.

"Okay, time to get up and get going. You're getting married in eight hours!" Emily practically yelled into her sister's covered ears. "Get up!"

"Oh my gosh, only eight hours left!" Amy laid on the sarcasm, slowly exaggerating each word.

Emily picked up her own pillow, smacking Amy upside the head.

"Okay, okay, I'm up. I'm up!" Amy practically rolled off the bed and into the bathroom.

* * *

Everyone was dancing, pounding on the giant dance floor; Amy was noticeably intoxicated, loving every minute. The sound of the base speaker closest to Emily was so loud that she had to cover her ears and head to the back. Mark stayed close to Emily every chance he could. The crowd was not his type of people; they were younger and too over the top for his taste. Rick and Amy once again stole the spotlight. The lighting bounced off her stunning, diamond-beaded gown in every direction, forcing an array of rainbow colors that just added to her elegance.

Although the music did not suit such a dance, Mark and Emily enjoyed the hectic day coming to an end with a close, slow dance. She rested her head on her husband's shoulder, closed her eyes, and smiled. All she could feel in that moment were Mark's soft lips pressing into her crown; swaying softly, blissfully in the moment. Before there was a chance for the couple to finish their private moment, the music volume lowered and everyone stopped dead in their tracks. Emily stepped back from Mark, only for him to put his arm around her shoulder, and steer her in the direction of the stage.

The newlyweds were center stage, their faces flushed with excitement. "It must be time," Emily whispered, looking down at her watch. It was ten p.m., the scheduled time for the bride and groom to give their thanks, and encourage people to stay and enjoy the party, while both headed upstairs to change into their honeymoon attire. Amy, with the assistance of Emily and her bestie, Julia, had only a short while to get out of her extravagant dress. At eleven p.m., they would need to leave for the airport. Rick looked dashing; his finely pressed suit accentuated the soft copper in his hair. His tie was now discarded, leaving the top three buttons of his shirt open, with a sprinkling of chest hair poking out. He towered over his new bride, even in her heels.

While Rick babbled on about how it was the best day of his life and further confessing his love for Amy, Emily turned to Mark. "I shouldn't be too long, probably twenty minutes. Stay and enjoy yourself. I will be right back, and then we can go home," she encouraged him, as she started to back away, turning.

At that moment, Mark grabbed her wrist, spinning her back around to face him. She looked up, stunned and confused by his reaction. Her concern ebbed as he proceeded to cup her heart-shaped face, and slowly sealed his lips over hers. Gently, his tongue brushed against hers, deepening the kiss. He playfully bit into her lower lip, tugging, as his hands pushed back into her hair, his grip growing almost painful. His intensions became obvious as his hand dropped to the small of her back, tugging her closer and into his hardness, making her knees weak. She grinned, thankful that the lighting didn't betray the growing heat of her cheeks.

His eyes heavy-lidded, drunk with lust, Mark pulled back to rest their foreheads together. Waiting for her to open her eyes before speaking, he whispered, "I love you," between soft kisses. "And I can't wait to tear you out of that dress."

She gasped at his blatant authority. His wink did nothing to discourage the twinge of excitement racing through her core. Suddenly warm and flustered, all she could do was nod and smile back. "I'll be quick."

She spun on her heels and headed towards the exit, where Amy and Julia were standing, staring, all wide-eyed and noticeably jealous of such affection. Emily grinned at their reaction and took one quick glance over her shoulder to her statuesque husband. His smile widened at her gaze, his hands gesturing for her to go ahead. She quickened her pace, following the girls to the waiting hotel room.

∗ ∗ ∗

"One more picture," Julia demanded. "You look absolutely stunning!"

Amy stood still and smiled for the hundredth picture of the day. It had been such a long day, and Emily knew her baby sister was running on low. They stole a quick smile before Amy announced, "Okay, enough, get me out of this thing!"

"Hey, now!" Julia chastised her, in a sarcastic, yet amused tone.

"I'm sorry, Julia, but was your goal to sweat me to death?"

"Yeah, yeah. You're lucky I didn't go with your first idea. You would have been rolling on the floor trying to crawl out of that thing."

"It wasn't that bad, it reminded me of your prom dress. Remember? I always loved that dress; took us months to find it. It was beautiful and I seem to remember we still partied hard and you were able to hold your own."

Julia just rolled her eyes.

More than happy to oblige, Emily, who had been there two years ago, almost suffocating in her all-silk, embroidered dress, tugged on the last button of thirty, enabling Amy to momentarily lose thirty pounds in excess fabric. Helping, Amy pulled off her half-length sleeves and slowly backed up, dropping the dress into Julia's waiting arms.

Standing straight, fanning her face twice, taking a deep breath, and smiling, she said, "Now, for the next one."

This dress was a lovely, deep emerald, bringing out the color of Amy's eyes. It flowed as a simple, three-quarter length, silk piece, fitting around the bust, and hanging loose around the hips and thighs. Amy slipped out of her white flats into a sleek pair of black, strappy heels, as Julia tightened the straps, and Emily took the jeweled pins out of her sister's hair, to let Amy's semi-curled blond locks fall over her shoulders, in soft billows.

Jumping up, Julia almost hit her head on the floating shelf behind her. "All right, I think you're ready, your bags are in the car; Mark is just bringing that around." She paused, smiling through new tears. "You look amazing. I'm going to miss you!"

Amy rolled her eyes, but stepped into her friend's warm embrace. "I'm only going for two weeks; you can survive that. Plus, somebody needs to stay behind and clean up!" Both Emily and Julia remained deadpan, until Emily poked Amy in the nearest rib, and then all three burst into immediate laughter.

Three knocks to the door pulled the trio apart.

The door was already propped open; all three heads turned to the intrusion. Anne, Emily's close friend, stood in the doorway, smiling brightly, "Everything's ready. Mark has the car out front and Rick is already waiting downstairs."

"Thanks Anne," Emily praised her. "We'll be right behind you."

Anne smiled again, curtly nodded, and backed away, calling back through the open door, "Julia, you coming?" Julia looked surprised at the request, but then realized why, when she took in the faces of the two sisters. She followed Anne out the door to give them some privacy.

Once alone, Amy propped herself carefully on the end of the unused bed, and patted the area next to her. Emily already had tears in her eyes; tears of joy, of course. The minute her rear hit the sheets, Amy threw her arms around her big sister. "I wish they were here," she whispered into the crook of Emily's neck.

There was no need for explanation. "I wish they were here too." She kissed her sister's temple. "Mom would have loved your dress, and Dad would have laughed until he cried, at James' speech."

Amy pulled back, wiping the back of her hand along the bottom of her nose; a small sniffle was chased by a giggle. "Oh, I can imagine." They sat and smiled at each other for a short while before Amy continued, "Em, you know I love you so much. I'm so glad you're here to share it with me." Fresh tears fell onto her rosy cheeks.

Emily tried to pull herself together. "Of course I'm here. I wouldn't miss this day for the world." She laughed and brushed her thumb under Amy's left eye. "Now, stop crying or you'll ruin your makeup." They both laughed and wiped each other's tears. She playfully smacked her sister's knee. "Are you ready, Mrs. Michaels?"

Amy laughed aloud at her new title. "That's going to take a while to get used to. Come on, let's go!" They stood up and held each other's hand, making their way to the door.

CHAPTER ONE

As they made their way along the narrow corridor, smiling and glancing at each other, there was a loud bang followed by two more. "What was that?" Amy cried, covering her ears and looking back and forth down each end of the hallway. The lights began to flicker, went out completely, and then flickered on again, gradually getting brighter and brighter.

Emily cried out, shading her eyes from the intense brightness, "I don't know, let's just get downstairs." A few light bulbs burst over their heads. "NOW!"

A loud droning noise began to fill the hotel, followed by more banging, then nail-biting screeches. Emily tried to rationalize the mania, but there was no explanation; the noises made no sense. They were coming from what appeared to be the hotel rooms along the corridor, but the entire floor had been booked out for the wedding, and no one was currently in the rooms. Scared, Amy began to run for the elevator, pressing the down button repeatedly.

"No, not the elevator!" Emily yelled, above the noise. "We don't want to risk it breaking down, let's head down the stairs!" They both spun around and began to run to the other end of the hall, where the emergency staircase was hidden around the corner.

Emily got to the door first, yelling to her sister to hurry up. She held the door open wide, intending to let Amy go first, and then run down behind her. Amy passed, frantic fear filling her wide eyes, as a thick vibration filled the air. In desperation, Emily turned her body to follow; her feet moving of their own volition. Just as she did, out of the corner of her eye, she saw a closet door blow straight off its hinges and smack into the door across from it; forcing that one to buckle and split into two. Emily froze, her head spinning in that direction; eyes wide and mouth open.

Then another, even louder noise came from that very room. It was so loud that Emily screamed and covered her ears, desperately willing her eyes to squeeze shut. A white light consumed that empty doorway; an unnatural light. almost glowing, hitting the opposite wall, and covering the entire hallway. Whatever it was, it was getting closer to the doorframe and seemed intent on coming out. Strangely enough, at this moment, Emily began to feel calmer, almost as if the light was soothing her. Without thinking, she felt her body begin to straighten up, so it was now in line with the hallway. Her near foot lifted to take its first step towards the intriguing light. Almost as in a daydream, Emily no longer had control of her body or thoughts; she felt no stress or worry and was completely at ease, as she began to smile and back away from the open exit doorway.

After she took two steps forward there was a cry behind her. Sluggishly, Emily spun around to see her sister, gripping one white-knuckled hand on the doorframe and stretching out the other towards her. Amy's mouth was moving; her faced distressed, but Emily could not understand anything. No sound pierced her ears; her only desire was to turn back to the beckoning essence, and she stared, unmoving, at her tearful sister. It was as if everything was in slow motion – fascinating to witness. More and more, Emily tried to focus on her sister, attempting to understand what she was trying to say. Sound began to rush into her ears, like the aftershock of an explosion. There was sound but nothing made sense. Distant noises were meshed together, but nothing was coherent.

The overwhelming onslaught on her senses became nauseating and confusing. Emily shook her head from side to side and really began to focus. She could now hear every word her sister was so frantically trying to say. "What are you doing? Emily, get over here! Come on. Hurry up. Emily... EMILY!!" At that moment everything was clear. Emily ran towards her sister, who then turned and ran back down the stairs. She took one last glance over her shoulder, then followed Amy down the first of nine flights of stairs.

*   *   *

Next to the exit door on the fifth floor, Emily's hand-held clutch began to buzz. In a panic, she yanked it open and found her cell phone; the caller ID displayed, "Mark."

"Em, Emily are you there?"

"Mark, oh thank God, what's going on? We're just heading down the emergency exit. We just passed the fifth floor," she forced out, breathless.

"Stay where you are!" he yelled.

Emily automatically grabbed her sister's passing arm and pulled her to a stop.

Amy mouthed, "What?"

Mark continued, "There are these things, I don't know what they are...Stay where you are, I'm coming to find you. I'm with Rick and some others."

"Mark, I don't understand what's go..." The line went dead.

Amy began to panic, looking back and forth from her silent frozen sister, to the remaining stairs leading them to freedom. "Emily, what is going on? Why have we stopped? Let's go. Let's get out of here!"

"Stay where you are!" Emily replied, pulling harder on her sister's arm, her fingernails digging into soft flesh. "Mark and Rick are on their way. They will explain everything when they get here!" She saw the disbelief in her sister's eyes. "Please, just trust me. We stay here; they're coming. They're coming, it's all right, just sit down!" After a disapproving stare, Amy obeyed and they both sat at the top of the stairs.

Roughly five minutes passed and Emily began to feel panicked. Something was wrong; something just wasn't right. As if to answer her silent prayer, the third-floor door burst open, light covering everything. People were screaming and crying, and footsteps ran in all directions. Both Emily and Amy jumped to their feet, and leaned over the railing, attempting to get a glimpse of what was happening down below.

"EMILY!!" She recognized Marks voice instantly.

"MARK! What's...." she yelled, and then stopped, seeing a rush of movement below.

"RUN!" With Mark's voice, they also heard Rick's directing others. "Run, Em, get upstairs. Get up to the roof!" The voices were getting closer and closer, footsteps banging on the steps below. "Move... MOVE!" Emily and Amy looked at each other, then began ascending, two steps at a time. After a short time Mark, Rick, and three others were within sight.

"Keep going, keep going. I'm here, I'm right behind you!" Mark could see the shaking fear vibrate throughout his wife's stiff back. Just as he finished his words of encouragement, another loud bang came from the first floor. The door sounded as if it had just blown off its hinges. This was followed by the same strange light, but this time, there was also a loud noise accompanying it; constant, like two or three people yelling but saying nothing intelligible. The footsteps got louder below; this time in perfect sync with one another.

Almost to the top floor, three people; a man and two women, pushed their way into the open stair entrance and ran to the other end of the hall. Emily stopped for a second, wondering if they should follow. Mark just ran up behind her, spun her around, and yelled, "Forget them. Just get to the roof. Come on!" He grabbed Emily's hand and practically dragged her up the remaining flight of stairs.

Amy tripped on the fifth step from the top; her strappy heel had got caught in the grating, twisting her ankle with the forward momentum. She cried out loudly, clearly in pain as she fell to the ground. Emily stopped next to her sister, pulling her heel out of the grating below, and lifting Amy's arm around her shoulders, as she helped her up the remaining steps. Rick was holding the exit door open, slamming it behind the girls as they made their way through.

Still not knowing what was going on, Emily watched straight ahead, as Mark ran to the other side of the rooftop, held onto the railings of the fire escape ladder, and looked over the edge. It was silent for a moment, as Mark's head swiveled side-to-side, observing down below. Then out of nowhere, he threw his head back, looked to the sky, and cussed at the top of his lungs.

Before anyone could comment, Rick took Amy's arm off of Emily and supported her himself. "What? What is it?" he shouted.

"We're surrounded," Mark announced not looking back. "The escape ladder is broken off three floors down!"

Rick closed his eyes and exhaled sharply. "Fuck, what do we do?"

Not only was Emily confused, she felt a dull ache in her chest. Every pore of her body wanted the intoxicating pull of the light. Her right leg inched back towards the door. Focused frustration caused her to force it back into place. She became overcome with anger and unease. "Mark! What the fuck's going on?" She forced herself to step forward. Motion helped with the unexplainable pull. "Tell us what's going on? What was that light? Those noises?"

Mark didn't answer. He began to run back and forth across the patio, looking from side to side. Emily couldn't understand what he was looking for. There was nothing on the roof; no patio furniture, nothing. Rick took Amy around the side of the metal entrance and leaned her against the back. He then bent down, unstrapped her shoes, and threw them in the corner of the rooftop.

Emily was beginning to become infuriated, her skin crawling with pure adrenalin. Spinning around as Mark ran right in front of her, she reached out in time to grab his arm and spin him in her direction. He was still looking away, everywhere but at her. Using her free hand, she guided his unwilling face until he had no choice but to look into her eyes. Slowly and calmly Emily said, "What is happening, Mark? Where is everyone?"

Emily knew from Mark's pained look that this was definitely something serious.

"Everyone…they've all been taken."

Her brows pulled together in confusion and her hand fell to her side. "What? What are you talking about?"

"Kidnapped!" His eyes darted around again.

"Kidnapped! By who? Mark, there were over one hundred people in this hotel."

"Not by who! By WHAT!" he exclaimed back to her.

"What?" Completely lost, she drew Mark's face back to hers, cupping it with both hands. She whispered, "Mark, you're making no sen…"

He grabbed her shoulders. "Em, I don't know who or what they are! The guests and I were all waiting downstairs for you, when there was a loud bang, the lights went out, then all the windows blew out around us." He looked straight into Emily's shocked eyes. "They just blew, Em. I was with Rick and some others. We were standing ten steps from the emergency exit, then these THINGS..." He closed his eyes and shook his head. "They're not human, Emily!! First, that light came from all directions. The hotel entrance doors blew open. We were blinded, and then people started screaming." His eyes lost their focus as he remembered. "Smoke started to fill the room, and we all started to feel dizzy, but at the same time..." He paused. "I felt calm, like everything was fine, like it wasn't real or something."

This shook Emily, reminding her of the light coming from the hotel suite on the ninth floor. Her gaze turned to look back at Amy and Rick, also listening intently; Rick more interested in Amy's reaction.

"And then what happened? How did you get out? What about all those people?"

Mark looked up once again. "The screaming got louder. I put my hand in front of my face to cover the light, when I saw the things come through the smoke." He swallowed loudly. "They were hideous; at least seven feet tall. Monstrous. Their skin was dark and burnt – they looked strong, powerful."

Before Mark could finish, the dull noise coming from inside the building began to get louder. Whatever it was, it had followed them. The noise now trembled with rapid vibration. Small rocks began to bounce around their feet. The vibration was so close, it was as if it was being blasted from the other side of the nearby door. Everyone turned to look. Mark stepped in front of Emily, blocking a large portion of her view. All four stared in the direction of the door, and for a long time there was nothing; just noise. Then the iron began to tremble; the hinges began to shake.

Mark turned, grabbing Emily by the tops of her arms as she looked up, but he was looking away. Amy's sudden squeal pulled their attention back to the door. The very same light from before began beaming into the night's sky, illuminating the door.

Mark's eyes did not stray from the door. "Go!" he directed with his chin and lightly shoved Emily.

"There's nowhere up here to hide."

"Get on the back side of the entrance!" Three bolts from the top hinge shot off and flew, cracking one of the far tiles. Everyone watched in disbelief. Then Mark began to push harder, spinning Emily back around. "MOVE!"

Rushed and panicked, she obeyed. The four wedged themselves between the back of the arched metal frame and the low wall bordering the rooftop. The heavy vibration throughout their expanding chests made them all struggle for air. There was just enough room for them to sit, bent-kneed, squashed side by side. Amy was visibly distressed and about to fall to pieces. Rick and Mark took the outside, barely covered by the door.

Emily grabbed her sister and pulled her head into her lap. "Shush, just close your eyes," she whispered, trying to sooth whilst not giving their position away. Less than two minutes later, the iron door blew off its hinges. Amy tried to scream in shock, but Emily quickly covered her mouth. Shaking uncontrollably, Mark reached around and held Emily, with Amy, covering them in a giant embrace. He closed his eyes and buried his face in his wife's hair. Emily had her eyes squeezed shut as tightly as she could, until she heard the noises as she'd heard them before, in the stairwell. Footsteps followed; at least three pairs of feet.

Amy began to squirm in her sister's arms. Emily could see she was trying to get away. All she could do was tighten her hold and look down at the non-existent space in front of her. The noises got louder; closer on Mark's side. Emily reached over and grabbed his far leg, pulling it in as tightly as she could. As she did, she could not help but stare into the small reflection displayed on the bottom of Amy's discarded heel, the bottom giving off an almost perfect mirror image. At first she just saw the reflection given off the side of the metal frame, with the patio below. It must have been around midnight by now, so the only source of light was the dim, hanging lantern in the corners of the patio and the unearthly light, now accompanied by smoke, coming from the ruined doorframe.

Still nothing. Emily could hear footsteps, but see nothing. Then a large, dark figure appeared in the corner of the reflection, making her jump lightly; it was moving slowly, attempting stealth movements. Emily could not see a face, it was far too dark; and whatever it was wearing seemed to camouflage its flesh and true appearance. Mark was right – it was at least seven-foot tall, easily three hundred pounds, but not overweight; its mass was somehow evenly distributed throughout its body. Whatever it was, it was definitely getting closer to their position. Emily drew in a swift breath. Mark looked up and saw his wife staring wide-eyed at the corner of the building, only four feet from them. Mark followed her gaze, his body becoming rigid.

Pulling closer together, Mark grabbed Emily's shock-stricken face and pulled her into his chest, then once again squeezed his eyes shut and covered his face in her thick hair. Two more steps and whatever was coming would surely be alerted to their position and do with them whatever had been done with the rest of the wedding guests. *Too close,* was all Emily could keep thinking.

Suddenly, a strange, shrieking noise like a high-pitched car alarm pierced the night's air, clearly coming from the entrance. The couples lifted their heads and stared into the sole of the shoe once more. Then a noise like the others started, mechanical in nature – like joints of a robot moving up and down with many more than two legs. The creature, which was so close to their not-so-hidden hiding spot, swiftly turned on its feet and ran back to the door, out of sight. The footsteps on the far patio seemed to pick up their place. The noise, which seemed to be speaking, became louder, though this time it appeared to be coming from one origin, like a recording or radio announcement; possibly coming from the so-called robot. The four struggled to keep their shaking bodies silent.

The machine swiftly silenced, as the creatures were obviously running back through the doorframe. The harsh vibrations from the door almost knocked the four survivors into the patio railing more than once. Minutes later there was nothing; absolutely nothing. The noises had stopped; the voices were silent. The light beaming from the open doorframe was drawing back, making the night sky seem eerily too dark. Then the light went out altogether, causing Emily to pull her family closer.

Darkness surrounded the two couples. Immediately, they looked up at one another; Mark's head peeking ever so slightly around the corner to make sure the coast was clear. Could it be that easy? Could they really be gone?

The sisters, bewildered and unsure, couldn't pull their eyes away from one another. Suddenly, what felt like an earthquake started to shake the building's foundation. The four clung onto each other, staying low to the ground. The shaking was so severe that the hanging lanterns in each corner of the patio shattered in loud bangs, one at a time, causing both women to jump with each small explosion. Then the shaking ceased.

Overwhelmed, Emily burst into tears, followed by her sister. From what appeared to be the side of their building, on the other side of the railing, so close to them, a new noise began to generate, getting louder and clearer.

With shock and an unsuccessful grab from Emily, Mark leapt up and began to peek his head over the railing. A loud whooshing sounded in the night's sky, with Mark's head pulling back. Leaning back and still holding on, he took a deep, loud breath, as if coming up for air after almost drowning. He dropped back down next to his wife. The others, still confused, looked up at Mark's expression. Immediately, some sort of vessel rose from the side of the building. It was easily three floors deep, and double the width of the hotel. A large light, surrounded by many smaller, focused right on the four, so strong it nearly blinded them. They could not see anything, not even one other.

The wind created was so strong that it forced each to press his or her back against the doorframe once more. Right as Emily lifted her hand to cover her eyes, what felt like a physical shock-wave, along with a sound much like a foghorn, blew. The light became brighter. Was that even possible? Emily began to sweat, her head swaying side to side, and gradually drooping. The last thing she remembered was the feeling of Amy's head hard-hitting her shoulder and the large amount of smoke surrounding them, coming from vents within the giant object. It was too much for their bodies to take, and each was swiftly knocked unconscious.

* * *

June 17th

A drop of cold water landed on Emily's face, so cold that it woke her instantly. She gasped for air, forcing her body to twist uncomfortably so that she could support her upper body on the cement tile below her. Her hands spread out, her forehead lightly touching the cold surface as she continued to take in large, cold, deep breaths.

Amy's head, still collapsed onto Emily's lap, began to stir. Her eyes burst open and she instantly sat up, pressing her back to the doorframe and looking around frantically. Her breathing accelerated into a full-blown hyperventilation attack, as she started to grab at Emily's shoulder. Emily's head lifted up as she twisted to stare at her sister silently. Suddenly, her instincts set in and she flew towards Amy, wrapping her arms around her and holding her head to her shoulder.

"It's okay, we're okay... Just breathe Amy, breathe!" Amy's answer was deep, more controlled breath, and it relaxed Emily's tight hold. "That's it. Deep breaths. It's okay."

Another drop of cold water hit the top of Emily's head, causing her to react instantly, and look straight up. The clouds were dark and fierce-looking; almost no sunlight broke through. As her senses came back to her, she began to feel extremely cold. She remained looking up for a long time.

Another two drops hit her shoulder and the cement below.

Amy felt the tension in her sister's neck and followed her glance, first looking at her face, then drawing her head up, so she too could look at the storm brewing above. A loud rumble of thunder made Amy tremble, causing Emily to unconsciously tighten her grip. They both stared as lightning bolts danced from one cloud to another, not appearing to touch the ground once.

Emily's head dropped instantly when she remembered that they were not alone. On either side, both of their husbands lay still unconscious on their backs. Emily's hand flew across Mark's limp body to his opposite shoulder and she shook him, lightly at first, then with more force, calling his name. Mark began to regain consciousness, his head rolling back and forth. His face pulled together into a bunch, eyes still closed until, without warning, his eyes flew open. He let out a gasp and stared into Emily's shocked expression. Remembering the night before, he frantically started to look around, scanning the immediate area.

There were four more drops of heavy rain, one ricocheting off the tin roof, framing the iron doorway, making a loud echoing noise. The unnaturally cold air around them started to pick up, as wind blew, causing their hair to stand on end.

Emily turned in Rick's general direction, where he was already beginning to wake. His eyes opened and his right arm came up to cover his face. His long, narrow fingers brushed through his dark hair, pulling it away from his forehead. Once Amy's eyes met Rick's, she practically clawed herself free from her sister's grip into his waiting arms. Emily sat straight up and took one long, deep breath to clear her head. What had happened last night?

By this time, the rain had really started to come down, heavily. This is when the lack of shelter and protection became evident. Goosebumps rising on her bare arms and legs, Emily gave one agonized look to Mark, and then directed her eyes to the side of the frame. Mark instantly understood the look on her face and gradually edged himself up, focusing on the open patio. Slowly, Emily pressed her back to the frame and shimmied her way up, staying as flat to the wall as possible. Rick and Amy glanced up at the two standing, and Emily's hand gestured at them to follow. They looked around then helped each other up. Once standing, Amy took Emily's outstretched hand, and then the three stood huddled together as Mark led them towards the open door.

All four stayed with their backs to the frame, making their way around. At the very edge, Mark looked at his wife's panicked face behind him, then quickly popped his head around the corner, looking directly down the stairs. He drew his face back, the movement not lasting more than five seconds, then again; this time more effectively.

"It's clear," Mark whispered into Emily's ear.

She looked up into his eyes. "What do you think?"

He made an indecisive face then looked up at the stormy sky above. "Well, it's hard to tell if it's really safe." He looked back down at her. "But we definitely can't stay out here and I can't hear anything."

Emily also looked up at the sky, then down at the couple behind her. Both were wide-eyed, nodding frantically with hunched shoulders, and shivering uncontrollably. Emily looked down at the ground below. The rain was becoming a torrential downpour. This is when she realized that Amy was barefoot and stepping from foot to foot, making sure that one was not on the bare ground longer than the other.

With a loud exaggerated breath, Emily abruptly looked up at Mark, squeezed his hand, and nodded her approval. He gave a humorless smile, then turned his body into the direction of the open doorframe, taking his first step.

The first few steps were quiet and guarded. Mark kept glancing down over the railing to look for any immediate danger. Everything fell silent, apart from their scared, heavy breathing. Emily looked back at her sister a few times before turning forward. Right on Mark's heels, she followed him; her eyes almost boring a hole in his back, too scared to look anywhere else. Four floors down, the exit doors were wide open and the light from the hallways appeared much weaker than before. Continuing down the staircase and finally reaching the bottom, Mark, still facing forward, pushed Emily back, and gestured that the others stay by the wall while he looked out the head-sized, circular window. Slowly, he gazed through the hole, scanning the room, then down on the ground. His eyes widened and his jaw dropped ever so slightly.

Taking a deep breath, he turned back to the others. "It looks clear. No smoke."

It was Rick who spoke next. "But?"

Mark's vision seemed to blur for a short second, then he focused on Emily as he spoke. "But...There are bodies. I can't tell if they're dead or alive." Then looking over to Amy, he said, "I recognize a few people from the wedding."

Holding tight to Amy's shoulders as big tears swelled in her eyes, and flowed down one cheek, Rick stared at Mark.

Apart from the tears, Amy surprised Emily, who felt close to her own hysterics, by appearing somewhat stable and showing little emotion.

Mark turned back to the door, placed his hand around the handle, and looked through the window once again. "The main doors are wide open." Looking back, he whispered, "We need to get out of here and figure out what's happening."

"Agreed," Emily said, taking a deep breath. "Let's just get out of this building before whatever that was last night comes back." Looking back at her sister and brother-in-law, she smiled in weak encouragement. Amy reached down and took Emily's hand.

Slowly, Mark pulled back the door, trying to make as little sound as possible. Taking a step away from the wall, Emily placed her right hand on the small of her husband's back, as he guided them forward. He dropped to one knee, as he checked the person lying face down on the floor, directly in front of them. Emily looked around the room and was startled when Amy dropped her hand and she and Rick practically ran across the room. She knelt down next to what appeared to be a female's body. Rick pulled to his left and ran over to the body of his friend, James, who was still wearing his wedding attire.

With Rick's movement, Emily could clearly see the person Amy was frantically leaning over. Mark's voice then interrupted Emily's internal screaming, causing her to look down. "He's breathing; he doesn't appear to be injured, but he won't wake up." She looked over Mark's shoulder, then down at a man now rolled onto his back, with his mouth wide open and eyes shut. He did not look familiar, but Emily hadn't recognized half the people who had been at the wedding, yesterday.

Amy cried. "She won't wake up!"

Mark stood as Emily spun and ran over to her sister, who was shaking the seemingly lifeless body of Julia. Emily bent down over Julia's head, checked her pulse, and then glanced up into her sister's eyes. "She's fine, Amy," she said, straightening up and looking around the room. "They all are. For some reason they just won't wake up. It's like they're in a deep sleep." Then looking down at Julia: "Or a coma of some sort." Amy stroked Julia's hair and made a whimpering sound of fear and confusion.

That was when Emily noticed her husband was no longer in the lobby. "Mark," she cried, panicked, and looking around. "Mark!"

Ten seconds later, he jogged back into the foyer, coming from the main entrance. He took in the overall grim appearance of the room before continuing over to Amy's side, holding her arm, and gradually pulling her up. "We need to get out of here, Amy. Julia and the others will be fine for now, but we need to get somewhere safe so we can figure this out."

Looking back at Emily and Rick, who were now standing next to each other, he said, "It's stopped raining. The streets are deserted; I think we're the only ones awake. There are a few cars outside that have crashed and are smoking. I found a truck parked out front; let's just get out of here."

Amy stood stricken to the spot. "Mark, I get it." She tugged her arm free of his grip. "But I'm not leaving her here, not if whatever that was is coming back!"

Rick responded before anyone else could. "Okay," he said quickly, then looked over at Mark. "If whatever that was does come back, we can't just leave them." His arms spread wider, turning to the limp bodies surrounding them. "How many can we fit in the back cab?"

Quickly glancing over his shoulder and out into the street, he turned back and rushed towards Julia, where he picked her up into his arms and turned back to the group.

"As many as we can." Mark passed Rick, making his way towards the street. "Hurry."

Emily scanned the room and noticed two small children no older than three.

"Amy," she said, pointing and running towards the children. "Come on."

Rick hurried after both women, who were now running with the unconscious children in their arms. Breathing heavily and cursing under his breath, he ran out of the main lobby with James over his right shoulder. When they reached the dark-green GMC 1500, Mark was in the truck bed. Julia was half-falling out of the front seat as he hastily threw chunks of rubber, wood, and tools out into the abandoned road. Emily held the small boy's head close to her neck, as she scanned the streets. Turning back to the hotel, she gasped. Rick and Amy followed her gaze.

"Look." She pointed to the fifth-floor balcony, on the west side of the building.

Mark had laid out a blanket he found crumpled behind the driver's seat and rear window. Jumping down, he carefully placed Julia in the truck bed.

Still pointing but facing back now, Emily cried, "Mark, look!"

He ran up to her side and followed the direction of her finger to a man's body, hanging upside down over a balcony. The man's shoe and pant legs were caught on the metal bar, which was buckling under his weight.

"Get them into the back, then get in the truck," Mark said, taking a step forward and focusing on the man. "Rick, I might need your help," he blurted, before running off into the building.

Rick dropped James, less lightly then he should have, into the back next to Julia and ran after Mark.

Left outside, Amy looked back and forth, in every direction, then down to the girl in her arms. "What do we do with them?" Looking up at Emily, she said, "We can't just throw them in the back!" Her gaze turned back to the hotel. "What if their parents wake up? They'll be so worried." Emily glanced into the cab of the truck.

"There's not much room in there." She looked back at her sister and the child in her arms. "But we can hold them on our laps. Come on, let's just get in." She opened the passenger door and slid as far over as she could while Amy followed her in, slamming the creaky door shut behind them. They both looked around the dark cab, then back out the passenger window.

"Emily? Are you okay? You look kinda green." Amy raised her hand to her sister's forehead.

Emily brushed her away. "I'm fine, just a bit dizzy. It's making me nauseous." Looking back out of the window, she said, "I don't know about you, but I don't even remember seeing any people next to these kids."

Amy turned to face her then, thinking quickly before her gaze dropped to the little boy in her sister's arms. "No, actually I don't remember seeing anyone. Why would they be alone?"

"They were close to the doors; maybe the parents went to find a car or something?" What she had just said starting sinking in; both sisters looked out the front windshield, at the smoking cars and mini-vans littering the streets. Silently, both women held each child closer to their bodies, hoping their tighter grip would somehow shield the young ones from reality. Emily glanced back through the passenger window in time to see Mark and Rick on that fifth floor balcony.

* * *

"Okay, how do you want to do this?" Rick asked, without taking his eyes off the middle-aged man still dangling in front of them.

"We need rope or something." Frustrated, Mark looked around the deck and back into the room. "If we try leaning over, that bar's going to break." Still looking, he focused on the bed that was thrown awry, sheets lying in a mess. "Okay, I hope this actually works and can support his weight but…" Grabbing the nearest bed sheet, he started ripping it down the center. "Let's tie these sheets together, then if you can hold on to me, I'll try and wrap it around his ankle or something; then we'll just shimmy him up?" he said, eyes wide, and unsure of his own solution.

Rick gave a quick smile and raised one eyebrow. Letting out a loud, held breath, he muttered, "At this point I don't think we have much of a choice." He yanked a second sheet, ripping it down the center, and then helped in fashioning a makeshift rope. Both headed back out onto the deck, grabbing onto the unaffected side railing, and getting as close as possible. Mark, rope in hand, began to reach for the man. As he leaned slightly on the damaged railing, it bent further forward and the fabric of the man's pants slowly started to fray, dropping his body lower and lower.

"Grab my belt!" Mark yelled, letting go of his side support, reaching both arms over the railing, and tying a knot around the man's nearest leg as fast as possible. Almost as soon as the knot was tied and stable, the last remaining fabric tore, the man's foot released, and he began to plummet.

Mark lost his grip and began to fall, a loud "Shit!" following his descent. The wives, watching from the truck, let out a short scream.

Rick dug in his heels and heaved. Mark was yanked back toward the balcony door, dropping onto his back, with his lungs grasping for air out of shock and panic. They reached for the delicate rope, which they had, thankfully, already tied to what was left of the stable fencing. The man just stayed unconscious, dangling by the fourth floor balcony below. Rick strained and attempted to lift, with next to no success, until Mark was at his side assisting. After a few minutes of grunts and tugging, they had the man's body within their reach. In no time, they each grabbed a leg of the man and hauled him over the bent railing, dropping all three of them to the balcony floor.

Sluggishly getting to their feet, they attempted to drag the man into the room. Mark witnessed an odd reflection in the balcony door window. Dropping the man's feet and turning around, he went back onto the balcony. Far to the west, coming down towards them, came Hummer after Hummer; each completely white, taking up both lanes and ignoring any speed limit. Mark counted eight before Rick came to see what he was looking at.

"We need to get out of here. NOW!" Mark had started turning back into the room when Rick grabbed his arm.

"What do you mean? They're probably here to help us."

Mark shook his head and grabbed Rick's other arm, spinning back towards the vehicles and pointing. "If they're here to help us, why do those three have military grade machine guns strapped to their roofs?" Rick stopped to take a closer look, as Mark backed into the room. "Why not send police or ambulances? I don't like it." Rick's eyes widened as he noticed the guns and what appeared to be the men standing behind them, in full white uniforms, faces masked, holding their own machine guns. "Come on," Mark yelled, pulling at Rick's shoulder.

They both ran as fast as they could, jumping and tripping over the remaining bodies. Emily and Amy knew something else was wrong when they saw the seriousness and fear in their faces. They must have been unconscious for most of the day, because it was getting late now and the sun had already set over the ridge. Mark automatically ran to the driver's side, yanking the door open wide, as Rick got in the passenger side, with the women in the middle on the bench seat. The engine started and the vehicle pulled away before anyone spoke. Spinning the truck east, Mark hit the gas.

Emily moved the boy's head to the right side of her neck so she could stare at Mark. Placing her hand on his thigh, she asked, "What happened in there?"

It was Rick who spoke: "Nothing new inside, it was what was coming down the hill." Emily looked at her new brother-in-law as he continued to speak. "Back there, coming down the west highway about five minutes from the hotel, last we saw from the balcony, were fifteen Hummers." He turned to look over at his very concerned wife. "All white, with machine guns and men in white masks." Amy's jaw dropped and she looked across to her wide-eyed sister. Emily turned her head towards Mark, who was only interested in getting out of there. His eyes were trained on the road, looking at his rear view mirror every two seconds. Not a working car in sight. He didn't appear to blink as he pushed the gas pedal down to the floor and made his way east, turning down narrow roads, and eventually getting on the northbound highway heading for Tucson.

The truck's cab had grown very quiet; no one could piece a sentence together to fill the growing silence. All four adults sat as still as they could manage, staring out the windshield. It got so dark that Mark had no choice but to flick on his headlights, still frantically looking out his rear-view mirror. Emily got a sudden wave of exhaustion and let her head rest on his welcome shoulder. Refusing to take his eyes off the road for too long, Mark merely tilted his head down, pressing his puckered lips into her hair, gently. Emily smiled to herself and closed her eyes. She knew, no matter what happened, she would be safe with Mark. This comforted her so much that she was able to fall asleep, surprisingly quickly.

CHAPTER TWO

June 18th

"John, hit the alarm ALREADY!" Kristine poked her husband's ribs as he jerked and laughed, staring over at her. Lifting his hand he smacked the bedside alarm clock which was shrieking six a.m. "Thank you!" she whispered, gesturing with her chin towards the shower, as she rolled back onto her side.

John rolled onto his back. "Yep," he said to himself, rubbing his eyes as he slid out of bed, bathroom in sight.

* * *

Jonathan Stark and his wife Kristine were born and raised in Phoenix, Arizona. They had relocated to Sierra Vista for John's work shortly after they got married. John had received his PhD in Archaeology and Linguistic Anthropology; his area of specialty and fascination was Ancient Mesopotamia. Physically, John was six-foot and slender. His dark-brown hair was cut short and spiked. In recent years, he had taken to working out three times a week, simply as an escape.

John shared a research lab with his best friend, Abel Jones, who was a qualified chemical engineer. Though their research subjects and work ethic were very different, they were able to convince their funding parties to allow them to pick their own work settings. Abel had been recently employed by the government to work on some classified research, which even John was not privy to. Thankfully, the office space filled more than two rooms, allowing for a wide work split.

They had met each other during their first year at Phoenix University and carried on fraternizing through graduate school. Though two years older than John, Abel had always acted decades younger. He prided himself on being, "the eternal bachelor," with no immediate desire to get married. Even at thirty-three and busy at work, Abel took his physical appearance quite seriously, taking good care of his health. He was six-foot one and two hundred pounds of mainly muscle, with light-brown hair and hazel eyes, Abel was the last person anyone would guess was a chemical wiz. He wore expensive brands and held himself as more of a movie star than a lab nerd. No thick eyeglasses required.

John's wife, Kristine, had qualified as a paleontologist, but chose to take extended leave to be a stay-at-home mom for their six-year-old twins, Erik and Tess. Kristine had first enticed John with her luscious, thick, auburn curls, which only added to her dark-green eyes and few freckles. It was love at first sight for John. She had more of an athletic body, but was still feminine in her curves. They had met at the gym in the fall semester of their third year at Phoenix. She was on the treadmill, red faced and sweating, but John just couldn't take his eyes off her. She was stunning. Finally, gaining enough confidence, he intercepted her as she made her way towards the changing room. At first she thought he was insane. She was standing there, practically coughing up her lungs, with baggy workout clothes sticking to her heated skin, and John couldn't stop smiling. Kristine figured she'd give him a shot and three years later they were married.

* * *

John took his usual twenty-minute-long shower before hopping out just as the phone began to ring. Wrapping himself in the nearest towel, he ran for the phone just in time to smile at his wife who had the pillow tightly covering her head and was dramatically kicking her legs at the sound.

"Definitely not a morning person." He dropped to the side of the bed, laughing to himself, and lifted the phone to his ear. "John speaking."

Abel was on the other end. "Hey it's me. Tell Kristine, I'm sorry for waking her."

John smiled, turned his head, and said, "Abe says sorry for waking her highness up!"

Kristine lifted her head from under the pillow, turning slowly towards her husband. Her right hand began visibly tracing her body under the sheets. When it finally appeared, she raised her middle finger, and then quickly pushed his back so he fell off the bed. John heard her bellowing laughter as he reached for the phone that had dropped from his grip, put on a clean pair of boxers, and threw his wet towel in his wife's general direction.

Still laughing he said, "Sorry, about that, what's up?"

Abel let out a single laugh. "No problem, so yeah don't bother getting dressed for work."

"What do you mean? What's happened?" John, now serious, stopped mid-step.

"Turn on channel five, I just got a call from my boss."

John made his way to the living room and turned on the TV, as Abel continued, with melancholia filling his words. "Something's happened at the lab. Apparently it got broken into over the weekend; some radical green-group or something. They trashed the place and some of my chemicals were spilt." John turned the volume up on the TV, as the field reporter stood in front of their office building, surrounded by crime scene tape, security, and police. The camera then focused on the white plastic that was covering a makeshift tunnel to the entrance, attached to a solid, white plastic tent.

Abel continued, "I guess a few things were taken. Some surrounding buildings were broken into too. They were playing with some pretty bad stuff."

John watched as one after another, white, unmarked Hummers drove up to the entrance of the white tent.

"Apparently, they attacked the Sierra V. Hotel too."

John gasped, his eyes momentarily pulling away from the television. "What did they do at the hotel?"

"I don't really know. The news doesn't say much, other than a lot of people were hurt and possibly infected with whatever it was."

"Do you have any idea what they could have taken?" John asked, almost shyly, knowing much of Abel's research was classified.

"I honestly don't know, John. There are a million and one things in my lab that shouldn't be fooled around with by anyone."

John just shook his head, his gaze returning to the screen. "Either way, I got a phone call saying to stay away until they hear more. Looks like the military is researching a possible terrorist attack."

"Seriously? Wow, this is big." John didn't know what else to say.

"Pretty much. Okay, well I'm glad I caught you before you headed out. I've got to go, so I'll just speak to you later, okay?" Abel finally said, interrupting John's mental monologue of questions and concerns.

"Okay, sounds good. Keep me informed, talk to you later!"

Abel muttered, "Later," as John hit 'end.'

John sat there watching the men covered in white come in and out. He prayed that none of his research documents had been taken or destroyed. He was filled with self-pity and fear for his research, until something on the screen caught his eye. A group of men, still dressed in white, but with their faces now showing, left the shelter of the tent and walked towards the people on the outskirts of the police tape. These men were carrying machine guns strapped across their heavily armored chests. They gestured for the public to move back. One spectator ignored their request; raising his camera, he continued to take numerous pictures. Clearly angered, one of the armed men obstructed his view, pulled the camera from his hands, and took a long step back as the man complained. Finding the device's memory stick, he removed it, not taking his eyes off the man. Then he surprised everyone by snapping it in two, and throwing the camera back at the shocked man's feet. The crowd took many steps back as he gave a wave of his hand and now rested his other hand on his gun.

CHAPTER THREE

June 18ᵗʰ

Emily awoke to the sound of the radio, skipping though the stations, and then Mark's voice. "Oh sorry, babe. I didn't mean to wake you."

She lifted her head from his shoulder and looked around drowsily. Rick and Amy were still fast asleep. "Where are we?"

"Just coming up to Littletown." He grinned down at her staring face and kissed her on the lips, before his eyes were back on the road. "I'll stop when we get to my parents'. They're out of town, but I know where their spare key is."

Emily just nodded, and then seemed to remember the small weight on her lap. She pulled the boy from her grasp and held him out in front of her, so she could get a good look at him. He still hadn't woken and had barely moved.

Mark spoke as he noticed her examine the boy's breathing. "I don't think we need to worry about them, they both started snoring a few hours back. Amy's little one actually started talking. Well, make noises." He smiled, "It's weird, but I think they are just sleeping; they'll probably wake up in a few hours." Emily listened as Mark spoke, still staring at the boy's face. Suddenly, his eyes fluttered and his head started to move from side to side. He was obviously still sleeping, and she pulled him back into her embrace and smiled up to Mark.

"Any news?" Emily noted the clock on the dashboard; it was just after six a.m.

"Yeah," was all Mark stated. His angered expression had Emily confused and she began to tell him to continue, but he needed no encouragement. "The news is saying a nearby chemical lab was broken into and vandalized. They're saying that whoever it was took things and attacked a few buildings, including the hotel, and let off toxins or whatever." He shook his head. "They've evacuated five square blocks."

Emily looked out the windshield, as she contemplated the news. "But that makes no sense, how do they explain the light, the noises, those THINGS on the rooftop?"

"It's bullshit, that's all it is! They're hiding something; something big."

"At least we know not everywhere was attacked," she said as she watched the second car pass by.

"Yeah, it only seems to have affected where we were last night. Twenty minutes after you fell asleep there were cars on either side of the road." Mark yawned.

That's when she remembered he had been driving all night; he was exhausted. She straightened back up in her seat. "How much further?"

"Only another hour or so."

"Okay, how about we pull over and you let me drive for a bit, you're exhausted," she suggested, rubbing his shoulder.

"No, I'm fine," he said, looking down at his wife. "Seriously. I just want to get there, and then I can get some shut eye." Emily was about to protest further, when he kissed her hard on the lips, turned back to the road, and reached his arm over her shoulder to pull her close into his side.

* * *

After forty-seven minutes of silence, other than the low-volume radio, the truck pulled up onto Mr. and Mrs. Claybourne's driveway. Mark's parents, Jim and Mary, were currently in the Dominican for their thirty-fifth anniversary.

Mark turned off the engine, and glanced around the truck, before he made any other movement. Even though it had not yet hit seven a.m., the sun was already high in the sky; heat beading in through the windows. Thankfully, it being a Sunday, not too many people had left their homes, let alone beds, yet.

"Stay here for a sec. I'll just go unlock the door and make sure no one's home." With Mark being an only child, there should have been no reason for anyone else to be in the house.

Emily sat in silence for a short moment, before Mark came back around to the driver's side. He pulled the door open and held out his arms. "Pass him over."

Carefully, she raised the child up, so that Mark could lift him to his chest. Placing the boy's head on the left side of his neck and wrapping his short legs around his ribs, Mark only needed one hand to support the boy. Once Emily had shimmied her way across the remaining seat and jumped down to the cement, Mark lightly closed the truck door on the three still sleeping inside. His free right hand took a firm grip on his wife's and led them into the house.

Laying the boy down on the nearest couch, Emily was next to speak, looking back out to the truck. "We really should bring them into the house." Then back at Mark; "We need to get Julia and James out from the truck before people start to notice."

Mark smiled to himself. "Yeah, I guess that wouldn't be the best thing," he said, walking towards the door. "Random, stolen truck, filled with bodies." He laughed. "Definitely, not the best way to be inconspicuous."

Walking out onto the path, Emily sat on the side on the couch, as the boy rolled onto his side and began to suck his thumb. She smiled and her eyes followed her own body, until they reached her feet. "Why am I still wearing these God-awful shoes!" was the only thing she could think. She lifted her legs up, one by one, yanking the strappy shoes off, and threw them by the door just in time to see Mark struggling with James' limp body. Mark tossed him on the other couch, not before his head bounced off the nearest side table, and back onto the cushion.

Mark's eyes widened and both he and his wife made scrunched up faces. Emily turned to her husband as he mouthed, "Ooops!"

No matter how painful it looked, and it was definitely going to leave a bruise, she couldn't help but laugh at her husband's expression. "Maybe I should help." Looking back at James, she saw that his blonde curls just barely disguised the growing red mark. Grabbing her husband's arm, she spun him back in the direction of the door, and took a few steps. Looking up at her husband, she made an inch-gap between her thumb and index finger, sarcastically commenting, "Just a little!"

He grinned, lightly shrugging. "That dude weighs a ton. He's got height and bulk...He's easily got fifty pounds on me. He's lucky I didn't take him by the ankle and drag him in."

As they reached the truck, Mark jumped into the back, raising Julia up into his arms. Emily raised her eyebrows, in another sarcastic reaction, while she rested her hand on the passenger door. Mark looked at the woman in his arms and back down at his wife, "I'm pretty sure I can manage this one." Spinning around, he jumped down from the truck in one fluid motion, walking straight past his wife with a beaming smile, and rolling his eyes. She too rolled her eyes, as she turned her body flush with the truck and yanked the passenger door open.

Rick, who was closest to the door, jumped at the loud, creaking noise, which shook Amy awake. Trying to comfort the startled couple at first, that's when Emily noticed the small girl in Amy's arms. Emily gasped, her eyes unmoving, and took a small step back. Rick and Amy turned to stare at the small girl who was wide-awake, frantically looking around, her face crinkled with fear. She scanned the space before her gaze froze in Emily's general direction.

The two-year-old's eyes were completely blood red. She blinked frantically, trying to see, squinting and squirming in Amy's less restricted arms. The adults still frozen, still staring in shock, when she reached up with her small hands and covered her eyes. Screaming loudly, she thrashed her head from side to side, as she began mumbling things that began unintelligibly, but slowly morphed into what sounded like, "Mama."

Still stationary, Emily noticed Mark out of the corner of her eye, at first walking, and then when he heard the child, running to her side. Looking back at her husband with his wide eyes and open jaw, then back at the crying child, something clicked inside of Emily. Reaching over Rick, Emily grabbed the frantic child, and held her close to her body. Mark moved out of her way, as she walked over to the front yard, lightly bouncing the child; humming and shushing her, while holding her small head close to her neck. "It's okay, sweetheart, you're okay. I'm here." She continued to soothe the toddler, as she slowly turned to glance at the three adults now leaning against the side of the truck, looking at each other, and then back at Emily.

After five long minutes of tears and hiccupping, the small blonde began to relax, becoming silent and burying her face into Emily's warm neck. Her left hand reached up, softly playing with the long tendrils of Emily's hair, swirling it between her tiny fingers. Emily took a deep breath, slowly looking down at the completely relaxed child in her arms. Blowing out slowly, she looked back at the group, who seemed as shocked as she felt. Turning, she walked into the house and out of sight.

Mark quickly followed. "Let me take a look at her," he said, reaching carefully to take her from Emily's light hold.

As soon as his hand touched her back, the child stiffened and became panicked, thrashing and screaming, before holding tighter to Emily.

"It's okay sweetie, we just want to look at your eyes and make sure you're okay." Emily gripped the girl lightly under the arms, attempting to pry her out of such an intense grip to hand her over to Mark's waiting arms.

"No!" she screamed, "Mama," crying once more in Emily's arms and jerking her body in a tantrum.

Lightly rolling her eyes and patting the child's back, Emily looked up at her waiting husband, and walked towards the over-sized armchair in the corner of the room to sit down. With the child on her lap, Emily pulled her away from her chest. "Okay, let me see." The girl, who had her eyes tightly shut, loosed them gradually. Finally, eyes opened wide, she began rapidly blinking.

Intently staring, without moving her eyes, Emily called for her husband. He slowly walked to the side of the chair and dropped to his knees, without touching either of them. The girl, who was focused on Emily's face, turned to look in Mark's direction as he cowered ever so slightly. Rubbing her back, Emily said, "It's really okay, sweetie. Please let him take a look at your eyes."

The girl turned back to Emily. "Abby."

Emily glanced in confusion at Mark then back at the girl. "Abby. Is that your name?" The girl smiled ever so slightly, squinting uncomfortably, then began continually nodding her head. "Okay, Abby," Emily slowly said, placing her hand on Mark's shoulder. "Abby, Mark needs to take a look at you to make sure you are okay. Mark is a doctor." In encouragement, Emily smiled widely at Abby's confused face. "Do you know what a doctor is? They are people that help other people feel better." Abby's eyes widened and she turned her body, still lightly holding a strand of Emily's hair between her fingers, to face Mark who was now smiling too. "So, will you let Mark make you feel better?"

Slowly, still guarded, Abby began to nod her head and reach both arms up so Mark could take her. Mark's smile widened as he got to his feet and slowly lifted her into his arms, holding her with one arm against his hip. "I just need to take you into the kitchen where there is more light, okay?"

She nodded.

As Mark took a step away from Emily towards the kitchen, turning his body, Abby started breathing heavier. She stretched her small hand out, which had been resting on his shoulder, grasped the air where Emily was sitting, and let out a small, panicked cry.

Emily got to her feet instantly. "It's okay. I'll come too," she said, grabbing Abby's outstretched hand with her own. "I'm here. I'm right behind you. Don't panic."

* * *

The three went into the kitchen, leaving Amy and Rick standing there, silently staring after them. Once out of sight, the newly-weds turned to each other. Amy closed the space between them as soon as she could, and held Rick close, as they simply held each other in a tight embrace. After a few minutes, Amy pulled back and looked up at Rick's face. He brushed the loose strands of hair away from her forehead. Leaning forward, he pressed a light kiss between her brows.

Before a single word exited their lips, James began to stir on the couch behind them. Amy closed her mouth, and looked around Rick's shoulder, just as he turned and ran over to James' side.

James' head was swaying side to side, his arms flailing as if to swat away something in front of him. Rick dropped to his knees. "Hey buddy," he soothed him, placing his hand lightly on James' nearest shoulder. "Dude, you're okay."

James, with his eyes still shut, raised his hand to the top of his head, feeling the small bump just under his hairline. "What happened? My head is killing me."

Rick began to explain, but was interrupted by James' sudden loud scream. Both of his hands flew up to cover his face. James lifted his body into the sitting position, placing his feet on the dark-green, shag carpet. Hunching over, balling his hands into fists, he covered his eyes and cussed loudly. "My eyes!" He squeezed his eyes tightly. "My eyes are burning!"

Emily came running from the kitchen, towards the pained noises. She had a confused expression on her face and stopped in her tracks as James was still screaming on the couch, now rocking back and forth. Taking two more steps into the living room, she noticed that Julia and the small boy had awoken. The boy began to scream, much like his sister had earlier. He began rocking back and forth on the couch, almost rolling off the edge. His hands alternated from scratching at his face, squeezing his eyes as tightly shut as he could manage, to smacking down hard on the couch below him. His whole body shook in pain. Emily ran to him, taking him into her arms and rocking him like she had done with Abby, soothing him with comforting words.

Still holding him tightly to her body, which was getting hard to do as he struggled forcefully, she turned to see Julia sit upright, mirroring James as she too rocked back and forth.

"Mark!" Emily cried. Both Amy and Rick were seated next to their friends, trying unsuccessfully to be helpful. Amy began to rub Julia's back as she rocked. Emily yelled for Mark once more.

Mark, with Abby perched on his hip, came running around the corner. Abby's eyes had started to clear. Though still very pink, the iris was now visible. Her eyes, as did Mark's, began scanning the room. Their jaws dropped slightly as they took in the scene. Mark focused on James, who was nearest, while Abby stopped on the boy cradled in Emily's arms, his body now relaxing into her embrace.

"Maaatt!" she shrieked in her babyish voice.

Mark's head turned in the direction, following her outreached arm, to stare at his wife. Emily looked at Abby, then down at the boy, "Matt. Is that your name, sweetheart?" Emily dropped back down onto the couch, sitting on the edge of her seat, letting the boy's legs fall on either side of hers.

Mark placed Abby on the seat next to Emily. Looking down at the girl, he said, "Stay here," and put his hands up as if surrendering. "I'll be right back."

Mark nodded once, obviously in doctor mode, closed the curtains in a hurry, and jogged back into the kitchen. Matt leant back from Emily and curled into himself, hunching over, his hands covering his eyes once more.

Abby was on her knees on the couch at Emily's shoulder, wide eyed, and in a panic, staring at her brother. "Matt," she said softly. "Matt." She reached over, ever so gently, and touched the side of his face. He did not react to her touch, but remained preoccupied with his discomfort. Emily began to lightly rub his back, as Abby looked up with teary eyes at Emily.

"Oh, Abby, don't cry sweetie. He's going to be fine. Just like you." Abby looked back at her brother, as Emily spoke again. "His eyes just hurt like yours did, but you're feeling better now, right?" Abby began to nod slowly.

Just then, Mark came running back into the room. His hands

were filled with what looked like wet washcloths. He passed them off to Rick and Amy, who quickly reached over, pulling their friends' hands out of the way, and covered their blood-red eyes with the cold cloth. James and Julia seemed to instantly begin to relax, holding the cloth as close as they could, letting the excess water squeeze out over their laps. Mark came up onto Emily's free side and lifted the boy. Abby crawled into Emily's vacant lap and they both watched silently, as Mark raised the last cloth up to the boy's eyes. He too began to relax, holding the cloth closer. Mark placed his free hand on top of the boy's to keep it in position.

The room fell silent, and Emily, Abby, and Mark sat still, as Amy had Julia in her arms, and Rick had his arm lightly slung over James's shoulder. Those who could, just looked up and stared at each other; when was this going to end?

CHAPTER FOUR

Once the news report had ended and yet another rerun of *Friends* had begun, John got up from the couch, turned off the TV, and headed back into the bedroom. Kristine was on her side, facing away from him, fast asleep and snoring to herself. John smiled, sliding back into bed. He reached over to his wife and pulled her close against his body.

She woke lightly. "Oh goooood morning," she said with an exaggerated smile. He let out a dry laugh. Kristine rolled over, placing her hand on the side of his face. "Aren't you gonna be late?"

John's face fell, pulling his face back so he could talk to his wife. "No work today." She looked confused, as he let out a deep breath. "The lab was broken into last night." Her eyes widened and brows rose. "Yeah, that's why Abe called. Apparently some of his chemicals got spilt or something. The whole building and half the block got quarantined. They broke into some other buildings too." He shook his head. "They attacked a hotel, Kristine. I really hope no one was seriously hurt." Then he dropped his head back on the pillow.

"Wow, that is weird." She looked straight into his distant gaze. "Your research!" He closed his eyes and nodded as she continued, "What about your research? I hope they didn't tamper with it."

"I know. It's killing me. I need to find out but I can't; the building is surrounded by men in white uniforms and hazard masks." Her eyes widened. "I guess it's pretty bad, cuz they all had oxygen tanks. At the outskirts, where the caution tape is, they have armed guards."

"Armed!" she gasped, looking both shocked and confused.

"It's gotta be serious, they obviously don't want anyone near that place. They even destroyed some guy's camera." He raised his free hand in defeat. "I just don't know what to do, I was getting to...possibly the biggest breakthrough of my career with this stuff and now what?" He looked down at his wife. "They won't even let Abe near it, what can I do?"

Kristine chewed on her bottom lip for a minute while she thought, then she looked John dead in the eyes, stroking the side of his face. "Well babe, there's not a whole lot you can do. Obviously, this is serious, so we have to just let the professionals deal with it."

His eyes dropped to stare off into space as the realization hit home that he really could do nothing.

"Why don't you come out with me and the kids; I've gotta do some shopping, we'll be gone most the day." She grabbed his chin and pulled his sad face down, so he had no choice but to look at her. "Okay? It will be nice, a family day out; we haven't had one in a long time." She raised her eyebrows and smiled, waiting for a response.

He finally gave in, with a glum smile. "Sounds nice."

Her beaming smile made his smile even wider. Rolling both of them until he was on his back, she laughed down at him. "Good." Her smile turned to a devilish grin as she cocked one eyebrow, glancing over to the clock. "It's a shame the kids won't wake up for another couple of hours," she said with a grin, hitching her thigh up and rubbing herself suggestively against him. She pushed out her lower lip to make a sad, puppy dog face. He laughed loudly at her expression and rolled them both once more until her head hit the pillow.

* * *

John awoke, rolled over, and saw that it was now nine a.m. The pounding of small feet outside the bedroom door made him roll over to his side. Kristine was gone, which meant the kids were definitely up. "Family day," he chuckled to himself. By nine-fifteen, John literally rolled out of bed onto the carpet below, completed ten consecutive push-ups, then jumped to his feet and got dressed.

"John," Kristine called from the kitchen. "Breakfast is ready!"

He strode into the kitchen, running his fingers through his hair, and stopped at the edge of the table. He watched his twins shove down as many blueberry pancakes as they could; obviously, a competition was underway.

"Done!" Erik called, putting his right hand as high in the air as he could.

John sat at his regular spot at the end of the table and reached over to high-five his son. "Nice!" They both laughed.

Kristine turned from the oven and walked over, placing a plate full of pancakes in front of John. Then she sat at the other end of the square wooden table with her own plate. "You shouldn't encourage them." She winked at John as she looked down at her daughter, who was still trying to force her last two pancakes into her mouth. "Tess, you don't need to rush anymore. Eat normally, or you'll feel sick." Kristine reached over and cut the remaining pancakes into small, bite-size pieces.

Erik laughed and sucked on the non-existent chocolate milk that was at the bottom of his plastic cup. John took a gulp of orange juice as Erik spoke; "Dad, are you gonna be home all day today?" His eyebrows were raised and enthusiasm etched his face.

"Nope," John quickly said, as he took a bite. Erik's smile faded as he turned back to stare at his empty plate, and Tess poked at her food while Kristine opened her mouth to protest. John continued; "Cuz, the four of us are going to be out all day." He smiled down at his son, who punched him on the shoulder.

Kristine shook her head in disapproval, and grinned into her coffee mug.

"Cool, we haven't hung out in ages, Dad." Then looking over at his mother; "What are we doing today?"

Kristine swallowed her mouthful, then took a drink of orange juice. "Well, we've got to pick up your sister's prescription, then get you guys some new shoes." Looking up at John, she said, "Your father desperately needs some new clothes."

John looked down at what he was wearing, then back up, attempting to say, "What?" with his mouth full. Kristine continued, looking over to her son, "And we need to get some food shopping done."

Erik rolled his eyes and slouched back in his chair. "Fun," he said sarcastically.

"That stuff won't take all day, and we don't have to do it in that order. What do you guys want to do today?" she asked, looking back and forth between her children and then to her husband. "We're going to have some fun today," she promised, as John grinned, taking another mouthful and waiting for their answers.

"Bowling!" Erik yelled.

"Swimming!" Tess shouted shortly after, bouncing up and down in her chair.

Kristine smiled at them both, looking back to her husband, cocking one eyebrow as he spoke, "How about both?"

"Both it is," Kristine finalized their plans as the kids jumped around with excitement and they finished eating.

∗   ∗   ∗

By four p.m. the Stark family had only one thing left on the day-trip plans: grocery shopping.

"Can I just stay in the car?" Erik moaned, as his wet hair soaked his t-shirt. He pushed back into his car seat as they parked out front of Jane's 24-Hour Groceries, a family-owned food store.

John and Tess were already getting out of the car as Kristine unbuckled her seatbelt and sighed. "Erik, get out of the car. We're almost done for the day. We're all tired, so the sooner we finish the better." He let out a groan and loudly got out of the car, slamming his door behind him. Kristine rolled her eyes and tried to ignore him. John was waiting at the front of the car to meet her, taking her hand as they walked into the store. Erik walked in front of them, kicking rocks as he went.

"Erik, can you grab a shopping cart?" Erik turned his head in their general direction, obviously still having a tantrum. "Please!" John exaggerated the word. They continued into the store as Tess grabbed Kristine's right, free hand. Erik was already behind with the cart.

Kristine let go of John's hand to put it on the shopping cart and started down the first aisle. She looked down at Erik who was still pouting. "Knock it off," she said sternly.

John was the next to speak. "Hey, Erik," he said, reaching over and messing up his son's hair, "Why don't we go look at the fishing gear?" Erik finally smiled up at his father, as John turned to Kristine. "We'll come find you guys," he said, as he and Erik walked around the corner.

"This is so cool!" Erik lifted up a very large hunting knife.

John turned to see. "Whoa!" John ran over, taking the knife as fast as he could. "Be careful with that!" As John recovered from his mini-heart attack, Erik started to play with the ready-prepared fishing rods. John walked around, picking up tins of fishing bait, reading the contents, then placing them back down on the nearest shelf.

"Dad, isn't that your office?" Erik spoke from behind. John spun on the spot to look down at his son, who was pointing up to the outdated TV hanging in the far corner. The news was on and the reporter was standing in front of the yellow police tape again, reading from a white piece of paper. John went to stand directly under the TV, listening carefully.

"...few people are missing from the quarantined area. These people must be found immediately. They need to receive medical attention. They may appear delusional; even violent. They are extremely contagious and will harm others with prolonged exposure. If they're found, be careful, and stay in well-ventilated areas. This is of high priority. The sheriff has just issued a statement. There will, in fact, be a reward for finding these missing people, although the dollar amount has not yet been released. If they are not found within forty-eight hours, Governor Stone will take immediate action to protect his people.

Once again, if viewers are just tuning in, five-square blocks in downtown Sierra Vista have been shut down and quarantined. Trained professionals have entered the area, and saved more than fifty individuals; transporting them to designated hospitals and lab facilities while they recover. These individuals vary in age and gender. Thankfully, most have been accounted for, however a few are still missing. Following are the names of the known missing."

A list of thirteen names covered the screen, and after they disappeared, a paragraph of contact information appeared with a statement: "Pictures to follow shortly." John didn't recognize any of the names, though he was relieved that at least no one he knew was hurt. But he did worry for those who had been infected by whatever, and might be on their deathbeds for all he knew. A sudden burst of guilt hit John. He needed answers.

"John," Kristine called from behind. He had totally forgotten where he was. He turned to see his family staring back at him. "We're all ready to go," she said, looking more closely at her husband. "You okay?" she whispered, placing her hand on his shoulder.

He stared for a second. "Oh yeah, yeah sorry." Kissing her forehead, he smiled down at the kids. "Just daydreaming, I guess." Kristine smiled as they made their way to the checkout counters.

* * *

"Hey Abe, yeah it's John. Heard any more?" John spoke more quietly on the phone than usual, as he sat in the leather chair in their home office. "Did you see the news?"

"Hey, yeah, I just watched the new report. I feel terrible. I've spent all day trying to figure out what could have been mixed together – how bad it could be. I really don't have any more news. I've tried contacting my team three times, but their phones are all shut off." John heard the TV in Abel's living room abruptly shut off. "God knows what they're dealing with. Those bastards are probably dealing with PR, just trying to find ways to cover their own asses. But like I said, I'll contact you as soon as I know more. Right now I'm like you. In the dark." Letting out an exasperated breath, Abel could be heard tossing the remote onto the coffee table with a sudden crash.

John took a deep breath. "I just can't stand it. I need to know what the hell is going on down there. I hate to sound self-centered, but my life is in that building, Abe. Everything. I was on the verge of a breakthrough with this dialect and now...Fuck!" He stopped his rant, then took a calming breath. He spoke more softly now. "Even just moving certain pictures around, messing up the notes.

Kristine's been telling me to type up that shit for weeks, cataloguing my day. Fuck, Abel, I'm going insane with 'what ifs.'"

"I know. I know. Trust me, I know!" Abel repeated in quick succession. "Me too buddy, and I can't even get a hold of anyone for answers. A few of my compounds in there…" he paused, thinking, "if they even get moved, spilt, or played with in any way, I'll have to start all over again…Months of research and trials John – months down the fucking toilet."

"This is ridiculous," John blurted out. "That's our office building, we pay the rent, and we have a right to know what's going on inside there. Have the police contacted you at all? Asked for a statement? Anything? Is that how you originally found out?"

"Actually, I never thought of that. No, nothing at all. I heard directly from my boss," Abe said, blowing another round of air into the speaker. "Aren't they supposed to contact us and fill us in?"

"You'd think," John answered, nodding into the receiver, knowing full well he couldn't be seen. "Okay, that does it, I'm calling the police."

"Okay wait, give me until the morning. If there isn't any more news then we both go into the station. Deal?" Abel asked.

John considered that for a second. "Okay, fine. Deal; but come eight a.m. and no news, we go find out what the fuck is going on."

"That sounds perfectly reasonable," Abel replied, almost laughing at John's determined state.

"I'm serious, Abe. Eight a.m."

Kristine knocked twice on the glass door. John looked over, switching the phone to his free ear, as he looked over at his wife. "Dinner's ready," she said through the door.

"Be right there," John yelled, as he covered the speaker of the phone. Once she had walked back into the kitchen, John continued, "Okay, I've got to go, so phone me as soon as you hear anything at all, okay? I don't care what time."

"Sounds like a plan. I'll talk to you later. 'Night, John."

"G'night." John hung up the phone, and went to sit at the dinner table.

CHAPTER FIVE

A few hours had passed since everyone had awoken. Mark was on the loveseat, with Abby and Matt on either side. Their eyes had completely recovered; the whites of their eyes were clear as day. James and Julia had recovered as well and they were now sharing the big couch with Rick and Amy, who were snuggled close together. Rick had his arm slung over Amy's shoulder. That left Emily sitting alone on the single rocking chair. They were all watching reruns of the *Looney Tunes* and then *The Simpsons*. While the others remained distracted, Emily couldn't help but let her mind wander, exploring and hypothesizing numerous explanations as to their current situation.

The others remained silent, staring at the TV screen, as Emily glanced around the room, stopping on the small children clinging to her husband's side. She jumped to her feet and all eyes followed her as she made her way to the kitchen. Once she was out of sight, they looked at each other then back once more at the colorful screen, but Mark turned back in the direction of the kitchen. Shimmying forward until he was on the edge of the couch, Mark took his arms from around the children and stood up. "I'll be right back," he said to their raised eyebrows, and then they went back to watching the television. Nobody watched Mark as he strolled into the kitchen.

"Em?" He walked up to the giant granite island in the middle of the polished room. Just then she walked out from inside the pantry, carrying a pack of uncooked spaghetti and a tin of tomato sauce.

"I'm here." She continued to place the two ingredients on the counter and walked over to rummage through the fridge. "Is their kitchen always this empty?" she asked, speaking into the fridge. "Mark?" She spoke after a few minutes of un-answered silence. She leaned back, after no reply, to see her husband smiling widely back at her from the other side of the door. "What?" she asked, looking up confused.

"I love you," was all he said back, before closing the fridge door and pulling her into his arms.

She lay her head on his shoulder. "You know, you can be really difficult sometimes, but I love you more."

"Impossible."

She leaned back to smile a cocky grin, shaking her head from side to side. He slowly tilted his head down to kiss her plump lips. After a minute, his hands caressed the curve of her spine; his hands settling to splay over each of her silk covered buttocks, squeezing playfully.

"I also love this dress." He smiled at her growing blush. "Doesn't leave much to the imagination."

She ran her hands down his white button-down shirt, resting her forehead onto his chest. "Hmmm, you know I love a man in a suit." She smiled as the gentle vibration she felt from his chest was expanding into a chuckle.

"That I do," he said. She pulled back in time to see his playful wink. "You did amazing today. Well, I guess it was yesterday." He continued kissing her after ever other word.

She took a deep breath, and her teasing expression settled into a serious mask. His brows pulled together in concern. "No, you did," he started to protest.

"Mark, YOU were the one that got us off that roof. YOU were the one that found the truck, saved the man on the balcony, and drove us safely here." She moved her not-so-free arms around in exaggeration. "I was just along for the ride," she ended, with a sarcastic tone.

He smiled back down at her, turned his head to look out the back window, thinking; then quickly turned back. "Yes, but it was only you who kept me going. I had to keep you safe." His smile faded ever so slightly. "Nothing else matters."

Emily grabbed the sides of his face with her hands. In response, he pulled her more tightly into his embrace. "A team effort," she said, making a face, which made him laugh. Mark dropped his arms and pulled away, going to rummage through the refrigerator. Emily continued over to the sink, filled a big pot with water, placed it on the oven top, and set the heat to high to boil.

"And to answer your question…Yes." Mark turned towards the island, placing a few vegetables on the counter, and grabbing the loaf of crusty bread from on top of the fridge. "Mom likes to get fresh food every couple of days, so they rarely have anything in the house." Looking in the pantry, he muttered, "I should probably go get some things. The kids will need some milk and stuff too."

"Is it safe?" Emily forced past a growing lump in her throat. She clutched at the counter and looked out of the kitchen window into the enclosed back yard.

Mark turned to look at his wife, instantly recognizing the panicked expression on her face. "I think we're fine, for now, I don't think anyone saw us come in. If anyone is looking for us at all, it will be back at Sierra."

Emily began to relax as she waited to pour the pasta into the water when it boiled. "Okay, but after lunch, and when it gets a little darker." She noticed his grin. Continuing more shyly, and without making eye contact, she lightly swayed from one foot to the other. "Just in case," she said with a shrug, fiddling with the wooden spoon.

"Yes dear," he laughed as she poked him in the ribs with her index finger. They laughed there together, as they began to prepare lunch.

Mark began setting the large dinner table, as Emily dished out equal proportions of pasta; the children's in smaller bowls, when a call came from the living room.

Rick came running around the corner, still gripping the wall, never fully leaving the hallway. Without looking directly at either of them, and looking very panicked himself, he said, "Mark! We need you." Then he was gone. Mark glanced over to Emily who stared back, dropped the pan of boiling hot sauce on the counter, and then ran towards the hallway.

Mark got the living room first. "What? What is it?" he said, looking around with his hands up, ready for action. Rick and Amy were the only ones standing. Mark looked around them to see Julia and James, collapsed back into one couch, and the two siblings on the other. Their bodies were limp, sprawled around the cushions, but their eyes were wide open, not blinking, as their pupils dilated and contracted.

Mark pushed Rick to the side, as he reached James first. "James!" He spoke directly into his face. Mark had his head between his hands. "James!"

Emily went straight over to the children that were also staring off at nothing. She grabbed Abby by the face and looked closely. Her eyes seemed to move slightly, as if watching something. Emily gasped, as the little girl's pupils began to increase in size, completely consuming her blue irises. Abby's eyes started moving more freely now; her face reacting to whatever she saw.

"James!" Emily heard Mark, still calling, from behind her. She looked over her shoulder, and then back at the child below her. Abby's eyes were moving often, focusing on one thing, then moving to focus on something else. Finally, her gaze focused on Emily.

Abby took a deep breath, as her pupils went back to normal. She began to blink frantically as she tried to move her head, which was still in Emily's grasp, from side to side, looking round the room.

Out of the corner of her eye, Emily saw Matt sit up and start to move. Picking up the girl, she spun and sat back down on the couch. Abby sat upright on her lap as they looked over to Julia and James, who were wide-awake and looking around the room. Mark stepped over to Julia, who still seemed to be a bit dazed, and looked at her pupils. "Did you see that?" she whispered, her eyes wide.

Amy dropped to her knees, next to the couch, as Mark continued his examination. "See what?" she asked, turning and looking over her shoulder in the random direction Julia seemed to be staring.

"Those images. What were they? Did you get what he was saying?" Julia continued.

Amy turned back to her friend. "Images? Who's 'he' Julia?" she asked with a very concerned look on her face, while she brushed Julia's hair out of the way. Mark checked Julia's pulse.

It was James that spoke next, drawing the other adults' attention. The others still seemed to be subdued and unresponsive. "The guy, the old dude with the grey beard. He was standing next to a street sign." James's eyes seemed to focus on nothing, as he remembered. "He was just standing there, smiling."

Rick sat on the couch next to James, "A road sign? Dude, what the fuck are you talking about?"

Julia answered, "Old Hondo Cannel Rd, Sherman Place."

Rick looked over questioningly at Julia as James

muttered, "Roswell."

Mark stood up and looked down at both of them. "What are you two talking about?"

They seemed to relax back into their sitting positions, blinking more normally. Eventually, they both looked up at Mark, and Julia asked, "You guys really didn't see anything?"

Amy answered, "No. We were all just watching TV, then the four of you…" She looked at the children who sat silently with Emily, then back at her friend, "… just collapsed back into your seats and started staring off at nothing. Your eyes got all big and blurry, then you were back, staring around at us."

Julia looked across at James, who was seated at the other end of the couch, when he spoke. "Yeah, well I remember watching the show, then all of a sudden I saw desert." He looked around at everyone as he spoke. "Like, literally a bunch of sand all around me. I couldn't move, but I could feel the heat of the sun above. Then I saw the guy's face, with a beard." James leant forward, resting his elbows on his knees, and counting with his fingers, as he continued; "More desert, then back to the guy, but this time he was standing next to the sign that said…"

He gestured to Julia. "Old Hondo Cannel Rd, Sherman Place."

Emily noticed the children listening intently as James and Julia spoke, nodding to everything they said.

James also nodded, then continued. "Exactly. Then desert once more, then a table full of paperwork, or like…newspapers, then a big sign saying…" He air-quoted with his fingers. "Welcome to Roswell, the dairy capital of the southwest." He dropped his head down and held it there with both hands.

"And then what?" Mark asked.

"And then nothing. I saw the inside of this room and you leaning over me checking my pulse," James answered with his head still between his knees.

Mark turned to Julia next, "You saw the exact same thing?"

She nodded, "Exactly the same." She paused, looking unsure, then whispered, "Are we losing our minds?" She ended by turning to gaze at James.

Mark turned to the children. "And you? Did you see the pictures too?" he asked, in more of a child-like way.

They both nodded. Matt smiled and started waving from side to side. "The man waved at me."

Mark opened his mouth to comment, but James added, "Yeah, the guy had a odd smile on his face and just waved at us."

"It started as a wave, but I think he was gesturing for us to come, like…" she used her head as an example. "…he was calling us."

Mark turned back to his wife. Concern and confusion filled their features. Before the conversation could escalate, Abby's stomach grumbled audibly.

Emily grinned, bouncing Abby on her knee once. "Okay, well she's obviously starving. Why don't we go eat and talk about this in the dining room." She stood up and maneuvered Abby until she was perched on her left hip, then she spoke to the room. "Okay?" They sat or stood where they were for a second then began to move, walking in the general direction of the kitchen.

Lunch was surprisingly silent, considering what needed to be discussed. The small children were balanced on Emily and Amy's knees, so they could reach the table properly. Clearly famished, they ate quickly, not taking their eyes off their bowls. Julia and James both stared down at the table in front of them, one elbow on the table supporting their heads, as they merely poked at the food in front of them. Rick ate, while Amy kept looking back and forth between Emily and the two daydreamers.

Matt pushed his bowl into the middle of the table and spoke. "TV!" he yelled, gripping the table and jumping up and down on

Amy's knee.

Rick, who was sitting next to his wife, had already finished his meal. He looked over at Mark, and then to James, then back down at Matt. "Sure bud," he said, reaching for Matt and taking him into his arms. He turned and left the room. Amy began to eat again, as she noticed Abby hastily finishing her last bites and staring after the two that had already left. Standing up and reaching for Abby, she said, "Come on kiddo, let's go watch some cartoons too." She smiled down at her sister, leaving only the four adults.

Mark was the first to break the silence. "Okay, so what are we gonna do about this?" He spoke across the table, to Julia and James, who lifted their heads for the first time since they'd sat down.

Julia answered. "Well, what is there to do?" she said sluggishly.

Looking at Julia and then to Mark, James joined in. "Yeah, I mean this is weird." He exaggerated the last word, raising his eyebrow. "Believe me, but yeah; so what?"

Emily finally entered the conversation. "So what?" she muttered with a critical tone to her voice, placing both hands on the table and leaning forward. "So, all four of you saw the same thing. Obviously, this means something. You were literally given some sort of address. You know what the guy looks like." She looked back and forth between them. "Soooo…"

"What are you saying?" Mark asked, looking directly at his wife.

"I guess I'm saying, whatever happened to us at the hotel doesn't make sense." Emily pointed her right hand at the other two. "Now you guys are having some sort of vision." Then back at Mark; "I don't know about you, but I want answers, and from the sound of things those answers are in Roswell."

"The old guy." Julia nodded, looking back down at the table.

Mark looked down at his wife for a long while.

"Roswell? Tomorrow?"

"Roswell," she finished, nodding, turning back to the table.

"Seriously?" James looked around the room as if the company present had grown extra limbs. He ran a hand through his short blonde hair. "Some crazy fucker does something to mess with our heads and you wanna just show up at his doorstep?"

"You got a better idea?" Emily folded her arms protectively over her chest. "We can't just sit around here and twiddle our thumbs. What if next time we're out in public and you guys go into another fit? We need answers, James."

He turned to Julia. "What do you wanna do?"

She chewed her bottom lip, staring at the table as she thought. Glancing up at the others, she shrugged. "I wanna know, don't you?" She gripped his near thigh as it bounced under the table.

He stilled, his eyes becoming slits as they scrutinized her face. Abruptly, his features smoothed. "Sure. Why not?" He squeezed her hand reassuringly.

The four pushed away from the table and walked into the living room to join the others. They sat down quietly and stared at the screen. Rick was flicking through the channels for the tenth time. "Wait, go back," James said, sitting on the far edge of his seat.

"What?" Rick asked, looking over.

James reached over and stole the remote straight out of his hand, smiling at Rick, then looked back at the screen, turning the channel back to the previous one. "It was the news, they were standing in front of that office building on the corner of Machol Avenue." He shook his head at his best friend's confused expression. "Sierra Vista. Two blocks from the hotel?" He laughed, as he could see the light bulb click in Rick's expression.

Everyone became silent and for the first time, actually interested in the news report. Gradually, everyone in the living room moved to the edge of their seats, closer to the TV. At first the report gave the same details that Mark had heard on the radio, in the early hours of the morning. He rolled his eyes and leaned back in his seat, as the others continued to watch, but then the reporter began describing people that the cleanup crews were missing. The words, "Missing members of the Wedding Party" caused James to unconsciously turn up the volume as everyone's jaws dropped with a few popping noises.

"...five square blocks in downtown Sierra Vista have been shut down and quarantined. Trained professionals have entered the area and saved more than fifty individuals, transporting them to designated hospitals and lab facilities while they recover. These individuals vary in age and gender; thankfully, most have been accounted for. However a few are still missing. The following are the names of the known missing:

    Lilly Andrews
    Emily Claybourne
    Dr. Mark Claybourne
    Ian Hunter
    Abigail Johnson
    Elizabeth Johnson
    Mathew Johnson
    Ryan Johnson
    Julia Paine
    James Pinter
    Amy Michaels
    Patrick Michaels
    and Dr. Charmaine Shannon

Some of the names also had pictures to follow. No one recognized Lilly Andrews' picture, but there was a family photo of Matt and Abby, with their parents. Elizabeth had chest-length amber curls, with green eyes, and was pictured with Matt in her arms. Ryan had Abby in his; he had dark brown hair and blue eyes that matched his daughter's. They both looked roughly about thirty years old. Abby turned on Emily's lap, looking up as she pointed to the screen. "Mama."

They had no pictures for Charmaine or Ian yet. Then there was a wedding picture that must have been taken from a discarded camera. Obviously, Amy and Rick were in the center, all smiles, with Emily on Amy's right, then Julia behind her. James, being Rick's best man, was on Rick's left, with Mark behind him. They all looked flawless; so happy.

The news report finally ended and James turned off the television. Slowly, everyone seemed to turn to each other simultaneously. James, Julia, Rick, and Amy slid out of their seats. The men were sitting on the floor and Amy went to sit on the edge of her sister's seat. Emily put her arm over her shoulder, while Julia just stood there.

"So, five thousand dollars goes to anyone that finds us. Each of us." James spoke while staring at the curtained windows.

They were all silent for a long time until Mark took a deep breath. "Well, what they are reporting is…" He looking down at Matt on his lap, then back up, "Bull poopy." Emily half smiled. "And we're all physically fine, from what I can tell." James raised his eyebrows, and opened his mouth in protest, so Mark quickly added, "Physically. And the lab setting sounds a bit funny to me, so I think it's in our best interest to lay low and get to this bearded guy to get some answers, before we do anything else."

Rick nodded and answered the fear in Julia's eyes; she was obviously scared. "This whole situation is a bit crazy, but you guys weren't awake when we left the hotel." Pointing to the blank TV screen, he said, "Those guys in white, going in and out of the office building. They were coming down the highway towards us;

in big white Hummers that had machine guns on top."

This was news to James. He said, "What?" while his brows raised.

"Yeah, there were more than thirteen Hummers; all the same, coming towards downtown." Shaking his head, Rick looked at the TV, as he spoke. "That doesn't scream chemical cleanup crew to me. No, Mark's right, screw them. We need to get the hell out of this state."

Leaning back against the bottom of the couch now, James asked the room, "So the New Mexico plan is still in effect then?"

"First light," Mark finalized.

Each seemed to ease back into their seats, while Rick and James spread out on the floor in front of the large couch. James turned the TV back on to *The Simpsons* and everyone watched. Abby crawled on the floor along with Matt. Both shimmied closer, to sit less than a meter from the screen. Julia lay across the love seat, as Amy rocked back and forth in the single chair, off to the side. Emily scooted over, putting her feet up on the couch at the same time Mark lifted his arm to put it around her shoulder. They all seemed to be quite cozy, as they sat watching for two straight hours. No one moved.

The sun had finally gone down and Mark glanced to his right. Above where Amy was sitting, a large grandfather clock stood next to the wall, stating that it was eight-thirty at night. Mark looked down at his wife, who still had her eye on the television, and rubbed her shoulder. "I should probably go pick up some things," he said, starting to lean forward as if to stand up.

Emily's eyes widened as he dropped his arm off her shoulder. "Oh, okay I'll come with you."

"No," Mark said, too fast, startling his wife slightly. She instinctively leant back, recoiling from his harsh expression.

Mark began backtracking immediately, leaning over and

kissing her forehead, "You stay here with the kids and get some sleep." She didn't speak, so he dropped his head down, forcing their foreheads together, as if they were the only ones in the room. "I just need you to stay here, so I know you're safe."

Emily then understood. Rolling her eyes, she kissed him quickly. "How do you think I feel? I don't want you anywhere out of sight, so I know you're okay." She leaned back, smiling this time. "Also, we all need a change of clothes and a man's touch, even a doctor, is still hopeless."

"Thanks," he joked. "But you're still not coming." He raised his eyebrows while smiling, daring her to argue.

"Well I'm definitely going," Julia blurted out, as Mark spun his head around to look at her. She was now sitting upright on her couch. "No seriously, I need to get out of here and get some fresh air. Plus, Emily's right, men cannot buy clothes." She smiled back at Emily.

"Yep, I'm coming too." James was off the floor in seconds. "We'll wear baseball caps or something." Looking out the window, he said, "It's dark enough anyway."

Rick stood up and was just about to offer to accompany them, when Amy reached up, pulling him down on the seat with her. "Oh no you don't! You're definitely staying here with me!" She smiled as James made two whipping sounds and laughed.

Rick joined in. "Yeah, I guess the REAL man has to stay behind and protect the women and children."

"Yeah. That's it, protect the women and children," James repeated sarcastically.

Five minutes later, the three were ready to go with James and Julia already in the truck. Emily watched as her husband unbuttoned his suit and exchanged his white formal shirt for one of his father's t-shirts. Unfortunately, Mark was a few inches taller than his father, so the pants had to stay. She smiled when his head popped back through the neck hole. "Hurry back." Emily tugged at the bottom of his shirt.

"Always," Mark answered, while putting a baseball cap on before running off to the truck.

Emily lightly closed the door behind him, locking it, and walked over to join the kids on the big couch, as Amy and Rick cuddled on the love seat.

* * *

An hour and a half later, Emily couldn't help but glance over at the door, then the clock, every other second. They were still watching the TV; the news reports had repeated four times in the last hour, with their pictures being blown up each time. Emily was getting very nervous.

Three loud knocks on the door made Emily jump in her seat, then practically run to the door. "Finally," was all she could say, looking over at the clock. It was just past ten. Without looking though the peep-hole, she flung the door open, with a big smile on her face. "Final..." she began to repeat, but stopped abruptly as she saw that a man in his late forties stood alone on the front steps.

"Excuse me?" he asked.

"Sorry, I thought you were my husband," Emily blurted out.

He smiled, taking one step up to stand in the doorframe. "Oh, no ma'am." Taking his cowboy hat off and holding it over his heart, he reached out to shake her hand, "I'm Dean Tomas, I live three doors down."

Emily shook his hand. "Emily," she awkwardly smiled, as Rick got up from the couch slowly.

"Nice to meet you, Emily. So, how do you know Tim and Mary?" Looking around the room, his eyes widened ever so slightly.

"They're my in-laws. My husband and I," she said, looking back into the living room, "and our friends are just staying here for the night while we travel up-state."

"Oh, you're Mark's wife then, Emily Claybourne?" he asked quickly, looking her directly in the eyes.

Her eyebrows creased. "Yes…?" she had a questioning tone to her voice.

He smiled, looked down and quickly yelled over his shoulder, "It's them!"

Emily lifted to her tiptoes to look over his shoulder. "What?" she began to say, as Dean dropped down rapidly, lifting her over his shoulder and turning back down the path. Emily screamed for Rick, kicking and punching as hard as she could.

"Emily!" Amy screeched from her seat, jumping up and running behind Rick.

Rick ran fast and he almost caught up to Dean, who was halfway across the front yard heading to a running, maroon minivan with the side door propped open. "Hey!" Rick yelled.

Dean quickened his pace, with Rick on his heels, reaching for Emily's outstretched arms. Out of nowhere, Rick was hit hard in the stomach with a baseball bat. Amy screamed, as he folded in half, the bat coming down on his back this time, knocking him to the ground.

Meanwhile, Emily lifted her body straight up, grabbing the back of Dean's head, and twisting her body so that her bare knee smacked right into his nose. He began to drop instantly, throwing her to ground below him. He cried out in pain and kicked her hard in the ribs. As she curled up on her side, Dean reached down to pick her up once more. His nose was already bleeding to his chin. Fighting the pain of a broken rib, Emily reached up with both hands, her nails digging into the top of his scalp, and dragging their way down, digging into his eye sockets.

He screamed, even louder this time, lunging for her throat. "Bitch!" he yelled, raising his right fist and bringing it down hard across her left cheekbone; instantly breaking her nose. The force caused her to bite her lip in a garbled cry. Blood poured from her nostrils and lip as she screamed out in pain.

Rick was now on his hands and knees, clawing at the grass, in the general direction of her cries for help. A second man stepped out in front of Amy, with the bat in his hands, his back to her, going to take another swing at her husband. Amy took two bounds and lunged at him, jumping on his back and smacking his chest with her fists. He grunted slightly, and slammed both of them into the side of the garage. He spun his torso, so his elbow hit her left eye. Amy hit her head and lost her grip, falling to the path below.

Dean spat out more blood as he started to punch Emily, while her vision slowly began to blur and her body became numb. With her last effort at freedom, she managed to kick him hard enough so that he tripped backwards, over the large boulder rock; inoffensive as a garden display. Emily screamed; the blood had spread into her vision, and covered a large portion of her dress. Rolling onto her stomach, she dragged her body, pulling at the grass, until she got to the bottom step. She lightly raised her head to see Abby and Matt, screaming and crying in the doorframe, as Dean grabbed her ankle and flipped her over onto her back. This time she had managed to grab a handful of gravel lining the grass, flinging it up into his face. He cried out, closed his eyes, and reached down, grabbing her by the shoulders. He picked her up and threw her weak body onto the grass. Kneeling on her chest, he reached for her throat and began to choke her. The wild commotion of noise cascaded in waves in Emily's ears.

The other man, a lanky man with hunched shoulders and shoulder length greasy hair, targeted Rick, kicking and stomping him as he was forced to the ground. Amy got to her feet, as fast as she could, and lunged for the man once more. This time, she grabbed him around his waist, knocking him over Rick. She landed on top of him and began slapping and scratching at him as hard as she could. Eventually, he reached around her waist and spun her body, so it hit the very same boulder. She gasped and fell to the ground. He managed a kick to her face, knocking her out instantly. This gave Rick enough time to get to his feet. Just as the stranger stood straight and turned around, Rick jumped at him. They both fell and began exchanging punches.

Emily flared her feet around; her eyes were wide as she tried so desperately to breathe. Her hands scratched at his. The blood was making it hard to see. Her heart was pounding loudly, the children's screams began to fade out, and her own pulse became the only thing she could hear. Her whole body was numb. Her eyes began to roll to the back of her head, as she let out her final chokes and whimpers.

Suddenly, her body shook to the left – she could breathe. The pain on her chest had stopped and she could fill her lungs more evenly. Her weak head dropped to the side. Emily blinked sluggishly and saw Dean lying on his back with Mark on his chest.

Emily continued to watch, as Mark's left hand took a strong grip on the top of Dean's shirt. He raised his right fist over and over again, bringing it down hard on the left side of Dean's face. Emily couldn't hold on much more; her vision began to tunnel, as everything went black.

A gunshot sounded in the night sky, ricocheting off the buildings, and making an echoing noise. Rick stopped punching the man below him and ran over to his wife. He lifted Amy into his arms as she began to stir.

James lowered the gun and pointed it at the near stranger. "Get up!" he yelled, then without turning away he called, "Mark!"

Mark was still pounding on Dean.

Rick set Amy on her feet next to Julia, who was standing behind James, and ran over to his brother-in-law, grabbing his bloody fist, as he raised it one more time. "Mark, enough!" Mark turned his head, pure hatred in his eyes. He pushed away from Dean, dragging to his feet. He ran around Rick to drop next to his wife.

"Em?" he whispered, as he leant his head down on her chest to hear her faint wheezing, then reached up to cradle her head, holding it in his lap. Watching her blood-soaked face, tears began to collect in his eyes. "Emily?" he spoke louder. She remained unconscious in his arms.

Her nose was broken and swollen, her bottom lip had ballooned almost twice its size, and she had many more cut marks across her cheek and temple, which was now starting to bruise. Mark lowered her head back to the ground, and then raised her into his arms. He walked down the driveway, and stepped into the empty minivan, laying his wife across the back seat. James followed Mark with his eyes, then nodded. Julia and Amy ran into the van too, taking up the middle row. Rick ran to the house's front door and turned off the internal lights, quickly grabbing both children up into his arms. Closing the front door, he headed to the waiting van, passing Matt and Abby to the distraught women in the center seat. Rick closed the van's sliding door and jumped into the passenger seat. The stranger watched James, occasionally testing his resolve, as he held the gun still pointing towards them. James moved around the front of the van and jumped into the driver's seat. As he knocked it into drive, they took off down the dark street. Rick looked over his shoulder back at the man, who finally ran over to Dean's limp body and dropped to his knees, attempting to care for his friend.

CHAPTER SIX

The silence was overpowering. Five long minutes down the road, Rick spoke, turning to James. "You got a gun?" he asked.

James smiled with no humor. "I figured there is a pretty price on each of our heads, so we'd need some protection." Then he glanced in his rear-view mirror and all sarcasm was lost.

James turned the radio on softly; Bon Inver's "Flume" was playing. Finally, the situation seemed to sink in, and no one said another word. They just sat there feeling the gentle bump and sway, as they fled.

* * *

Roughly six hours later, Emily began to wake, her body hurting absolutely everywhere. She opened her eyes slowly, to see Mark smiling down at her, encouragingly. Her head was in his lap and all she could tell was that they were in the back of a fast-moving vehicle and that the sun was beginning to rise from the left-side window. As more sensations came back to Emily, her body began to move, causing more pain. Her face automatically scrunched up and she let out a light yelp of agony. Mark's face showed sympathy, then concern, as he looked her up and down.

Her right hand reached up to feel her extremely swollen face, but Mark gently held it and pulled it back down to her chest. "I know it hurts, baby. Try not to move." Big tears filled her eyes as she tried to stay still. Finally, the pain became too much and she lost consciousness once more.

Amy, who had a black eye, had turned around on the middle seat, watching her sister and feeling completely helpless.

"Is she going to be okay?" She directed her question at Mark, who had balled his right fist up, leaning on his elbow, looking out the window. She could see he was obviously lost in his own guilt and brewing anger.

He took a deep breath, dropping his fist, and turning to speak, said, "She'll be fine." Looking down at his wife and squeezing his eyes shut as he took in her brutalized face, he said through pursed lips, "But she's gonna be in a lot of pain for a while. I'll give her some morphine first chance I get, then hopefully when she wakes up, she will be able to function somewhat." Then he turned back to the window. Amy just nodded, tears already filling her eyes, and turned back to face forward in her seat, dropping her head and leaning it against Abby's back.

"James," Mark called from the far back seat.

James looked in the rear-view mirror.

"First chance you get, we really need to change and I need to reposition Em's nose." He grimaced as he said the last part.

"Yeah, sounds like a plan. I need to stretch my legs anyway." Glancing down, he remarked, "We need gas anyway."

Ten minutes later, James turned into a gas station and pulled up to the nearest pump. Everyone but Emily was awake now, as the sun began to rise higher in the sky.

"Okay, well I'll fill up then I guess we can go to the bathrooms and change," James advised, as Julia grabbed the three bags filled with new clothes from the space between her and the door. She passed the clothes to each person.

"Um, I think I'll change in here," Mark quickly responded.

74   LAUREN SOMERTON

"Amy, when you get back, do you mind helping me change Em?"

"Do you want to change her first?" she responded.

"Well, I gotta fix her nose, which will bleed some more, and I doubt you wanna see or hear that," he muttered.

She grimaced at the thought, jumping out of the van and lifting Abby into her arms, while Julia lifted Matt. "We'll go get changed, the guys can go change and wait inside. When you're ready come grab me."

"Sounds like a plan, I'll be ten minutes."

She nodded, closing the sliding door and heading towards the ladies' restroom. Rick was already in the men's room changing, while James had finished pumping the gas and was heading into the station, leaving Mark alone with his unconscious wife.

He lifting her head up as he slid out of his seat and placed it back down. Taking a step to the right, he pulled her legs up to balance at the top of the window, so that her head lay in the middle of the seat, "I'm so sorry, baby," he whispered.

He positioned her body on the edge of the seat, so that he could rest his knee on the other side of her body, effectively positioning himself directly over top of her. He leant down, examining his patient, and then pulling back, he placed the side of both palms on either side of her deformed nose. He sucked in a sharp breath, closed his eyes, and pulled his hands quickly to the right.

A loud crunching noise, followed by a crack, and her cartilage snapped back into place. Fresh blood was flowing down the right side of her face, as her head flopped. Mark quickly lifted her under the armpits and sat her upright. Her chin dropped to rest on her chest. He ripped off his father's borrowed shirt, balled it up, and raised her head straight, using the shirt to sop up the blood. Holding her still, he saw the blood begin to clot and eventually stop. Mark slowly lowered her head, to rest on the right window, and used this opportunity to jump into the middle row seating and change into a pair of beige khaki shorts and a black t-shirt, then lace up a pair of Nike runners.

Laying Emily's clothes out on the middle seat, he turned and opened the sliding door, waving Amy over. She passed Abby to Rick, and left the group standing just outside the station doors as she got into the van and closed the door behind her. Amy got into the far left back seat and pulled her sister over. She then pulled Emily's body down so that her head was on her lap and Mark reached down, sitting on the edge of the far right seat, and lifting his wife's feet into his lap.

Amy lent over the seat in front, grabbing a clean pair of underwear and socks, holding them in her hands. Mark lifted his wife's dress up so that it rested halfway up her thighs. Tracing his hands up either side of her legs, he reached for her underwear and shimmed them down past her knees and off the end of her toes. Amy passed the new underwear to him, and he replaced the last pair, trying to move her body as little as possible. He then covered her feet with black ankle socks. He reached over, grabbing a pair of cut-off denim shorts. One foot at a time, he managed to get the shorts halfway up her bare legs. Amy reached down and grabbed either side of her sister's lower back. Mark nodded, and she lifted as he quickly pulled the shorts into place, buttoning them up as he finished. They rested just above her knees. Mark lightly dropped Emily's feet to the floor as Amy sat her back up.

"Can you hold her arms up for me?" he asked as Emily's chin fell back onto her chest. Amy barely managed as Mark carefully felt down her torso, stopping and concentrating on her right ribs.

Cussing under his breath, then looking up at Amy who had her eyebrows raised, he said, "I think this rib is broken. Maybe more than one." Looking out the window towards the station, then back, Mark said, "Okay, hold her there, I'll be right back."

Mark flung the door open with more force than needed. No

one was around, so he left it propped open and ran into the store. Less than a minute later, he was back with a large, thick, tensor bandage in his left hand and a pair of scissors in the other. Climbing back in, he closed the door behind him again, taking the seat next to his wife. Amy had Emily gripped under each arm leaning away from the seat.

"Okay," he said, more to himself than Amy.

He reached up, grabbing the top of Emily's ruined dress, and carefully pulled the scissors down. Then telling Amy to lean her all the way forward, he cut down the back side of the silk dress, successfully splitting it in two. Sitting her up straight, they both took a half of the fabric and slid it off her arms. Mark reached back and unclipped her bra, sliding it off her arms and throwing it in the bag on the seat in front.

"Hold her arms up, again. Keep her elbows out of the way," he instructed, as Amy lifted. He reached down to the seat, grabbing the bandage and unraveling it roughly six inches. He held the beginning to her left rib cage, and holding the bandage taut, he wrapped it across her bare breasts and completed three turns around her torso before he clipped the end back on itself.

He grabbed her new, plain, black t-shirt and put her hands through each of the arms and pulled it to her shoulders. Amy rested her sister's body back against the seat and guided her head though the shirt's neck as Mark pulled the shirt down the remainder of her body.

Letting out a deep breath, they finally leant Emily's body back into her seat, as Mark spoke. "Thanks," he said smiling.

"Don't mention it," she said, smiling back, stepping around them both. Amy collected the bloody clothes in an empty bag, and dragged the van door open. Stepping out, she waved the rest of the group over, as she threw the bag in the closest trash can and got back into the vehicle, sliding back over to her own seat in the middle row.

Mark pulled his wife into his side, wrapping his free arm around her waist, as her head dropped onto his shoulder. They each got back into their seats. Wearing new, more summer-appropriate clothing, Matt took up the free space on the other side of Emily, as Abby sat in between Amy and Julia.

"How's she doing?" James asked, looking in his rearview mirror.

"Better," Mark stated, looking down. "Now, all we need is to pick up some pain killers for when she wakes up."

Just as he finished, Julia rustled a plastic bag and turned around in her seat.

Way ahead of you." She beamed, passing him some water and two bottles of high-end painkillers.

Looking at them, he said, "Thanks." He smiled back, taking a closer look at the labels. "Where'd you get these? You can't get these ones without a prescription."

"Really?" She shrugged, turning and looking at the gas station. "Well I just asked the guy if he had any strong stuff, so he gave me those." She turned back. "I guess we are in the middle of nowhere." Mark just smiled and placed the bottles in his side pocket, and the water in the drink holders next to him. James started the engine and they drove off, passing a sign saying '380 East.'

Another two hours later and Emily began to wake. Her cheeks held more color than previously. Without moving her head from Mark's shoulder, she glanced to her left at Matt, who was sitting quietly, staring out the window. Looking around, everyone seemed to be silent, listening to the radio, either staring out the window or straight ahead.

Emily slowly leant away from her husband, causing him to lightly jump. She pinched her eyes shut, as she pulled her body straight. The pain was excruciating. Mark had his hands less than two inches away from her, not wanting to touch anything, as if to support her. She stayed there for ten seconds, before she finally opened her eyes. Attempting to take a deep breath, she winced, and reached to her right side. Making sure to not push down, she noticed her change of clothes. Mark reached into his pocket, pulling out the two bottles and taking a pill from each.

"Here," he said, as he passed her the white tablets, and unscrewed the cap of the water bottle. "These will lessen the pain."

She took them quickly, throwing them back, as he raised the bottle to her mouth. She took a big gulp, and another.

"Thanks," she said inaudibly.

He brushed the hair from her face. "How do you feel?"

She considered his question for a second, creasing her eyebrows. "Better than last night," she said slowly, adding a faint smile at the end. She slouched back in her seat. "My head is killing me, but it's bearable."

He nodded, considering. "I know, but give those pills fifteen minutes and you shouldn't feel much." He smiled back at her, placing his hand on top of hers. She glanced over his shoulder, seeing the sun bright in the sky and desert around them. Looking down, as Mark intertwined his fingers with hers, she lightly gasped and raised their hands up to her face. His were terribly swollen, and blackened, with large gashes around each knuckle.

He turned and frowned, as she examined his hand. Big tears began to fill her eyes, as she turned his hand to see more. He untwined their fingers, cupping the far side of her face; she turned to kiss his palm, squeezing her eyes shut, as the tears overflowed down her cheeks.

Amy and Julia turned in their seats. Emily turned to face forward and was caught off guard, as Amy leant over the back seat, grabbed her sister by the nape of her neck, and kissed her forehead as hard as she could.

Emily was the first to speak, noticing the purple bruise under her sister's eye. "How are you?" She was concerned.

Amy shook her head and let out a soft laugh, pointing to her own face. "Oh this? I think I'm gonna make it," she said with a smile. "All that matters is that you're going to be okay,"

Emily rolled her eyes, and without looking, grabbed Mark's hand again, intertwining their fingers. "I am going to be just fine! Just gotta be a little careful and I'll be right back to normal in no time." Her lip was thankfully back to normal, though deep blue danced just below the skin and a scab was forming where her teeth had sunk in.

Amy lowered her head slightly, raising her eyebrow, as Emily nodded and said encouragingly, "Really!"

Amy smiled and opened her mouth, to add her final comment, as the van suddenly swerved to the left, flinging Amy into Julia and Emily into Mark. Amy turned forward in her seat, as Mark gripped the seat in front of them, pulling Emily into his side. They gawked at the driver's seat, as James' head collapsed into the steering wheel and his hands fell to his lap. Rick reached over and grabbed the wheel, attempting to steer it straight, as he barked his friend's name over and over. Julia had fallen out of her seat and into the open space in front of Mark. Emily momentarily looked to her left, to the seat occupied by Matt, who was wide-eyed, with his mouth hanging open, as his head collapsed back on his armrest.

Emily stared down and listened to Rick, as Matt's pupils consumed their irises, and his body reacted to whatever he was seeing. She clung to Mark, as hard as she could, her broken rib screaming out under the skin.

"James!" Rick yelled one last time, as Matt took a deep breath and blinked continuously. Turning her head, she noticed Julia beginning to blink, reaching for her head, and Mark helping her back into her seat. James had sat back up in his seat, breath heaving in shock, as he tightly gripped the steering wheel.

"Pull over now!" Rick bellowed.

James did not take his eyes off the road, as he took the first exit and stopped along the curb, leading to an abandoned children's park. He cut off the engine, yanked the door open, and angrily stormed around the front of the van, marching up the grassy hill. Rick turned to his wife in the seat behind him. "Go!" she said, gesturing with her hand, for him to follow. "Make sure he's okay!" Rick nodded, and then opened his door, running after his best friend.

"Is everyone okay?" Mark asked, after a few seconds.

Amy nodded, looking down at Abby. Julia turned around in her seat, rubbing the top of her head. "Yeah, I'm fine."

Mark looked down at Emily, as she tightly gripped his waist. "And you?" he asked.

Pulling away, she tried not to show the true amount of pain she was in. "Yeah. I'm good." She could barely catch her breath.

The others now turned to Julia, and Emily spoke. "Another vision?"

Julia nodded.

"What did you see?" Amy prodded, leaning across the seat.

"The same as last time, just..." she stopped, creasing her face deep in thought, "Just a little more." They all nodded, encouraging her. "Same guy and stuff, but then other people; people in white masks staring at us, then other people." Looking over at Amy, she said, "Some I recognized from the wedding, locked in a dark room." She started to shake her head as she remembered. "Then... What looked like surgical tools, needles, and blades." She gasped, looking over the seat at Matt who was pale white and still. "And blood."

She stopped, closing her eyes, and spinning around to face the door. She pulled it open and began walking up the hill, joining the others. Amy watched after her, before turning to her sister, unsure. Emily directed her chin after Julia as Amy leapt from the van, hurrying after her friend.

Emily watched after her sister, until she disappeared over the ridge. Mark stood, bent over in the van, and went to examine Abby.

Emily turned to the boy next to her. "Matt," she spoke slowly. He gradually raised his eyes to look at her. His small features mirrored an aged man. The fear she sensed in him made her reach down and lift him to her chest. She edged her way forward and out of the van, just as Mark did the same with Abby.

Closing the sliding door behind them, Mark reached up to rest his free hand in between his wife's shoulder blades, gently guiding and offering his support as they both began to ascend the grassy hill. Once they reached the top, they noted Julia and Amy were seated on the grass to the right, talking, while Rick and James were at the bottom on the other side, throwing rocks in a small pond. Mark lightly patted Emily's back, and then reached down to take her hand. They walked to the green metal bench on the edge of the graveled playground. Sitting down, the children collapsed onto their laps, their legs falling to the side and their heads resting on their chests.

The four sat there for five minutes, before Mark began bouncing Abby on his knees. "Would you like to go play on the playground?" he whispered in her ear, loud enough for Emily and Matt to hear. She raised her head, slowly turning towards the park, then dropped it back down. Pouting, she shook her head.

"How about the swings?" Emily suggested, Mark smiled as both Matt and Abby raised their heads, and looked at each other then back at his wife. They nodded, starting off slow, then gaining momentum. "Well, then."

They stood and walked to the swings, lowered both children

into the baby swings, and began pushing. After a half a minute, both children were giggling and smiling brightly. Both Mark and Emily faked a smile every time the children looked back at them, while they were really glancing past the park over at their friends and family. Both sets of friends were deep in discussion for more than twenty minutes. Finally, James stood up with Rick, and they made their way over to Julia and Amy. As they also stood up from the grass, Rick grabbed Amy in a tight hug, while Julia and James silently stood by. Five seconds later, James shook his head and closed the gap between Julia and himself. They held each other equally as close and as long as their married friends. Minutes later, those four made their way over to Mark and Emily, who were still pushing the giggling toddlers.

James smile dropped first. "I am so sorry." His head then dropped, as he took over for Emily, pushing Matt.

"Hey!" Emily said taking on an annoyed expression. "You did nothing wrong! You couldn't help it." Then reaching up, she grabbed his head and kissed his cheek, then leant back. "And you saved my life," she finished. Stepping back, she put her right arm around her husband's waist, as he put his arm around her shoulder, and kissed her hair.

James grinned, a light pink covering his cheeks. "So, now what?" he asked, as Abby giggled, breaking their silence.

"We continue on to see the old guy?" Rick kicked the gravel in front of him. They all turned as he lifted his head and spoke again, shrugging his shoulders and holding Amy's hand, "Well, from what I can tell he's obviously still important. Maybe he can give us some answers about this new..." looking over to James who was now frowning, "...stuff."

"I agree," Amy said, squeezing his hand. "I mean we have no new helpful information, so I say we stick with our original plan." She then looked over at her sister for advice. "Em?"

Emily took a slow, deep breath, wincing as pain shot across her chest, garnering a concerned look from Mark. Looking at the group before her, she said, "Well, it's not like we really have a choice any more." They all nodded in agreement.

Standing around the children, as they seemed oblivious to the situation, Julia changed the subject, "Is anyone else hungry?"

James laughed, taking a step towards her. He rolled his eyes and said, "Starving." They began walking shoulder to shoulder down the hill, less than an inch between them, their arms brushed together. Halfway, James twisted his hand, and grabbed hers. Their fingers twisted together and their arms began lightly swinging back and forth in synchrony, as they made their way to the van.

Rick turned with his wife, as they followed their friends. Amy glanced back, over her right shoulder, and raised her eyebrows up and down mischievously, while she grinned. Emily and Mark laughed quietly, shaking their heads at the inevitable will of Amy Michaels.

Emily reached her far arm over, resting her left hand on Mark's chest, tracing soft kisses along his jaw line. Toddlers freed, the final four made their way down to the van. The sliding door was propped open, with James and Julia staring at each other in the far back seat, and Rick and Amy in the middle. Emily passed Abby off to her sister, and got in the passenger seat, as Mark did the same, closing the sliding door then jumping into the driver's seat.

"So, what's everyone in the mood for?" Mark asked, starting up the engine and fastening his seatbelt.

"Anything fast," James called from the back seat.

"Mickey D's sounds good right about now!" Rick said.

Mark laughed turning back around in his seat. "McDonald's it is!"

They drove ten more minutes down the road and pulled into

the drive-through. After they each yelled their order into the half-rusted speaker and got their food, Mark drove to the nearest parking spot and parked. They sat and ate their food, more slowly than expected, savoring every bite. The children played with their Happy Meal toys, while the others sat and finished. When they were ready, Mark turned back onto the 380-East highway and hit the gas. The children continued to play with their toys as the two couples began to talk in the back. Emily watched out the windows, while Mark silently drove.

After two more hours, Mark unexpectedly pulled the van over to the side of the road. "Is that what you saw?" he asked, pointing at the windshield.

James leaned forward, with Julia comfortably under his arm. They both looked out the windshield at a giant sign that read: "Welcome to Roswell, the dairy capital of the southwest." Julia read each word aloud, then nodded. James' smile turned to a frown, and he nodded too.

Mark's face stiffened as he nodded. Turning back around, he pulled back onto the road. "We're getting closer," he finally said, as the van became silent again.

Pulling into the first gas station without a word, he went inside. They all looked at each other for a minute as he made his way back. Closing the door behind him, he passed a giant map of Roswell back to Rick, who then passed it back to James.

"Where did you say it was again?" Mark asked.

"Um..." James muttered, trying to remember, as Julia spoke.

"Old Hondo Channel Rd.," she said, looking down at the map in front of them. After a minute of scanning, James pointed down.

"There!" he said, leaning down and squinting closer. "Yeah, right there." He pointed, passing the map back to Rick.

Rick forwarded the information on to the driver, showing him with his fingers. "Right here. It'll be easier if you go through here and down there." He traced his fingers along the map, directing his brother-in-law through back roads and shortcuts. Mark finally turned back around in his seat, passing the map to Emily, as he put the van in drive and got back onto the highway.

CHAPTER SEVEN

John woke up to the phone ringing at his bedside. "Hello?" he said groggily.

"It's Abe, sorry to wake you, just thought you might want to know. I just got off the phone with my bosses and they say they want to arrange a meet as soon as we both can." John sat straight up, waking Kristine, who saw that he was on the phone and rolled back onto her side.

"I'm free, as soon as you are." He spoke a bit too loudly, causing Kristine to groan and kick him in the leg. "Sorry," he whispered, getting out of bed and walking out of the room.

Abel laughed on the other end. "I thought you'd say that, so I arranged a meet in one hour."

"Great." John smiled into the phone. "Where?"

"I'll come pick you up in forty-five minutes, okay? They suggested going for breakfast so we're gonna meet them at Ducky's."

John turned and walked back into the bedroom. "I'll meet you outside." Hanging up the phone, he dropped it on the chair, and headed into the bathroom.

Twenty minutes later, John snuck out of the bathroom, and began to rummage through their large dresser, trying to make as little noise as possible.

"And where do you think you're going?" Kristine's voice startled him.

He slowly turned around, and shrugged his shoulder, keeping a straight face. "To see my other wife." He remained still for a second, then dodged the king-sized white pillow hurtling across the room at him, as he laughed out loud. In between laughs he managed to give her a true answer. "That was Abe, his bosses want to meet with us, and discuss everything that's going on." He finished with a smile.

She kept a straight face, then squinted her left eye into a sly expression. "Okay," she said, thinking. "No, that's good, hopefully you get some good news." She pulled his pillow over to the center of the bed, and flopped back down.

"I hope so." He finished getting ready. Walking over to the bed and starting at the foot, he crawled his way up until he covered his wife, who had her eyes shut and a big smile on her face. Eventually, she opened her eyes. "I shouldn't be long," he stated, leaning down and kissing her sweetly.

"Okay, call me if anything comes up." Then she light-heartedly pushed him off, closing her eyes, and turning her head into the pillow. "You may leave," she embellished, eyes shut. "Her Highness is not done with her royal sleep."

John rolled his eyes and kissed her cheek, then went to wait in the living room. He turned on the TV, skipping to the news channel instantly. The same reports were on as the day before. The only new news was that members of the wedding party had been intercepted at one of their parents' homes in Littletown. They had sadly acted violently, beating a friendly neighborhood citizen, and stealing his maroon mini-van. The anchor then continued to emphasize the importance of their capture. Still no others had been found.

John glanced up at the small clock above the TV and noticed it was exactly eight a.m., when Abel pulled up in front of his house. Turning off the TV, he ran out the front door and jumped in the passenger side.

"Morning." John spoke past an unexpected yawn.

"Good morning, let's hope we get some good news!" Abel smiled, pulling away from the curb.

Ten minutes later, they were parked out front of Ducky's breakfast house. No other cars were in the parking lot, so they sat for a few minutes before heading in.

"Do you have a table for a Jones or Mr. Neil?" Abel scanned the open floor plan of the '80s style interior. Three random men sat alone, scattered throughout the restaurant.

The waitress studied her table arrangements and shook her head. "No sir, no one by those names."

"Oh okay, could we just get a table for four then?" He took the opportunity to check out the perky waitress. The buttons on her uniform seemed to be missing the top two loops, exposing more cleavage that necessary.

She smiled, taking four menus in her left hand. "Table or booth?"

"A table is fine, thank you." He smiled back at her, following her to a round table in the far right corner of the restaurant, under a large window. She took their drink order, coffee with two creams and one sweetener, and left them sitting in silence. Two minutes later, their drinks had arrived, but their company had not.

Looking around the restaurant, John glanced back out the window. "Where are they?"

"They'll be here." Abel took a drink of his coffee. "Would you relax?"

John turned to look at Abel, who was staring down at John's hands. Looking down, he noticed his vice-like grip on the coffee mug. He was holding it so hard in his right hand that it was shaking. Every little movement threw burning hot coffee over the table. His screaming senses came back to him, and he gasped at the heat and released the cup, shaking his hand on the carpet below, and then wiping it dry with his napkin. He examined his hand, and then looked over at his best friend, who had both elbows on the table. Abel had his cup to his mouth and his eyebrows raised high; John dropped his head slightly, and spoke in a defeated voice. "I'm sorry, I just need know when I can get back in there."

Abel placed his coffee on the table and reached over to grab John's shoulder, nudging him lightly, waiting for him to look up. "I know John, not long now, and hopefully, everything will be back to normal. Honestly, some people would welcome a short vacation, considering you've spent the last three months holed up in that cold office."

John smiled and nodded back, fake-punching him on the shoulder.

"Are we interrupting?"

The intrusion made Abel and John turn and look up instantly, their smiles fading to serious form. Abel pushed back his chair first, standing, as John copied him.

"Oh, no sir." Abel gestured to the seats in front of them. "Please, have a seat."

The two men wore black business suits, finely pressed and professional looking. They sat formally, one ordering tea instead of coffee.

"So, what's the news?" Abel relaxed into his seat.

Both men turned to each other. One nodded, then lifted a black leather briefcase onto the table, while the other, the man Abel recognized as his new superior, Jacob Neil, answered their questions. Neil's words were stiff, and forced. Though he had been in the position for two months now, he had rarely spoken to, let alone acknowledged, Abel.

"Dr. Jones."

Abel put up his hand, "Please, just Abe is fine."

Jacob nodded, "Lansing Foundations has decided to relocate you," he said, looking over at John, "and Dr. Stark, to a brand-new facility, a few blocks away from the original."

John turned to Abel, with a confused look on his face, then back to Jacob. "Relocating? Where? What about our research?"

John had leant forward, resting on the table; his voice was gradually rising, as the waitress returned and Abel patted his back, and whispered, "Calm down."

John fell back into his seat, glancing up at the waitress as she spoke. Taking out a pen and holding a small piece of paper, she tapped it twice, "Okay, what can I get you guys to eat?"

No one spoke so she looked around the table and stopping at Abel. Raising her eyebrows, and pushing her chewing gum to her right cheek, she said, "What can I get you?"

Abel had not had a chance to look over the menu, so he asked for the daily special. She nodded, chewed twice, then continued to the right where Jacob was sitting. This time she didn't ask, she just tapped her pen lightly on the paper. "I'll have scrambled eggs, two slices of bacon, three sausages, grilled tomatoes, and mushrooms. Sourdough toast, with the crust cut off." Only John noticed her light roll of the eyes and he smiled down at his lap.

She turned to the gentleman next to him, "And you?"

"I'll have the same," he said, not taking his eyes off the table.

Lastly, she turned to John, who forced a smile and asked for the special. Leaving, she stood by the computer, placing their order for longer than the average time needed.

Keeping a close eye on the silent man in front of him, thinking something just wasn't right with this guy, John leaned onto the table and had to ask, "I'm sorry, what was your name?"

The gentleman took a deep breath, swiftly looking up from the table straight into John's prying eyes. He was roughly fifty years old, with salt-and-pepper coloring to his hair. His stare was intense enough, without adding the looming scar which traced from the left side of his nose and down across his cheek. After a few seconds, his shoulders seemed to relax and he extended his right arm across the table, with a forced grin on his face. "Tom Edwards."

Abel then asked, glancing back and forth between the two men, "Well, Tom, I have had the pleasure of meeting Jacob before in my last briefing, but what do you have to do with our research?"

Tom let out a small cough, making John and Abel lean back in their seats and glance at each other in confusion as he continued. "I'm..." He paused to think of the right words; "the specialist." They still had blank faces. "You might call me new security, solely for your old office building."

"Security?" John muttered in a disbelieving tone, arching one perfect eyebrow and glancing over at Jacob.

Jacob began to shake his head lightly. "Dr. Stark, don't worry about anything. None of your research was touched." Then looking over at Abel he said, "You know, a few unstable elements were tampered with and we need to make sure everything is okay." Patting Tom's back, he smiled. "So, let's just let Mr. Edwards do his job."

John's jaw dropped open to ask another question, but shut quickly as two waitresses came over to the table and placed their breakfasts in front of them. One stood there, refilling their coffee, and adding a new tea bag to a metal water pot and placing it in the center of the table. John looked over at Abel, who had already begun shoveling his eggs into his face and smiling at the waitress. John cut a square of bacon, added some eggs, and lifted the fork to his mouth, taking a big bite. The others joined in, devouring their meals.

"How does everything taste?" she asked.

Abel smiled. "Oh everything is fine, thank you."

Then he winced, as John pressed hard on his toe when the waitress walked away. John leaned over, whispering, "Would you stop flirting, for once, and be serious!" His face was serious, too serious. Abel swallowed loudly, as he took in his best friend's mood; but then blew a sigh of relief as John's angry face turned to a mocking grin. He rolled his eyes and turned back to the men in front of them.

Before either Abel or John could further comment, Jacob continued, "Okay, so all your things have been successfully moved into the new building. You each have double the space you had before." Abel grinned over at John.

Jacob glanced down at the paperwork that had been taken out of the briefcase, as Tom sat silently eating, widening his smile as Jacob continued "And best of all," said Jacob, looking over at John, "we understand the importance of your research and the stress this incident must have put on you, so we have contacted the university and with some…" he glanced sideways at Tom, "… persuasion, we have added fifty-thousand dollars to your personal research and added an extra year to your sabbatical."

John's jaw dropped and his eyes seemed to pop out of his skull, as Abel spoke up. With an obvious shaken look on his face, Abel grabbed John's shoulder as he sat silently in shock. "What? That's amazing." Looking over at John and shaking his shoulder, he said, "John, that's unheard of."

John's eyes didn't move from the table, as he just sat in a daze. Jacob continued, "And Abe, we haven't forgotten about you. You have been granted an extra year as well, and a fifteen-percent increase to your yearly salary." He stopped to let everything sink in. "So, are we good?" His overly friendly and engaging enthusiasm felt insincere to John and Abel. Something still felt wrong with the whole situation, but they weren't going to pass up on such welcome compensation.

John and Abe shot a look at each other, giant grins spreading across their faces, as they turned back and both merely said, "Yes."

Abe added, "Of course."

Tom finished his last bite and pushed away from the table, standing and surprising them all. Jacob looked up at him, and nodded, dabbing the side of his mouth with the paper napkin and then tossing it onto his empty plate. He stood, saying, "Well, this has been great gentlemen, but we really must be going."

John stood up and reached over the table, to shake his hand. "Thank you, so much."

As they shook hands, and Abel finished his last bite, Tom pulled a wad of bills from his left pocket, took out three twenty-dollar bills and threw them on the table. Abel quickly reached for them, stood up, and tried to pass them back. "Oh no, please let me get this."

Tom smiled, lifting the briefcase off the table and he took a step back, raising his free hand up, holding his palm out. "No, my treat." Without another word he turned, walking out into the parking lot, while the other three watched after him.

"Forgive Tom. He can be a little strange sometimes," Jacob said, taking the money from Abel's still outstretched hand and throwing it back on the table. "You boys stay and finish up." Patting John on the shoulder, he said, "Congratulations." John just smiled and nodded once more. Jacob separated the pile of white and yellow papers on the table into two piles, then passed a pile each to John and Abel. "These are your new contract agreements, and such. Have a read-over and don't hesitate to call me if you have any questions."

Jacob shook his hand, turned, and took two steps for the door. Abel began to sit down, as Jacob quickly turned and lifted his pointer finger on his right hand, as if he just remembered something. "Oh, and I'll swing by Abel's place later tonight, to drop off your new keys and grab your old ones."

They both just nodded, as he turned and joined Tom in the parking lot.

John and Abel sat there in silence for a minute, glancing down at the pages in front of them, without really looking at the words.

"All finished?" the waitress asked, startling them.

"Oh yes, yes. Thank you, it was great." Abel winked, reaching over and helping pile the dirty dishes in her arms, not taking his eyes off of her. John just sat, still looking down at his paperwork, and lightly laughed to himself.

Finally, Abel sat back down, watching her walk away, and noticed John staring at him with a grin and shaking his head. "What?" he said, exaggerating the word. "She's hot."

This time John laughed out loud, "And half your age." He continued to laugh, as Abel punched him hard in the left shoulder.

Their laughter gradually stopped, as the table was cleared and they took their forms, making their way back to Abel's black, 1967 Shelby Ford Mustang. They sat in their seats, silent for another minute.

John turned in his seat and practically yelled the words with excitement, "Can you believe this?" His smile beamed, as his best friend answered.

"This is crazy, I've been complaining about our work space for ages, and it wouldn't hurt to have a little more money, and supplies," Abel mentioned.

"And time," John quickly added. They were quiet for another second. "That Tom guy was weird though."

"Oh yeah, something about him didn't feel right," Abel commented, "but who cares!" He cheered, throwing his papers on the back seat and knocking the car into gear.

They drove around for an hour, just listening to music without a care in the world. John surprised Abel with, "Hey, head towards the old office."

He did, and twenty minutes later they were at the end of the street; no one could get through still. Police barricades consumed the street, with bright orange tape and armed men ten paces back. Abel stopped the car and got out, attempting to get a better look. John followed him to the first cement barricade, as an armed man began walking towards them. With what time they had, they glanced down the road, going on tiptoes, trying to see.

The man started waving them back. "Get back in your car," he called, still walking towards them.

They stood there, still looking as the man neared. The large white tent was still erected, out front of the entrance, with even more armed men wearing full white. The man reached them, clearly agitated, with only a meter between him and Abel. "Get back in your car, sir, and drive away. It's not safe for civilians here." Abel did not answer. "Both of you move, now," the soldier demanded with more force in his tone, tapping the gun on his side.

John looked back and forth between his friend and the stranger. Breaking the silence, he turned and grabbed Abel's arm, "Come on, let's go." At first Abel still stood there, not moving, with a confused look on his face. John pulled his arm again. "Abe, come on!"

Abel finally pulled out of his semi-trance, starting to blink, and shaking his head quickly from side to side, as if trying to lose a thought. He turned and walked back to the car, with John. Once they were inside, John spoke. "What was that?" He sat staring at his friend, who seemed deep in thought. "Abe?" He waited.

"Nothing," Abel answered quickly, reversing down the small street and turning around. "It's nothing."

"Didn't look like nothing. What were you thinking?" John

asked. Abel did not answer; he just stared out the windshield and drove straight, "Abel!" John said his full name with force.

Two minutes later, Abel pulled into a near parking lot, parked swiftly, and turned to sit sideways on the seat with his right leg bent. His head was still down as he leant back in the seat, supporting his body with his elbow wedged in the headrest. Gesturing with his hands, he slowly raised his head to look John square in the face. "It just seemed too easy."

"What do you mean?" John burst back, more concerned, though he sounded angry and frustrated.

Abel grabbed John's papers. "This." He threw them back in his lap and gestured to where they had just driven from. "All this!" He stopped for a minute, searching for the right words. "Why in the hell would they need armed guards? Fifteen of them. And block off five full blocks?"

"Because of the chemicals and..." John answered, as Abel started shaking his head and cut him off.

"No, John, I was going over that stuff last night. Yes, there were some bad chemicals in there that could definitely hurt some people, but not to this magnitude." He took a deep breath them blew it out. "The quantities I was working with, if mixed badly, would have harmed twenty to thirty people at most. Even then, it would have to be in a closed, confined space for more than a few hours. It's not like the stuff would have no smell or anything. Unless they introduced an outside source, I can't think of anything being contagious either.

"Did you see? It was only our building that had most of the tape around it and all the lights still on. They're not even touching the surrounding buildings that are supposedly infected and dangerous. What about those missing people? The whole state is out looking for them."

"So, what are you saying?" John finally asked, when it seemed

Abel had said everything.

"I'm saying, our little payout, the new lab, the missing people, the armed men... It's all too much for just a chemical spill. Something else is definitely going on here, that we don't know about." Abel turned back in his seat.

"So, what are we going to do about it?" John said.

"I don't know yet, but you are going home to your family." John started to protest, but Abe cut him off. "I'll call you later on tonight." John looked at him questioningly. "Don't worry, I'm not gonna do anything tonight. Just a little research, that's all."

Fewer than ten minutes passed before Abel had driven to John's house, and they were sat idling in his driveway.

"Abel," John's voice seemed to chastise.

Abel dropped his head back, resting it on the seatback, and then turned to face his friend. "I promise, okay? I won't do anything stupid."

John squinted, scanning him up and down, and then he opened the passenger door, taking one step out. "Okay, you better not... Or I'll kick your ass." He smiled, scuffed up Abel's hair, and got out of the car quickly.

Closing the door and walking towards the house, John paused when Abel called his name. As John bent down, leaning into the car, Abel said, "Don't forget these. Make sure you read the small print." He handed John his pile of the paperwork. "And I need your keys, remember."

John, still leaning into the car, pulled his keychain from his pocket and slowly peeled the correct key away, then passed it over to Abel. "Okay, thanks." Taking a step back, he paused again, bending down. "Nothing stupid, not until we know more, okay?"

Abel grinned, shifted into reverse, and reached over to shake John's hand once. "Deal." He placed his outstretched arm over to rest behind the passenger seat and looked over his shoulder. John took a step back, as Abel reversed off the driveway and down the street, turning the corner out of sight.

John watched after him, long after he was gone. Slowly he turned, shaking his head, and walked back into the house.

CHAPTER EIGHT

"Mark, can you stop at the next exit? Abby needs to go." Julia laughed from the back of the van. Mark smiled as he looked in his rear-view mirror to see the small child bouncing up and down on her seat, and looking around frantically.

They had been on the road non-stop for two hours now, and everyone was getting a bit fidgety. The conversations had died down, and everyone seemed to feel uneasy heading towards the unknown. Two minutes later, Mark pulled into the nearest gas station, as all but Mark, Emily, and Rick went to the bathroom.

James took a quarter out of his pocket and announced, "I'll be right back."

Nobody said anything as he closed the sliding door, and snuck behind the van. He stayed there for two minutes, and then walked around the side of the gas station with something white and roughly the size of a piece of paper in his hand, and then he went out of sight.

"All righty, then... Weirdo." Rick laughed, watching his best friend act so strangely. He shifted over his seat, and slid the door open. "Actually, I gotta stretch my legs and get a drink. Did you guys want anything?"

"No, thanks," Mark replied, smiling up at him, and then turning back down to smile at his wife.

"Em?" Rick asked.

"Nope, I'm good, thanks."

"Cool, be right back." Rick closed the door behind him.

The couple sat there alone, enjoying the silence, when Emily looked up and out the window then back to her husband. "Babe, how much cash do we have left?"

Without any hesitation he quickly pulled his wallet out of his khakis' pocket and counted the bills. As he counted, he noticed Emily lightly touch the side of her swollen face and feel her lip. "How do you feel?"

His sudden question surprised her, making her drop her hand instantly. "Oh, I'm fine."

Mark didn't believe her. He leaned over and lightly grazed the good side of her face, "Sweetheart, you went through a lot back there."

She frowned, fidgeting in her seat, at the flood of recent memories. She placed her hand over his. "I know Mark, but I honestly feel fine, considering…" She raised her right eyebrow at the last word. "I'm still just a little shook up, is all. Plus, I don't like this." She pointed her chin in the direction of the highway. "We have no idea what to expect and we don't even really know where we are going, or why."

"I know, I don't like it either, but at this point we don't really have an option. Do we?" He turned, reaching for her hand. "But I promise you, I will never leave you again."

Emily, shocked, pulled her head back. "That wasn't your faul…"

"Either way, I'm not leaving your side from now on. At least until we have more answers." Interrupting himself, he said, "And we have five hundred dollars combined."

"Really, how?" Emily asked, surprised. "I only brought fifty to the wedding with me. Did you bring all that money?"

"No, I only had eighty dollars, but I found some of my parent's emergency money. I don't know how much the others have.

Why?" Mark asked.

"Because I think we should get a hotel for the night, just so we can rest." Looking back out the window, she added, "It will be dark in an hour and we still don't know exactly where we are going. Plus, even if we did, I'd rather wait until sunlight."

He was quiet as he thought for a moment. "Yeah, that's probably for the best," he agreed. "God, knows what we're going to do, so I think a night of rest for everyone would be best."

As he finished, they watched James smiling back at them, and walking along the side of the van and back down to the back. The sliding door flew open, and the two other women and the children got back into their seats.

Rick stood there, with a plastic bag in his free hand, as he faced James. "What the hell are you up to?" he asked, sarcastically.

A "Shush," came from the back of the van, then James ran to the door, nudging Rick's back. "Get in, get in."

He did, followed by James. Feeling a flush of panic from James, Mark turned onto the highway. Rick turned back in his seat, "Okay, what were you up to back there?"

James had a giant grin on his face, as everyone turned to look at him; Mark looking in the rear mirror.

"Well, the latest news said practically the whole state is looking for us, so I figured changing the license plates to a Roswell plate would draw less attention." They all slowly, one by one, started to grin back at him. "So, I just switched the plates with another van. Hopefully, no one saw. They might not even notice."

"The quarter?" Rick asked.

"Screwdriver." He winked.

"Wow, James. That was actually pretty smart... For once." Then he turned to face forward. James took his arm off of Julia's shoulder and smacked the back of his friend's head. Then everyone laughed.

* * *

"Okay guys, I think we should head to a hotel and continue on, in the morning."

"Good idea." Amy spoke, but her mind was elsewhere.

"Yeah," James added.

Five minutes later, they turned a corner and parked outside of a Motel Eight. "Okay, how should we do this?" James asked.

"Obviously, cash only," Mark said.

"Okay, how about Julia and I go since we're the only..." glancing around the car, "normal looking ones"

"Okay, just get two rooms with queen beds," Emily said.

"How much money do you have?" Mark asked James.

"I've got about one hundred and thirty," he answered, as Rick pulled out his wallet.

"Here." Rick passed James a small wad of twenty-dollar bills, as Mark passed him another one hundred.

"Okay, stay here, we'll be right back," he said, sliding the door closed and walking into the front foyer.

* * *

The motel office was small, not much larger than the inside of the van. The desk took up most of the room. Even as the doorbell rang, the receptionist didn't look up from her magazine. She continued to pop her bubble gum, and turned the page.

"Excuse me," Julia said, reaching the desk before James.

The girl, no older than twenty, blew out her breath and dropped her magazine, staring up at Julia. "Yeah?" she asked, with a disgusted look on her face. When Julia didn't speak instantly, she continued, "Yeah, can I help you?"

James came up, and slid his arm over Julia's shoulder, "We'd like to get two rooms for the night." James leant down on the desk. "If it's not too much of an inconvenience for you."

She rolled her eyes, and pushed back from the desk, dropping her feet to the ground. She dragged her seat over to the computer, and then pushed off, rolling to the near wall behind her, and grabbing two keys. Her shoulder-length red hair barely covered what was clearly a half-shaved scalp, on the left side.

Throwing the keys on the counter she mumbled, "One hundred and ninety-eight dollars." She sat there with her hand stretched out.

James squinted at her, then threw the money in her hand. He took the keys, turned, and he and Julia both walked out of the building.

"What a bitch!" Julia muttered.

James laughed.

They got to the maroon van, which was parked around the corner. They slid the door open and jumped in.

"Pull around the side. We have rooms Nine and Ten."

Mark parked in front of room Nine as James passed a key to Emily. "Okay, how about Mark and I will take the kids and you guys take room Ten?" she thought aloud.

Rick slid the door open, saying, "Sounds like a plan."

They grabbed their things, walking as a group to the rooms. Mark opened the door, as the two couples continued walking. "Hey, when we're up, I'll come get you guys, okay?"

"Okay," Amy agreed, as Rick and the others continued to the room next door.

Mark closed the door behind him. Amy got inside, and locked the door behind her. James was already lying on his stomach on the far bed watching TV, with Julia at the top end of the bed, on the pillows. Rick had stepped out onto their ground floor balcony to check things out.

"I'm gonna jump in the shower," Amy muttered as Julia smiled, and James waved her to go ahead, not looking away from the television. She went into the bathroom, lightly closed the door and started a hot shower. After examining her bruised face, she stripped, then stepped under the welcoming water.

Julia and James had started talking, when Rick interrupted, "Where's Amy?"

"Shower." Julia turned her chin towards the bathroom.

Rick's face slowly transformed. Raising his eyebrow, and with a devilish grin looked over at James. James laughed, as Rick started towards the bathroom, taking his shirt off and dropping it to the floor. "I think I need a shower too."

James just laughed as Julia watched him enter the bathroom, closing the door. Then a few seconds later she could hear Amy's schoolgirl giggles. They attempted to start up their conversation again, until the giggling turned to laughter and moans. Finally, the banging on the shower siding made James say, "Feel like taking a walk?"

Julia jumped to her feet, "Yes, please!" She took James' outstretched hand, and they both ran from the room, locking the door behind them.

* * *

"Cartoons," Matt called, as soon as Mark locked the door behind him.

Emily looked down at her watch, "Okay, but only for a little bit." She lifted them both onto the farthest bed from the door, and they both sat silently on the edge, watching the first cartoon show Emily could find. She settled them in, passing them a juice box each, before sitting on her own bed.

Mark came and sat on the edge of their bed, resting both

hands on her shoulders. He scooted over, so he was kneeling right behind her, as he began to rub her neck and shoulders. Emily smiled to herself and let her head drop. They sat there for five minutes, before she raised her hands, and lightly patted his. She pulled her head back and smiled and he leant over and kissed her.

"I need a shower," she stated, pulling away.

A deep growl vibrated through his chest. "Mmm, I'd love to join you, but..." Then he turned his head to the side, to stare at the smiling toddlers, who were still watching *Bugs Bunny* and clapping their small hands together every so often. Emily turned her head to watch as well.

She laughed with Mark, as the children seemed to be overjoyed by the simplest things. Stopping, Emily winced and grabbed the side of her temple. Her eyes scrunched. "My head is killing me."

Concern etched on his face, Mark pulled her onto his lap. "Rate the pain from one to ten."

Rolling her eyes, she said, "Sorry, Doctor, I didn't realize you were on duty."

He nuzzled into her chest. "I'm always on duty." He pulled back with a mischievous wiggling of his brows. "Providing an array of services, 24/7." Giggling, she playfully smacked his chest, as he continued, "But seriously, do you need more pain killers?"

Already shaking her head, she replied, "No, thanks. The last batch made me so nauseous. I think they made me feel worse." Crawling off his lap, she waved him off. "I'll survive without your services, for one night."

Grinning at his exaggerated pout, she walked into the bathroom, and closed the door behind her. Like her sister had before her, Emily went straight to the shower and turned it on full blast, before walking over to the mirror. She gasped at her reflection. Her face was still swollen with varying degrees of bruising. Almost the entire left side of her face was purple and black but the swelling had gone down. "Thank God," she whispered to herself. The scratches on her forehead and right cheek had begun to scab, and her nose, thankfully, looked pretty straight, but still bruised and tender.

The steam began to fill the room as she began to remove her clothing; taking note of added injuries. Raising her arms above her head to take her shirt off made her take in a deep breath to stop from screaming out in pain; instead, her teeth ground audibly. She examined the rest of her body. Unraveling the bandage slowly, her eyes drew back to the mirror. Turning to get a better view, and raising her arm up slowly, she saw that her entire right side, from her armpit to her hip, was colored in blotches of blue and red. The majority focused around her broken rib, which she could still feel pulsating under the skin.

One more once-over, then she decided there was no time to waste playing over her memories. Turning back, she walked into the hot shower, standing directly under the steady stream, relishing the heady steam as she closed her eyes. She stood there for fifteen minutes, barely moving.

Two sudden knocks on the door made her jump slightly. "You okay?" Mark called.

"Yeah, I'll be right out," Emily called back.

"Okay, no rush." Mark sat with the sleepy children on the edge of their bed. His eyelids began to droop. Glancing over to the bedside clock, he noted it was 9:52 p.m.

Emily cut the water and grabbed the closest towel. Taking five minutes to dry off and get redressed, she walked out into the bedroom, towel-drying her long brown hair. Mark turned to smile at his wife, and then got up from the bed. The children watched him slowly walk up to her and kiss her on the forehead, passing her as he headed into the bathroom. A few seconds later, and the shower started up again.

Emily smiled down at the two, as they turned back to the TV. An interactive children's show, with hand puppets and large colorful characters, charged across the screen. Abby yawned loudly, as Emily joined them on the bed, still drying her hair. Abby's mouth seemed to consume her face, making Emily laugh to herself.

Seven minutes later, the show ended, and Emily quickly turned off the television. The children looked up at her with shocked faces. "Come on you two. Bed time."

Emily stood, as the small twosome crawled their way to the top of the bed. She pulled back the top cover and they both took a pillow. Lying on their sides, facing each other, they closed their eyes as she raised the cover back up. Matt started to suck his thumb. They looked comfortable enough, not even filling half of the giant bed. Emily went around closing the curtains and switching off the lamps, until only the small lamp on Mark's side of their bed was still lit.

Emily pulled off her shorts, keeping her t-shirt and panties on. She slid onto her side of the bed, facing the children, and laid her head down on the pillow. As she closed her eyes, everything slowly became calm and relaxed. Two minutes later the bathroom door cracked open, letting a beam of light fill the room for a second. A minute later and the top cover on Emily's bed lifted up, on the far side, and the bed lightly drooped. The sheets strained underneath her, as a warm arm reached around her waist, and pulled her back into a tight embrace.

She smiled at how comfortable Mark always made her feel; his body feeling like home along her back. He started to kiss her shoulder, making his way along her collarbone and up the side of her neck. His hand, resting on her hip, slowly traced the curve of her side, dragging forward to cup her full breast, making her giggle and squirm against his front. She turned just as his lips got to her jaw line, to kissing him softly.

"Good night," he whispered in her ear.

She kissed him once more then dropped her head back on the pillow. "'Night."

*   *   *

Emily and Mark awoke to both Abby and Matt crying out of control and screaming. They both ran over, to either side of the children's bed.

"What? What is it?" Emily cried, sitting on the side of their bed, and pulling Matt into her arms. He shook violently in her grip.

"Abby?" Mark gently pulled her into his arms.

Loud panicked banging came from their right side. The couple looked up, as the door handle of the connecting room started to shake.

"Mark, Em it's us. Open up," Rick called, from the other side.

Emily lifted Matt into her arms, and went straight to the door. Unlocking it, she took a step back as Rick yanked it open, forcing Julia into the room ahead of him. She was cradling her right hand, holding it close to her chest. A cream towel covered her hand, streaked with a line of dark red. She too, had tears in her eyes, as the others started to file into the room. James was last, closing the door behind him, his face distraught.

Julia walked straight to Mark. Letting Abby lie there, still in tears, he carefully examined her outstretched hand. "What happened?"

Rick answered, rubbing sleep from his eyes. "We were still in bed." He gestured to his wife, then back to Mark. "Julia went into the bathroom, and James started to watch TV. We sat up, as James collapsed back onto the covers with his eyes wide open." He looked over to his friend with concern. "Like last time." Pausing, he took in a shaky breath. "Then all of a sudden, his body started to convulse." His eyebrows rose with the severity of his words. "His eyes rolled to the back of his head, and then there was a loud crash in the bathroom."

Amy continued, "A few seconds later, he was wide awake again; he just sat up, and stared at us with no color on his face."

"Julia started screaming, in the bathroom." Rick glanced over to Julia, who was staring down at her bleeding hand. "She fell into the shower door when it happened." He motioned towards the bathroom. "The door didn't break, but she fell on the metal thing that you slide the door open with."

Mark started to nod, as he sat Julia on the children's bed. They seemed to be distracted by the conversation and had stopped crying. Mark proceeded to tear a long strip from the bed sheet below, tying it around the hand, which had already been cleaned. As he did so, the others seemed to fall back onto the nearest surface. James didn't say a word; he just sat there, silently.

While the others all seemed to be focusing on Julia, Emily walked over to James, in the far corner seat. His head had dropped down between his knees.

Placing her hand lightly on his right shoulder, she asked, "What did you see?" She quietly studied his stiff frame.

His head raised to stop three inches from hers, and the first thing she noticed was big tears covering his red face. He looked scared; his features betraying his usual persona. Shaking his head, he slowly dropped it back down, between his knees, knitting his fingers together behind his head. She moved her hand from his shoulder, to lightly pat the top of his head, and turned to see the others staring after her; they all sat on the same side of the far bed. Julia's head was in her lap now too. She began to lightly weep, as Amy put her arm protectively over her shoulder. Emily and Mark locked eyes, as the group stayed put, until someone spoke.

"Okay," Rick said softly, five minutes later, going to sit on the other side of Julia, and looking around the room at the four people who were clearly traumatized. "We really need to know what you saw."

No one spoke.

"Julia," Amy rubbed her back slowly. "Tell us."

It took a few more minutes for Julia to blurt it out, "Dead, we're all dead."

"What?" Mark blurted.

He switched to sit on the children's bed, right in front of her, placing his hands on both of her knees. "What did you see, Julia?"

She slowly raised her head, wiping the tears away from her face. Stopping, she gazed his way. "It was the same vision as before, but more," she said, fearfully, wiping at her eyes. "The same people were in the rooms, but they were getting slaughtered. There was blood everywhere." Her eyes seemed to drop and focus on nothing.

"People were screaming and running. There were loud gunshots, and the sounds of blades coming together. I seemed to BE one of them. Everything was in slow motion. I saw everything through their eyes. We got out of the white room, and started running to the stairs. I looked to my right, and there was Emily." Everyone glanced over at Emily, as Julia continued to speak. "She was running with me. She had a gun, and was yelling at people to run. Then, I went straight and you were standing there too." She looked up at Mark. "You were helping people up some metal stairs. There were gunshots, behind us, hitting the walls around us." She tried to keep speaking, but a violent hiccup made it hard to understand. "Then Emily flew forward, and fell. Light blew past her."

Mark's jaw clenched.

Julia turned to Emily. "Blood was all over us. Amy came running out of nowhere, and lifted your arm over her shoulder.

We got to the door, where Mark was waiting, but then everything went numb. I dropped to the ground. Rick tried to lift me, but I was too heavy." Julia's head dropped into her lap, as she continued. "You all left, with others, running up the stairs. I couldn't move, but I could see everything. You got to the top of the first set of stairs, and the door flew open. Everything lit up and your screams..," She cried harder now. "Your screams were unbearable. You all dropped, where you were. Then these people came through the light in the door. I could feel my body being dragged backwards. Something was strong, wrapped around my ankle, pulling me, and then I couldn't see any more. I couldn't see."

She shook and Amy pulled her head into her lap.

"I saw the same," James spoke for the first time. "From the same perspective. Feeling the same things, hearing the same things."

Emily turned to look at him; her hand was still resting on the top of his head. "It's going to be okay."

"No, it's not. You're going to die. I saw it." He yelled back at her, making her pull away. "We all are."

Tears started to fill Emily's eyes, as she sat there staring at him. She slowly stood up, not looking at anyone, placed Matt on the bed and passed through the connecting door. She slammed the door behind her, as Mark called after.

Mark instantly got up and ran around the bed to follow his wife. When his hand gripped the doorknob, as he turned it to open, James muttered sincerely from behind, "I'm sorry."

Mark shook his head and opened the door. "It's okay," he breathed, understandingly, as he ran in after his wife, and closed the door behind him.

"Emily?" Mark called, when he didn't see her straight away.

Her sniveling drew him to the small space in between the beds. She was sitting on the ground, leaning against the bed, looking away from him. Knees pulled up, she had her arms crossed on top of them, with her head resting on her forearms. She was crying heavily, her shoulders slumping with each gasp. He immediately fell to his knees next to her, and wrapped her in his arms. She eventually loosened up and held his body close to hers, as she continued to cry, soaking his t-shirt. Mark felt so helpless. He hated watching her in pain. They both sat there for a long while, as she continued to weep.

"I can't do this," she mumbled incoherently, between sobs.

Her face was red, black, and blue, covered with tears. Mark leant back, and lightly lifted her head with both hands, so he could see her face. "What?" he whispered.

She took a deep breath, lifting herself up, and away from his embrace. Taking three deep breaths, she wiped her eyes. "Mark." Her eyes were pained. "I don't know if I can take much more of this." Her head dropped, as she shook. "It's too much. I'm scared," she cried.

He reached over, without a word, lifting her under her knees, cradling her back, as he pulled her onto his lap. He rested his chin on her crown, as he gently rocked them. "I know, sweetheart. This is all too much for anyone to handle, but we have to, Em. We don't have a choice. We need to see this through, so we can get back to our lives."

Her head shot up as she gestured back to their room, "You heard what they said. If we see this through, we all die," she said, choking at the last part. "There is no going back to our old lives."

"Listen to me. I won't let that happen. Nothing is ever going to happen to you. I promise. We don't even know what any of that really means, or why we're even supposed to be there, in the first place." He held her there, tightening his grip. "I promise, Em. Nothing is going to happen."

Tears filled her wide eyes, but her face seemed to slightly relax. She reached up with her free hand, touched his face, and looked from his hairline to chin and back to his eyes. "I can't lose you," she whispered, as the tears overflowed down her warm cheeks.

He shook his head quickly. "That's never going to happen, so don't even think about it." He pressed his lips to her creased forehead. She couldn't control her reaction. Reaching up, she cradled the back of his head with her left hand, pulling his lips down to hers. She repositioned her body, without breaking their kiss, as her thighs straddled his hips. His hands traced down the side of her ribs, lightly, stopping on either side of her lower back. He pulled her body closer, leaving no space between them. Her left hand cupped the side of his face, as did her right.

The tears still flowed down her cheeks, as she rocked her hips and he deepened the kiss. Unconsciously, they pulled and pressed each other closer, into their embrace. Nothing at that time seemed to matter. His hands splayed out on her upper thighs and their breathing sped, as he kissed any part of her body that his lips could devour. Tracing down her jaw, he kissed his way along her collarbone as she whimpered.

Two minutes later a few knocks made Emily pull back, scrambling off her husband's lap, to focus on the connecting door. Mark lifted his head, and looked over his shoulder, as Amy popped her head around the open door. "You okay?"

Emily took a deep breath, and wiped away the resistant tears. "Yeah." The corner of Amy's mouth pulled into a sympathetic smile. "Just a little shook up. You know?"

Amy began to nod. "Yeah, I know." Glancing down at Mark, he smiled in encouragement up at her, then back to her sister. "Well, when you guys are ready, we'll be in the van."

"Thanks," Emily muttered, as Amy closed the door once more. Emily took another deep breath, and then looked over at her husband.

"Come on, let's get out of here." He playfully squeezed

her thighs.

Rick and Amy had taken up the two front seats, while the other four took up the back. Emily stepped in first, and slid across the middle seat until she was at the other side. Mark closed the door behind him, as he joined her.

"What's the plan?" he asked, as they pulled out of the parking lot.

"Breakfast first. We'll find somewhere where we can sit and talk this out, while we eat. Then, we can all decide our next move," Amy answered.

Mark nodded and they all sat in silence, as Rick drove.

"Em," James said quietly from the back seat. She instantly turned, looking over Mark's arm. "I'm so sorry about back there. Please forgive me. I was, am, messed up."

Her brows creased as she started to shake her head, disapprovingly. "There's nothing to forgive, James. We're all in this together. It's hard. We needed to know. So, now we can try and change it." She forced a smile, turning back to face forward in her seat.

Amy turned the radio on to the first station that had any music. A new song, that no one recognized, was playing quietly in the background. A few minutes later, Rick pulled into the back end of a Wal-Mart parking lot, and opened his door.

"Hold on." He spoke to his wife, "I'll be right back."

Jumping out, leaving the others to stare after him, he ran into the store. Five minutes later, he returned with a bag filled with baseball caps, women's decorative scarfs, and sunglasses. He passed Amy a black baseball cap, and big sunglasses. Taking a pair for himself, he passed the bag back to Emily, who divvied them up, as he started the van up again. She passed Mark his sunglasses, and a dark blue cap. Putting the two small caps on the children, she took the purple scarf and sunglasses; finally, passing the remaining supplies to Julia.

Three stores over, Rick parked out front of a restaurant that had big flashing signs saying, "Bee's Breakfast, Lunch, and Dinner!" Once they were inside, the waiter took them to the nearest round table, which easily sat eight. He left for a moment, and then returned with two toddler seats that he pulled up and parked next to Emily and Amy's seats.

"Thanks," Mark added.

"No problem." The young man quickly placed a menu in front of each of the adults. "Are there any drinks I can get you right away?" He glanced around the table, trying not to focus on their obvious wounds.

"I'll have a coffee please, and can you grab two milks for them?" Emily gestured to Abby and her brother.

"Of course." He pulled out his paper and pen. The others took their turns ordering drinks, and then he left, heading into the kitchen. After he had returned with their drinks and taken their food order, they made sure no one could hear their conversation, as they started devising a plan.

"Okay, well aside from the new stuff, you guys saw the same guy right? The same road sign and stuff?" Rick asked, focusing his question more at James.

James nodded, "Yeah, all that stuff was the same." Then his forehead creased. "Only thing is, we were going over the map, and Old Hondo Channel Rd, is actually a bunch of roads that come together. In the middle of nowhere."

"So we don't actually have an address or direct destination," Julia added.

Rick leaned back in his seat. "Great," he said sarcastically, "So, now what?"

"Well, it's all the same," Emily spoke up. "I think all we can do is go to that general direction and hope for a sign or something." She looked over at Julia and James. "Maybe, if we drive around the area a bit you guys will remember more?"

Mark nodded, agreeing with her plan, and shrugged his shoulders. "Unless, you guys have a better idea?"

The table fell silent, as the waiter returned with their orders. He placed the food in front of the right people. "Is there anything else I can get you?"

Amy looked up at him and smiled, "Oh, no thank you."

No one else said anything more, so he smiled down at them, saying before he left, "Okay, well I hope you enjoy, and don't hesitate to grab me if you need anything else."

They each took a mouthful, while Amy and Emily cut the children's pancakes into bite-sized portions.

"So, that's the plan?" Rick took a gulp of his orange juice, and looked around the table.

"Yep," James merely muttered, focusing on his warm food.

After one hour, everyone had finished, and was ready to go. The waiter brought the bill over, placing it onto the table. Mark glanced down at the price, took out his wallet, and forced a few bills into the faux-leather receipt case. Standing, Mark took Matt into his arms, as his wife lifted Abby, and they walked back out to the van.

Taking a right, then a few minutes later, a sharp left, they were back on the highway. Amy examined the map on her lap, and directed her husband to their destination. It took only twenty-five more minutes before they reached the end of the first Old Hondo Channel Rd turnoff. Rick slowed to almost a crawl speed, as they all leant forward in their seats. Almost expecting a neon sign of clues, they all moved around in the seats, trying to find some scrap of information.

"Do you recognize anything?" Rick called back.

"Yeah, I think you go to the far end, down there." James pointed straight ahead. The roads were completely deserted.

"There!" Julia yelled, getting closer to the right rear window. They all followed her finger, as she pointed to a random tree in a large field. There was nothing else around. A path seemed to follow along the side of the field, as the land dropped on the other side of the tree.

"What?" Rick glanced between her and the field.

"There...I don't know." She paused, shrugging. "The only thing I recognize is that tree."

"Yeah, Rick, we gotta go over there," James called from beside her.

Parking the van on the edge of the path, Rick and the others slowly got out, looking around dubiously. There really was nothing else out there; not a bird in the sky, nor any distant cricketing of the usual insects. Amy took her husband's hand and followed James and Julia, who had the children in their arms. Mark and Emily followed close behind, as they made their way closer to the centuries-old tree. Reaching the partly desiccated oak, James and Julia placed the children on the ground, and the four circled the stump; touching the sides with shaky hands, then looking around the immediate area, as the others stood back and watched.

"Now what?" Rick asked.

James shrugged, almost embarrassed, with a dumbfounded look on his face.

Within one minute, the entire scene changed.

A sudden whooshing came between them, and Julia stumbled two steps back. Taking a deep breath, she raised her hand to her neck. Shock covered her features as the group noticed the three-inch, green dart sticking out from her throat. She looked up with fear at the others, losing her balance, as she began to collapse and fall.

"Julia!" James cried, reaching out for her.

Three more consecutive whooshes and a dart stuck out of

his outstretched forearm. One hit Amy in the back of her right thigh. Rick caught her as she fell. James and Julia collapsed into a pile on the ground below. The others watched, in slow motion, as Rick and Amy did the same. Abby and Matt began to back up, fear covering their faces, as they frantically looking around, still standing at the base of the tree. Emily attempted to run toward them. Another whoosh, and Mark watched as a dart hit her in the center of her spine.

"Emily!" Mark roared, lunging for her, as she fell forward. Three more whooshes, and everything went black.

CHAPTER NINE

Abel parked his Mustang in the garage of his three-story residence. No matter what he did, he couldn't help but feel like he was being watched. Jumping out of his car quickly, he went up the four steps and hit the garage door opener. He turned to watch it slowly go down, not moving until he was sure he was alone. Taking a deep breath, he grinned to himself, shaking off his paranoia, and turned into his entranceway.

A loud thud came from directly above. Abel glanced up and then smiled as he followed the fast footsteps of four large paws, running down the main stairs, accompanied by two deep huffs and heavy panting. Abel took three fast strides, out of the mudroom, and into the entrance, as his five-year old bloodhound jumped off the last step and landed right by his feet. Abel dropped to the ground, playfully nudging her over until she flopped on her side, spread out on the floor in front of him.

"Tess, you lazy girl!" Abel laughed, as he rubbed her belly and around her ears. "Have you been sleeping on my bed all morning?"

When Abel first got his dog, he let John's daughter, Tess, being his goddaughter, decide the name. "Tess Two" was the first thing that came to her mind. John and Kristine had tried to get her to change it to be more canine appropriate, but she'd refused. From that day on, they shared the same name.

Five more minutes of mutual loving, and Abel lightly pushed

her away. Standing, he walked around the corner to his kitchen, tossing a small bag on the counter. Tess followed, circling the island, going directly to her empty food bowl. Abel grabbed a glass from the cupboard, and poured himself a glass of cold water. Tess blew out a deep breath that ended with a huff.

Taking a step back, Abel peeked around the corner, chiding, "Is somebody hungry?"

Tess nudged her bowl around the floor, in answer. Finally, after finishing his second glass of water, Abel went into the pantry and came out with a large scoop filled with her favorite dog biscuits.

"There you go, girl," he muttered, rubbing her ear, as he tossed the scoop back down.

He cranked the air conditioning on the near wall before sitting at the counter. Quickly rifling through the plastic bag, Abel pulled out a small, eight-by-eight inch, black block. Leaning back, he stretched out, so that he could reach into his pocket, and pull out his key chain and John's key. Sitting back up, he slowly turned his office key around on the chain until it popped off, and then placed both office keys on the counter before him. Back at the box, he found a little clip on one side. Popping it open, he unfolded the square into a rectangle double the original length. Inside was filled with a greyish-blue putty.

Concentrating, he carefully lifted a key and placed it on one of the squares. He pushed it down slightly, attempting not to move it too much, and then folded the box back together, with the key still inside. He held the two sides closed together for two minutes, then he slowly peeled it open, exposing the key; leaving a perfect impression. Without disturbing the imprint, he closed the box one last time, locking it into place, and taking it down into his basement where he kept all of his tools.

Fifteen minutes later, he came back up empty-handed, grabbing another drink before lounging out in his entertainment room, which was across the hallway to his open kitchen. Abel flopped across one of his long leather couches, and turned on the flat screen. Two minutes later, Tess joined him, taking up most of the room on the couch. Abel got so hot he slid off the couch and onto the carpet below. Grabbing his ice-cold drink from the table and taking another long sip, he flicked through the channels; there was never anything good on. He came across another news report.

"...Eight remain missing as police continue to search."

Abel turned up the volume.

"For those of you that still don't know, five square blocks in downtown Sierra Vista have been shut down and quarantined due to a dangerous chemical spill..."

Abel shook his head disapprovingly as he continued to listen in.

"Six individuals; three male, three female, from the main wedding party, and two small children are still unaccounted for by police. Once again, these individuals need medical attention quickly to avoid any permanent damage."

Their images covered the screen as the anchor continued.

"If you have seen or know of the whereabouts of any of these individuals please contact this number."

Abel rolled his eyes and shut off the TV, just in time for his doorbell to chime. Tess let out a wolf-like howl and jumped off the couch, barreling into the hallway, before Abel could get to his feet.

"Tess, shush!" Abel chastised her, pulling her away from the door as he glanced through the intricate glass detailing centered on the door, before opening it.

"Jacob." Abel took a step back, opening the door to its fullest, as he pinned Tess behind him to the wall. "Please, come in!'"

Jacob smiled back and stepped over the threshold, into the

main entrance, his eyes wide as he scanned the room.

"Your house is beautiful, Abe." He glanced down at the dog that had forced her way free. "Nice dog."

"Well, thanks, Jacob. How are you doing?"

The two stood there, exchanging pleasantries, then made their way into the kitchen.

"Here you go!" Abel said as he lifted the two keys off the counter, placing them in Jacob's outstretched hand.

"Thanks a lot, Abe," Jacob said throwing them in his right suit pocket.

"Can I get you anything? A drink?" Abel said, gesturing towards the fridge.

Jacob raised his hand, shaking the offer off. "Oh, no. No, thank you. Actually, I must get going. I'm late for another meeting."

"Oh, okay... Well, thanks for everything," Abel muttered, as they both made their way back to the front door. Placing his right hand on the handle and pulling it open, Abel said, "Feel free to come back any time. John and I will sign our new contracts, and I'll bring them over on Friday."

Jacob patted Abel's near shoulder, saying, "Sounds like a plan." He took two steps out the door. "You enjoy the rest of your day. Have a good one!" He weakly waved, making his way down Abel's driveway and into his car.

Abel's bubbly facade quickly faded as he closed the door, heading back down into the basement.

Around eight p.m. John called.

"Hey, just making sure you're still good," John said, by way of a greeting.

"Yep. I'm all good, no new news. Nothing."

"Thought up any plans for dealing with our little problem?" John questioned.

"No. Not yet," Abel barely replied, distracted.

"Okay, well tomorrow if you want, I'll come around and we can think this through. Figure out a logical plan of attack."

Abel almost laughed; John always wanted to over-analyze things and think them through.

"All right, sounds good. How about I call you when I'm up?" Abel suggested.

"Sounds great! Okay, have a good night. Have a beer or two, just relax, and loosen up," John insisted.

Abel laughed. "Yeah, all right, you first."

"Yeah whatever. 'Night!"

"Night, say hi to Kristine and the kids for me!"

"Will do!" John hung up the phone.

* * *

Abel was wide awake as Tess loudly snored at the end of his bed. Glancing over at the bedside table, he saw it was only 11:52 p.m. He was mentally exhausted, but couldn't keep his eyes closed. Finally giving up, he rolled off the queen-sized bed and stepped into the bathroom, turning on the light as he entered.

"Fuck!" he whispered, cringing away from the bright light.

After his eyes had adjusted, he leant most of his weight on the dark granite top and turned on the cold faucet, cupping the water in his hands. After two refreshing bursts, he leant back, wiping his face with a towel. Turning off the light, he went back out into the dark bedroom. Tess awoke, lifting her head, as Abel strode out of the room and down the stairs, before dropping her head and falling back asleep.

Abel went straight to the kitchen, grabbing a cold glass of milk before heading into the TV room. He flopped onto the couch and turned on the screen; still nothing on. Finally, he gave up and stopped on the first movie channel. One of his favorites was playing: Paul Newman in *Cool Hand Luke*. After sitting there for half an hour, still not able to fall asleep, Abel slouched down into his seat. Lowering the volume until it was almost inaudible, he began to scan the room; from each floating bookshelf, to his random ornaments. Finally, his attention stopped on a black Nikon D5000 digital camera. Taking a deep breath and thinking for a few minutes, eventually he placed his empty cup on the coffee table and stood up, making his way to the basement.

The basement was large and undeveloped, cold, and filled with various tools. The walls had shelf after shelf of supplies and extension cords. Abel switched on the light, pacing over to the near freezer, then to the table in the middle of the room; focusing on his workspace. He placed the small, frozen, black box on the surface. Very carefully, testing, he unclipped the edges once more and slowly separated the two sides, to reveal a perfect replica of his original office key.

* * *

It was now one a.m. and Abel, fully dressed in black clothing, began packing a small backpack on the edge of the kitchen table. Tess eventually came downstairs, and was now sitting by his chair, staring with a look of intrigue. Abel glanced down and lightly laughed at her expression; she honestly looked concerned.

"It's okay, Tessie. I'll be back as soon as I can."

He rubbed her head and played with her ears. Proceeding to zip up his backpack, Abel pulled it over his shoulder. As he stood, Tess followed close behind. He went over to her food bowls, filling her water and placing more biscuits into her oversized bowl, much to her delight. Turning off the light, he walked purposefully into the mudroom. Tess sat in the doorway, watching, as he tied his hiking shoelaces.

"Aw, come on! Don't look at me like that." The growing slobber pulled the corners of her mouth down in a pout, as her eyebrows twitched. "I'll see you soon, girl!" Bending down, he kissed her head, patting her twice on the side.

His mint condition Mustang roared to life as he threw the backpack on the passenger seat, and put it into reverse. In silence, Abel slowly made his way to the old office, stopping and parking two blocks away from the first barricade. He sat there, constantly glancing out the windows, as if he was waiting for someone to find him. When he'd managed to calm his heartbeat, he reached over for his backpack and pulled out his camera, making sure any old pictures or video were deleted, leaving plenty of free space. Abel zipped his pack back up, and lifted it onto his back, securing the straps.

Slowly and carefully, he got out of the car, trying to make little sound as he locked the vehicle, and pushed his keys into his back right pocket. Bolting down the near path and through the various alleyways, he hid behind the closest tree, near the first cement barricade. There didn't appear to be anyone around – no armed security. The streetlights were the only form of guidance. Trying not to waste time and push his luck, Abel ran as fast as he could, jumping the barricade and into the first lot of trees.

It took him seven minutes, and six more blockades, before he was within reach of the office. It was pitch-black. Abel could only see the small space illuminated below each lamppost, other than the office building itself. All of its lower lights were on, with the white tent drawing most of the attention with its bright, freestanding lamps. He crouched down, lifting up his camera. Looking through the lens once, he pulled back to focus on the display screen; the image was useless. After hitting menu and going through the many options, he finally found a night vision mode.

Once set, Abel took more than a few general pictures. Then

running across the street, he inched closer. Lying on the ground next to a short brick wall, he managed to take various photos of shadow movement within the camp-like tent. Finally, Abel could see the two guards that were on lookout. Snapping a few more pictures, he crawled along the wall, managing to hide in a small grouping of trees only a few meters from the first guard. Abel stayed silent, as the man flicked his cigarette, and started to walk a few steps away. He would have used this opportunity to move closer if it weren't for the third, previously unseen guard, stepping right out in front of the trees not three feet away; back turned. Abel held his breath, as he heard the man unzip his pants to relieve himself.

"Hey, Chris!" the other guard called.

"Yeah, yeah! One minute!" Chris called back, shaking his leg twice and zipping up his pants as he ran over to huddle with the others.

Two minutes passed as the men stood talking, not moving, enthusiastically swapping war stories. Abel snapped two photos before he ran silently in the opposite direction, towards the back side of the building. There was surprisingly no immediate security to guard that door; possibly as a key was needed to enter. There was minimal lighting, but Abel still hesitated by the door. Quickly, but efficiently, he glanced in through the small glass window and saw that the hallway was completely empty. Abel smirked, knowing exactly where all the security cameras were. The far back side of the building had no real importance, other than supply rooms and open warehouses. There was no real need for security or surveillance, given the security stops along each hallway.

Taking one last, deep breath, Abel pushed his replicated key into the lock. Wiping the excess of nervous sweat off his hands as he turned the lock with a audible click, he yanked the door open. With just enough room for him to slide through, he ran into the closest room, not turning on any lights. His heart pounding in his ears, he tried hard to control his panicked breathing. Eyes wide, he searched the room. Slowly, he forced his head back around the corner. His eyes stopped at the end of the hall, at the closed heavy metal door that led to one of the main hallways on the first floor. Keeping low to the ground, he forced himself onward, stopping next to the door. The lights were bright and flickering, visible through the small window; the only form of light in Abel's abandoned hallway. Quickly, he turned the sound off on his camera. Fiddling, he switched the controls until it was back to normal settings. This time, with no flash, he sat there for a few more minutes, deliberating his next move.

Abel knew the only security cameras were at each end of the next hall. The building was so large, even on the first floor, the majority of the available space was vacant at any given time. He figured there would be no real reason to guard this area. The only reason there were locked doors in this hallway was simply out of precaution and containment. Slowly sliding his back up the near wall, trying to keep as flat as possible, Abel glanced through the open window into the large open hallway. Left and right, there was nothing. The only room doors were closed, and the cameras were currently facing the other way. Every half-hour, they turned to face down this hallway. If he could just get down the hall, unlock one end, and make his way to one of the control rooms, he could take a look at what they were really doing.

There was a security room on each floor; three on the main floor. Abel knew, of course, that any real surveillance would be controlled in the main room just off the front entrance. It was the largest and had all the equipment. But Abel also knew about the last room. The smallest control room in size, it just had a small desk, couch, and the camera screen. The security people used that room more as a nap room than anything. Obviously, the usual security guards would have been told to stay home, so whoever was controlling the building now would have no need to use all three.

Abel prayed that was the case, as he drew back and slowly, quietly, turned the doorknob and winced as it creaked open. He peeked around the corners, making sure he hadn't missed anything, then quickly ran to the other end, the brightness blinding in comparison. The hallways were all the same on each level; decorated more like a hospital than an office building. Staying just out of sight of the near camera, he peeked around the corner. Nothing in sight; just another locked door. Abel blew out a deep breath, and steadied himself. Looking across the hall, into the empty room, he was surprised to see it was not empty at all. His forehead creased as he squinted, trying to look past the blinds. The room was filled with metal tables, in eight by four rows; long and narrow. After making sure no one could see him from either end of the hall, Abel ran across the narrow hall, stopping directly under the security camera, to look into the near window. Turning around, taking a closer look, he noticed more. Without thinking he raised his camera and took three shots. Unsure if the door would open, Abel took a step to the right and placed his hand on the door handle. Pulling down, he discovered that the door was surprisingly unlocked. Quickly and efficiently, Abel made his way into the dark room, closing the door as he went.

Taking many more pictures now, focusing on the tables, he noticed one row had black ankle and wrist straps attached to each. Turning to the back wall, he saw that many smaller black tables held covered trays. Continuing, he made his way to the back of the room, taking pictures as he went. Nearing the closest table, he pulled back one of the sheets, unveiling a tray filled with various surgical tools. More pictures. Abel went to the next table, finding more tools along with syringes, gauzes, and plastic gloves.

"What are they doing?" he whispered to himself.

Covering the trays again, he made his way back to the door, and glanced out the window. The hallway was still empty. With more confidence now, Abel opened the door, sliding into place in the corner of the hallway. Any minute now, he knew the security camera would rotate to survey the hall he had just come from. Sure enough, three minutes later, Abel smiled, as the camera slowly turned and he ran down the opposite hall. Dropping to the ground below the window again, he reached into his pocket, and pulled out his new key. Hoping he wouldn't trigger any sensors, he slid the key into place and cranked it to the left.

"Yes!" Abel quietly cheered as the door unlocked, and he retrieved his key, placing it back into his pocket as he got to his feet.

On the other side of the door were two narrow hallways. One carried on straight, with rooms on either side, to the staircase. The other hall began with a sharp left turn, leading to an elevator at the far end. On the right side of that hall, before the elevator, was the empty security room. Abel could see no one; he couldn't believe his luck as he slowly opened the door. Quickly though, he began to panic as footsteps neared and voices filled the air, coming from the open staircase at the other end of the hall. Fearfully, he ran to the left and slid into the first room, closing the door. Abel stayed facing the wooden door, holding tightly to the handle and pressing his ear to the cool frame. The room was pitch-black. He decided to wait until he knew it was safe, and then continue down the hallway, into the security room. As he focused, his breathing slowed, and his shoulders began to relax. The coast seemed clear; pulling himself together, he took a step and attempted to leave.

Freezing on the spot as he heard a light cough come from behind, his head automatically recoiled back, and he spun, dropping to the ground. His gaze frantically searched the room. It was too dark. Nothing was visible as he tried to catch his breath. The only window and source of light, belonged to the door he was cowering against. Sucking in a deep breath, while remaining on the ground, Abel's hand reached as high up the wall as he could. Finally, he found the light switch and pushed it up. The long florescent lights began to buzz and flicker to life.

Abel covered his face, shielding his eyes from the sudden intrusion, as he continued to blink, his eyes adjusted. His eyes widened as he took in the room around him. His jaw dropped, as he sucked in a sharp breath. Jumping to his feet, sticking close to the door, he couldn't believe his eyes. The space was filled with ten of the same metal tables, with scattered smaller trays.

The walls and floor were white, with random splotches of red and pink. The floor was wet with deep red pools, as the stench of rotting flesh finally reached his senses. He gagged, quickly covering his nose and mouth with his covered forearm. A second cough drew his attention back to the six people, lying still strapped down, covered in their own blood. Abel raised his camera one last time, taking at least a dozen more pictures. Anything he could find, he took shots of, as he make his way to a faint voice.

"Help me!" A female voice whispered. Five of the six were laying still, their skin so white, with their heads to the side. They were either unconscious or dead, their heads shaved in asymmetrical patterns, clearly examined and studied.

"Please!" another whisper.

He then made eye contact with a woman in her mid-forties. She was very slender with dark hair and grey roots. She lay bound, at the back of the room. Running around the others, making sure not to touch anything, he found the woman.

"I'm here," Abel frantically whispered, as he pulled at the restraints around her nearest wrist. "I'm gonna get you out of here."

Abel moved away from her face, freeing her arms and legs. Coming back to her head, he really took her in. As her head rested on its side, she tried so desperately to keep her eyes open. He noticed a black dot at the side of her temple. Looking closer, he saw the dot was actually a wound, beginning to heal. Lightly, he lifted her head, and rested it to the other side where he saw another, perfectly symmetrical circle. Feeling the back of her head, the shaved skin felt prickly against his bare hands. Bringing it forward, trying not to move her too much, he saw that the back of her skull had been marked with various surgical markers, signifying future experiments. Both of her shoulders had large, deep lacerations as well. Her forearms, cut down the center, revealed deep red stains where her arms had rested against the lower sides of her t-shirt.

She coughed once again, and her face reacted to a sharp pain. Concern filled Abel as he quickly scanned the room, then reached for her nearest arm, pulling it over his shoulder. "Let's get you out of here!"

Before he could slide his other arm under her knees and lift her off the table, he felt her pull her arm back. He looked down confused, as her eyes widened and focused on something behind him.

"What?" Abel asked, twisting around and glancing over his shoulder.

Before he could see it, he felt it. One hard blow hit him on the back of his head, as his body went limp. His vision blurred, and his head hit the metal table, hard. Seconds from unconsciousness, falling, he heard distant screams.

CHAPTER TEN

Amy awoke with a sudden jolt. Something strong and present inside of her, told her to keep her eyes closed and breathe normally. Even then, she knew if she did open her eyes, not much light would find her. Darkness filled her eyelids. Her head was uncomfortably turned fully to the left, resting on a rough piece of material, which seemed to be taut under the weight of her body. She could feel a warm, woolly blanket covering her legs. As she took in one slightly deeper breath, she noticed the air was stale, cold, and bitterly moist.

A strange, musky scent filled her nostrils, and something feeling like a thin layer of dirt or dust covered the free side of her face. A light breeze blew over her, tickling the small hairs on her arms, as a sickly, putrid smell followed. Her eyes tightened, as her nose wrinkled in revulsion. Her shoulders locked, and she had to focus on her steady breathing.

In control, using her hands by her hips under the covers, she lightly felt the material beneath her. It was not the most comfortable of beds. Obviously only big enough for one, it seemed to encase around her. It reminded her of the small, one-man, foldable, military style beds that she and Rick had taken camping last spring.

Rick! Amy screamed in the back of her mind.

The light breathing of two others in the room behind her made her internal panic halt, as she attempted to listen more closely. Others were in the room. From what she could tell, two pairs of footsteps were walking close next to the top of her head, and to her right.

Although the breathing remained constant, Amy noted that it was not coming from where the people were walking. From them, she could only hear their shoes rustling around, at a faster than normal pace, from one end of the room to the other. Just before she decided to lightly open her eyes, something brushed up against the length of her right arm. It took all of her concentration not to flinch away from the unknown. Her eyes remained shut. Desperately, she tried to appear as if she was still sleeping, though whoever had touched her arm appeared to be hovering over her, unmoving.

Constant deep breaths, in and out. That's all Amy could get her panicked body to do. Every pore screamed for motion, for freedom – to roll to her left, get up, and run as fast as she could. Suddenly, the air around her face became very thick. The small hairs on the back of her neck rose, and she knew someone or something was leaning over her. Trying to stay as still as possible, she felt that something was rested on top of the blanket above her right arm, wrapped as much around the top of her wrist as it could, holding her down. Feeling icy cold, a finger lightly touched down onto her temple, sliding a strand of her hair behind her ear. Wanting to cringe away, the contact unbearable, she had to focus on keeping her body still.

A noise behind her started; a light buzzing noise transformed into a gentle hum. Through her eyelashes, Amy could tell a small light must have been turned on. The air seemed to loosen up around her, as the touch pulled away. Whoever it was took two steps back, swirled around, and walked swiftly out of the room, closing a heavy door behind him or her. Shortly after, a different pair of footsteps entered the room; these were lighter and more controlled. Distracted, all that Amy could hear were the two people breathing steadily behind her, and the gentle humming of the faint light.

Letting her curiosity get the best of her, Amy thought this was a better time than any to open her eyes, and figure out where she was. Carefully, ever so slightly, her eyes crept open. Her body remained unmoving, as she took in what was available of the darkness. It was almost pitch black, if not for the light coming from behind. Whatever she was lying on, which did appear to be an army bed, was positioned less than a foot from an old brick wall. The brick had obviously darkened with age, becoming brittle and cracking.

Her eyes followed the wall, roughly eight feet up, until it reached a small window that was exactly the same as the windows in her parents' old house. Then she knew she was in a basement. That would explain the cold, damp feeling she could not shake. There was absolutely no light coming from the window; it must have been the middle of the night, wherever they were. Following the wall, as far right and left as she could, she could see nothing more than mud and brick. One thing Amy could tell was that the room was huge. Obviously, they were in an undeveloped basement taking up most of the width and length of the house.

Slowly, she noticed the light behind her flicker, get brighter, and then fade. One person, closest behind her, seemed to hiccup and jolt awake, his or her breathing momentarily accelerating. From the gasping, Amy recognized her sister's heavy breathing. Without hesitation, she pushed back her blanket and twisted her body to the far right, jumping up from her cot.

She was then facing a woman in the center of the room, five meters away from her, as the women stood tall and skinny, directly over Emily's body. Taking two steps, Amy watched the woman's arms, outstretched, with both hands less than two inches away from Emily's face and torso. Her fingers stretched wide, almost holding Emily down, without any touch. What shocked Amy was the light. The light did not come from a lamp, but from the woman herself. It seemed to generate from her feet, up her legs and body, and out of her palms. Her eyes were closed and she did not seem to be fazed by Amy's presence at all. With each wave of light, her chest seemed to swell with breath. Amy could not move; she was frozen by shock and fear. Her eyes glanced down at Emily's, which were now focused on the woman's face.

Amy could not help but analyze the woman. She was beautiful. She had to have been at least six foot tall. She was wearing all black; with more of a business suit appearance, and her sleeves rolled up to her elbows. Her nails were long, and her hair was an amazing shade of dark ruby red. Thick and full, it curled perfectly just past her breasts. Her skin was porcelain, her facial features perfectly proportioned; but her eyes seemed to be her best feature. Even closed, Amy could tell they would be surreal.

Movement behind the woman made Amy glance over at Julia, in a matching cot against the far wall, as she rolled over, still appearing to sleep. Then Emily's breathing increased and she began to shake. Panic-stricken, Amy stole two more steps, quickly gazing down again. Emily's face appeared agonized now, and her eyes searched around the room. Her breathing turned to pained cries, and then her eyes rolled to the back of her head. Before she could think, Amy let out a blood- curdling scream as her sister's body seemed to lift from the cot, levitating, following the pattern of the woman's hand movements. The light grew stronger. Amy's scream grew louder. Now they were accompanied by Julia's screams, as she had gotten up from her bed and taken in the situation.

Loud banging began echoing throughout the room and yelling

came from the wall behind Julia. The wall must have been thin and metal, as the noises carried. Finally, the woman was pulled from her trance, her eyes locking with Amy's. Emily's body continued to jerk, unnaturally, above the cot, as she opened her eyes wide. The light continued over her, as Amy cringed back, still screaming, as all she could see were the woman's wide eyes; they were completely black.

Forehead creased, the redhead turned, looking over her left shoulder. Julia appeared frantic, arms flaring, and running towards her. In one swift movement, not taking her left hand from Emily, the woman turned her body to the right until she was in line with Julia. As Julia continued forward, the other glowing hand flicked in the air in front of Julia, in the space between them, as if to flick away a fly. Julia's screaming suddenly stopped; her voice cut off. As the banging continued, Julia's body lifted off the ground, and flew backwards into the wall behind. Hitting high up, with a thud that dented the wall, her body fell hard to the ground.

"Julia!" Amy screamed, trying to take two steps forward as the woman turned on her.

Amy could hear the door burst open behind her, but remained facing forward. Footsteps flew in. The woman nodded, looking straight past her. Confused and afraid, Amy turned on her heels. There was only darkness. Out of nowhere, a white, male face, eyes completely black, appeared inches from her own, and then he smiled. It was not a friendly smile; it appeared sinister. One last scream, a step back, and then a gust of cold air hit her body, forcing her farther back until she fell to the ground below. The face drew back into the shade. Amy scanned the area, but only darkness filled her vision.

Flipping onto her stomach, she started to drag herself towards her sister's loud panting. Amy's vision still escaped her. The redhead merely smiled, however, this time apologetically, at her persistence and went back to her current interest. Amy tried to raise her body to her knees, as she clawed at the soil below. Inching closer, suddenly a strong hand restricted around Amy's right ankle and with one last screech, Amy's body was dragged back and into the darkness.

* * *

Mark awoke, lying on his left side. He took a deep breath as his eyes burst open. Less than a foot from his face there was a stuffed red fox, displayed with its mouth wide open, nose wrinkled in a vicious expression. Mark's immediate reaction was to jerk his head back and yell. Pushing away into the middle of the small, poorly lit room, he relaxed when he understood the animal was in fact dead. He stared at the animal for a minute, until a smell in the room made him gag. It reminded him of his first year in university; his first cadaver lab.

Coughing behind him drew his attention, causing him to recall his last memory of Emily falling to the ground, and their current situation. Glancing around the room, he turned to see James and Rick propped up against the metal wall in front of him. Rick was still unconscious, as Mark ran over to James, who was practically coughing up his lungs, gagging at the smell. He helped get James up and breathing. As James stood bent over, holding his knees, Mark told him to breathe as steady as possible. He held James's shoulder, as he scanned the remainder of the room.

"Emily?" Mark called.

The room was no bigger than his parents' living room, equally dark and clammy as the room before it. The only light was from a naked light bulb in the center of the ceiling, which illuminated only so much, displaying lots of clutter around them. Two large, wooden tables took up the majority of the space. Mark called for his wife one more time with no response. James, breathing calmly now, got to his feet. Rick began to stir on the dirt flooring. Jumping slightly where he sat, wide-awake, he scrambled to his feet. The smell did not completely affect him until he was standing next to James. Both covered their noses and mouths with their free hands, as they too searched the room.

"Amy?" Rick's cry was muffled by his own hand.

"Julia?" James called.

"They're not here." Mark was solemn, pacing from the other side of the room. Both men squinted, as they followed Mark's voice. He was standing next to a heavy, metal door, with a circular window at head height. White paper had been taped on the other side, distorting a bright light coming from the corridor on that side.

James lightly pushed Mark out the way, pressed his face up against the window, and banged on the mental door three times. "Hey!" Two more bangs, "Hey! Let us out!" he bellowed.

A dark figure passed by the window, appearing to lean against it, making James pull his face back. The person stilled for a moment before continuing on his or her way.

"Hey!" All three yelled and kicked at the door.

"Where's my wife?" Mark beat on the door.

"Yeah. This is fucking kidnapping. Open the goddam door!" James kicked the door once more, wincing as he jammed his toe.

Amy's sudden loud outburst from the room behind had them running to the metal wall across the room.

"Amy!" Rick was so panicked and fearful. "Amy!"

All three began banging as hard as they could on the makeshift wall. It swayed and dented under their attempts, but would not budge. As the other two continued, Mark stepped back and tried to find a way in. Searching, he hoped to find some form of gap in the wall or a sliding handle. Julia's added scream made James beat harder, frantically trying to get attention. It wasn't until Mark recognized Emily's cries of pain that he anxiously began searching the room for anything; something heavy or sharp that they could possibly use to break through to the women. More screams and cries from all three. Emily's cries cut off prematurely.

"Emily!" Mark screamed, running back to the door and banging once more.

Another cry pierced the air. Muffled by the wall, "Julia!" was all they could make out, and then a loud bang hit the wall just above Rick. The three men took a few steps back and stared. The wall shook in its entirety, as whatever it was slid down to the ground. Silence. One last cry from Amy, then complete prolonged silence.

"Amy!" Rick kicked and punched the metal wall. "Amy!"

Still no other sound, as Rick fell to his knees on the sand-dirt below. A few more weak punches and his shoulders slumped, his forehead rested on the cold metal before him, and he began to weep, sobbing his wife's name. James continued to aggressively kick, bang, and scream at the metal divide, while Mark stood frozen to the spot. He was in shock. Searing hot tears defiantly slipped down his cheek, his fists clenched at his sides, as he kept glancing at Rick on the ground in front of him, to James, and then back at the metal door behind. Mark slowly started to step backwards, edging closer into the shadows. Rick pulled his head away from the cold vibrations. Spinning his body so that he was seated with his back to the wall, James refused to stop, but his blows came with less force. Rick finally raised his head and leant it against the wall, as he stared at the expressionless Mark. They just stared at each other, defeated, as James finally gave up and turned to face Rick and Mark, cussing under his breath. Looking over at Mark, he said, "What do we do?"

Mark was still staring at Rick. Taking a deep breath, he went to answer, when two pale arms reached around his neck and waist, and pulled him further into the shadows. Mark, letting out a gasp, attempted to struggle, he was pulled backwards out of sight.

"Mark!" James cried, creasing his forehead, and taking two lunges after him.

"Mark!" Rick yelled, and scrambled off the ground.

Just before they both leapt into the shadows in pursuit, the one and only light went out, leaving them all in complete and utter darkness.

* * *

James woke first this time. He was seated upright at the end of a long, cherry wood, rectangular table. He was not bound, but he could not move one muscle below the neck. Looking up, he noticed he was not alone. To his right, Emily was still unconscious, her chin resting on her chest. Next to her was Amy, then Julia, Rick, and at the other end of the table, Mark began to stir.

"Mark," James whispered loudly. "Mark!"

Mark opened his eyes and raised his head. Looking directly across at James, he whispered back, "I can't move!"

"I know. Me either."

Then Mark saw his wife. "Emily!" he called out loudly.

He called once more, but she made no show of waking. James glanced around them. They were now in a moderately well-lit room, which only contained the table and nothing more. White tiles from ceiling to floor further illuminated the room, accentuating the dark, wooden flooring. Looking up, James noticed there were five spotlights on them. On the opposite side of the table, three wooden chairs sat alone, with a large steel door behind them, two meters back. Light moans and stirs drew him back down to the table where the others, all but Emily, were beginning to wake.

"Argh!" Rick cried, not looking around, as he unsuccessfully attempted to move.

"Rick, you're stuck! We all are," James called, from the end of the table, making Rick glance up.

Rick was just about to add a snide comment, when he noticed his wife at the middle of the table. "Amy!" he gasped, relieved.

Her eyes were still closed, and her head shook from side to side as she began to fully wake. Her forehead creased, and then her eyes surged open when she heard his voice.

"Rick?" she burst out, scanning the room and turning her head to beam at her husband. Big tears swelled, as she glanced around the room quickly.

"Are you okay?" he asked.

Amy tried unsuccessfully to move. "I think..."

"Julia?" James interrupted.

Julia's eyes opened and then she squinted, cringing away from the bright light. Looking back down at the table, she finally spoke in relief as her eyes focused on him. "James!" Looking around, she noticed that like herself, they were all seated along a rectangular table with both hands stuck to the table, palms down.

"I can't move," she muttered.

"None of us can." Mark's eyes were trained on his still-unconscious wife, "Emily!"

"Emily!" Amy cried, as they all turned to stare at her; her head still resting on her chest, unmoving.

"Her face!" Julia cried, turning to the table. "Look at her face."

"What? What is it?" Mark frantically scanned his wife, not understanding Julia's expression.

"It's fixed! She has no bruises..." and she added, glancing around the table, "None of us do."

They all seemed to notice then, looking around at one other, that it was true. There were no cuts or bruises, and from what they could tell, no pain. Mark began to start by calling his wife once more, when the doorknob began to turn and the creak, causing them all to become silent and glare at the door in front of them. They each took deep breaths, no blinking, as the door gradually crept open. Slowly, a man in his late-fifties entered the room. He had a pair of light denim overalls on, with a bright red t-shirt underneath. He had grey hair and a long straggly beard; obviously a farmer of some sort. Julia and James glanced at each other for a second then looked back at him.

"Who are you?" Mark barked.

The man merely smiled, walked over to the chair in the middle of the empty row, and sat down. Continuing to smile, taking in each of the faces, he made his way to Mark, "My name is Thomas. Nice to meet you all."

They each seemed to recoil from his odd, friendly introduction. Considering the situation, it just didn't seem right. Thomas leant back and crossed his arms, as Mark responded.

"What do you want with us? Where are we? Where are the children we came with?" The last question made Amy and Julia focus more clearly, glancing around the room and at the open door. Mark continued in a more panicked voice, "What have you done to us? My wife?" He gestured to Emily, with his chin, as Thomas followed, then finally raised his hand to stop Mark from asking another question.

"Remember you came to us. You needed to find us. In regard to your wife," he glanced at Emily quickly, then back to Mark, "and yourself, I'll leave the detailed explanations for later, but first I have a few questions of my own. To begin with, what are your names?" he asked around the table, now smiling again. No one spoke, so he continued "Well... We know your name is Julia." His smile widened to show an off-grey set of teeth. "And yours is James."

He went to continue, but James interrupted, "How?"

"Well other than the events that ended on a bad note, a couple hours ago," Thomas turned to Amy, then back, "you both have been shown. Like myself and the people close to me."

"Shown?" Rick joined the conversation with a confused expression.

"Yes, shown." Thomas focused on Julia, then James. "The visions…that told you two to come here."

"YOU did this to us? Why?" Julia asked, in an agonized voice, clearly still straining against her invisible bonds.

"Oh no. No, not me. THEY! They did!" He smiled, "And please do stop trying to get free. It is impossible at the moment, and I wouldn't want you to hurt yourself."

"They? Who's they? Why are you being so fucking cryptic?" James demanded.

Thomas shook his head, still smiling, and leaned back in his chair. "Questions, questions. In due time." He then leant forward onto the table, a serious spark crossing his gaze, "Honestly, we mean you no harm." Gesturing to their uncomfortable positions, he said, "This is really for our protection."

"Your protection? You attacked us, did God knows what to us…threw me across the room." Julia trailed off, clearly fuming. "Fuck you."

Blowing out and taking a deep breath, Thomas turned to James. "I just have a few questions, and then when I decide it is safe, two others will join me." Glancing around the table, he said, "You will be released from your hold and your questions will all be answered." Then he turned back to Julia. "But first, give me the answers I need. Please."

Julia studied his face for a while. Glancing at the people trapped next to her, she finally surrendered, and turned back to Thomas realizing they really had no choice either way. "Ask!"

"Thank you." Turning to James, he said, "All I need are your names, how you got injured, and what visions you have seen. And if anyone else knows where you are." Thomas spoke directly to James, and then glanced around the room at the others.

James answered each in turn. Thomas watched Emily, as James gave details of the horrific fight. Then he focused on the details of each vision. Finally concluding, he analyzed Thomas's reactions, which barely faltered in his neutral stance.

Thomas nodded, smiled, and pushed back from the table. "Thank you. Please give me a few minutes, and I will be right back." He disappeared from the room.

As soon as the door closed behind him, their physical holds relaxed and they could now feel their full bodies. Two seconds later, James managed to reach over, just in time to catch Emily, as her head was about to hit the table below. Mark kicked out of his own seat and ran around the table to grab his wife.

"Thanks." He pulled her out of her chair and onto the solid floor below. "Emily?" he called, lightly shaking her shoulders.

The others got up from the table and spread out around the couple on the floor; making sure they could all see without getting in his way. Mark's training set into action, as he checked her pulse, her breathing, then lifted each eyelid for a pupil response. It all seemed to be fine, but no matter what he did she wouldn't wake.

Just then, the door opened, Mark raised Emily into his arms, and twisted his body in a protective hold. Amy and Julia stood behind him, as James and Rick took a flanking stance, blocking them. Thomas walked in and taking in their reactions; he took two steps forward with his eyebrows raised and his arms up in a surrendering display.

"Please! Please don't be afraid. We won't harm you. You are perfectly safe." No one moved, as two others entered the room cautiously. James and Rick's gaze followed them, as they casually walked up to the empty seats on the other side of the table. They were wearing all-black, stylish business suits. One was male and one female. As they sat, the woman looked up and smiled.

Gesturing to the table in front, Thomas went to sit in the middle. "Please. Have a seat. Please."

The three sat there for a minute, until James and Rick looked at each other, then back at the group behind them, and then went to sit at each end of the table. The girls took their sides, as Mark sat, with Emily still in his arms, in the middle seat directly across from the others.

CHAPTER ELEVEN

Sitting in silence, the two groups analyzed one another. Thomas appeared the same; still in his farm-like attire, seemingly under dressed compared to the other two. To his right, closest to Rick, sat a pale woman in her mid-twenties. Her raven hair was slicked back into a tight ponytail, resting heavily down her back. Her skin looked tight across her forehead, with a dusting of freckles across the nose, her lips had a pale pink hue, her bottom lip was full and pouty. Her eyes seemed to take up a large portion of her face, but the irises were a unique shade of deep-ocean blue, clear, and mesmerizing. Mark had never seen anything quite like it – it was as if they shimmered along with the lighting. His eyes took in the woman's entirety. She wore a brown, silk shirt, which came right up to the base of her neck in a straight-across-the-collar neckline, with a fashionable black blazer. Her fingers were interlocked, resting on top of the table, with long, black-painted fingernails.

Passing over Thomas, to his left, sat a man. He must have been in his thirties, with a round face, with more of a Slavic appearance. His eyes were dark and serious. With hair buzzed, his general appearance screamed military and controlled. Though he appeared stiff and withdrawn, he was anything but. A welcoming smile drew in the others, as he glanced around the room. His dark-brown shirt and business jacket matched that of the women, given the obvious male-female differences in shape.

Then Mark noticed the other nagging connection. Even though there was no way they were biologically related, other than having perfect, albeit pale, skin, they both had three matching, tiny, dark freckles creating a sideways-V on their left temples, just off the corner of their eye. The man's were darker in coloring, but the connection was clear.

"What have you done to us?" James broke the silence.

Thomas seemed to draw back in his seat at the sudden outburst, but the others did not seem to react. The male slowly turned his head, still smiling, and answered. "James, we have taken away the visions, so you and the others will be perfectly fine. And will feel no further pain."

"Why the darts?" Rick copied James's tone.

"That was a precaution, on our part. We needed to make sure you were really one of the affected and not an intruder. We could not give away our true location so easily." His answers remained calm and focused.

James leant forward and opened his mouth to ask another question, but Amy beat him to it. "Where are the children?"

She had directed her question to the man, but it was Thomas who leaned forward, and answered for him. "Rest assured," he said, reaching his palms out. "The children are perfectly fine. Don't worry, they are resting upstairs with the others."

"Others?" Rick interrupted,

"Yes," the strange male intervened. "More of our kind. We do hope more of yours will come. Those that have been given the same directions, that is. We hope they arrive soon."

This upset Julia, as she leaned on the table. "Directions?! You call watching your friends die over and over again..." She wiped a defiant tear from her cheek, as James rested his hand on her shoulder, and eased her back into her chair.

The man's brows pulled together and he frowned down at the

table, as he seemed to search for the right words. "That was..." Looking into Julia's moist eyes, he finished with, "one of many possible outcomes."

Her jaw dropped, letting out a burst of breath. Shaking her head, she looked disgusted. Mark, finally, had enough and had to ask, "How did you fix us? What is wrong with my wife? Did she have cranial injuries? Bleeding?" He held Emily close to his body, keeping her head held against his left collarbone. Her gentle breath eased some of his panic.

The woman and Thomas turned to the male at the end, as he stilled himself, and leant on the table. "From now you have obviously concluded that we are not of your Earth."

"You don't say? Most people don't have fully blacked out eyes and shoot flames from their fingertips!" Amy burst out.

"What?" Rick turned to his wife.

Gauging their reactions, the man continued, ignoring the interruption. Placing his left hand over his chest, he said, "My name is Amadeus." Then gesturing to the woman on his far left, "This is Amelia." She merely nodded, with a humorous smile. Amadeus then spoke directly to Julia. "Earlier, you met our healer Isobel and her protector Riley."

"Didn't look like she needed much help," Julia huffed, still angry, leaning into James. "She attacked me!"

"I know and I am so very sorry, but once Isobel starts working on an individual, it is very dangerous to break the link." Amadeus spoke softly and indicated Emily, "She could have been killed if they had not stopped you." He finished, glancing at Amy.

Amy's eyebrows furrowed as she shot back, gesturing to Emily. "All I saw was my sister crying out in pain and after the last thing I remembered...God knows who she was or what she was really doing!" Then she folded her arms and leant back into her seat, as Rick wrapped his arm around her shoulders, squeezing with reassurance.

Amadeus was already nodding, with his lips pursed in a tight line. "I understand that, but for what it's worth, any recovery is usually painful is it not?" Amy merely looked him dead in the eyes, then after a few seconds slowly began to nod in defeat. "But once again, I am truly sorry for the fear and panic, which seeing that must have caused you. Please forgive us. We didn't have much time." He honestly appeared saddened as he waited for a response.

She huffed, still not fully convinced.

Julia took a deep breath, adding with a hint of sarcasm, "What about the eyes? You expect us to believe there was nothing bad happening, there?"

Amy remembered; "That guy…Riley, he grabbed me and dragged me away, he was laughing!"

Amadeus's brows knit together. It was clear when he glanced at Amelia, that that was not how things should have been handled. "Again, I apologize. Riley can get a bit carried away sometimes." As if he had forgotten. Shocking the rest of the group, he leant back and blinked. The group froze as a third, cat-like, black eyelid slid from the inner edge of his eye, sideways. It remained, solid black, before his smile widened as it retracted, and his pupils reappeared. He blinked twice, and then shrugged. "We evolved slightly different in our human-like forms. Our planet is much harsher in certain areas." He paused, watching as their jaws visibly clenched and unclenched. "We also use it when we are focusing on something. To you it looks black, but to us it's more like night vision. We use it to think and focus. We can also utilize other abilities."

"Abilities?" Mark chose to bypass the obvious insanity of the situation, storing it for later. "So you have a special healer?"

"Yes. Well we all possess such abilities, but as on your planet, we each specialize in different areas."

"So, what are your specialties?" Rick asked, exaggerating the last word, as he glanced between the two.

"Well, I am what you might call the ambassador for our planet. I am also in command of my people. My..." He moved his hands, grasping at the air, searching for the right words, "...fleet."

"Like a general? A president?" James offered.

"Yes. Something along those lines."

"And you?" Rick continued, gesturing to Amelia with his chin.

She smiled, obviously amused by their probing, "I am the ship's communicator and pilot." She lightly giggled at the last word. Then becoming slightly more serious, she leant on the table and spoke matter-of-factly. Still amused, she hitched an eyebrow. "I am also head of security and training."

"Training?"

She glanced at her leader, and then leant back into her chair. "Amadeus will explain more, soon."

Rick just stared at her, unsure, and nodded, as Mark intervened. "You still haven't answered my questions. So you have the ability to heal flesh at a rapid pace. What medicines do you use?"

This time Amelia answered. "We have no need for material medicines."

She glanced over to her leader, who nodded, and then turned back raising her left hand up into the space in front of her. Suddenly, a light buzz entered the room, followed by gasps and shocked awe. Amelia's hand seemed to go up in flames. An array of colors coated her flesh, swirling in silent tranquility. Not burning, as it would seem, the bright light appeared to mimic a flickering fire. As she slowly turned her hand around and moved her fingers, everyone but Thomas and Amadeus, stared at the light show.

"Our race is known as the Jarly. Over many millennia we have visited your planet in secrecy, in an attempt to learn and in discreet ways, advance your own technologies." Gradually, two by two, the eyes shifted from Amelia's hand to Amadeus, as he continued. "At first we only watched from a distance, until the order was given. We received permission to..." He stopped searching their faces. A faint flush ticketed his cheeks.

"Test," Amelia finished, as she watched her own light show.

"Test?" Mark asked, in a critical tone.

"More like practice, to blend in, and get involved. Some were given permission to stay behind and create a new life." Amadeus continued, as Amelia once again cut him off.

"Their interbreeding and ancestry have led to your modern-day geniuses, savants and those with extra abilities such as foresight; mediums and so forth." She said this while rolling her right hand, a bored expression on her face.

"Anyway," Amadeus lightly smacked his hand on the table and raised his eyebrows in an obvious, *shut up, now!* look.

She rolled her eyes and closed her left palm, causing the light and the buzzing to cease, before intertwining her fingers and becoming still.

Amadeus then turned and smiled apologetically at the mystified people in front of them. He opened his mouth to continue, but James interrupted with a questioning expression, directly at Thomas; "What part do you play in all this?"

Thomas smiled. "Ever since I was young, I have known these two." He gestured with his head, left and right.

Instantly the others were confused. James asked, "These two?"

Thomas nodded.

Still confused, Rick added, "But they are easily half your age."

Amadeus smiled, as Amelia answered, "I am two hundred and thirty-two, human years old." Once again the friends were stilled by the new jaw-dropping revelation. She continued, "Amadeus is close to four hundred."

The others could say nothing, so Thomas continued. "They age very differently from us. They look roughly the same, as when I met them at seventeen." He winked at Amelia, as she offered a knowing smile. "I'm one hundred and twelve."

"What?" Mark burst, "but you're human."

"I've adapted in my own ways. Learnt things." He shrugged, "We'll never live as long as them, but they can definitely help. On paper, I'm my own grandson."

"One day we will die. But as you can see, not for a while." Amelia added.

Amadeus coughed, lightly drawing the attention back to himself. "So, like I said before, we have many abilities Our kind works with a sort of energy we are all born with. We can harness this energy, at any time, to do many different things. Isobel has mastered rapid tissue-healing. Riley, her protector, has been trained by Amelia to fight in a very effective way. Our physical and mental abilities are almost one hundred times greater..."

"And faster," Amelia interrupted.

"Than that of a human." Amadeus finally finished.

"Okay, so you healed us," Mark muttered, under his breath, now looking at Emily.

"Yes, Mark," Amelia answered. "But Emily's injuries were much more severe than your own." Mark nodded, as she continued, "In order to save it, Isobel was forced to put your wife in a coma-like state, so that it could feed from her bodies' energy and survive."

"What do you mean, 'it'?" Amy asked, clearly confused.

"The child," Amelia answered quickly with no hesitation, as if the answer was obvious.

"What?" Mark blurted, wide-eyed and panicked.

Then it was Amelia that was confused. "Emily," she said, turning to Amadeus, then back. Speaking quickly, she added, "Mark, you didn't know your wife is pregnant?"

The room went silent as Mark gasped and looked down at his love, frozen, showing no emotion. Amy burst out in joyous tears, covering her mouth, as she grabbed Mark's right shoulder and looked down at her sister.

"Are you sure? How do you know?" Mark whispered, as he forced back his own tears.

It was Amadeus that answered. He smiled, tilting his head to the side, as if to listen intently. "Your wife is fifty-seven days pregnant." He smiled encouragingly, "She will only be in this state for three more hours, then she will awake and both of them will be fully healthy and safe."

One single tear rolled down Mark's right cheek, as a sniffle turned into a smile.

Amelia leant onto the table and let her hand reach across. "Would you like to know what it is going to be?" she offered.

Amy laughed and wiped away another tear, as Mark smiled, shaking his head. "You can do that?"

Amelia merely smiled.

He smiled back. "No. Not yet."

They were all grinning now, as they looked down at Emily. James grabbed Mark's free shoulder and shook it, as Julia smiled past her tears. Amadeus, Thomas, and Amelia seemed to be having a silent conversation. Abruptly they stood up from the table, drawing back the attention.

"Please, come with us." Thomas gestured for them to follow.

Rick smiled and stood up with the others. "Where are we going?"

The two Jarly left the room, as Thomas continued. "We will let you eat, rest, and..." looking at Emily in Mark's arms, "Recover. Then tomorrow morning we will all meet again and discuss your involvement." He smiled then turned away.

"Involvement in what?" James asked, walking behind him.

Thomas glanced over his shoulder, with a grin. "Involvement in their global unveiling."

They followed him slowly out of the room and down a well-lit hallway. Painted light-beige, with a black-stone tiled floor, the hallway was bleak and clean at best. There were absolutely no windows, and the girls all seemed to shiver and hug closer into their lovers. Mark glanced down and saw the goose bumps rise on Emily's bare arms, causing him to hold her even tighter. James wrapped his arm around Julia and held her close, as he spoke. "Where exactly are we?" he asked the back of Thomas's head.

Still walking straight, not turning, "Right now, we're in the basement of my farm."

James looked over his shoulder at Rick and Amy. His brows rose, skeptically, and then he turned back. "A farm?"

Thomas let out a single laugh, gesturing to the clean walls and closed doors as he went. "I guess this must not look much like a normal farm. Over the years, the Jarly have blessed my family with many underground rooms and supplies. This, for instance, is one of the wings they use to house their own and others. My underground tunnels are cleaner and easily three times the size of my own house, above ground." Then he glanced over his shoulder, continuing, "THAT, is more of a farm house, that I use to keep up appearances."

Abruptly, he stopped out front of a closed black door, turned the handle, and gestured for them to go ahead, flicking on the light as he went. They followed him into a large room, a lot like a small apartment. In the shape of a hexagon, it displayed five closed doors on each red-painted wall, but one. The carpet was thick, cushy, and chocolate brown. In the middle of the room, lowered by three steps, was the biggest couch any of them had seen. It easily sat ten people, in a U-shaped dark suede, facing the non-door wall, which had a huge, seventy-five-inch plasma screen television, enclosed by a mini fridge on its right and a shelving unit filled with food, drinks and movies on the left. In the middle of the couch, a solid dark-wood coffee table, held a large vase of flowers.

Filling the room, the group gawked. Thomas continued, "Okay, so you all can stay in here and rest, for the night. The children are fast asleep in that one." He indicated the first closed door behind them, "And the rest of you can take the other rooms. Each room has its own bathroom and mini-fridge. There is plenty of food." Taking two steps back, towards the open exit, he added, "I'll be staying upstairs, and if you need anything at all, don't hesitate to come find me or knock on the doors next to you, but I doubt you will need to. Get a good night's sleep and whenever you wake up, follow this hallway to the dining area, where we'll have breakfast for you and we can start."

Nodding, as he finally said, "Goodnight," he closed the door behind him. They all stood there listening as he walked down the hallway, until they could hear nothing more.

Finally alone again, Amy quickly ran over to the children's room and peeked in. She stood in the middle of their cribs silently, as Julia joined. From what they could tell, the kids were perfectly fine. Matt was even sucking his thumb, as usual. For a split second, Abby smiled in her sleep, and rolled over. The women grinned, as they slowly backed out of the room, and closed the door. Returning to the living room, they sat on the couch, between Rick and James. Mark still had Emily in his lap, and he sat in the far corner. The others seemed to huddle close together and couldn't help but continue to scan the strange room.

Eventually Rick spoke up, asking Mark; "Still, no movement?" They all glanced over at him brushing the hair from her face.

"No, but he did say she would be completely healed, in a couple more hours."

Amy began to beam, as she tried to lighten up the situation.
"I'm going to be an aunt!"

Mark let out a single laugh, smiling, still not taking his eyes off
his wife's face. "So they say."

"What, you don't believe them?"

"I'm not sure. I need to get her to a hospital, check her out
myself, and take tests." Then he looked up and began backtracking, when he saw her smile drop ever so slightly. "Well, it could
be possible." Then he seemed to stare off into space, as he continued, obviously thinking; "She has been complaining of head-
aches lately." Then gradually he started to smile, with each added
comment. "And has had some dizzy spells. She's been more sleepy,
than usual. Nauseous."

Amy began to smile again. "And she's eating more, and I
remember her throwing up a few weeks back and again a couple
days ago."

Mark was beaming now. "Well, from the sounds of it..." He
looked down, then up again. "It sounds like...She. Could. Be.
Pregnant." Amy's smile got wider, with each subsequent word.

The others all smiled, as James added, "Congrats buds, you're
gonna be a father!" Amy, still smiling, wiped another tear of joy,
as Rick kissed her cheek.

Mark laughed, as he grinned down at his sleeping
wife. "Thanks."

When the cheers finally faded, Julia yawned, causing a
chain reaction.

Shaking his wife's shoulder, Rick whispered, "Bed time."

Amy yawned, comically wide.

"Yeah, I'm gonna lay her down too." Mark muttered rising to
his feet. The others nodded, watching, as he went to the first room
closest to him. "Good night," kicking the door closed behind him.

* * *

Mark peeked over at the bedside clock. He had stayed awake, waiting for Emily to wake. Excitement bloomed in his chest, as he ran over ways to break the news. It was now midnight, and it had been three hours since they had first awoken in the white room. Their bedroom was a calming shade of mint-green, with dark brown furniture. The bed was an oversized king, padded and covered in pillows. It came up higher than Mark's waist, with dark-purple sheets and dark-green accents. Emily was lying on her back, under the covers, on the left side of the bed; hands resting on her stomach. It worried Mark how pale and still she still was. He was on her right side, propped up by his elbow, not taking his eyes off her face.

Starting to smile, Mark watched as her eyes began to flutter, squeeze shut, and then burst open. In a panic, she began flaring her hands around trying to get free. She didn't focus on anything, as she scanned the room, frantically. Mark filled with concern and he grabbed her wrists, to stop her from hitting him.

Just as she took a deep breath to scream and tried to pull out of his grasp, he quickly whispered, "Em, It's me. Babe, it's me, Mark!"

Still shaking her head, she pulled her body away, taking a closer look. Saying nothing, she just stared straight into her husband's nervous eyes. Her breathing slowed, as he let her hands free, and her body finally relaxed.

"It's all right, you're fine. We're all here." With his words, and not moving her head, she glanced over his shoulder, then back to his face.

He waited for her to speak, but nothing came. Her body was still internally in shock, and they just lay there for a minute, staring into each other's eyes. Finally, big tears swelled as she pinched her eyes tight, and gave into her emotions; weeping softly. Her hands came up and covered her face. Her spine curved and her head leaned forward until it rested on his shoulder. Mark was shocked by the amount of anger the flowed through him at that moment. He had failed her. All he wanted to do was protect her. She was still so terrified. Slowly, he wrapped his arm around her waist and pulled her back into his embrace. Together, they stayed unmoving, for the remainder of the night.

Around seven a.m., Mark woke first. For one minute, eyes still closed, he had completely forgotten everything around them. It was just him and his wife in the most comfortable bed he had ever slept in. Pulling Emily tightly into his arms, he kissed her forehead, and rested his head back in her hair, taking a deep breath. Too soon, it was over. Mark's eyes burst open, as he quickly glanced around the room. Everything was just as they had left it. They were, thankfully, still alone. Pulling back, he critically examined his sleeping wife's face.

Emily appeared as comfortable in his arms as she had always been; not yet affected by his stiff hold. Her face was still lightly red and puffy, from the hours of body-wracking tears, but her face looked soft and at ease. Slowly, she began to wake. Mark didn't move, as she seemed to fidget in her sleep. Blinking a few times, she merely smiled, closed her eyes, and then pressed her face into his warm chest. Copying her husband, a few seconds later, eventually the scene sunk in and her head pulled back and quickly looked around the room.

"We're okay," Mark whispered, as her head spun back around and she focused on him.

"Are you sure?"

He nodded, kissing her forehead.

"Where are we?"

"Remember the old guy from their vision?"

She nodded back, confused. "Yeah?"

"We're in the basement of his farm. The people that gave them the visions are here too." Then he focused on her face, as he continued, scrutinizing her response. "They're aliens, Em." Her eyebrows raised and her lips parted, as she sucked in a sharp breath. "They had to sedate us, so they could transport us, to this facility. They took away whatever it was that was causing James and Julia and the kids' visions. Then they told us to rest and tomorrow. Meaning today, they will give us some real answers."

Emily was speechless, completely in shock, shaking her head deep in thought. Worry now replaced the confusion. She flicked back the sheets and lifted her torso up onto one elbow. Still on her side, she scanned Mark's body up and down, then lifted her far hand to brush through his hair and rest on the side of his face. "How are you? Are you okay? Did they hurt you?" Panic covered her face, as she continued to search for scratches, bruises, anything on him.

Mark quickly understood, sitting up, and pulling her into his arms in a tight hug. Holding the back of her head and kissing every bit of face he could reach, he reassured her, "Sweetheart, I'm fine, I'm perfectly fine. Don't worry about me."

She pulled back to scrutinize his face. He was always so good at covering up any real pain.

Smiling he cupped her face, and resting their foreheads together, crossed his legs and pulling her onto his lap. "Really, I'm fine!"

Abruptly, he gripped her nape, tilting her head up, so he could seal his lips over hers. Breathless, he pulled back to stare into her bewildered green eyes. "How, do you feel?"

She took a deep breath and actually considered his question. "I feel fine." She shrugged. "A little dizzy, I guess. And hungry."

He smiled at her.

"But I feel a lot better actually." She pulled back out of his grasp to look down at her body, and then touched her face. "Actually, my face and ribs don't hurt at all." After a few minutes, with no comment she watched the flush of Mark's amusement and excitement return. A look of awe prompted her question. "What?" she asked slowly. "What?" again, more quickly.

Shaking his head, Mark grabbed her by the hips, and thrust her into his embrace. Face to face, he reached up, brushing a stray strand behind her left ear, grazing her cheek with his fingertip. A shallow gasp escaped her lips, as a sudden heat pulled at her core. His finger brushed down the side of her neck, leaving a longing tingling.

"Em, the rest of us woke up, all at the same time. A few hours before you."

She just stared, not understanding.

"These beings have the ability to rapidly heal each other." His eyes strayed from hers, as he remembered. "They use some sort of energy, a glowing light..."

She winced, pulling back slightly at his words.

Shocked by her reaction, he looked her up and down, then grabbed her face. "What is it?"

"I remember the light. That's what she used to torture me." Emily answered.

"Oh no, no babe," he muttered, rubbing up and down her arms, trying to explain. "She was healing you. Apparently it can sometimes be quite painful, but that means it's working."

At first she was still upset, but then she seemed to understand. After all, she was clearly healed and feeling better than she had in a long time. "Okay," she drawled, as if to say, "continue."

He grinned, brushing his lips against hers, as his hands snaked around her lower back. Shuffling them backwards, dislodging pillows, he settled with his back against the headboard and her thighs now straddling his. He repeated, "So, yeah, they have these abilities and such."

"So, because I was injured more severely than you guys, I took longer to recover?" she asked, wrapping her arms around his shoulders.

He raised his knees, effectively cradling her against his body, caging her to him. She now desperately tried to focus on the topic of discussion and not on sudden urge to undulate her hips. His smile cracked, as he knew that look all too well. Resting his hands on her shoulders, he pulled her attention back to him.

"Yes, but it wasn't your face or ribs that took longer to recover."

Fear covered her face. "Then what?" Her ribs and face were the only things that previously hurt. What else, more serious, could it be? Internal bleeding? Organ damage? Brain damage?

His smile broke into a beam.

"What is it?" She grabbed his ribs, shaking him for her answer. "Mark!"

"You're pregnant!"

"What?" A gust of breath forced from her lungs. First, Emily was confused, and then she began to think back, counting in her head, as she glanced back at her overjoyed husband.

Taking a deep breath, her words came with shaky skepticism. "I'm pregnant?" she asked, slowly raising her eyebrows.

Playfully squeezed her hips, he nodded, "We're gonna have a baby."

Her eyes glossed over, as she contemplated the thought. A slow and steady grin spread across her face. Amidst her breathless laughter, new tears filled in her eyes, brimming, then over-flowed down her cheeks. She grabbed his face and pulled him into a heated kiss. Wrapping her arms tightly around his neck, she held him close.

Mark, satisfied with her reaction, smiled, wiping away the forgotten tears, as he waited for her to speak. Clearly deep in absent thought, Emily stilled, concern intruding on her happy thoughts. Without thinking, her hands went straight to her lower stomach, as her gaze dropped to the side, focusing on the intricate patterns of their bed sheets, as her mind wandered.

Eventually, she spoke in a rush. "How do you know? How far along?" Her eyebrows drew closer and her face became more and more concerned with each question. "Are you sure, it's okay? I went through a lot back there." More tears overflowed, this time the tears scorched by fear.

He grabbed her face, dragging her back to him, his brows creasing. "Shush," he whispered trying to comfort her. "It's perfectly healthy, Em. Look at us. Our recovery was perfect. You're healthy. They said, the minute you woke, you both would be completely healthy, as if nothing happened. They said you are just under two months. And when I think back, you have all the symptoms of morning sickness. Did you miss last month?"

Thinking back she began to nod. "Everything's been so hectic with the wedding and work. I just thought it was stress, or that I was just coming down with the flu."

Mark began to nod, understanding, and then he smiled. "So, don't panic anymore. We're going to have a baby." He brushed the hair from her face and held her close. "A perfect. Healthy. Baby." He deliberately stopped with each word. Finally, her body relaxed, and her shoulders slouched, as she forced another smile. Pulling herself back into his embrace, she rested her cheek on his shoulder, as he gently rocked them; both becoming silent, contemplating the future to come.

*   *   *

With hot showers and changes of clothes, Emily and Mark felt rejuvenated and ready to face the day, and they headed into the living room. The other adults were already awake and sitting on the large couch. Before a word could be spoken, Amy leapt up the three steps and lunged at Emily. Knocking her back a few steps, she held her in a tight hug.

"Em!" she cried. Kissing her cheek she whispered, "I was so worried."

"I know," Emily held her sister's head at her shoulder, and ran her hand over her hair. "Me too." Then pulling back to take a look at her, she asked, "Are you okay?"

"Yeah. I'm fine." Amy looked like a child, as she stepped back, slightly twisting on her feet.

Emily held the side of her face. "The black eye's gone."

Amy let out a light laugh, unconsciously touching her own face. "All better." Shrugging, she reached over to brush Emily's cheek. "You too! Perfect, as usual."

Emily let out a laugh, and lightly nudged her backwards, right into Rick. He smiled, stepping around his wife to take his sister-in-law into a friendly hug, whispering, "You okay?" into her ear.

She stepped back and nodded, smiling up at him, as James nudged him out of the way and grabbed Emily tightly, into a bear hug, lifting her off the ground.

"Can't.... breathe." Emily gasped exaggeratedly for breath, as he laughed and placed her back down. Then finally, Julia appeared to his right, stepping around to lightly hug Emily, and kiss her cheek.

"I'm so glad you're okay," she said. "You had us worried, there."

"I know. Sorry, about that." Her answer was mocking, yet serious in a way.

They all stood silently, anticipation in the air. The others glanced back and forth between Mark; Amy with a wide grin and raised eyebrows, and then Emily. Mark let out a quick laugh, lifting his arm over his wife's shoulder. "She knows."

Amy squealed, flapping her hands with excitement as she

practically bounced on the spot. She couldn't help herself, pulling her sister into another tight hug, grabbing and lightly shaking her hips, as Emily smiled and rested her hands on Amy's shoulders. "You're going to be a mommy!" Amy practically screamed in excitement. "I'm gonna be Auntie Amy!" she quickly added, giddily.

"Uncle Rick," Amy's husband blurted out, nodding, and turning to James. "I like the sound of that." Amy stepped back, as Rick put his hand on her shoulder, holding her close, and she wrapped her hand around his waist.

"Yes, well let's get this over with, so you can be Uncle Rick! Shall we?" James broke into the joyous conversation. Gradually, their smiles faded. One by one, they began to nod, turning and staring at the door leading to the mysterious hallway.

Then Emily turned, looking up questionably at Mark, "Where are Abby and Matt?"

He jerked his chin at the door next to their exit. "In there. I guess they're still sleeping." He glanced at the others for agreement.

Emily took a step away from him, "I'll get them, so we can leave."

Mark smiled back, as Amy added, "I'll help."

"We'll wait here," Rick added, taking a step back down and going to sit on the couch. The others joined him, turning on the flat screen.

Slowly, Emily opened the children's door and peeked in. Amy lightly pushed it wide open, so they both could see. Moving to stand in between both cots, they grinned down, as Matt continued to suck his thumb and Abby lightly babbled in her sleep. Nodding lightly at her sister to go ahead, Emily reached down and raised Abby, still sleeping, into her arms. The child's little head rested on Emily's shoulder, her tiny lips pressed against her collarbone. She smiled to herself. Amy slowly raised Matt into her arms. At first, he stirred slightly, still not opening his eyes, but he eventually calmed down and rested both arms around her neck.

CHAPTER TWELVE

Holding Julia's hand, James took the lead, as they slowly opened the door to the hallway. Not taking a step, James pushed his head out into the hallway and glanced left and right. Empty. Pulling back with his head, he gestured for the others to follow. Mark and Emily, with Abby in her arms, followed closely, with the other three behind them. James took a left out of the doorway and into the hall. The hall was well-lit as it had been the night before. All doors remained closed, as the hall came to a sharp turn, leading to a shorter hall. At the very end, they saw the only door in that hallway to the right, wide open, with the light from inside hitting the wall across from it.

Emily couldn't help but hold Abby slightly tighter and hold her breath. Mark could feel the sudden tension and lightly rubbed her shoulder. He smiled down in encouragement at her, as she blew out sharply and smiled back. They edged their way closer to the door. Eventually, voices could be heard and Emily noticed. Julia lightly started to shake and her free hand open and closed. She wiped it against her pant leg. Finally, James reached the doorway, but Julia held back. James understood and nodded. Taking the final step, he lined himself with the frame and looked in. The room became silent. The others analyzed his face.

"Please, come in." A strange husky voice came from the room.

The others froze where they were. James nodded and then

turned back to his friends, gesturing with his hand. "It's okay. Come on."

Mark dropped his arm from his wife's shoulder and quickly took her shaking hand. Emily squeezed his tightly, and then copied Mark as he took the first step forward. Slowly, two at a time, they entered the room with wide eyes, obviously nervous. As they filed in, they stayed close to the wall, not far from the door.

They were in a fairly large room, the walls again beige, with the same dark flooring as the hallway. There were four large tables with chairs; the only furniture in the room. Three were parallel to the length of the room, while the fourth, closest to them, stood across the end of the others. The friends stood there, as eight people looked up at them from various tables. Two burly men were seated at the far left table. Both of them had dark hair and dark clothing. They were too far away for Emily to notice any real details about them. Looking up at the new arrivals, the men quickly appeared bored, and turned back to their conversation.

In the middle table were three others; two women, sitting on the right side of the table, talking to a male across from them. One woman, the farthest away, was stunning, with her long blonde curls and curvaceous figure. The woman next to her had a blunt, black bob-cut; her pointed nose, and plump cheekbones, revealed beauty in another form. Emily watched as the woman's long, painted fingernails tapped rhythmically on the tabletop.

The man across from them had broad shoulders, and his light-brown hair was cut shorter on the sides and longer on the top, spiked into a rounded bouffant. These three too wore dark clothing, which was emphasized by their pale skin. No one in the room looked over thirty, though the others knew that meant little given yesterday's revelations.

Eventually, Emily focused on the three people sitting opposite them at the nearest table. On the far left, sat a man with dark-brown, spiked hair, and a chiseled jaw. He was quite possibly the most attractive man she had ever seen. His eyes were dark-green and smoldering. In the middle of the table sat a woman, with equally dark hair, slicked back into a tight ponytail, which rested over her right shoulder. When Emily looked to her left, at the other end of the table, she took in a sharp breath and squeezed Mark's hand; surprising him, as she took an involuntary step back. The woman at that end was smiling, like the other two, but was focused solely on Emily. Emily recognized the tall, red-headed beauty, from before.

"Please, join us." Amelia gestured to the seats across from them.

Emily refused to take her eyes from the woman, who had stopped staring, and had turned to the cooked breakfast of bacon and eggs in front of her. Slowly, the friends sat down, leaning far back into their seats. Amy lightly jumped in her seat and let out a little cry, as a strong arm came out of nowhere, placing a breakfast in front of her. She glanced up to see one of the tall, burly men from the corner place it down. He continued to give the others meals, leaving dishes of baby food in front of Emily and Amy, as they whispered "Thank you."

The man didn't utter a word, but he returned their smiles and nodded as he returned to his seat.

"Please, eat." The smoldering male spoke, gesturing for them to begin.

One by one, they took their first bites, and realizing how hungry they were, they quickly finished their meals.

Amelia was the first to speak. "Let me introduce each of us."

Turning in her seat, to face the men at the far table, she pointed. "This is Damon." He nodded, "and his brother Caleb." Caleb smiled and turned back to his brother.

Then she turned back to face the others. "Damon is the ship's chef." She smiled. "By choice, and he is also the linguistic specialist. He speaks every known language on Earth, even dead languages." They all raised their brows, in amazement, as she moved on. "Both are our weapons and combat specialists, though Caleb spends most of his time in engineering."

Then she turned to point at the table directly behind her. "The blonde is Selene, my sister. She's the religion specialist and historian. Next to her is Aella. Aella is our tactical specialist and negotiator, though she dabbles in many things. And across from them, is Pike." Finally, she turned back to face the group. "He's the ship's recorder and second communicator with our home planet."

Emily and her group all sat silent, listening intently, waiting for her to continue. Amelia gestured to herself. "Most of you have met me already." Emily glanced up at Mark, then back to her. "My name is Amelia, and I am the ship's pilot and head of security." Amelia placed her right hand on the shoulder of the man next to her, and he smiled at her touch. "This is Riley; he is a famous warrior on our planet and is ordered to protect our healer." Dropping her right hand, then lifting her left to rest on the woman's shoulder, she added, "Isobel." Isobel smiled and nodded once.

Then there was silence. Emily was surprised by Isobel's sudden question to her; "How do you feel?"

Emily understood that Isobel had healed her, as opposed to intentionally harming her, but she could not shake the memory of the pain. "I'm fine, now. Thank you." Practically whispering, she kept her eyes trained on the table, as she lightly leant into Mark's side; taking his hand in hers, under the table.

She saw Isobel smile, lean back in her seat, and nod to herself.

When the silence of their table was overtaken by the other conversations in the room, Amelia spoke up. "Well, please relax and enjoy a conversation or two, while we wait for Amadeus. Our leader," she explained to Emily. "Then we can begin." Slowly the

conversations did begin. At first they stayed in their own group-
ings, but gradually the humans and the Jarly began questioning
each other in innocent curiosity.

* * *

"Okay, so hold up." James sat there, interrupting an intense conversation between Amelia, Riley, Amy, and Rick. He literally held
his hand out, to stop their conversation. "If you've been coming
here for thousands of years, how come there's no evidence? No
writing of direct encounters?"

Amelia laughed quite loudly, as Isobel smiled and answered.
"Who do you think gave the ancient Egyptians the idea for the
pyramids, or the Chinese the Great Wall of China, or the ancient
Ziggurats of South America? Or taught the Mayan's astronomy?"

James and the others looked completely dumbfounded and
amazed, with jaws dropped open. With no answer, Amelia continued. "The first human book ever written was about one of
us." All eyes were suddenly on her, looking like a kindergarten
class, fascinated with their pre-nap-time story. She took a deep
breath. "In 2733 BC, a man from one of our earliest outposts
was given permission to stay behind and integrate into society.
Gilgamasiean, was his name; later known as Gilgamesh, on Earth.
The book was simply about his life."

"With a couple myths and boogiemen, here and there." Riley
spoke for the first time, smiling at Amelia. Amy, nearest, felt a pull
between the two. She let out a tiny giggle that only Rick seemed to
notice. Glancing sideways at her, he raised a questioning brow, to
which she responded by grinning and discreetly shaking her head.

"He was already a well-known leader on our planet,"
Amelia added.

"And warrior," Isobel joined in, while Amelia continued,

unfazed by the interruption.

"The humans living in Uruk at the time..." She stopped glancing around at the others, who looked confused at each other.

Riley raised his eyebrows with each question; "Babylonia? Sumer? Mesopotamia? First cities EVER formed on Earth? Any of this ring any bells?"

"It's modern-day Iraq." Amadeus smiled, as he entered the room. Everyone stopped, watching as he made his way over from the large, open doorway, sitting in the only remaining seat at the giant table. "Oh, no. Please continue."

"Geez, you guys need a history lesson," Riley muttered under his breath.

Amelia smiled, nodded, and went on. "Anyway," she said, trying not to laugh. "Gilgamesh encouraged the people to work together and unite under common goals. He showed them many farming techniques, how to create simple account records, and how to irrigate their fields effectively. Obviously, even at that point in time, we had much more advanced technologies than you have even today, but the one condition on his stay was that he could not advance the people beyond their time and mental capabilities."

"Why not?" James had to ask, while his friends nodded and waited for an answer.

Riley leant forward in his seat, onto the table, and seemed to think for a few seconds. "In terms of technology, at the time, picture an anatomically modern human, handing over a ray gun or any advanced technology, to a small group of cave men that had just been playing with sticks and stones, and were still fascinated with the idea of fire." He raised his eyebrows at the end, letting it sink in.

The others thought about it, so Amelia and Isobel used the silence, as an opportunity to continue.

"Eventually, he was so vital to their daily lives."

"And loved." Isobel grinned at Amelia to continue.

"That they thanked him by making him their king and their true leader. From that day on and until his death, he led them to build the cities, develop greater trade, and slowly advance their technology."

Riley took over. "As you know, our kind don't exactly age like yours. After many years, Gilgamesh knew the people were beginning to get suspicious. When the next crew came back to study..."

"He faked his own death and returned home, leaving many sons and daughters. When he returned hundreds of years later, he lived out his days in peace," Amelia ended, quite bluntly.

The human crowd was caught off guard, as they heard Thomas clapping from behind. Their heads spun to see him leaning against the open door. "I love these historical stories."

Julia stole a glance at Amy, *What-a-special-little-man* was written right across their grinning faces, and they had to force themselves not to burst out in laughter. Thomas stayed where he was, as Amadeus cleared his throat and shuffled the pages in front of him.

The room went silent, as all the heads turned to listen.

"May I interrupt?" asked Amadeus, with obvious, friendly sincerity.

"Please." Amelia smiled and gestured to the table. "It's all yours."

"Thank you." He turned to face the curious humans.

"How are you?" Amadeus asked in general.

Emily and the others were taken back by the sudden formality in his words. He waited for an answer.

"We're fine, thank you. And yourself?" Mark answered on behalf of the group.

"Oh, very well. Thank you. So, shall we begin?"

Mark leant back in his chair, resting his left arm along the back of Emily's, as Amadeus began.

"I am sure you all have many questions that, rightfully need answering, and hopefully I can answer them all for you." He glanced around the room. "Okay, so Emily, I'm afraid you missed our general introduction yesterday. I'm sure Mark has filled you in on the basics. We are known, as the Jarly. We come from a distant galaxy, though our kind evolved much faster than your own, being an older species, and therefore we have mastered space travel. So the minute we found life on your planet, we set out to learn and observe your kind. For a while now, we have hidden in the shadows, unable to unveil ourselves." Emily nodded, when he seemed to pause, waiting for a response.

"So, where would you like me to begin?" Amadeus asked around the room.

"How about the hotel? What happened to us? What was that light?" James blurted out.

Amadeus turned to directly address him. "Just like your own planet, we are governed by a form of politics, as well. We have studied the inheritance of this planet for thousands of years, and now our journeys come at greater costs. We have attempted to make contact on previous occasions." He let the papers in his hands drop to the table below, as Julia gasped.

The others turned to face her. "What? What is it?" Amy grew panicked.

Julia pointed, "This was one of our visions."

James turned to look at the table. "Yeah, I've seen those papers before."

Amadeus was already nodding, turning a couple of the old newspapers around, and he tossed them down the table to them. The headlines read, 'July 8, 1947 A Flying Disc.' It was a local newspaper, describing the crash landing of an unexplained object near Roswell. The other newspaper attacked a second article, written two days later, stating that previous reports were incorrect and it was in fact a weather balloon.

"So, the Roswell crash was real. Area 51, all that stuff, is real?" Rick's eyes seemed to widen as Amadeus grinned.

"That was one of many attempts to make contact in the recent century. That specific crash was one of our smaller research pods, which was shot out of the sky by your military. The two Jarly inside were quickly transported and studied in a private facility, south of Colorado. I'm afraid what you and many others have come to believe as "Area 51" is just another form of distraction."

"So, why set up your training base here? Roswell. Isn't that kinda obvious?" James asked.

"Think of it as hiding in plain sight," Riley offered, a mischievous grin plastered across his face. "Kind of a joke, I guess. But also, this is where Thomas grew up. His family is from here, so why move?"

"Why would they cover the crash up?" Julia naively asked, changing the topic.

"We have tried to make contact throughout the globe, not just in the United States, and every form of government, to date, has acted the same. I guess they wish to study us and determine if we are a threat to your kind, before they go public, possibly causing hysteria."

"Okay, so why Sierra Vista? Why now?" Rick asked again.

"As I said previously, I follow orders on my planet just as you do here. My leaders have decided that now is the last chance we'll have to attempt to communicate and learn. If we are unsuccessful, we have been ordered to leave Earth. Indefinitely."

Amelia cleared her throat. "Sierra Vista in particular is close to many military bases, on both secrecy and high magnitude. The Grand Hotel, where you were staying was chosen as the best spot." She shrugged. "The most humans in one area, for a connection."

"You say connection. You mean the visions?" James asked.

"Yes. Those visions were part of our little experiment." Amadeus turned apologetic. "It was more curiosity, than anything. Our goal was to enhance your abilities, connecting you, so that you could see one possible future of our visit and involvement with your planet."

James nodded. "Right, okay, and the light? What was that?"

"Ah," Amadeus said, as if he had hit the key subject. "We call it Nona. Nona is our planet; our life, our control. Like Earth, Nona, is consumed by energy. When an individual is born, Nona loses a small amount of her core energy. When a person dies, that energy is replenished. It's a cycle of life, a physical bond with our planet. At first we were like you, unaware of our surroundings and true potential. More than a millennium ago, our kind began practicing what you may call a form of meditation. When we reached a certain level, things became clear and we could control the energy within our own bodies. We could draw on that energy and the energy of others to protect, heal, and support ourselves. With each new ability we gained, new technologies were created to work in unison with our energy, or light, as you call it. With such a strong bond with Nona, the average life span tripled. At first, it was a day-to-day connection, but throughout the generation, our kind has evolved with such abilities at birth."

The others were silent, as they took in the information. "So, that was the light that consumed the hotel? You can teach us to connect with our own Earth?" Rick asked.

"Yes, the light that consumed the hotel was actually from one of our ships. That ship was created by, and runs materials and energy, drawn from Nona. In your own training..." He searched for the right words. "It is possible, but it will take true time and focus. Hopefully, your future generations will evolve like we once did."

Then he turned quickly to the others. "We only had a certain amount of time to complete the task before we had to leave. I'm guessing you four found good enough hiding spots to escape our touch."

Mark laughed slightly, nodding. "The roof."

"I see, well in any case, we did this with the added choice for you to all find your way here for more answers and a group tutorial on our history and purpose. But then the next morning, when you began to wake, it was too late. Your military had already begun to invade. We had no choice but to stand back and watch as they were taken."

"So, the other visions. The later ones of dark rooms, blood..." Julia trailed off.

"Being connected, those visions changed and you saw through the eyes of the people that were not fortunate enough to get away. That was their possible futures," Amadeus answered.

James cut him off. "What about the vision of us in the room too? We were running and getting killed."

Amadeus's eyes saddened, as he glanced around. "That is one possible future, now."

The group became silent, as they thought about more questions, "What about those things that came and implanted these visions in our heads?" James asked. "They looked more like those big ugly things from those movies – like goblins."

"Predators," Julia interrupted, looking down at the table.

"Yeah, they looked more like predators than you guys."

"Yes. Well, believe it or not they were once like us. Over sixty thousand years ago, before our kind became instinctually peaceful and diplomatic, and only used violence as a form of defense, there was a time of global war. We had all learnt how to become one with our planet and nature. We learnt to wield the energy around us, to use it to heal, but also to destroy. Those beings you call predators are known as Birons. Back then, their ancestors used their gifts to create havoc and fight amongst themselves. They looked like us, but their power had greatened and overwhelmed them, until it physically deformed their bodies. After the Great Wars, eventual alliances tend to conferences, and the remaining fighters were stripped of their abilities to connect to Nona. They were banished to a remote geographical region.

"For centuries, the Birons stayed to themselves, learning their own ways and lifestyles. Adapting to different surroundings, their bodies further changed, making their appearance almost completely unrecognizable. It was as if they were a completely different species. Generations later, they gradually left their lands and tried to interact with our kind again. Of course, we accepted them back into our society, but with gene pool dilution, the energy that was once forcefully blocked could no longer be adapted or controlled in their new bodies.

"A lot of our technology is taken for granted by those of us that can use the planet's energy. The Birons were forced to keep to themselves, even within our company. Eventually, when we began our space expeditions, our government came up with a plan to give them purpose and a good living. I am sad to say that the Birons are the perfect subjects for war. Their bodies are tough and can withstand much more intense environments than our own. Therefore, our leaders have commissioned the majority of their kind to be our first wave of attack and protection."

The group remained speechless.

"So, what does this have to do with us? Why are we here?" James asked, after a few minutes.

"Well, as I said previously, this was supposed to be a group meeting. It was meant to be a choice. You could all come as a group, finding your way here out of curiosity. If you decided not to come, after a week, the visions would have stopped and you could have continued on with your lives. We were going to reveal ourselves, with the help of your group, which would speak for us and welcome us publicly.

"We thought civilian involvement would finally work. But after their militarized efforts, our orders quickly changed. Now we are to train whoever does make it here, to go, and retrieve the others. If and when you're successful, you will have proven yourself. We have been given permission to unveil ourselves on a large scale... Large enough that we can do so peacefully."

Amadeus took a deep breath, releasing it in a huff, as he absently tapped his fingers. "You have to understand. Our leaders were frustrated with our initial results. We're going out on a limb here. When they see initiative and willingness to risk your lives for your own kind, to reveal a higher nature and the truth, they will believe Earth is worth it. Then, no matter how badly the governments of Earth wish to conceal us, they won't have the option anymore."

"So, let me get this straight." Rick leant forward, pressing both palms against the table surface. "You come without warning. Cause a number of people to get kidnapped and tortured. Send us on this wild goose chase to find you, having us beaten and broken in the process." He glanced at Emily. "And now you expect us to take on a militarized compound to retrieve them. Getting shot at, captured, or even killed, all on our own. So, your leaders, God knows how far away, can be satisfied that the human race is worth their time and effort?"

"I'd say that pretty much sums it up." Riley shrugged.

"Geez, how could anyone decline such an amazing offer?" James couldn't hide the disdain in his voice.

Emily, spoke up. "And what if we say no? What if we decide that we don't want our lives or anyone else's to change? That maybe the Jarly/Biron/Human alliance isn't for us. Are we the only six people on Earth, to make the decision?"

Amadeus's smile faded. He answered her questions and this time he was more pleading than before. "Please understand, we have spent centuries on your planet. We could bring you technologies to save lives that don't need to be lost. We can extend lives. Cure world hunger. Abolish the need for weapons. Uniting our two worlds would be in your best interests... But of course the decision must be made willingly. Neither I, nor any of my crew, can force the decision upon you and we understand if you decide to sway your decision more towards another cover-up. And, yes, I understand that this is an amazing decision to have on such young shoulders, but over the last few days, you six have proven to be the last ones remaining who can help us.

"But please know that this is our last chance. Your planet will go down in our history books, but your kind will never know of us. Everything will be lost. Lives will be forfeit for nothing. If you do choose to leave, we cannot help the others that have been taken. We must leave within twenty-four Earth hours and never return." Amadeus stopped his rant, and sat back in his chair. "I have visited Earth since I was a young man. I can't imagine not seeing her beauty again."

Though he made a compelling argument, the group needed silence to think.

"Hate to rush you, but we do need an answer today," Riley pushed.

"This isn't something we can decide in five minutes. We're putting our lives at risk here. Give us some time," James argued.

"I'm afraid time is not a luxury that you have now."

Mark eventually spoke. "I don't know about you guys, but I say we go for it." He glanced at the others, "If they really are who they say they are, we could improve life for millions of people."

"And what about the risking our lives, part?" James

asked, sarcastically.

Mark quickly turned to Amadeus. "You said we were now here to train. Train, how?"

Amadeus sat up straight, excitement blooming, as he spoke. "Yes. If you were to agree, you would go through a one-day physical training where we will advance you in defensive abilities."

"You expect us to take on the American government, after one day?" Mark burst out.

"Trust me, you won't need more than that, with this kind of training. We will show you how to use your own strengths and highlight weaknesses. You will bond with one of my team; accelerating your abilities and duplicating our own. Basically, by the end of the day, you would be able to retain the knowledge and abilities of a seasoned, trained warrior."

Mark turned back to the group. "So?" He looked at his wife.

She stared at him for a minute, scrutinizing his face, as she thought. "I think we should continue. Even if just to save those innocent people. We can't just sit back and let them be slaughtered."

"Well, either way, you're sitting this one out."

"What?" Emily leaned back. "You think I'm letting my husband and sister...all of you, put your lives in danger while I sit back?"

"Yes. We can talk about this later," he muttered, then crossed his arms and leant into his chair.

"Screw that. We're talking about it now." Her voice grew louder with each word. "You made me a promise, Mark."

His brows creased as he thought.

"With all the crap that has gone down in the last few days, you promised you wouldn't leave me. That you'd be at my side until this is all over."

"That was before we found out about the baby. No, way I'm letting you anywhere near that place."

"And, no way I'm letting my family risk their lives, when I could be there to help." He went to speak, so she continued in a rush. "Baby or not, I'm not sitting this one out."

"If I may," Amadeus pulled their attention back to the others, who sat in silence, gawking at the couple. "Mark, I can assure you that with the training ahead, Emily and the child will be quite safe. She will have rapid healing and added strength."

Emily thrust out her hand, toward Amadeus. "There, see. Problem solved."

"Not likely," Mark muttered under his breath.

When the couple fell silent, eventually the remainder of the group agreed to help.

"Perfect. You have no idea how happy this makes us." Amadeus beamed at them.

The tension in the room gradually faded as Rick spoke up. "So, we're seriously going to be able to do all this? God knows how many guys they'll have against us. We have to deal with that, while we try to release the remaining captives." He paused briefly, "Only then, do you have permission to intervene further?"

"Yes. I know it sounds hard."

Amadeus was interrupted by James. "More like impossible."

"Yes, one might say that, but you will receive extensive training and may gain help from other humans. I believe that once you reach the prisoners, they will revolt if given the chance, and help you. Remember, this operation is top secret, so they can't risk too much publicity by bringing in more enforcement. I'm working on ways to help you, as best we can, without facing our own form of court martial. You may use any of our technology that may be useful."

"Well, all we can do is try." Amy spoke up. "I'm with Em. Regardless, we can't just leave them there."

Amadeus nodded. "Like I said, I'm working on ways to help

more. In the meantime, if you are serious, we should start training as soon as tomorrow."

Amadeus's crew had remained quiet throughout the short meeting.

"So, you're going to fight for humanity and save the world?" Riley lightened up the room, with his joking tone.

The others laughed, as James answered with a smirk, "I guess so."

"Well, this is great news. I will inform my commanders. Please feel free to stay or head back to your room and relax. More food and entertainment has been taken to your room. You will need your rest for tomorrow." Amadeus got up with the others to leave the room, but stopped in the doorway, turning around with a huge smile. "Thank you. I know this decision doesn't come easily."

Their faces appeared glum again, but they did attempt to fake a smile and nod as the room emptied.

Amelia stopped in the doorway. "Training starts early so don't stay up too late." Then she disappeared with the others, down the hallway, leaving the humans alone to reflect.

"So, we're really doing this?" Amy asked around.

Rick pulled her hand from the table to intertwine his fingers with hers, resting their hands in his lap. "Sounds like it."

"I think we made the right decision..." Julia trailed off.

James leant back in his seat. "Yeah, but we might be regretting it tomorrow."

Once again the conversation trailed off to silence. The group sat staring off at nothing, deep in thought, for a while.

"All right." Mark said, taking Emily's hand and getting to his feet. "We're committed now, so let's head back to the room, and try to forget about it for one night."

Slowly, sluggishly, the group got to their feet. Abby and Matt were awake and obviously bored. When Mark opened the front door, they noticed the coffee table had been pushed over to leave a wide space on the carpet, which was filled with age-appropriate children's toys. The sibling's eyes widened, as they took in the room. Pulling away from Amy and Emily, they grabbed the air in front of them in the direction of the carpet.

Julia took Abby, following Amy to the play space, as they began to play and entertain the children. Rick and James, accompanied by Emily and Mark, relaxed on the large couch, flicking through the channels. The clock above the television informed them that it was only eleven-thirty in the morning. The group spent the rest of that day watching movies, T.V., playing board games and entertaining the children.

By eight-thirty that night, the toddlers had been put to sleep and Emily hovered by their bedroom door. Instead of returning to the couch, she walked around the upper lever to her bedroom door.

"I think, I'm gonna call it a night," she announced to the room.

Mark looked up at the clock and got to his feet, walking towards her. "Yeah, me too."

"All right, well night guys. See ya in the morning!" Emily opened the door, as the others said their "Good nights," not taking their eyes off the screen.

CHAPTER THIRTEEN

The three couples woke up to loud banging on their bedroom doors. One by one, the men jumped out of bed. Mark and James, were shirtless in black boxers, while Rick wore an additional white t-shirt. They went straight for their doors.

"You have fifteen minutes before we meet in the dining room. Here are your clothes. Be ready!" Riley placed three large, brown paper bags on the coffee table, as he walked back out of their small home and closed the door behind them.

"Yeah, he's definitely a morning person," Rick noted sarcastically, as he strolled over to the table.

"Yeah, tell me about it." James rubbed the sleep from his eyes. Glancing at the clock, he groaned when it displayed five a.m.

Mark and James joined Rick at the center of the room, hovering over the paper bags, picking them up and reading the print on the outside.

"Mark and Emily," Rick passed over their clothes. Mark grinned, took the bag, then yawned widely making Rick grin.

"What time is it?" Rick squinted at the room's bright lighting.

James didn't turn, as he muttered, "It's five a.m." All three let their shoulders slouch, as they grabbed the correct bags, and headed back to their rooms.

"Okay, remember, we have fifteen minutes. Tell the girls," Mark reminded his friends, closing his door.

* * *

"Emily," Mark whispered, holding himself directly above his wife, who was lying on her back.

Pinching her eyes even tighter, she tried to pull up the comforter, lightly moaning. Emily never was an early bird. Mark grinned, leant down, planting a tender kiss to her bare right shoulder. She gradually smiled, as he gently traced her collarbone with his nose, sucking and licking as he went, pausing at the hollow of her neck, then following her jaw line.

"We gotta get up and ready." He tugged at the sheets, exposing her bare flesh.

Two seconds later, Emily slowly opened her eyes, adjusted to the light, then focused on her husband. "Morning," she whispered. "What time is it?"

"Early." Leaning down, he kissed her with more force.

With the index finger on his right hand, the hand not supporting his weight, he traced around her earlobe, down her neck, and along the length of her body, before reaching her knee; the corners of their kiss breaking as he brushed over her bare ribs, causing her to giggle and pull away. He pulled back, dragging Emily with him, as she sat up in bed, letting the sheets pool around her waist.

Mark relaxed, humming contently, as he appreciated the view. Emily went to entwine their hands, but stopped short of his left, as he held something dark in it.

"What's that?"

"Your clothes for today," he muttered, pulling away and getting up from the bed.

Standing at the foot of the bed, Mark riffled through a large paper bag and pulled out his own outfit. Emily examined her set. She had been given a simple, tight-fitted, white, short-sleeve t-shirt, sports bra, and panties, with a pair of three-quarter-length, black sweat pants. As she finally slid her black socks on, Mark passed her a pair of black running shoes and a hair band.

"They think of everything." Smirking, she laced her shoes, and pulled her hair back into a loose ponytail, watching Mark tie his laces, sitting in the only chair in the room. "Ready?" she asked him.

Walking over, he said, "Ready."

"Okay, let me just brush my teeth. I'll meet you in the living room." She stood up from the bed and strode into the bathroom.

Mark went to wait in the other room; Julia and James were already sitting on the couch waiting.

"Ready?" James asked, as Rick and Amy came into the room. Mark couldn't help but notice the baby-blue t-shirt Amy was wearing and the bright pink Julia had on, both with white short-shorts, as they came into view.

"Yeah, Em will just be another minute." Mark shot a look at the girls' clothing. "Obviously, they know what we each like...clothes-wise."

The others laughed, as Emily silently walked out of their bedroom. "What's so funny?"

Mark just stepped back, took her hand in his, and gestured around the room. "Just commenting on the fact that even aliens know our fashion sense."

Emily smiled, confused at his comment, but then she smiled wider as she glanced at each person in the room. The girls were in light, bubbly clothing. James had a white, sleeveless shirt, which showed off his rock-solid arms. Rick and Mark wore casual gym wear, which was still very flattering and showed off some forming ab-muscles.

"Nice."

"All right, well, we better get going. There's gonna be some serious training if they have to get us up this early!" Julia broke their laughter.

"What about the kids?" Amy quickly asked.

"They're fine here, we'll let them sleep some more, then we can grab them later," Mark answered.

Slowly they filed out of the room, heading for the dining room where they had spent most of yesterday morning. Six plates had already been set out on the table in front of their chairs. The table was filled with plates of toast, boxes of cereal, bowls of oatmeal, bacon, eggs, juice and coffee. The group sat down and ate while they waited for further instructions.

Fifteen minutes later, one of the brothers, Caleb, knocked on the open door behind them. The friends glanced back, over their shoulders, as he spoke.

"Amelia is ready for you now," he said in a matter-of-fact tone.

Caleb waited patiently as they swallowed their last bites. Finally, they pushed back from the table. Rick reached down and quickly finished his orange juice, as they followed Caleb back down the cold hallway. The couples walked, hand in hand, as they passed their room and continued on.

This reminded Emily. "What about the children?" she asked of Caleb's back.

He turned and smiled warmly. "When they wake up, someone will go in and entertain them for the day."

Emily merely nodded after him, and after a few left turns, they finally came to the end of the hall, to a large, black door. Caleb pulled back the handle and pushed the door, until it opened wide. He stepped in and gestured with his arm for them to continue. Their eyes appeared to bug out, as they stepped into what appeared to be a traditional Japanese Dojo training room. The room was easily two floors deep.

James thought he had fallen into *The Matrix*, as he lightly laughed to himself, half-expecting Morpheus to step out from behind one of the pillars. The floors were light hardwood with a large, brown padded mat, consuming the majority of the room. The walls were even decorated with large Japanese writing and makeshift windows. James's eyes followed to the far back wall. It was filled with various weapons; wooden and metal, along with shields and body padding. The only items that seemed out of place were a small row of handguns at the very end.

"Please, come and sit on the side of the mat." They jumped, as Amelia's voice came from the other side of the room. She was standing with Riley in an open door, which led to a different hallway.

They did so and Mark asked, "Where are we?" as they all sat down and continued to glance around.

"This is our training room. We are still underground, in case you were wondering. This is another one of Thomas's rooms that he so graciously lets us use." Amelia walked across the mat until she and Riley were standing directly in front of the small group. "So, shall we begin your training?"

Both stood ready in their own workout gear. A sizzle of excitement passed through the women, as Riley absently flexed and released his biceps. The members of the group sat smiling, each nodding, as James almost began to bounce where he sat, obviously excited. Amelia smiled, nodded once, then held a hand out in front of Emily.

"Emily, could you please join me up here for a second?"

"Sure." Emily spoke cautiously, taking her out-reached hand.

Then they, along with Riley, turned and walked to the center of the room. Amelia nodded once, to Riley, as he began to walk towards the end wall.

"Can you all see us clearly?" Amelia asked the people on the edge of the mat.

One at a time, they yelled back, "Yes."

"Good," she responded, and then focused her attention on Mark. "Mark, before we begin, I know you worry about the safety of your wife and unborn child." Before she continued, she waited, as his face became serious and he began to slowly nod. Emily smiled down at him. She completely understood his fears, because they were also her own, in reverse.

"Okay, well I'm going to show you that such fear is not needed." Amelia quickly turned back to face Riley, at the other end of the mat, and grabbed Emily's wrist firmly. "Riley," she said, as in giving an unspoken order. "Ready, when you are." Her feet drew the same light Emily had seen Isobel use. Emily unconsciously pulled back, trying to get away from the flames. The light grew up Amelia's legs, into her torso, and along her arms. Where her hand touched Emily's arm, a light tingling feeling accompanied.

Emily and the others watched, wide-eyed. Emily looked down at her arm, across the room to Riley, back to Amelia who seemed extremely focused, then back to her arm. It was Amy's cry, which caused Emily to look over at her sister, and then follow her gaze to Riley, who slowly raised a Glock handgun, pointing it directly at Emily.

"No!" Mark screamed loudly, along with the others, as they tried to scramble from the floor, trying to reach them. Some unyielding force forced them back, making them unable to touch the mat. Riley raised his left hand and pulled back the top of the gun, knocking one bullet into the barrel, and then pointing back at Emily and Amelia.

"No! What are you doing? Let go of me!" Emily screamed, twisting her arm, trying to pull free.

Amelia's grip was unyielding and viselike. She quickly traded hands, grabbing Emily's other wrist, spinning her around, and holding her directly in front of her own body, in line with Riley's aim.

"No. Stop!" Mark angrily cried as he, and the others, repeatedly ran into the invisible wall, getting knocked back onto the floor below.

Mark quickly got back to his feet, but it was too late; it happened so fast. Emily cried out and cringed to the side, squeezing her eyes shut. The gun went off and Mark screamed for Emily. All of a sudden the bullet stopped.

"Mark. Come." Amelia's voice was soft, too calm for the situation, as she still held tight to Emily.

Mark took two strides forward, stopping just before the invisible wall, and put his hand up to feel the air.

"My shield is gone. You can go."

Riley turned, placing the gun back on the wall.

Mark could barely control his voice, as he started to run over to her without looking at the others. "Emily?"

"I'm fine." She spoke with a squeak, staring down at her stomach, her arms still held back by Amelia. "We're fine."

"Look." Amelia stepped around Emily, only holding one wrist.

The others joined Mark, as he reached his wife. "Emily?" he asked again, not taking his eyes off her hanging head.

She lifted her head up, eyes red from the previous tears, but now she was smiling. "I'm fine, Mark, really." She glanced down again. "Look!"

Then he saw it. The bullet was still there, but it had stopped, frozen, five inches from her stomach.

"Wow," James chimed in, absently staring.

"You see, Mark?" Amelia spoke, as he glanced up at her angrily. "I'm sorry we had to do it this way, but there was really no other way to show you." Then she gestured with her free arm, "Step back." They all did.

Emily and the others watched, as Amelia eyes grew distanced, and she raised her free hand. She held it straight out with her hand in a fist. The others kept glancing between the two, as Emily took in a sharp breath and looked down at the bullet. The light began to wave through Amelia once again, but this time passed through Emily, who inhaled in an exhilarated rush, focusing on the space between her body and the bullet.

Amelia's eyes focused on Riley. His brows rose, and he grinned in an almost seductive manner, directly at her. Amelia pulled her hand back a few inches, and then forced it forward. This time her fingers spread open. The bullet shot back at him, needing no gun or trigger. The same light drew from his feet, in record time, creating waves across his own body, before the bullet hit a similar shield two inches from his face. A sudden course-correcting had the bullet spinning, to stick in the wall to the left of him.

Amelia let go of Emily's hand, taking a step to the side. The others could not believe their eyes. No one moved, not even Emily, who still had her hand held out, as if Amelia still held her grip. Eventually, James and Rick turned to each other, grinning like school boys, as Amy and Julia just stared at each other.

When Mark regained his senses, he turned and closed the space between Emily and himself. He pulled her into a tight hug, grabbing the sides of her face. He knew there was no damage or injury, but he couldn't help himself; he took a step back, and seriously looked her over. It only took a few seconds, but Mark held her hand and he twisted her body in the artificial lighting.

Emily watched him as he dropped to his knee and grabbed the sides of her hips so that her body was positioned only a few inches from him face. Slowly, he slid his hand under the bottom of her t-shirt, sliding it from right to left, and then he lifted the left corner and raised the t-shirt diagonally just below the bra-line. This is when the others noticed his inspection and all glanced down at her bare flesh.

"You feel hot," Mark muttered, more to himself than the others.

Emily reached down and held his hand flat against her stomach. Slowly, he glanced up at her and she whispered down at him. "We're fine. Mark," she said slowly, raising her eyebrows to give more emphasis.

They stared in each other's eyes, before Mark promptly dropped her t-shirt, and got to his feet, taking her back into his arms. When Amelia spoke again, Riley now at her side, Mark couldn't help himself. Before he could think, he spun Emily around, so that he was positioned between her and the others.

"Now, do you see? With training, Emily... All of you, will be safe, if you actually listen to our words and don't do anything irrational." She raised her brows at Mark and Emily, as he continued to block her. "And trust us. This should be fairly easy."

Mark was still unsure, as Amy spoke up. "Okay, just don't do that again," she said, reaching for her sister's hand.

Riley's head dropped, with a huff. "Guys, I hate to break it to you, but if you do need to defend yourselves, I highly doubt it will be from flying fruit. You need to be prepared for anything." He was emphatic.

"So, now what?" James interrupted.

"Now you all go sit on the side of the mat again, listen, and watch." Amelia gestured, with her chin, for them to get back as she and Riley turned and walked to the middle of the mat.

The group had not realized they were no longer alone. Others had come into the room, from the same entrance they had; one after another. Isobel was first, followed by Caleb, his brother Damon, and Selene. Amelia smiled and nodded 'welcome' to each of them, as they crossed the mat and came together in the center, talking amongst themselves. Slowly they walked back over to the curious humans and lined themselves in a row in front of each. They all stood a meter away, and Isobel stood in front of Emily grinning, as Riley joined her, across from Mark. Caleb stretched his arms across from James, Damon across from Rick, Selene with Julia, and Amelia slowly stopped in the middle, across from Amy.

"All right, so as you already know, we deal with individual energy. We rarely need hand to hand combat, at all. However, on this planet, that seems to be the primary source to defeat one's opponent, along with weapons usage. So, you need added practice." Amelia spoke loud and clear, to everyone in the room.

"As part of our training," she gestured to herself, "we are trained in most forms of human warfare, along with technique training. I have paired each of you up with individuals best suited to your own abilities." Amelia took a step back so that she could address everyone, as she spoke pacing back and forth along the line-up.

"Now, considering we only have a day to get you ready, obviously we cannot teach you much." Then she hesitated; thinking. "We have discussed and decided to train you in a different way."

"Different how?" Rick interrupted.

"Rather than teach you all the same thing, we believe specialization will help, if you plan to fight as a team with each contributing as a unit. Sure, we will teach you all the very basics, but we have decided to copy our own unique training and abilities into each of you." The humans glanced around at each other, confused. Mark opened his mouth to ask one of a million questions, but Amelia raised her hand up to quiet them all. "As you have seen, we are able to share our powers, for a short period of time, so hopefully by the end of today, you will each be able to utilize our individual abilities."

From the far left she began. "Emily, I've partnered you with Isobel. We will be training you in basic self-defense, but we cannot turn a blind eye to your weakness. Being our healer, Isobel's own healing abilities are greater than normal, giving you extra defenses. She's going to focus on her healing. In case anything does go wrong, you will be the one to heal your loved ones."

Emily nodded, at her named responsibility.

"It then seems to fit that Mark is partnered with Riley, Isobel's protector, because only he knows her physical and mental state, through their bond. Like Riley, Mark, your job will be to protect Emily, the group's healer."

Mark nodded to Amelia, as she carried on down the line.

"Amy, you will be training with me. Although I see you do not have the same confidence as your older sister, you are the most physically comparable with myself and I believe you will do well with my personal military techniques."

Amy smiled at Amelia and could not hide the excitement in her eyes.

"Rick, you're with Damon." Amelia grabbed Damon's shoulder from behind. "Damon is strong, fast and good on his feet. I believe you two will pair well together. James, you have been partnered with Caleb. Out of your own group, I believe you are the most physically prepared for hand to hand combat and weapons usage."

James grinned over at Rick, who rolled his eyes.

"Caleb is our weapons specialist and is a great fighter. Even though you are not biologically related, I see a bond between you and Rick that is similar to Damon and Caleb's. They rely on each other, are bonded, and feed on each other's energy to gain more control. The four of you would do well to train together."

James and Rick smiled while Damon and Caleb remained serious, nodding at her suggestion.

"Finally, Julia." Amelia smiled at her and placed both hands on the shoulders of the woman across from her. "I've partnered you with my sister, Selene. She's stubborn, vicious, and sometimes annoying." Clearly mocking her sister, Amelia grinned, as Selene rolled her eyes. "But she is also protective, kind, and will do anything for anyone. Over the years, I've trained her in various techniques and I feel you two will get along very well."

Julia grinned back at her partner.

Amelia then backed away and went to the middle of the mat. "Now, please break into your groups, take a spot on the mat, and get to work. Please feel free to ask any questions. We're here for you."

Slowly, the line broke up. Amelia smiled and waved Amy over to the center. Emily and Isobel took the far corner, with Riley and Mark nearby. James, Rick, and the brothers took the opposite end of the mat, while Julia and Selene went to the last corner.

*   *   *

When Amelia explained a sharing of energy, she meant that literally. Each of the groups spent the better part of the morning exchanging energy. The Jarly could actually copy their unique abilities onto any human, like burning a music list onto a CD; all you had to do was practice. The duplication would only last a few days, but it came with vast knowledge and techniques. The room would glow and flicker. Each had managed to control the energy, though much more weakly than their trainer. If any of them did manage to utilize their new skills, the energy boost would only last for a few seconds, then fade off frustratingly. Each group would be briefly distracted, as another would practice.

Rick and James spent most of their time learning how to shoot the energy from their own bodies, while Amy and Julia's training focused on the defense; the ultimate goal, a well rounded defense and offence. Rick and James would do most of the attack and physical aspects of the rescue, while Amy and Julia would be close behind, blocking any attacks on the group; a perfect team.

As they proceeded into weapons training, Mark was at the opposite end of the mat learning similar techniques, but in more fluid movements. He had been in a few scraps in high school and college, even a bar fight or two, so he knew how to throw a good punch. With the protection of Emily being his main job, even without the added power of energy, he was physically charged and focused. Emily on the other hand, had less physical and more mental preparation, than the others. It was equally important, but admittedly a more trying and exhausting focus.

"Okay, show me one more time." Emily watched, as Isobel sat cross-legged, on the last corner of the mat facing her.

Isobel had a large slab of pigskin sitting on a tray in-between them. Emily watched closely, as she lifted the sharp scalpel in her right hand and created a deep cut from one end of the pig to the other. Placing the knife aside, Isobel closed her eyes, and raised her hands to one end. She held out her palm, fingers spread wide, just inches away from the flesh. The light seemed to burn up around her. It looked exactly like an amber flame, as her legs became engulfed and it traveled down her arm and out of her palm. Isobel's head tilted lightly to the left, focusing. Her breathing remained deep but constant, as the sliced skin seemed to fill in the crack and the wound closed, solid and fresh again. Slowly, her hand traveled the length of the flesh and it was as if untouched.

Emily smiled, as Isobel opened her eyes. Examining the healed flesh, she ran her fingers over the length of the previous line. The only thing she noticed was the warmth that came from the center, as the rest of the meat was still cold to the touch.

"Okay, now you try," Isobel encouraged her, spinning the surgical scalpel around and placing it in Emily's hand.

Emily looked unsure of herself, raising the knife slowly. Before, she had only managed to close one end of the flesh before the energy quickly faded and depleted.

"Just concentrate. Picture the light consuming you, like I've shown you. Guide it from your feet to your chest, along your arm, then out of your palm. Feel the warmth. I know you can do this, Emily you're doing really well, you just need to learn how to control your emotions and focus on your goal. Many humans fail when we try to train them, because their natural instinct is to fight it. You need to give your mind and body over. Accept it."

Isobel paused for a few seconds, as Emily hesitated. "Okay, instead of picturing a slab of pig's skin, picture one of your loved ones." Emily cringed, as a flood of horrific pictures filled her mind. "It doesn't have to be life or death. Think of Mark; picture that he has fallen and cut his arm or leg, it's a deep cut and he is in pain."

Emily nodded sternly, focusing on the flesh in front of her. She picked up the scalpel and made another cut. "Now, close your eyes and take your husband's pain away." Isobel whispered her last bit of advice.

Emily did as she had said. Isobel was right, although there was no danger, everything in Emily was screaming at her to fight the intrusion and protect herself. She started with her breathing, deep and smooth, in and out. Her mind's eye filled with images of gashes and bloody wounds. She drew on a memory, last spring, when Mark had tripped while hiking. A jagged rock had cut him deeply along the length of his shinbone.

Thankfully, the added enhancements allowed for detailed visualization and memory manipulation. Emily took another deep breath, as she raised her right arm, spreading her fingers. She imagined Mark, lying on the dirt track in front of her, holding his leg. The blood flowed, turning his white sock into a sickly red sponge. Emily watched her own hand extend out past her, hovering over his leg. After a few seconds the same light generated through her arm and out of her palm; further manipulating her memory.

As she concentrated, a perfect replica of Isobel's flame consumed her legs and waved across her body. The light produced was so strong and vibrant, that the others in the room couldn't help but turn and silently watch. The light grew ever brighter. Amelia beamed from across the room. The others moved across the floor, standing a meter away, as Emily continued. Mark sat mesmerized by his wife.

The light came up to consume her face, heat flushing her cheeks. She didn't seem to notice her audience, as she continued. The light pulled from her face and body, pooling by her shoulder. A few seconds later, the light traveled in short bursts of energy down her arms. Emily seemed to strain, willing her control to be more prominent. Isobel gasped, as her own buzzing noise came with the light, created by Emily. None of the others had mastered her source to gain that amount of power. Watching intently, Emily's entire body sparked with light, remaining constant in her one outstretched hand.

Still in her own imagination, Emily opened her eyes slowly, trying to replace the pig's flesh with her own visions. Watching the light grow, she lowered her hand to almost touch Mark's broken skin, focusing, as the blood slowly defied gravity and drew back up his leg to collect around the wound. Using her light, like Isobel had shown, she saw his skin bind together. As the bottom healed, Emily slowly pulled her hand up his leg and smiled to herself, as the wound eventually closed. Grinning, she blinked rapidly, revealing a freshly healed slab of pig.

James's loud cheer drew Emily back to reality. Surprised, she turned to see eleven sets of eyes focused on her. She let out a sharp breath of air, as she released the energy, and the light in her palm went out. She traced her finger along its length, to feel the warmth, and looked up at Isobel for approval.

Isobel quickly leaned forward, her legs still crossed, and hugged a very surprised Emily. "Well, done Emily." She cheered, clapping her hands together.

They helped each other to their feet, just in time for Mark to pull his wife by the hip. "Great job, babe!"

Then a sudden, loud clapping from across the room made everyone in the group turn and face the door.

"Yes. Very well done, Emily! I believe you are the first of your kind to recreate our abilities with such perfection, so soon in your training." Amadeus beamed, making his way over.

"Thank you." Emily blushed.

"Oh, please don't stop for me. You will all need a full day of training, for what is to come." Then he paused shortly, and turned. "Amy, I hope you don't mind. May I borrow Amelia?"

Amy was already nodding with approval, before he had finished. Amelia spoke as she walked towards her leader. "Okay, we still have a lot to do. Boys, I would like you to join up with the girls to practice group work. Damon, Caleb, you know what to do. Riley and Mark, can you start to work with Isobel and Emily?"

They nodded, as she and Amadeus walked from the room.

CHAPTER FOURTEEN

Separating into two groups, they began training and testing one another. Selene excused herself fifteen minutes later. Caleb focused with Julia and James first, as the others watched.

"Okay James, we're going to work on our defense. Julia, show us what you can do." Caleb gestured for them to proceed to center mat.

James and Julia followed, now in the middle of the mat facing each other. Caleb, standing a few meters away with Amy and his brother. Rick sat on the mat watching every move.

"First, let's see your hand-to-hand. James, go ahead."

James raised his brows and looked confused.

"I want you to punch Julia, as hard as you can in the face."

James turned to stare at him with disgust.

"Don't worry. If I feel her response is too slow, or you'll harm her, I'll block you before you even get close."

"It's okay." Julia encouraged him, shaking her hands and feet, and jumping on the spot twice, as if to get ready. James skeptically turned to look down at her. "Don't worry! I've got this."

He shook his head, still unsure, as he raised his fists in preparation. With creased brows, he paused, thinking, and then took a step back. The light burned at her feet, holding her hands in fists at her waist. The light grew and began to pulsate throughout her body.

"Now!" she yelled.

James squinted, lunging, aiming directly for her left cheekbone. Before he could take a breath, his body was knocked backwards, feet leaving the mat, as he began to fall. He landed hard on his back, but instead of crying out, he began bark with laughter, along with Rick and Amy. He turned to Caleb, his gaze questioning.

Celeb grinned back. "Oh, no!" Raising his hands, he said, "That was all her!"

James turned back to Julia, who was grinning up at him. She walked over and offered him her hand. As she pulled him to his feet, he didn't let go of her arm. Instead, he pulled her into a quick kiss, surprising their audience. "That was kinda HOT!" He smirked at her growing blush.

Caleb clapped his hands together once, and then turned to the floor. "Your turn," he said, gesturing to Rick and Amy.

Amy did the same as her friend except, before Rick hit the floor, she reached out farther with one hand and held his body hovering above the mat. Controlling her ability, she pulled her hand back, watching as Rick's body pulled upright, landing upright on his feet.

Caleb applauded. "Well done. I see Amelia has taught you her telekinetic skills."

Amy blew out her breath, as she let the light escape. "Yeah, I can't do it for long but, yeah." She beamed.

"Still, many of our kind have a hard time mastering that ability," Damon added, standing by the mat. Amy further smiled, proud of herself.

"Now, weapons offence." Caleb interrupted, as he gestured to the wooden manikin that Damon was sliding into place. "I want each of you to show me how much power of attack you really have. Use whatever training you are most comfortable with." The two brothers stepped aside, as the four humans lined up one behind the other, starting with Rick.

"Start with a distant attack and then close proximity." Damon gestured for them to back up a few steps.

Rick focused on the manikin, the familiar light bursting in more rapidly now, around his feet and up his body. The others took a few more steps back, so they could see more clearly around him. He held his palms together in front of his stomach. As the light flowed through his body and collected at his hands, he slowly separated his palms. His fingers drew back, as the light pulsated and generated a ball; a ball of light, which was getting bigger by the second. With one sharp breath, Rick forced his arms forward, blasting right through the manikin, creating a perfect hole.

James high-fived his best friend.

"Now closer," Damon commanded. "Something different."

Rick concentrated once again. "Weapons?" he asked, raising one brow.

"Whatever, you wish to use." Caleb gestured to the wall behind them.

Rick talked as he walked. "Well to be honest, if we use any weapon it will be a hand gun." Before anyone could say another word, Rick didn't appear to think, and without aim, he pulled the closest handgun from the wall. He loaded the first bullet into the barrel, as he spun on his feet, and shot one single round. His wife and friend ducked down slightly and covered their heads.

"Dude!" James yelled, angrily.

Rick remained unfazed. "Look." He gestured with his chin towards the wooden body. "Can you feel it?"

Their jaws dropped, as they saw the back wall through the manikin. Even with his rash movement, Rick had pierced a perfect hole in its right eye.

"Feel what?" Amy asked.

"It! The control..." He clenched and unclenched his fists. "The knowledge? I feel like I've done this a million times."

"That would be the bond. It brings a certain familiarity." Damon spoke clearly from the far corner. "Caleb and I have done this a million times."

Slowly they understood. The others could feel it too. It was as if their bodies were ready to handle anything, but their minds were constantly playing catch up.

"Next." Caleb called Amy's attention.

Rick placed the gun back on the wall and walked past his wife. "You got this, baby!" He lounged on the mat behind the others; confidence spewing from his every pore.

Amy shook her head, grinning sheepishly at him, then turned to focus on the deformed manikin. She stared at it, trying to think up something different to do.

"Once again, distance, then close up," Damon stated, and then smirked at Rick. "No guns this time."

Amy nodded, as she began to generate her own light. Taking a deep breath to steady her nerves, she turned on the spot to scan the wall of weapons. She laughed once to herself, as she noticed a row of kitchen knives stuck to one magnetic bar. Julia was about to inquire about what was so funny when Amy thrust one hand out and a nine-inch carving knife flew off the shelf. The handle rested perfectly in her palm.

"Cool!" Julia whistled, as Amy grinned back.

Gripping the handle and lowering the knife to her side, she next summoned a chef's knife, which flew into her other hand; her eyes finding no need to seek out the blade. She didn't grip it so tightly, holding it out in front of her, with the point closest to the manikin. Her next move shot the knife, with lightning speed, and it embedded itself in, more than halfway into the manikin's chest.

"Yeah!" Rick cheered from behind, hooting and clapping with more force than necessary.

"And close proximity?" Caleb asked with a questioning expression.

Amy turned back to her victim, walking casually towards it until she was only feet away. "Okay..." She let her actions speak for themselves. In two fluid movements, her light flowing through her arms, she let out one empowering scream. Raising her last knife, energy flowing smoothly, she sliced the manikin's head straight off and placed her hand on its chest. The light blew down her arm, one last time, as its torso shot backwards, embedding in the bare wall behind.

Amy turned to her trainers, and saw that Damon was wildly satisfied, and still staring at the manikin.

Caleb clapped. "Amelia was right, you two have very similar strengths."

Amy joined her little group, while Damon grabbed another manikin for James and Julia. The training continued, as James blew a similar energy ball to Rick's. This time, the only difference was that halfway in-between James and the manikin, his light turned to dozens of smaller balls, which blew many holes into the wooden torso. Julia focused and merely lifted the two hundred-pound manikin from the ground, roughly twenty to thirty feet, then swiftly hurled it back to the ground, where its limbs shattered.

Caleb was very pleased with their performances, but thought they needed more realistic training. "Okay, that was excellent work, but what I want to know is how you will act when it is a human as your opponent and not a wooden toy. Now Damon and I are going to watch. I would like the two women to fight each other."

Amy and Julia glanced at each other as James grinned; "Now you're talking. Maybe we should throw some wet mud," he said, gesturing to the mat. "Show us some wrestling skills."

Rick's laughter howled, as the girls rolled their eyes, Julia thrust out her middle finger.

Damon grinned, shaking his head, "Aaanyway." He drew the word out, still amused. "You will do some distance training. If at any time we think there will be any injury, we will block the other. Then we will move to hand-to-hand. I do encourage weapons usage because that's what you will utilize in your real battle. You both need to work on your controlled stops. Which means, Amy, I want you to shoot your knives at Julia, but you'll stop them a few feet away. If you fail to stop them, I will. There's nothing to worry about."

Amy looked too panicked to think, as Caleb turned to Julia who was also too pale. "Julia the same goes for you. I want you to raise Amy like you did the manikin, then shoot her down, but you will stop her a few feet from the ground, so there is no injury. It may take a few tries, so I will watch over you. Once I feel you are done, we will repeat this exercise with the men."

"What purpose does the ability to stop have to do with anything?" Rick asked, obviously trying to protect his wife from injuring herself or her best friend. "When we're there, we won't have the time to stop. It will be all or nothing."

Caleb took a deep breath, turning to face him. "Rick, any of you can attack a person. What if you threw an energy bolt and something goes wrong?" he said, gesturing to Amy. "She gets in the way, even by accident, and you would want to be able to stop, right?"

Rick went silent at the idea.

Caleb turned back to the girls. "Okay, so begin. Amy first."

Julia watched, as Amy was deep in thought. Quickly, she closed the space in between them. "I trust you," she said and she hugged her best friend.

"Maybe I should practice on the mani..." Amy began, as

Damon cut her off.

"We don't have time for that. You all need the extra push to make it real. Now!" he commanded.

Amy dropped her head and slowly raised her hand, as the small paring knife flew off the shelf and into her palm. She wanted to cry. Not wanting to break her concentration, she straightened up and held her knife directly in Julia's path. Amy closed her eyes, as the light formed at her ankles again. Her eyes flew open, as the light shot down her arm, and the knife flew forward. she tried to stop it, but she couldn't. The knife flew past its limit and stopped two inches from Julia's face.

The knife flew back, into Caleb's out-reached hand, as Amy let out a cry. "Julia, I'm so sorry." The pressure was too intense and she began to weep.

Julia didn't seem to be as upset by the mistake. She tried to take a step forward to comfort her friend, but Caleb raised his hand for her to stay put. "Amy, enough! Pull yourself together."

"Hey!" Rick scrambled to his feet. "Lighten up."

"Lighten up?" Before Rick could call upon his light, Caleb had him on his back, knife to his throat, his head forced up and away from the blade. The girls gasped, as James attempted to intervene. To his dismay, Damon was equally fast and thwarting. Emily and Mark paused, across the room, concern affecting their control. "Is that what you plan to yell at her attackers, while she cowers in the corner?"

Caleb practically spat, jaw clenched. "You need to take this seriously." Rick thrashed, to no avail, "This isn't a fucking game." He turned focus to Amy, as Damon threw James against the near wall. "You go in there and freeze, you're dead. There's no crying in war."

Within a blink, Caleb stood, the blade leaving his grip to lodge in wood wall, inches above James head. "Bravery counts for nothing if you're too stupid to know when to strike." He turned to Amy and Julia, frustration boiling over. "Again."

Amy didn't say anything, she just hung her head and shook it. "No," she said weakly.

"Again!" Caleb yelled with more force.

"Enough!" Rick attempted to gain his footing.

"Stay where you are," Damon commanded. James huffed, as he was released from his grasp. "Amy." Damon spoke with a calmness that Caleb had temporarily lost. "You need to practice this, again and again, because next time we won't be here to help."

"Please. Try again." Caleb spoke with a renewed softness.

Slowly, Amy drew her head up to see Julia speaking. "Just take your time and focus. I know you can do this."

Trying to smile through her tears, Amy summoned another blade, turning it towards Julia. *Focus.* Julia's words ran through her head. Pinching her eyes tightly shut, she stood, listening to the heavy intake of breath, and the rapid beating of her heart. After a few seconds of building light, Amy shot the knife one last time, this time, successfully stopping it one foot from Julia's head. As Julia beamed at her, Amy quickly forced the knife around Julia and back onto the wall.

The rest of the group took their turns practicing. Some attempts were uncomfortably close and threatening. Others learnt faster, with more control and steady hands. By noon, the group was ready for a short break, followed by intense physical combat and battle training.

* * *

Mark's group took a less dramatic route in their group training. The four sat in a small circle at the far opposite end of the mat.

"As Amadeus had mentioned, when healers are focusing on

their duty, they're most vulnerable and susceptible to attack." Riley sat across from Mark, as they watched Emily further practice. "You don't need me to tell you how important your wife is. Believe it or not, the six of you are going into a very hostile situation tomorrow, and you'll need all the help you can get."

Mark glanced up at Emily's focused face, her eyes closed, as Riley continued.

"People are going to be injured. Some lives will be lost. The hired goons protecting that building won't all be military. Many will be mercenaries. They know the importance of what's being hidden from your people; they'll be trained men; murderers, who will have no problem killing you and anyone that gets in their way."

Isobel interrupted. "Mark, I would like to spend a few minutes training you, as I have Emily. Not to the same extent, but enough to help or take over if needed. Likewise, Emily I'd like to show you a few things as well."

Mark nodded, as Emily's light faded, to reveal yet another slab of pig's meat slowly rotting in front of them. It was only then the sudden smell hit her. The constant warming of rotten flesh became intensified and her head began to spin, a green hue flushing her skin.

"Emily?" Isobel's concern, had the others watching.

"Em?" Mark grasped her shoulder.

Emily couldn't speak. She abruptly covered her mouth, forced herself back and to her feet, running into the open bathroom behind them, and slamming the door. Mark ran after her, waiting by the closed door; while he listened to her lose her lunch. He tried to turn the handle, but she had already locked the door.

"Babe, let me in." He spoke calmly through the door.

"No. I'm fine. The smell just got to me. I'm fine, really. Let me just tidy myself up. I'll be right out." She called back, before another sudden attack.

Mark waited there silently, before turning back, joining Isobel and her protector on the mat.

"Sorry, about that. The smell just got to her." Mark apologized.

"That's all right. Her body is going through a lot right now. Our powers do, in this case unfortunately, enhance human senses as well." Isobel understood. "Every time she utilizes my light, the child's bond will grow ever present."

"So, morning sickness is the least of her worries," Riley said with a laugh.

"Mark, Riley may joke," said Isobel, bumping his shoulder playfully, "but there is a serious note to his words. Emily has proven she is very powerful and mentally strong, but she is also a greater target in her condition. You will have to stay by her side, at all times. She'll need you there, in case she becomes too weak to continue."

Mark understood. Early pregnancy was hard enough. Tomorrow, he planned to keep Emily back and out of the way as much as possible.

"Sorry, about that." Emily rejoined the group. A slight sweat added a sheen to her skin as she absently brushed the back of her hand along her forehead. She sat back down, thankful that Isobel had already taken the liberty of removing the rotting flesh.

"Not at all," Isobel welcomed her back. "But before we switch pupils, I had hoped to get to some more realistic training."

"Realistic?" Emily asked skeptically.

"Yes." Isobel spoke to Mark. "I had hoped you would volunteer for a little trial and error."

"Of course," Mark answered, before Emily began protesting.

"No way. No!" Emily watched Isobel reach for a second scalpel.

"Emily, you need to practice on living flesh. On fresh wounds." Emily creased her brows, already shaking her head, as

Riley interrupted.

"You can start off slow. A pinprick and build up. Either way, sewing a piece of flesh back together is a lot different than a bloody wound."

"I know that." Emily huffed in frustration, fanning her slick hands. "But, I don't like this," she stubbornly shot back.

Mark turned to his wife, attempting to ease her nerves. "Em, you need to learn this. We can start off slow."

"I can't hurt you. I won't." She gestured to Isobel. "Pass me the blade, I'll practice on myself."

Mark pulled the blade from her reach. "I don't think so." Before she could stop him, he had sliced a clean line across his palm.

"Mark!" Emily cringed, as the thin red line grew, getting darker.

Mark shook his head, as he rest his wounded palm on one of her knees. "Now, heal me, woman." He said playfully.

"This isn't a game."

"No." He rolled his eyes." But you obviously needed the push." Glancing down at his hand, he urged her, "Just do it, before I get blood everywhere."

She shook her head disapprovingly, and then went to work. She closed her eyes and the buzzing came before the light, as she raised her right hand up and held it inches from his. The energy built, as her hand began to glow. Mark closed his eyes, relaxing his shoulders, enjoying the light tingle that chased away the sharp pain. Two seconds later, Emily looked up and Mark pulled his hand away. Opening and closing his palm, he grew fascinated.

"That was fast," he muttered. The wound was gone, leaving no trace that there had been anything there in the first place.

"Well done. Speed is equally valuable." Isobel grinned.

"How does it feel?" Emily asked curiously, as Mark continued to examine his palm.

"It got warm, while you worked. Kind of tingled, then the pain went away all together, and you were done."

"Okay. One more time, then I think you'll be ready to move on. Mark, I just want to quickly teach you the basics before we rejoin the group." They both nodded, as she continued, "Amelia will join us in a few minutes. She wants to do a group run through and scenario training."

"Scenario?" Mark questioned.

"It'll be fun. You'll see." Riley winked.

It took Mark an hour to learn the basics of Isobel's talents. Like Emily, Mark could heal the pigskin, but it took him much longer, with more attempts. While they waited, Riley went through a few defensive and attack drills with Emily. Like Julia, Emily was a quick learner at blocking, though understandably apprehensive when in the attack.

When Isobel was satisfied with Mark's session, the four walked over to the other group, which was waiting on the edge of the mat, while the others continued to train and wait for Amelia to return. Isobel and Riley were asked to join the other tutors, who attempted to add emphasis, while referencing previous encounters. This left Mark and Emily alone on the sidelines.

After a few minutes of silence and intense observation, Mark leant into his wife, wrapping his arm around her shoulder. "How are you feeling? You did great today."

"Thanks," Emily whispered, her eyes still on the current wrestling match that had James on his back, with Amy utilizing her light to overcome him. "I feel fine. Well, other than before." She side-tracked, referencing her recent bathroom trip. "All of a sudden, the smell from that meat just hit me. I don't know what it was. It just made me gag."

Mark brushed a stray brunette strand behind her ear "That's the baby. Your hormones and senses are going haywire. Given a normal pregnancy, a woman's senses are amplified. Smell can be very overpowering. But with all this extra stuff..." He trailed off, shaking his head.

She turned to him then, focusing. "I know. It's all a bit crazy. But surprisingly, I feel really energized. Like every time I tap into that power, a little battery is pumped into my muscles. It feels amazing, like I could do anything."

"Yeah, I get that same feeling too. Like every cell in your body is ignited." Then he really looked in his wife's eyes, serious. "But this is some powerful stuff that can be very draining. If at any time you get tired or need a break or..."

Emily cut him off. "I'll let you know – promise." She playfully pushed him down, his head hitting the mat, as she straddled his hips. Pinning both hands above his head, she completely ignored the loud grunts and groans coming from behind.

"Don't worry about me so much." Leaning down, she lightly tugged on his earlobe with her teeth. "What you should be worried about is what I plan to do to you, when we get back to our room." She grinned at the sudden intake of his breath, as she whispered, "These powers haven't just enhanced my healing abilities." A low hum in his chest vibrated through her torso, as their attention slowly dragged back to the training at hand.

Five minutes later, Amelia came back into the room. "Please, excuse my absence." She addressed the room formally. Gradually, the others joined Mark and Emily on the mat, while their trainers formed a line behind Amelia.

"I hear you have all done very well in your training. Now, there is one more exercise I would like to run through," Amelia continued. "James, could you please join me up here? Emily too."

James held his hand out for Emily, as they both got to their feet, and stood to Amelia's left.

"Okay, James if you would just come here." She gestured for him to join her on her right side, two feet away. "When you are in battle, you must always be alert and ready for anything. Being able to summon your energy at the blink of an eye is very important. I'm sorry, James."

He turned to her, opening a questioning mouth. With lightning speed, Amelia spun on the spot to face him, forcing her right arm up, her palm hitting the base of his nose, breaking it instantly.

He bent over, cradling his nose between his hands. Emily was two steps ahead, already having her light flowing through her, as Amelia spun, kicking her leg out, aiming for Emily's chest. It would have been a painful blow, if Emily had not raised her shield just in time for Amelia to hit the invisible wall, knocking her back a few steps. The others on the floor were attempting to intervene, but their trainers forced them to stay down. When Amelia relaxed back in her stance, James continued, defenseless, fretting over his injury. A small pool of blood began to collect where his head hovered over the mat.

"Well done, Emily," Amelia cheered, ignoring her tempered reaction.

Without another thought, Emily stepped passed Amelia, resting her hand on James back. "James, let me help." She tried to pry his hands away.

Slowly, he raised his body so he was standing straight, and he removed his hand, as his eyes were red and watering. Blood began to run down his chin and onto his shirt, as he tried to blink through the pain. Emily held her hand over his nose, being careful not to touch it, as she closed her eyes focusing. James closed his eyes too, letting his shoulders relax, as he breathed heavily through his open mouth. Momentarily, the blood stopped. With a light crunching noise, James winced, letting out a sharp breath. Emily stepped away, as he reached up to feel his perfectly reformed nose. It was completely healed and clean. The blood disappeared, with the only evidence left on his hands and clothing.

"Better?" Emily raised her brows.

"Definitely." He smiled down at her. "That didn't even hurt!"

Emily grinned, as they both turned angrily towards Amelia, who defended herself. "I did say sorry, James." He opened his mouth to protest, but she continued. "I was trying to prove a point; that you must always be ready for anything." Then she turned to the others on the mat below.

"You must always be ready to pull your power. For the next hour, I want you all practicing your reflexes and speed. I want lightning flash blasts, from head to toe. Then, when I feel you've trained enough, we'll grab some dinner, and have a little battle of our own." She grinned, with obvious excitement.

"Battle?" Julia asked, before anyone else could.

"Yes. We are going to use all available weapons, and no one is going to hold back. You need to be able to work under pressure and in dangerous situations. So, all of you will enter the battles training room, down the hall, and face some real situations."

Riley and Caleb's devilish grins did nothing to sooth the crowd below. When Amelia was finished, she had them separate off into their own space, practicing once again. After many solo attempts, Amelia brought over the weapons. She had her crewmates stand guard, as she threw knife after knife at each of them. Not hesitating in the slightest, the group grew weary that she was enjoying herself too much. They only had seconds to react. Eventually, she partnered each of them; the husbands and wives were partnered, leaving Julia and James. Each partner would stand in the middle of the mat, their backs together, as they stood alert. The others would watch mystified, as the couples prepared themselves. Their trainers would run around them, and without warning, an energy bolt, bullet, or knife would come their way. They'd be forced to protect themselves, and if need be, their loved one.

Amy cried out, crumbling to the mat below, as one of Selene's blades came from behind, hitting her outer thigh; embedding more than half its blade. She fell onto her good knee, as Rick turned to see.

Emily tried to run over to help, but Caleb grabbed her arm. "Wait." Then he spoke up, "You must continue, as if in a real situation."

"Fuck you!" Rick yelled back angrily, as he bent over his wife, completely letting his guard down.

"Emily!" Amy cried.

Emily tried to pull her hand free from Caleb's grip, but he continued as if she was not even there. "No, Rick. You must continue. What if this had happened there? What would you do?"

Rick looked up furiously, at him and the others, as Amy cried and held her hand around the handle. Before he could get back up, Selene threw a small paring knife into his right shoulder blade. He cried out in pain, as the others protested. Damon had to use more force in stopping James.

"Keep your guard up at all times. If one is injured, the other must defend them both," Selene chimed in, as Rick reached behind and pulled out the knife. With one jerk, he retrieved the blade, petulantly tossing it back at Selene, who blocked it with bored efficiency.

"Get up, and protect your wife," Caleb called from the sidelines. Amy's blood now covered the majority of her bare leg. She continued to cry, as Rick got to his feet. His shield burst even brighter, as he forced it up and around his body.

"Amy, bring your shield up!" Mark yelled, still standing defenseless next to his wife.

Amy turned her head towards her sister, then saw Selene and Damon beginning to run in circles around them, once again. Amy dropped to the mat, sitting upright, still unable to move her leg, as she raised her shield and watched bolt after bolt ricochet off Rick and her.

"Okay, enough!" Caleb called, after thirty more strikes.

Quickly, Rick turned and pulled his wife into his arms. She cried out; the movement having jolted the blade and sensitive flesh. Emily was already waiting on the sidelines, hands glowing, as Rick placed her down.

"James and Julia." Damon called for them to begin.

Rick nodded sternly at James, who had stayed back, to go ahead. Amy let out another cry, as Rick carefully placed her on the far corner of the mat. The four didn't wait and watch, as James and Julia began. The light show became a distant distraction from the corner of their eyes.

"What can I do?" Rick asked, fretting over his wife, who was still crying.

"Just hold her hand," Emily commanded, as she examined the wound.

"Amy... Amy, look at me," Mark said, as he held her wounded leg down with one hand. "Before Em can do anything, I have to take the blade out."

Amy let out another cry, repeatedly shaking her head, as fear and panic covered her face.

"Amy." Emily pulled her sister's wet face in her hands. "Just watch me. Mark?"

Two seconds later Amy cried out, much louder than before, and pinched her eyes shut.

"Rick, keep her occupied," Emily commanded, as she went back to work.

Rick distracted his wife, as Mark had both hands holding Amy's leg down to the mat; one hand above the wound, the other below. The wound was much deeper than Emily had originally thought. Amy's blood had completely drenched the space in-between Mark's hand and was trickling down either side of her thigh. Emily went into healer mode, this time using both hands, holding them out over the injury.

It took twice as long as it did to fix James's nose, but eventually Amy began to relax, her breathing becoming normal. Gradually, she sat up and wiped her cheeks, examining her leg. Emily pulled her hands away, to show a spotless thigh, in blood-stained short-shorts.

Amy wiped away the defiant tears that wouldn't stop. "Thanks," she whispered, with an added hiccup.

Emily laughed and kissed her forehead. "Anytime." That's when she noticed the small circular wound on Rick's upper shoulder. "Rick, hold still." He'd been preoccupied with Amy, he had actually forgotten about his own wound. Emily lightly gripped his shoulder, needing only a few short seconds to reveal his healed skin.

"Thanks." Rick smiled, glancing over his shoulder, as Amy absently pushed her pinkie finger through the small hole in his sleeve.

"No problem," Emily responded.

Slowly the four got to their feet, watching the end of James and Julia's match. No further injuries came from their match or Emily and Mark's.

"Enough. We'll break for a meal now," Caleb said to his shipmates. They nodded, coming to a standstill.

Damon, who was slightly out of breath, came running over to the humans who were now huddled together on the corner of the mat. "Go ahead. We'll get the other room ready for the group fight. Go straight to the dining room and eat. We will join you soon."

CHAPTER FIFTEEN

Mark and Emily entered the dining room first, to cheers from Matt and Abby. The children were bouncing up and down in their high chairs, at the end on the nearest table. Their arms were held high, grabbing at the air, trying to reach for the couple.

"Abby! Matt! We missed you!" Emily smiled, raising one chubby toddler into a tight hug, as Mark reached for the other.

When Amy and Rick followed, the children became overjoyed once again, reaching back to hug them. Emily smiled at her husband, as they both sat down in the nearest seats. Once the entire group was back together, they slouched into their chairs, feeling too exhausted to eat. After a few minutes, they began to look around the room. It was empty.

"Should we wait? Or are we supposed to go find food?" James sincerely asked.

The others shrugged. They had no idea. Before they could move, three people came into the room with two plates of food in each hand. Although the friends all smiled, no one could remember being introduced to these people.

A few seconds after the newcomers had left, Rick spoke the words everyone was thinking. "I wonder how many Jarly are actually here, and not JUST here. They could blend in anywhere. Be anywhere. They are probably all over the world, living as humans." Rick muttered his question, not expecting an answer. Gradually, the friends' appetites returned, and they ate with more gusto than they had expected. Emily didn't realize how hungry she was, until she had finished her second ham sandwich and large helping of tomato soup. The others laughed, as James went to the extreme of raising his bowl to his lips and drinking the last morsel of soup.

"I can't believe how hungry we are!" Amy commented, mouth full.

"Well, when was the last time you spent all day working out? Throwing knives and shooting energy bolts from your hands?" James joked.

They sat and laughed as their trainers and Amadeus joined the group. The mood remained relaxed, as the others ate their meals. Emily sat and enjoyed a hot Tetley Orange tea, as she snuggled into Mark's side. Random conversations started; it was if they were all at a family dinner. Emily continued to sit, silently thinking to herself, as she took in the room. Mark, holding her close, struck up a conversation with Rick, James, and the alien brothers. He was very curious about other planets and their journey to Earth. Julia and Amy were talking to the remaining Jarly, with Matt and Abby trying to follow the conversation from their stools.

By now, everyone had stopped eating, more focused on their conversations. After an hour the conversations died down.

"All right, now that everyone is fed and rested, we can head back for our final exercise." Amelia got up from the table; abruptly leaving the room without another word.

Riley and the bothers joined soon after, followed by Rick, James, and their girls. Emily took Mark's hand as they, along with Amadeus, made their way to the door. Glancing over her shoulder, she saw Matt and Abby sitting there watching after them.

Before she could ask, Amadeus spoke up. "Don't worry about them. A guardian will come back in a second and take them back to the playroom."

"Playroom?" Mark asked, grinning in amazement.

Amadeus smiled. "Yes, we have a room dedicated to the entertainment of children. It is almost the size of your dojo. Believe me, they are being well looked after."

Emily nodded, waving goodbye to the toddlers, as the three made their way back to the workout room. Amadeus stopped abruptly, turned, and silently continued down a different hallway. "This way," he called for them to follow. "The battle room is set up. It's much bigger than the training space."

Emily's mouth forced a silent, *Oh*. She and Mark turned to follow down the slightly darker hallway.

Mark gasped when he saw the new room. They continued in and stopped by their friends, who were just as amazed. The room was dark, clearly intentionally. They had covered the walls in large black drapes, constructed ramps, and adjusted the lighting so that it could flicker on and off. There was a second floor taking up half the room, with a weak, wooden railing. The second floor held mirrored rooms of various shapes and sizes, cement blockades, and randomly scattered weapons. To get to that floor, a makeshift metal ladder lamely stood, clearly only capable of handling one individual's weight, at a time.

On the main floor in front of them, was a full-sized maze of walls, mirrors, and indiscriminate objects. As the lights flickered, Emily felt as if she had been thrown into a horror movie. This was scary enough, not to mention the Halloween sound affects coming from all directions. Random bursts made the small hairs on the back of her neck rise. Blades, lightning, howling, bullets flying, and metal clanking distracted from all corners. A sudden chill crept down her spine, causing her grip on Mark's hand to tighten. As a whole, the scene reminded her of the laser tag halls they'd played in as kids.

James looked over at the couple behind him, and Mark

laughed, as his grin looked devilish in the lighting. All of a sudden, the lights went up and the sound effects stopped. Amelia stepped from the entrance of the maze, with Riley, Caleb, and Selene directly behind her. Amadeus had disappeared from sight.

"Pretty cool, huh?" Riley said. Even at two hundred and twenty three years old, he couldn't hide his schoolboy excitement. Rick and James were at the front of the group, both men grinning from ear to ear.

"Good. Well, this is as scary and challenging as we could make it in such short time." Amelia walked closer to them, beginning to give her directions. "Okay, so here's the plan. The six of you are going to band together. Riley, Caleb and Selene, along with a few others, will be hiding throughout the course. We have opened up the second floor above." She gestured to the makeshift balcony to their right. "That leads to rooms and a tunnel. At the end of that tunnel, Amadeus and I will be waiting for you. Your goal is to find us, and bring us back here." She then pointed to the mat below her. "Without harm, I might add. You have one hour to do so. Any questions?"

"So, if this is supposed to be the real deal, we fight back? No hold backs?" James questioned.

"Of course. We encourage you to use all your force. Unlike humans, we naturally heal much faster. Anyway, you'll need to attack them, to get past them. They won't be shielding them-selves or using much of their light, so you'll only have the time that they are down to continue. All I ask is that you don't inten-tionally aim for our heads or hearts. I want them to be realistic human opponents."

"So, you guys will be hiding throughout the course." Rick ges-tured to the three behind her. "We have to use any force and skills we have to get past you, to get to you." He pointed at the woman in front of him. "We get to you and fight our way back to this spot." They were all nodding, as he spoke. "In one hour."

"Exactly," Riley concluded his summing-up.

"Just remember that this is not training any more. We'll be using force, as well. We won't be holding back or shielding you, either. You're on your own for this one." Emily had to force back a nervous gulp at the prospect.

"Okay, so go back into the hallway and wait five minutes. When Damon opens the door again, the game begins," Amelia ordered.

Slowly, the six headed back into the hallway, as Damon closed the door on them. Those five minutes felt like five hours.

"Okay. Strategies people?" James had his back to the door and had his group huddled around him, like they were discussing a football play.

"Well, I say we keep our shields up at all times." Amy stated the obvious.

"Yeah, guys on the outside, girls on the inside. James and I will lead, while Mark brings up the rear." Rick suggested, as they nodded in agreement.

"Okay, but I think we should stick with our training." Emily joined in. "Amy, you and Julia watch over Rick and James. Move anything you can that's in their way. Rick you take the right. James you take the left. You're our fighting force. I can only really defend myself, and I'm here to heal, so I'm the last resort. Mark will follow me and protect our backs."

"Sounds like a plan," James whispered just as the door behind him cracked open. "Okay, we can do this. Stick together," he hurried to say, as he turned and pushed the door wide open, taking the first steps in.

The florescent lights were hanging now, flickering on and off, with a constant, static noise filling the room. The girls couldn't help but jump and lower their heads, as two hanging wires connected and sparked directly above. The mechanical noises had been changed to chainsaws. It was so loud in the room that Emily could barely hear her own thoughts. Without looking back, she held her arm out behind her, as Mark laced their fingers. The laser tag connection soon turned into a Freddie Kruger nightmare.

James started a chain reaction of light projection. Within five seconds they all had their shields up and ready to go. Amy, followed by Julia, raised their hands, as carving knives flew into their palms. Rick grinned at his wife, over his shoulder, as she lowered her arms and smiled back. James and Rick drew more light into their palms, as energy balls began to form. Slowly, they entered the maze. With black walls and mirrored corners, it was next to impossible to decipher an attacker from their own reflections.

Five minutes passed with no confrontation. Emily turned, as her eyes widened and focused. "Mark!" she yelled.

He ducked and tried to turn and see, but she pulled him closer, raising her glowing palm over his shoulder, blasting Selene in the shoulder. Blood hit the wall as Selene fell to the ground.

"Run!" James had seen her actions and ordered his group to pick up the pace.

They did. Three more turns and Riley shot off a round of bullets that ricocheted off of James and Julia's shields. James didn't think. He threw his light directly at Riley, managing to stop the ones aimed at his head, and chest. Riley let out a cry and fell to the ground. Rick turned the corner, almost running directly into a wall of blades, before Amy threw it back, clearing their path.

"Thanks, babe," Rick yelled, before blocking Damon's fist and punching him back.

James went to help, but was distracted by the two others; one male and one female that had not yet been introduced. The maze ended, opening up to a large room connecting to another tunnel. Julia and the woman began an energy bolt fight, three meters apart, as James and the large male threw punches, kicks, and the occasional bolt. Amy helped Rick until Selene popped up from behind.

The room lit up with the flows of energy and sparks of light. Emily took a step into the room, raising her fist and preparing to fight, when Mark stepped around her and backed her into a corner, so he was in between her and the danger. He took one step forward, so there was just enough space for her to see around him. She held her hands out, ready to attack. Mark waited. He let the fighting continue, as he drew his hands back and shot random bolts at the enemy. One surprising bolt hit Selene square in the back, as she had Amy cornered. Amy took her chance, while Selene was distracted, to shoot one last blow, into her right shoulder, knocking her straight through the near wall.

James and Julia had the others down, watching curiously; as the aliens closed their eyes and their wounds began to heal. James spun around and joined Rick to take down Damon. Mark and Emily had left their corner, and now were running towards the metal stairs, at the end of the hall.

"Stay here," Mark ordered his wife, as he quickly spun around and ran back for the others.

She stood by the base of the ladder, glancing down that tunnel and the deserted one next to it. Mark yelled for the others to join him. As they reached the entrance of the tunnel, Amy stopped and turned back, facing the room filled with apparently lifeless bodies.

"Julia, help!" Amy cried, as the men watched confused.

Amy held out her arms, and with her talents, she picked up random pieces of debris from the room, dragging it to create a crude barrier. Julia quickly clued in and helped. James watched the unnamed male begin to get to his knees and blindly search the room. In the space that was left, in the doorframe, James directed a swift bolt, hitting the man square in the back and knocking him to the floor again.

"Mark!" Emily screamed from behind.

The men spun where they were, to see the other end of the tunnel. Emily was standing on the spot, exchanging energy bolts with an unseen target. As they began to run to her rescue, the balls of light were joined by two fists, which Emily successfully blocked, until something pulled her legs out from under her. She dropped to the ground with a scream, as she was dragged out of sight.

"Emily!" Mark picked up the pace.

The energy around him grew stronger, as the air began to buzz and crackle. He reached the end of the tunnel first, eyes frantically searching the pitch-black tunnel to his right. Nothing.

"Emily?"

Her sudden scream and a flicker of light made him burst into a sprint. The light got stronger, as he saw it flicker from what looked like an open doorway. He reached the door, his gaze landing on Emily in the corner, as two men stabbed unsuccessfully at her shield. Her shield was clearly failing, her energy waning, as their fists made contact with her flesh. Blood poured from her nose, down her chin, as she fought back. She used her training to kick and punch, moving as much as she could, while her attackers had their work cut out for them.

Mark took a step into the room, but his shield didn't block Riley's fist. Mark hurled himself at his previous trainer, knocking them both to the ground. The others eventually reached the room. Instantly, Rick and James went to Emily's rescue. They each took a man and got in two punches, before the Jarly were pushed unnaturally against the wall. James and Rick looked confused, then glanced over their shoulders to Amy and Julia, who had their hands held straight out and were focused on the alien men. The aliens fought against the hold, but couldn't break it.

Julia let off one blast that split into four, hitting her prisoner in each limb, crippling him to the floor. The other watched and appeared to panic, as he turned back to Amy, who did the very same. Both girls ran over to check on Emily, as the men turned to helped Mark. Emily had already healed herself and was holding her stomach. She was bent over, as if trying to catch her breath.

"Emily?" Amy ran over and placed her hand on her sister's back.

"I'm fine. Just catching my breath," Emily responded, as she straightened, not dropping her hands.

Mark was literally buzzing with anger now. He and Riley had forced their way back into the hall. James and Rick waited for a chance to intervene, but that chance never came. Unaware of his own abilities and speed, Mark punched Riley smack in the chest. This time, his body didn't merely drop to the ground, but with Mark's boost of energy, Riley shot back more than ten feet, hitting a hidden wall. James and Rick watched after him, in amazement, but Mark didn't wait to see the end results. After the last blow, he ran back into the room straight over to his wife, his hands glowing; ready to heal her. Amy and Julia could see the strong emotion in his eyes and stepped aside.

"Where does it hurt?" he asked Emily, anxiously scanning her body.

Her breathing was still heavy and he saw a flicker of pain run across her face. His eyes stopped on her hand, unconsciously rubbing her stomach.

"What is it?" Even more panic filled his face, as she began to cry.

Before she could answer, he slid his hand under hers and held it there. He was attempting to heal, but he didn't know what he was healing.

Her hand rested on top of his, against her shirt, as she shook her head. "I took a hit to the stomach." He glanced down at their hands, as she continued. "But I can feel that everything is fine. I'm just tired and shook up."

He pulled his hand away and pulled her into a tight hug. The moment was ruined, by Rick's yelling, "I'm sorry guys, but we've got to keep moving."

Mark pulled away and took her hand in his. "Let's get this over with, okay?"

Emily smiled up at him through her tears. She took a deep breath and rebuilt her shield from within. Mark purposefully forced some of his light into her growing shield. Wiping her cheeks, she took the first steps, following the others from the room. They ran as a joined group again, until they reached the ladder. At that moment, no one was attacking them.

"Okay, I'll go first, then follow me up one by one," James barked, as the others glanced around, remaining alert.

Mark was the last one to start up the stairs. Halfway, he saw a flicker of light appear at the end of one of the tunnels. It drew closer, as Mark took two steps at a time. When he pulled his legs up, he saw Damon and Riley at the base of the ladder. With one last attempt, Mark threw an energy bolt, unintentionally melting the ladder in two. He looked back just in time to see Riley smiling up at him, as Damon attempted to shoot back. Mark pulled his head out of the way, as the others moved more objects to block the hole.

Mark cussed loudly, as he got to his feet and quickly took Emily's hand. The room was completely black, apart from their shields. They had entered a smaller room with concrete blocks scattered, with blades and bullets along the floor. Eventually, they found two closed doors, right next to each other. James went directly to the nearest door, on the right. Both he and Rick forced the majority of their strength into their hands, ready for anything. With one glance back, he turned the handle and the door opened into another room, seemingly leading nowhere. Closing that, he took a step to the left, and quickly opened it wide.

Just as the door opened to a pitch-black tunnel, a light flickered at the far end. James leant forward, and squinted to see what it was. Two blades came suddenly, reflecting off his shield, while another blew past him and stuck into Rick's chest. He let out a gasp, as Amy screamed, and tried to support her husband's weight as he fell backwards. James screamed for his friend, as he, Mark, and Julia threw scattered energy bolts back down the hallway, towards the unseen person, who eventually dropped to the ground.

"Rick! No!" Amy burst into tears, cradling his head, while he struggled for breath, already coughing thick blood.

Emily had already dropped by his side, and pulled the knife from his chest, making him strain even more for air. She placed her glowing palm over his blood-soaked shirt, closing her eyes to concentrate. Her face became tense and her breathing accelerated.

"Go!" Emily yelled, with her eyes still shut. "I need more time on this. They said they would be at the end of the tunnel." Her eyes burst open. "All of you go and get them, then come back for us."

"I'm not leaving." Amy irrationally screamed at her sister.

"Amy, they need your help and I need to concentrate. I can't do that with you screaming in my ear," Emily shot back. "He's going to be just fine."

She began to protest, but Rick raised his hand to grab the side of her face. He was no longer coughing blood. "Go!" he whispered, trying to smile up at her through the pain.

James and Julia had already left, as Mark pulled his sister-in-law to her feet, spinning her around to grip her shoulders. "Go! I'll stay behind and protect them. If Em needs help, I can heal him too. Now the sooner we find Amadeus and Amelia, the sooner we can get out of here. So go!"

He practically pushed her through the open door. She slowly nodded and ran from the room. Emily was still focused on Rick's chest. Mark had his back to them, as he watched the door and only foreseeable source of danger.

* * *

James ran as fast as he could, down the dark tunnel, throwing random bolts to direct him as he went. At the end there was a tight left, leading to their goal. James hit the corner and turned, before he saw many streaming lights cross the room at him. He pulled back into the hallway, and the bolts blew past him ineffectively, hitting the wall behind. He stayed flat against the wall, as Julia and Amy caught up to him.

"Okay, Amadeus and Amelia are sitting in the back, left-hand corner. In front of them, standing, are two women. And in the far right corner, Caleb is waiting." Six more blasts hit the wall across from the room. "Okay, so you guys get low and aim for the women. Caleb is mine." He inched away from the open doorframe, as Amy and Julia bent down beside him.

"On the count of three," Amy said, and then added to Julia, "I'll take the girl on the left."

"One, Two...Three!" James yelled the last word, and forced himself though the frame. He ran at Caleb, blocking his fire, as Julia and Amy burst in and distracted the woman before they could attack him, too.

Amelia and Amadeus were mesmerized by the light show, yet made no attempt to intervene. Amy was so upset she charged right up to the woman, using her power to knock her hard into the wall behind, almost taking Amelia with her. The woman was knocked unconscious instantly. Now, Amy and Julia teamed up and focused on the other. Caleb and James were in an all-out, man-to-man, fight. James's shields remained intact against any weapon attack, but fell just enough for a good-n-bloody fist fight. He eventually got the upper hand, pushing Caleb to the ground, and jumping on his chest. In blow after blow, James gained enough control and force to knock Caleb unconscious. Amadeus and Amelia nodded at each other and rose from their seats, as they had predicted this outcome. They waited, as Amy punched the remaining woman in the face, and Julia used all her force to fling her across the room, knocking her to the floor.

"Let's go," James commanded, blood trickling from each knuckle. The others followed him back down the hall.

∗ ∗ ∗

Mark held his glowing palm out, ready to fire, as three lights appeared at the end of the tunnel. "James?" he called, unsure.

"Yeah, it's us! Don't shoot!"

Mark let out a sigh of relief, rejoining his wife and Rick, who were now standing in the corner of the room. Finally, the others reached the room. Amy burst past the others, who were equally relieved to see Rick fully healed. She ran at him as he held his arms out for her. They shared a long kiss, while Mark and the others discussed.

"Okay, how do we get back?" James asked Amelia. It was obvious in his tone of voice that he was ready to be done with today.

Amelia shrugged, "You'll have to figure that out."

James let out a sigh of frustration, as he crossed the room to the only window that looked out to the broken maze below. He scanned the floor. No movement drew his eye, which wasn't as comforting as he'd expected. To the far left of the window, he could see the meeting point below. All they had to do was get back down and blow a hole in the tunnel below. He paced on the spot for a minute, thinking.

"Now what?" Rick interrupted James's mental monologue.

"Well, we just need to get out of this room, to below. Then if we can blast through that wall, we will be back to the start."

"How much of a drop is it?" Mark asked.

"About ten feet," James answered, looking over the edge.

Mark stepped away from Emily. His energy built with a light hum and the others watched as he closed his eyes and stretched his arms out wide. Without any warning, a blast of light drew from his body...more like a wall of light. Travelling across the room, in a wide line, it hit the near wall. The entire wall itself cracked and crumbled, breaking off, lightly shaking the room. Mark bent over, catching his breath, as James went to the very edge and looked down at the room below.

"Wow. That was some juice," James muttered to himself. "Now, what's the plan?" he asked the breathless Mark, as the others waited for a response.

"Now I'm hoping that if we jump, Julia and Amy can break our fall." He glanced over at the two women, "What do you think?"

They looked at each other and considered it for a minute. "I think we can do it," Julia grinned

"Maybe we should go in groups of four, just in case." Amy suggested.

"Sounds like a plan. Okay, me, Julia, Amelia, and Amadeus will go first. Followed by you guys," James insisted.

The first four lined themselves up with Amy close behind.

"Ready?" she asked Julia, with her hands out ready to back up.

"Yep!" Julia quickly shot back. "On three."

"One...Two...Three!" Amy counted down for her, as the first four blindly leapt out from the ledge, and plummeted to the floor below.

Julia didn't need the extra help Amy offered. Two feet from the ground, she used her power to freeze them in free-fall, then let loose, as their feet lightly landed, leaving them standing upright.

"Great job!" James cheered, kissing her cheek, and then he glanced back up at the others, who had lined themselves up for the next jump. "Okay, on the count of three. One. Two..." The group needed no, *Three* Just as he had said 'two,' they heard the footsteps running up behind them, and the growing buzz of power. Amy and Julia focused on their safe landing, as bolts of light blew past them, and followed from above.

"Mark. Wall!" James pointed to the wall behind them that needed a big hole in it, for them to finish.

Mark turned and focused once again, Emily staying close at his side, as the others blocked and threw back their energy bolts to the upper level. Added distractions now came down the tunnel to their right, where Selene and Damon stood, shooting handguns. Mark closed his eyes and spread his arms wide. The same hum returned and another blast of energy crippled the wall in front of them.

"Now run!" Mark turned and ordered the group to retreat through the open hole, as he helped James and Rick fight off the others.

All but the remaining three men were already at the finish point. Rick turned first, and ran to the spot where the others were waiting. James and Mark stepped backwards through the wall, as the others followed, still on the attack. Finally giving up and raising their shields to their maximum, they spun on the spot and sprinted to the so called 'Finish-line.' Caleb, Damon, Selene, followed by four men and women, pursued them, until Amadeus raised his hand, announcing the challenge was complete. "Enough."

CHAPTER SIXTEEN

Amadeus turned to the group behind him, who were all breathing heavily, apart from Amelia.

"Well done. Forty-three minutes. You passed. You're ready." He placed his hand on James's shoulder, and James slightly flinched away from the touch. "You can relax now."

James let his shield down, as his energy dispersed out his feet, and his action was followed by the others. The humans looked up, squinting when the lights came back on, and the noises stopped. Amelia stepped away from the group and began clapping. Soon after, she was joined by the others.

"Well done. I'm proud of you." Amelia cheered.

The group could not yet fully relax or smile. They scanned the faces of their previous attackers, stunned and unsure.

Finally, Riley came over and held his hand out to Mark. "Hey, no hard feelings right?"

Mark hesitated, but then he did relax and smile. He took Riley's hand and shook it firmly. "No hard feelings."

The others momentarily relaxed where they stood, smiling breathlessly. Emily grabbed Mark's shoulder, as he turned around to kiss her forehead. Her knees buckled and she began to fall. Mark began to panic, as he scooped her into his arms. The others watched, anxiety returning.

Concern covered his face, "Are you okay?" He spoke in a rush.

She took in one sharp breath and her eyes began to flutter as she nodded. "Yes, I'm just so exhausted. I literally don't have enough energy to hold myself up." Then she laughed at her husband, assuring him everything physically was still fine.

"That's okay, that's why I'm here," he said, cradling her closer to his body. He knew the concentration and amount of energy needed to heal was much more than that needed to fight. She was completely drained.

Amy yawned widely, which cause Rick to do the same.

"All of you go get some rest. You'll need your strength for tomorrow," Amadeus commanded, as the other Jarly left the room. Feeling as if their legs were made of lead, the gang forced their feet to move one after another, as they made their way back into the main hallway. "You can sleep in tomorrow morning. I recommend that you attack at night anyway. Enjoy your night," Amadeus recommended, as he walked past their housing door.

The group practically stumbled through the door, down the steps, and literally flopped on the humungous couch below. Mark walked to their bedroom door with Emily still in his arms. "We're going to bed. See you in the morning," he said over his shoulder, as he opened the door.

"Good night!" Emily called after.

Mark closed and awkwardly locked the door, before walking over to the bed and lightly placing his wife down on one side, then playfully rolling across her to flop on the far side, and letting out a long sigh of relief. They lay there silently staring at the stucco ceiling, for more than fifteen minutes. Emily reached over and intertwined their fingers, as she peeked over at the clock. It was 6:47 p.m., which caused her to laugh.

"What?" Mark grinned across at her. Her laughing made it impossible to speak, so she reached over, and lifted the clock up so he could see. "Wow, it feels like its midnight!" he replied, shaking his head.

"What a day!" Emily let out another sigh.

"What a day indeed. And you know what is always good at the end of a long day?" His face was straight, as he cocked one perfect brow.

Emily had already clued in, but continued to play along. "What's that?"

With no immediate answer, Mark rolled off his side of the bed and came around, raising his wife back into his arms. He turned, heading into the bathroom, "A warm bath."

Emily giggled, pushing the door closed behind them.

Each bathroom was exactly the same, though they were abnormally huge, bigger than the bedroom. The cream carpet in the bedroom ended at the bathroom entrance, leading onto large, dark-green tiles. The walls were a mint-green color, with stone and wooden highlights, creating a spa-like feel. When you entered, you had to walk across five tiles before you turned to the right and the room really opened up. The far wall glowed with white glass, trickling water from top to bottom, with two mirrors positioned in the middle. Below the mirrors were a narrow, cream granite shelf, that held two matching white glass bowls to use as sinks. The wall across, separated by a thin-tiled sectional, housed the toilet. On the left wall, a number of canvas paintings depicted landscapes and flora. To the far right, yet another sort hallway only five feet long, led to three distinct rooms; left, right, and straight ahead. These rooms were entered by a single step down.

The right opened to a room dedicated to a fancy shower, with twenty showerheads; four on each wall, seating, and built-in lighting. The heads were controlled by the user, and they were positioned overhead at the shoulders and lower back height. This was James and Julia's favorite room. The opposite room, solely held a black Jacuzzi, built for ten. This was definitely the room for

Amy and Rick.

The last room, straight ahead, was where Mark and Emily were heading. It was smaller than the others, and the walls were black apart from the back wall of small, cream tiles. In each corner, black metal shelves overflowed with white flowers, fallen petals and intricately designed towels. Each wall trickled with a similar waterfall, bouncing off cream pebbles that bordered the room. The temperature was set warmer here than in the other rooms; a light dew instantly coated their skin. On raised pedestals throughout the room, candles of all sizes flickered and dripped. The center held the masterpiece; a large, white, free-standing, claw bathtub with black iron legs, built for two.

Mark placed Emily at the entrance, as he went to turn on the taps. The bathtub filled quickly, as he added lavender-scented bubbles. Emily leant against the doorframe, enjoying the dimly lit room, smiling to herself as she watched her husband. She waited as he finally turned and beamed back at her. Leaping up the only step, he pushed her against the wall on the outside of the room. Slowly, she raised her hands, feeling every taut muscle and sinew, until they rested on his shoulders. Mark pulled her closer, his hands reaching under the fabric of her shirt. He raised it up, lifting her arms, as he slid it over her head.

They grinned at each other, as she grasped his head, pulling his lips back to hers. Stepping away from the wall, she ran her hands down his chest, before she pulled his shirt over his head, dropping in to the floor below. Mark turned them both and took a step backwards into the room, ripping off her sports bra and dropping it to the ground. Emily absently pulled her hair band, letting her head fall back, trailing down her spine. A moan escaped her lips, as he kissed and sucked his way down her chest, removing the remainder of their clothes.

He stood back up, quickly pulling her into his arms. Lightly jumping, she wrapped her legs around his waist, holding him close. Turning, with all of his focus still on her, he effortlessly raised each leg up and over the brim, until they both slid into the warm water. The water temperature was welcoming as he sat down, Emily straddling his hips, as his hands drew up along her spine, and his fingered threaded into the hair at her nape.

* * *

Mark spooned Emily that night, keeping her close, and comfortable. Her eyes drifted open the next morning, blinking to adjust to the artificial lighting, attached in a narrow line, bordering the top of each wall. The lights grew brighter gradually, over the course of the morning, as if there was natural light through a bedroom window. She stayed still, trying not to wake Mark, as she glanced up at the bedside clock. 6:52 a.m. Despite her best efforts, Mark, who had slept so close that his face was still pushed into the back of her hair, began to stir behind her. She stilled as he took a deep morning breath, stretched his legs, and pulled back his head. It was obvious he was still trying not to disturb her.

After a few seconds he whispered, "Em, you awake?"

She grinned, took a deep breath, and pulled away from him. He lifted his arm so she could turn around to face him. "Yep." She smiled, as he rested his arm back around her waist, his fingers lightly kneading her warm flesh.

"Morning," he whispered, brushing his nose against hers.

"Morning."

"Today's the day," he muttered, and both their smiles faded into a grim line.

Emily had no response. She nodded once, and her eyes strayed from his, becoming distant.

"Don't worry. I won't let anything happen to you." He

continued to whisper, as he pulled her closer, closing the space between them again.

Emily rested her forehead in the middle of his chest. "I know."

He kissed her hair, as they both closed their eyes, falling asleep in each other's arms.

* * *

Amy shook awake as Rick slid out of bed, walking gloriously naked into their bathroom. She rolled onto her back, covered her face with the sheets, and stretched out her arms and legs. The lighting had increased in the last hour, the room becoming brighter than mid-day. There were two improvised windows on the far wall, which even had mesh and blinds. Why did they need to have fake windows when everyone knew they were underground, Amy thought absently. When she thought about it, she hadn't seen the sky in three days and the artificial lighting started to comfort her nerves.

Suddenly pulling back the sheets, Rick found Amy grinning up at him. He smiled, and jumped back under the sheets; the cold morning air feeling uncomfortable on his bare skin. Rick reached across to his wife, pulling her into his arms, as she playfully screamed.

"You're freezing," she squealed as he deliberately pressed his stone-cold toes against her bare legs.

"Hmm." He dragged her close. "Maybe you should warm me up?"

"Get you all hot and sweaty?" She bit her lip, trying not to laugh, and he nodded, pulling her up and onto his bare chest. Skin on skin, she rested her cheek on the curve of his neck, as he wrapped his arms around her.

They lay in comfortable silence, with no immediate desire to move. "What time is it?" Amy spoke into his neck, brushing her lips along his skin.

Rick turned his head awkwardly to see the clock. "Eight-thirty." He dropped his head back onto the pillow.

"One week now." Amy was thoughtful. "We got married a week ago, today."

Rick was already nodding. "Some honeymoon!" he joked.

Amy let out a single laugh, but couldn't hide the feel of her warm tears pooling along his collarbone, running down onto the pillow below. Rick rolled to the side, dislodging them both, as he raised his free hand to rest on the side of her face.

"What it is?" he whispered.

She shook her head, and raised her hand to wipe the tears, as she tried to smile through her emotions. "Nothing." She wiped her face again. "It's nothing."

Rick rolled his eyes, let out a frustrated breath, and then further rolled, pushing her body into the mattress, and positioning himself above her. He nestled between her thighs, as his forearms braced his weight on either side of her torso, effectively caging her. With their faces only inches apart, she tried to turn her head so she wouldn't have to look into his probing gaze.

"Amy." He waited for her to give up and face him, watching as more tears came. "Talk to me."

She remained silent for a long while, as she tried to blink back her tears, and calm her breathing. Their eyes connected, and she could finally see his pained expression. "Amy," he whispered more loudly now.

Before he could finish, she couldn't hold back anymore; a flood of words came in a slew, with blubbering that sounded more alien than English.

"I'm scared Rick. I don't want to do this. What if you get hurt? Or Em or Jules or..." She lost track of her words, as she focused on his confused face. "We just promised to love each other and be with each other, for the rest of our lives and now that's sounding a lot shorter than I thought."

Rick opened his mouth to calm her down, but she continued, tears flowing down into her ears, her face becoming red and heated. Soon, she was practically yelling. "I want babies, Rick. Your babies. I want a family. I want to grow old and retire to a huge house in the country, surrounded by grandkids. I don't want to lose everyone that I love in some creepy military basement, for a bunch of people I don't even know, and an alien race that seems to have more fun playing with us than helping." She had a lot more to say, but Rick lightly covered her mouth with his, then shushed his hysterical wife.

"Breathe. Calm down," he encouraged her, as her breathing began to slow. "Can I say something?"

She let out an exhausted breath and nodded, her eyes wide and wet, as he spoke. "Amy, we're all scared. This stuff's enough to make anyone go crazy. But that doesn't change the fact that we're together and I love you. We're going to be together forever. We can have one hundred babies, if you want. We will grow old and retire. But we're here now and we have to see this through to the end.

"Amy, if we give up now, we lose everything. We have half the state.." He paused… "Hell, half the country is probably in on this now. They're all looking for us. If we're not captured and tortured by them, we'll be found by some redneck, who will just trade us in for their ransom and we'll end up in the same place."

Rick saw the tears begin again, so he began to backtrack. "But we're here now. We have these abilities. We're trained to kick ass, which was very sexy by the way." He trailed off, grinning and raising one eyebrow, trying to make her laugh. It worked, but only for a second. "And I'm not going to let anything happen to you or your sister or any of us. We're in and out."

Taking a deep breath, he pressed his forehead to hers. "And this isn't just about us, babe. What about those people that weren't as fortunate as us? Some of them could be our friends. They're all alone in that dark hole being poked, prodded, and tortured, Amy! We have to help them." A light seemed to flicker in her eyes then, and his words seemed to relax her. "Then we can get our lives back and you and I, we're gonna go someplace far away." His grin came back, "And we're gonna start on those one hundred kids."

She did laugh then, rolling her eyes, pushing at his chest.

Rick smiled down at her, as she grabbed his ribs, and raised her head so that she was close enough. "I love you, so much."

Their kiss began tenderly, but grew with passionate need.

Not breaking the kiss, he pushed her head back onto the pillow, his hands traced her sides and he hitched one of her legs around his. He pulled back, once more, shaking his head. "You have no idea."

* * *

By 10:00 a.m., Rick and Amy were dressed and ready in their previously assigned clothes. Amadeus wanted each of them to look casual enough to go about without being recognized, but also flexible enough for anything. Their clothes were very similar to those that they had been wearing when they first arrived.

Amy wore a pair of black cargo shorts that were perfectly fitted, with ties at the bottom, and added stretch, so that she could easily lift her leg above her head with one of her kick-to-the-throat moves. This was accented by a long, tight-fitted, white t-shirt and running shoes. Amadeus had also given the group their baseball caps, sunglasses, and scarves back, for further coverage. Rick wore a similar outfit of calf-length, black shorts and a baggy, white t-shirt.

Rick held the bedroom door open for Amy, as they both walked into the living room, where Julia and James were nestled on the couch watching a movie.

"Morning," Rick called, as they both turned their heads and smiled at their best friends.

"Morning," James answered.

"How'd you sleep?" Amy asked, as she and Rick joined them on the opposite end on the couch.

James grinned at his best friend, adding a wink, as Julia began to blush at Amy. "Very well, thank you." James continued, unashamed.

Rick grinned back, shaking his head, as Julia asked, "What about you?" Her voice rose higher than normal.

Rick winked at James, and the young men grinned at each other. Rick wrapped his free arm around his wife's shoulder, pulling her close into his side. Now it was Amy that was blushing.

"It was a good night." Rick stated, as Amy glanced at Julia then they both awkwardly turned to the romantic comedy playing on the screen.

"So, today's the day to kick some ass and get our lives back?" James blurted, as the others turned back to him.

"Just try and keep up with me!" Rick winced, as Amy elbowed him in the ribs.

"Yeah, right!"

"So when do we leave?" Julia wondered out loud.

"Soon," Mark answered, and the others turned to see him and Emily leaving their room. "It will take another eight hours to get back, anyway."

Then Emily smiled down at her little family on the couch below. "Morning."

"Morning," they each replied in turn.

"How you feeling?" Amy asked.

"Oh I'm great. I just needed a good night's sleep," she said as she and Mark shimmied in-between them and the coffee table, into the center seats.

"How are you guys?" Mark asked looking around.

"Good," Julia and Amy replied, too quickly.

"Hungry," James added, as they laughed.

"So, you think we need to leave soon?" Rick asked his brother-in- law.

Mark nodded and took a deep breath. "Yeah, well, Amadeus said it would be best to attack at night, and it's an eight or nine hour drive back, so I'm guessing we leave right after breakfast."

The others looked over at him and nodded, silently. Emily's eyes drifted from her husband to the only bedroom door that was still closed.

"What about the kids?" She gestured to their door with her chin.

"They can't really come with us." Amy trailed off.

"It's not safe," Julia agreed.

James joined in. "Yeah, the last thing we need is to be worrying about them, while we're there."

"Then what? We leave them here?" Emily asked the room.

"What choice do we have? They're safe here." Rick shrugged.

"They're right. I think Matt and Abby should stay here, in the meantime. When we have everything sorted out, we'll come back for them," Mark added, glancing down at his wife, who still didn't seem satisfied with his answer. "Well, how about we wait and see what Amadeus and Amelia have to say? Maybe they'll think we should leave with them."

Emily looked up at her husband, studying his face, then lightly smiled and began to nod.

"Okay, well, who wants to join me for some grub?" James got

to his feet.

The others smiled up at him, getting to their feet, as James and Julia headed out of the room.

"Mark and I will grab the kids. We'll meet you there," Emily said to her sister, who hesitated at the door.

Amy nodded, taking Rick's outstretched hand, as they joined their friends in the hallway. Mark rested his hand on his wife's shoulder blade, and entered the children's room. Abby and Matt were already awake, standing up in their cribs, overjoyed that someone had come to free them. Mark laughed, as Abby practically jumped into his arms and held on tightly around his neck.

He laughed down at her. "Good morning!"

Matt did the same to Emily, but only held on with his left hand, as Emily slid him onto her hip. He reached for his pacifier and threw it back into the crib.

"You're getting a bit old for that, aren't you?" She laughed then rolled her eyes, as he smiled and replaced his soother with his thumb.

She grinned at her husband, who was already waiting at the door. Mark took her hand, as they made their way past the living room, down the hall, and into the cafeteria, where everyone else was waiting. Amadeus and the others were there too. Damon greeted them with a genuine smile, then placed a large portion of bacon, sausage, and egg on their plates, as they sat down.

"Thanks," they said, sitting the children in their high chairs.

"You were right." James spoke with his mouth full.

"We're leaving at noon." Rick followed suit.

Mark turned to Amadeus, who was seated across and to the left of him.

"Enjoy your breakfast. We'll talk details when we're finished," Amadeus ordered, with a friendly smile.

CHAPTER SEVENTEEN

"I don't know how you do it, Damon, but that was amazing!" Emily finished her last bite of sausage, placing her knife and fork neatly across her plate.

"Well thank you, Emily. I do try." He took her plate and walked into the adjacent kitchen.

The table fell silent, as Amadeus spoke up. "All right, so you know what you have to do. If you succeed at rescuing the others, it's going to be a whole new world. We will be able to go through with our plans for contact and we can, hopefully, give your kind the opportunities we have." Amadeus had obviously waited for this day, for a long time.

"So, how long do we have these abilities? Your powers." James leant on the table, as he asked the Jarly sitting across from him.

Amelia took a deep breath and considered his questions. "About seventy-two hours, give or take." The humans all turned to her as she continued. "Hopefully, if this works, we can eventually teach you, and perhaps all humans, to gain and respect their own energy fields. But yes, for the time being, our copies will only last roughly three more days."

"We have been given strict orders not to interfere in your mission, but there are some loopholes," Amadeus began.

"Loopholes?" Rick questioned.

"Well, we are not allowed to enter the building and help save the humans or spill any human blood," Amelia added.

"But we can accompany you to our safe house in Sierra Vista and continue to mentor you along the way," said Amadeus.

"Plus, if need be, we have ways of NOT spilling blood," Riley offered, but he quickly stopped, still grinning at James and Rick, as Amadeus gave him a stern look.

"Amelia, Riley, Isobel, and the brothers have volunteered to escort you back to Sierra Vista, safely." Then Amadeus turned to focus on Riley. "Where they will then wait for further orders and your return."

Riley rolled his eyes.

Amelia seemed to remember something. "I watched all of you carefully yesterday. You each have strengths that even surprised me." Then she turned to Amadeus. "We have discussed and decided that Emily will be in charge of your mission, when you leave these grounds."

"Me!" Emily blurted out, surprised and uncertain.

Amadeus grinned in encouragement. "Yes. You were the first to completely replicate Isobel's energy and ability. You are the oldest female in your group, and it is obvious that your opinion is not taken lightly."

Amelia shrugged. "Being an expectant mother, your own senses are heightened more so than the others', and you appear to consider a more diplomatic approach, before violence. You are also the healer and therefore slightly more valuable to your group and the others. It just makes sense."

"Is the duty too much?" Amadeus seemed to be genuinely asking Emily.

"No, of course not."

"Do any of you disagree with our choice?" Amelia asked the others.

"Hell no!" James spoke up for the group, then turned to Emily.

"Em and Mark are the only grownups in this group," he joked

"It's a perfect choice." Amy grinned at her sister, as Emily blushed.

"Then it is settled." Amadeus beamed.

"Although you must know, when it comes to leadership and chain of command, if you accept her as your leader you MUST honor her word." Amelia spoke so seriously that it gave Emily goose bumps. "If you disagree or decide to go against her orders, you will not be able to use your energy for any purpose and may even feel physical pain. If Emily becomes your leader, her word is your command."

"So listen to Emily, and do what she says, or you get hurt," Rick stated sarcastically.

"Literally. If you accept, say so now, then we can bind your energy," Amelia said.

"What happens when you bind us?" Julia asked, curiously.

"When we bind you, Emily's every word will be listened to and acted upon. If she asks you a question, you'll have no choice but to answer truthfully. The bond will only last as long as you have our powers, but it's not something to be taken lightly. You will also all be connected on a higher level. You will be able to sense one another, when separated. You will be able to draw on each other's energy and even utilize some abilities that you personally have not yet mastered."

"When you become their leader, I will also have my crew answer to Amelia and you." Amadeus smiled across the table at Emily, who had still not been able to display any other emotion but fear.

"Two heads are better than one," Amelia added, snapping Emily out of her trance.

"Well, of course I accept," Mark stated.

"Me too." Amy spoke next, followed shortly by Julia.

"Definitely." Rick smiled at his sister-in-law.

James turned to Amadeus, nodding. "Go ahead. Bring on the bond."

They all laughed, as Amadeus gave his, 'Very well then' nod of approval to Riley.

"Okay, I need you all to stand and hold out your right hands, palms up, over the table." Riley stood, pulling a small knife up from the table.

Julia gasped before she could take it back.

Amadeus stood when he took in their unsure gazes. "Our energy starts in the core of us, in our hearts, so I'm afraid the bond must be made in blood." The girls' eyebrows all raised. "Only a few drops are needed for the connection."

"Why is it always in blood?" Julia grumbled, under her breath, as they held out their hands, in turn.

Starting with James and ending at Emily, Riley dragged the blade roughly two centimeters across their palms. Emily was shocked when the blade was so sharp that she barely felt a thing. The blood began to pool in their palms, as they looked up and waited for further instructions.

"Emily, hold your hand out into the center of the table. One by one, I want each of you to turn your hands over and gently press your palms against hers, so that your blood mixes. Then I want you to close your eyes and collect your energy throughout your bodies, until I say stop," Riley commanded.

James was first. He grinned at his new leader, as he turned his palm over. The blood had pooled enough so that it began to drip down the side of his hand and into hers. They stood, palms touching, for a few seconds before closing their eyes and then their light burst out around their feet, radiating throughout their bodies. After a few seconds, the others watched, as the light waved throughout their bodies, and came to focus on their hands.

"All right," Riley whispered.

Their eyes burst open and James pulled his hand away. He released his energy back through his feet and glanced down at a perfectly healed palm. Emily continued to let the energy flow though her as Julia raised her palm up and did the same.

"Well done." Amadeus spoke as the group continued until it was only Mark remaining.

Emily and Mark separated; Mark grinning as their energy released and both their hands were healed.

Julia shrugged. "I feel the same."

Amelia laughed and turned to Emily. "Test it out. Order one of them to do something." She turned to look at the others. "Then one of you, fight it."

Emily grinned devilishly at her family, as they all laughed; her plotting evident. "Hmm. Rick go give James a big kiss."

"So, this is how you plan to torture us!" James said sarcastically, with a fake disgusted face. "Dude, you kiss me and you're getting decked."

Amelia and Amadeus laughed, as she leant over, "Rick fight it. Tell yourself you're not doing it."

He was already jokingly squinting at his sister-in-law, as he turned to face James. He stared at him for a long minute, then let out a light gasp, squeezed his eyes shut, and clutched his head.

"Okay, I take it back," Emily quickly added, concerned.

James was laughing, as Rick relaxed. "Geez, it's like a million needles going off in your head." Rick reported.

Amelia clapped her hands together, once. "Well, at least it works. And it will keep you all in check."

"Thomas, will show you to the surface and help you with supplies, while Amelia and the others bring around the cars." Amadeus changed the subject, gesturing to Thomas, who still sat silently eating his breakfast next to him.

"What's going to happen with Matt and Abby?" Emily questioned.

Amadeus thought for a minute then turned to her. "We will ask them what they wish to do. They may either join you, back in Sierra Vista, where they will wait with my crew, or I am sure Thomas has no problem with them staying here, with us."

"Oh, of course not." Thomas spoke up, before Amadeus even finished. "They are wonderful children."

Amadeus turned to the two toddlers, who couldn't help but eavesdrop, smiling with their innocence. "Matt, Abby, your friends are going to go on a little trip, to go save some people from some mean men. Now you get to decide, do you want to go with them or stay here and wait?"

The group smiled at the children. They clearly understood the question; their little brows knitting as they thought. They even glanced at each other before turning back to the adults.

Abby spoke enthusiastically. "Stay!" she bounced in her seat.

"So, you would like to stay here with us?" Amadeus asked, in a child-friendly tone.

The kids smiled and nodded, but then something occurred to Abby and her little face fell. Turning to James, who was seated nearest, her little hand reached out. "You come back."

He laughed down at her, lifted her out of the seat and pulled her into a hug. "Of course, we're coming right back for you. It will just take us a day or two."

She examined his face for a few seconds, assessing his sincerity, and then seemed to believe him, pulling her arms around his neck. Emily felt relieved by the children's decision, and smiled back at them, as Mark squeezed her shoulder. Amadeus then stood, preparing his parting words, before he would leave the room with Amelia and the others, apart from Thomas, behind him.

"I hear you've all done very well in your training and are more than ready to complete this task." Amadeus focused his eyes and it aged him, suddenly. "You have no idea how long they've been waiting for this day. We know you're not warriors and didn't ask for any of this. For this, we truly are thankful. But we're also counting on you. I know you will make us proud. All I can say is, good luck, and I look forward to when we meet again." Then he shocked them all by noticeably holding back tears, as he swiftly left the room.

Emily's group sat back down and glanced around at each other.

"You have no idea how much they want to help us. To introduce lifesaving technology and teach." Thomas spoke up, as he finished his breakfast and pushed his plate into the center of the table. They had no response to give, so he stood up with a smile. "Well then, shall we get going?"

They all stood and followed him down the last hall, around two corners, and down another hall, before they got to an open staircase. As they began to climb, Thomas started to talk again. "I have prepared a few bags of food and we have arranged a number of purses and wallets filled with more than enough money for your journey."

They then got to the top of the five flights of metal stairs, before reaching a door that opened up into the stairwell ceiling. Thomas turned a combination lock and unlocked the two large metal doors, continuing up to the undeveloped basement of his house. Once they had all stepped out into the room, they watched as he closed and locked the doors behind them. To an unsuspecting eye, the door in the floor would just look like the entrance to a bomb shelter or underground supply room. As Amy looked around, she recognized the small windows that were at the top of each wall. She shivered slightly, taking her husband's hand. He didn't ask about her sudden reaction to the room.

As Thomas got back to his feet, he walked over to the other

side of the basement, around the corner, and up a set of wooden stairs that led to a closed, mundane, white door, no different than a bedroom door; nothing fancy. When he reached the top, he turned the gold handle, and walked into another room. Emily and the others smiled, as they walked into a typical farm house, with chipped paint, rooster paintings, plaid upholstered chairs, and wooden beams.

They continued to follow Thomas around the house and into the large dining room, which held a long, rectangular table big enough for twenty. On the table were three large hiking bags, filled with clothes, food, and supplies. Next to them were three woman's purses, which had the essentials, including three matching black-leather wallets.

Thomas walked into the room, resting his hand on the back of one of the chairs, as he gestured to the table's contents and spoke. "Hopefully, this will be enough. Each wallet and the ladies' bags contain over one thousand dollars of unmarked bills. You will need vehicles for the journey, so they're bringing them around now. You can break up into partners if you wish. You will be following each other, but each car should have one of these bags. They have everything you'll need."

James reached for the first big bag and took a look inside.

Thomas continued. "We also took the liberty of making you some fake identification cards, for the time being. Hopefully, no one will ask to see any. Any questions?" They looked at each other then back to him, their heads shaking. "Well, then let's get going."

Mark, James, and Rick each lifted a bag onto their backs and found the right wallet with their I. D, as the woman took their purses. Thomas took a different door out of the room, leading straight to his front entrance. It was then they saw the light. The front door was framed with an array of painted glass. It was just coming up to noon now and the sun shone brightly through every window in the entrance.

When he opened the door and made his way down the front steps, a light wind of fresh air hit their faces and the smell of trees and summer filled their lungs. Looking out, they discovered that the scenery was exactly how they had pictured it. From the outside it would appear they had come out of a white, three-story farmhouse, with brown shingle roofing, surrounded by fields of short green plants, which Emily could not recognize.

The paths were all dry and sandy, bordered by different-sized rocks. To the right of the house, there was a huge, New Mexico pine tree, with a child's swing. The land went on, as far as the eye could see. There was definitely no one living within five miles in any direction. As they adjusted to the bright light, Thomas seemed unfazed. When he reached the path at the base of the steps; he walked out, following another gravel track off to the right.

Emily looked farther down the path, one hundred yards away, where there was a huge, traditional, red and white barn, as tall as the house, and double the length, with its main-end doors wide open. The couples enjoyed the fresh air, as they practically skipped along behind Thomas. Amy looked back to the house, finally noticing mountains behind. Then, she looked out onto the fields. This was when the heat hit her, the first bead of sweat running down the side of her face. Looking around, she saw there were only varying shades of brown and beige. She glanced down at her feet and kicked a random pebble that danced around in the dust.

Finally, they reached the entrance of the barn.

"Fortunately for you boys, my friends have nice and expensive taste in cars." Thomas laughed at their expressions, as one by one the men's jaws dropped in awe, and their women looked at them, not understanding.

Thomas stopped in front of an army-green Jeep Wrangler.

Next to that was a silver, convertible Mini-Cooper, and to the far left, a black Ford Mustang. All three vehicles had heavily tinted windows.

Thomas tapped the Wrangler hood, and then threw the first set of keys at Mark. "These babies are yours."

"Aw, sweet. The GT California special-edition. I call this one!" James peeked inside the Mustang window.

"No way," Rick complained.

"Come on. Look at me," James spread out his arms, puffing out his chest. "Now, look at the Mustang. Now, back to me." He grinned, yanking open the driver's door. "It's a match made in heaven."

"Dude, you fucking suck." Rick looked down at the Mini with trepidation. "We could fight for it."

James's grin grew wider, as Rick's brow rose, dangerous thoughts apparently crossing his mind. Shaking his head, he said, "Face it, you haven't been able to beat me at anything since we were eight years old. Plus, Amy would kick both our asses." James chuckled, bending to jump into his driver's seat, "Enjoy the Coop."

Amy placed fists on her hips. "What's wrong with the Mini? I have a Mini."

"Nothing. It's just...a bit girlie, is all." Rick shrugged, "Plus, it's not the most comfortable ride over long distance." He jumped in the driver's side, forcing the seat back as far as it would go. "Automatic," he grumbled to himself.

Emily and Mark silently threw their packs into the open roll cage of the Wrangler and settled into their seats.

The entire barn had been converted into an automotive dream, equipped with lifts and a detailing bay. The interior was solid metal. Half of the building was dedicated to a parking lot; each car had its own little cubby hole, given that it could only be reached by a mechanical ramp. Amy and Julia couldn't stop laughing, as their men drooled over the view.

From left to right, James and Rick practically hyperventilated, as they recognized the vehicles. A red 1962 Ferrari, Porsche Carrera, 1968 Chevrolet Corvette, Dodge Viper, a burnt-orange Lamborghini Diablo, a silver Mercedes-Benz SLR McLaren, a 1961 Jaguar, and even a blue AC Cobra 427, with white racing stripes.

"Aw, can't we take one of those?" James called, still mesmerized, as Amelia and the others came farther in the room, laughing.

"The idea is to not draw attention, remember?" Riley muttered.

Amelia threw her things into the back of a black Mercedes. Caleb and his brother filled the trunk of a white Toyota Tundra Pickup, before getting in. Isobel smiled to the others, as she slid into the Mercedes's back seat.

"Okay, you're going to follow us, while Caleb and Damon bring up the rear. It should be a smooth drive. Take these." Amelia passed Mark three walkie-talkies. "Keep them set on channel two and message us when you need a break or anything. Riley predicts it will take about eight and a half hours to drive to our location. We'll figure out the main details tonight. Okay?"

"Yep, sounds good," Emily agreed, reaching over to take the spare radios, as she jumped out of her seat.

"Good luck, to you all." Thomas said his good-byes and got out of their way.

Emily ran in between their cars, handing over the radios. "Keep it on channel two." She said, glancing between each couple, "If you need anything, just say. Mark and I will follow Riley, then you guys follow us, and Caleb and Damon will follow you. It's gonna be just over eight hours, so we'll probably stop a few times to stretch our legs, okay?"

"Sounds like a plan," Amy smiled, leaning across her husband to see her sister.

"See you there. Love you all." Emily ran back to the Jeep, and fastened herself into the passenger seat.

Mark waved Riley to go ahead, as he started the engine. Thomas waved them on, when they pulled out of the barn, and onto the long driveway. It took five minutes alone to get out of the main lot and onto another dusty track. When everyone had settled in, Mark and Emily put on their sunglasses, and he reached over to intertwine their fingers, resting his hands in her lap. Emily grinned, as they stopped for Riley to turn, and he leant over to kiss her cheek, before focusing back on the road. After a few minutes, she looked down at the walkie-talkie in the middle console then picked it up with her free hand. Mark watched, as she raised it to her mouth.

"Just making sure you can hear us." Emily grinned over at her husband, when she let the call button out.

Amelia replied first. "Loud and clear."

Amy followed. "Yep, Gotha,"

"Yeah, we're here," Julia added.

Damon was the last one to check in. "Yes Emily. We can hear you just fine."

Emily finally relaxed back into her seat. She stole one more glance at Mark, and then let her head fall back against the headrest, enjoying the clear blue skies. Having only the roll bar above, Emily had the perfect traveller's view, and she casually watched the scenery go by. After roughly twenty minutes, the dirt tracks turned to paved cement, and the group made a sharp left turn onto highway US-380 West.

Not forty minutes had passed before Emily reached back for the sack, and rummaged through the contents until she produced a juicy red apple. Grinning, she threw the bag behind Mark, and took a big bite, letting the juice flow down her gin. His sideways glance and shaking head made her curious. Mouth full, she asked,

"What?" She forcefully swallowed.

"That's supposed to be our backup supply."

She shrugged, "Well, I'm hungry now."

He allowed a slow grin, followed by a generic hum of agreement, but she took another large bite.

There was little distraction for the next two and a half hours. Emily even managed to enjoy alone time with her husband. She tricked herself into believing it was just a hot summer's road trip, alone with Mark. She had to, because the thought of where they were actually heading had her stomach jumping into her throat.

"Em?" Amy's voice sounded over the radio.

"Hey, what's up?"

"Some of us gotta go pee and need to stretch our legs." She giggled.

"Got it. Riley, you there?" Emily asked.

"Yeah, we heard you. I'm turning off at the next stop."

"Thanks." A static-filled version of Amy's voice came through.

Two minutes later, the group pulled into a Shell gas station. Once parked, everyone got out of their seats, and stretched their legs. The girls, along with Rick and Mark, all headed into the bathrooms. Being careful not to draw attention, they wore large sunglasses and baseball caps. When they returned, James handed everyone a few liter bottles of water and treats. Slowly, the group crowded together, shielded between the Wrangler and pickup truck.

"How we doing?" Amelia asked, keeping her voice down.

Emily nodded. "Fine."

"Yeah, we're good," Julia added.

"Okay, well if anyone wants to take a short break or anything just let us know. In about an hour, we'll pull into a diner and grab something real to eat." Riley said.

Rick spoke up. "Great."

The group then split once more. This time Emily, Amelia, and Damon took over the driving. Amelia pulled out in the lead, as Emily followed. Mark quickly took his wife's hand again, resting his head back, and closing his eyes. Another left turn and they had started on the I-25 south, for another hour before Amelia pulled off into a restaurant, ironically named, The Diner. Emily parked, squeezing Mark's hand. He had slept the majority of the way, his jaw wide open for most the trip.

Misinterpreting her touch, he jumped a little. "What is it?" he quickly blurted out. Before he could think, he drew on his energy and his feet began to blaze.

Emily began to panic, praying no one was near. "No! No, we've just stopped for dinner. We're fine. Mark, Stop!"

He looked at her, confused, and then he looked down to see his legs were lit up. Someone was just heading out of the restaurant, but thankfully, his head was turned away, while he talked to a friend. Mark quickly released the light, and everything returned to normal.

"Sorry." He honestly felt terrible. Looking away, he ran his hands through his hair and shook his head.

She let out a sigh of relief and reached over, grabbing his chin, "It's okay, babe. We're all a little on edge." She smiled, leaning over to elicit a quick kiss, before pulling away and jumping out of the driver's seat.

Riley, Amelia, and Isobel were already getting a table inside. Fortunately, they had covered their signature Jarly freckles with makeup before leaving the farm. Later, Riley would explain that the freckles were actually tattoo markers of the district from which they originated. The darker points on Amadeus meant higher ranking and inner city dwellers, while the near-faded points of Isobel's temple meant that she was from the outskirts of their city; not necessarily poor or needy. The faded tattoo signified fighting and a greater bond with Nona. Damon and his brother had a distinctly obtuse triangle formation, while the rest of their crew revealed equilateral.

Caleb smiled and held the diner door open for the others to enter. The waitress had already seated the first few, and was taking their drink orders, when Emily and the others pulled out their chairs.

"Can we just have three pitchers of ice water, with lemon, please?" Isobel politely asked the waitress.

"Of course. I'll be right back for your orders, too." The waitress welcomed the others, and then backed into the kitchen.

James and the others relaxed and slowly took off their camouflage of glasses and hats, placing them in the center of the table.

"Everyone still good?" Emily asked around the table. She got a number of replies, but the general gist was that everyone was fine and comfortable.

Before they could start any real conversation, the waitress was back.

"So, where y'all headed?" She struck up a friendly conversation, raising Caleb's glass and filling it. Then she left him with a playful wink, making him raise his brows, as James stifled a laugh.

"We're just traveling through." Riley grabbed his glass, taking a long swig.

"Might head to the coast," James added, to flesh out their story.

"Oh, well I hope you guys enjoy yourselves. The weather is perfect for a nice long drive." She finished filling their glasses, then reached in her soiled apron for a pen and paper.

"So, what can I get ya'll?" She smiled, turning to Caleb first.

"Um, I'll just have the beef burger and fries, please." He grinned back, and then started a pile of menus in the center of the table.

When she had taken their order and returned to fill their pitchers, she left them alone long enough to talk.

"Okay, well we're making really good time," Amelia said, glancing at her watch, and quietly speaking to the table.

"Great. Well, hopefully if we get some long stretches of road we might be able to give'er and get there faster." Damon hoped.

"It would be nice to get there ahead of schedule." Riley seemed to stare off into space, as he spoke. "Just means for prep and planning."

"So, what IS the plan when we get to the safe house?" James was curious.

"Well, we get you ready for action." Then Amelia hesitated, glancing over at Riley, who was now looking serious, and staring back at her, nodding.

Their exchange wasn't hidden. "What?" Rick blurted.

"We have information on one of the men that works at the office building. We think that he can help us. He knows about the blueprints, the hallways, safe zones, and guarded areas. He will have a key and most of the codes to get you in."

"So? Why are we hearing about this now? Why the hesitation?" Mark answered with a tone of accusation.

"It's just, he has no idea about this; about us. And when he finds out, he might react differently." Amelia spoke slowly, concern covering her youthful features.

"Differently?" Emily asked.

"He may turn against you and risk your lives. If possible, we would rather not have to bring him in at all."

"All right, well then let's hope we don't need him," Mark said, leaning back in his chair.

After ten more minutes, the food came, and everyone seemed to relax and forget him or herself.

Forty minutes later, and they had finished. Riley threw a bunch of bills onto the table, as they all made their way to the parking lot. For this stretch of the journey, Amy and Julia took over the

Mini, while the boys filled the Mustang. Isobel took over the lead, as Mark followed close behind. Soon, Isobel turned onto the I-10 West, entering Arizona.

Emily didn't realize she was squeezing Mark's hand, until he raised it up and kissed the back of her palm. She looked over and awkwardly smiled, as she tried to loosen her grip.

"We're fine." Mark made sure she listened.

Emily took in an unsteady breath. "I know. Just nerves." She tried to shrug, but her shoulders still felt too stiff.

When she could, she pulled her hand back, and reached into the back, where the seat had been removed and replaced with a large storage pit, to get to the hiking bag. After riffling through it for a couple of minutes, she pulled out two bottles of water, and a pack of spearmint gum.

She passed Mark a bottle of water, and as he took a cautious sip, she passed him a piece of gum. After taking a few sips of her own water, she took two pieces of gum for herself, her hands shaking so much that she dropped a third piece on the Wrangler floor. Mark kept glancing over at his wife, getting slightly worried when she repeatedly rubbed her stomach, and chewed her gum loudly, taking in deeper breaths. When she started to look around, panicked, he took his foot off the gas.

"Babe? You okay?" Mark asked trying to keep one eye on the road.

Emily took deeper breaths, as she clenched and unclenched her fists, in front of her stomach. Clearly uncomfortable, she ran her sweating palms up and down the length of her thighs.

"I don't know. I don't feel so good." She practically spat out the words, with each breath. Her body rocked in the seat and she lowered her head to her knees. Mark reflexively reached over, rubbing small circles into her back. She fanned her face, as it gradually got paler with a green hue. She ripped out her gum, taking another sip of water, as Mark reached for the radio. "Hey guys. We gotta pull over for a sec!"

"Why?" Amelia demanded over the radio, straight away.

"Cuz, Em's gonna be sick," he answered, with a bite in his voice. Straight away, Isobel turned onto the nearest gravel track, and continued along just enough for all the cars to get off the main road. Emily pulled off the seatbelt, running from the jeep. When she reached the nearest tree; she supported her weight, and bent over to swiftly lose her recent meal. The others got out of their vehicles, coming to crowd around Mark.

"She okay?" Amy was concerned, looking up at him, then out into the field where her sister was still bent over.

"Yeah. I think it was just nerves or the baby," he answered, while Isobel nodded.

Mark made his way out to his wife. "Wait here," he called back to them, as they leaned against the jeep.

"Emily?" Mark came up behind his wife, just as she was spitting out the bile from her mouth. Emily didn't turn to face him, but bent over, placing both her hands back on her knees. Mark continued to step up to her, placing one hand on her back. "You okay, babe?"

She let out a frustrated breath, wiped her face, and then stood up with tears in her eyes. "Yeah, I'm fine. Either I just got hit with a sudden bad case of motion sickness or the baby didn't like dinner." She tried to laugh off her embarrassment.

"Here." He handed her a bottle of water, then pulled her into his arms.

She took a big gulp, as he lightly twisted their bodies from side to side, pressing his lips to her forehead. "You do feel hot." Pulling back, he raised his hand to cover her skin.

Pulling his hand away, she laced their fingers together. "I'll be fine. Just need to breathe."

Mark laughed. She had most her color back now accompanied by a light flush and sweat sheen. "The heat doesn't help." He glanced up at the bright sun, shielding his eyes, then turning back. "Ready, to go?"

"Can we just stand here for one minute?" Her gaze widened, begging.

"Of course."

She leant against the other side of the tree, head falling back, and closed her eyes, focusing on her breathing.

After three minutes, she pulled away and they slowly walked back to the others. Emily couldn't make eye contact with anyone.

"How you feeling?" Amy asked her sister, walking over and lightly placing a hand on her stomach.

Emily held her sister's hand there, as she spoke. "I'm fine."

"Here." James passed her another piece of gum.

"Thank you!" she answered with exaggerated chirpiness, as she reached around her sister.

"Are we okay to continue?" Amelia asked.

"Yes, of course." Emily seemed surprised by the question. Amelia smiled apologetically back at Emily, when she understood the harshness of her tone.

"Okay, well let's get back on the road then. Shall we?" Riley asked as the others agreed and got back into their vehicles.

Emily slowly got back into her seat, buckling her seatbelt. With a few more deep breaths to calm her nerves, she spat out her rotten gum, then leant back over to the middle console, and took another piece.

Mark turned the key, but made no attempt at putting it into gear. "You sure you're okay?" He wiped away a bead of sweat that was gathering at her forehead.

Though she was smiling, she already felt exhausted; her joints and muscles aching. All she wanted to do was crawl into bed. "I'll live," she answered as if she wanted to continue with, *I have to.*

Mark didn't like it one bit, and he turned back to glare out the windshield, jaw clenched. He could see she wasn't up for any of it, but was resigned to their fate. His face became a mask of frustration and anger. Riley, who was now driving again, did a wide U-turn at the end of the street, pulling back onto the main road.

"Come on, let's go," Emily ordered Mark.

He did as he was told, but she knew it wasn't the end of their discussion. She watched her silent and distracted husband drive, knowing his head was elsewhere. It was a two and a half-hour drive before they would take another left turn onto Arizona-90, which meant somewhere along the road, Mark would explode with whatever he was thinking.

His face showed no trace of humor, like it had before. She could practically feel the anger vibrate through him. His left elbow rested on the window edge, with his hand on the steering wheel. His right hand had Emily's fingers intertwined with his, with her hand resting on the top of his thigh. His whole posture was rigid and controlled. The silence was becoming unbearable, with only a few words in over and hour and a half. What had she done? Why did he look so mad?

Julia called for another bathroom break. As soon as the cars parked, Emily threw off her seatbelt and marched into the bathroom. Mark could tell she was upset, but he didn't push it. When the group met up once more, Emily spoke up. "Maybe Amy and I could take the Mustang? Switch it up a bit," Emily suggested, not making eye contact with her husband.

Before she could reach for the keys that Rick held out for her, Mark's face came to life, as panic overcame him. "No!" he burst out, shocking everyone. "Em, you're staying with me. If you wanna change vehicles, so can Amy join us, we can."

"Mark, I want some alone time with my sister. We'll be driving right behind you."

"No!" He wasn't looking directly at her, and his tone was more of an order than a comment.

Amy was just as confused as the others. She looked at her husband who lightly shook his head, as if to say, *Don't get involved.* He pulled her back under his arm, as Emily and Mark began a furious stare-down.

"What is your problem, Mark?" Emily burst out at her husband. The Jarly took their cue, heading back to their vehicles to wait it out. The others stayed by, albeit a few steps back.

"I can't…" Mark began, then paused, lowering his voice, taking another breath.

"You can't. What?" Emily confronted him. James glanced around the area. Thankfully, they had stopped at an old, practically abandoned, desert gas station, with no one in sight. Mark didn't say anything back. He just leant back on his jeep, and glanced down at the rocks and dust by her feet. "You can't, what, Mark? Ever since I was sick you've been acting strange. You haven't said two words to me in over an hour. What did I do?" Her voice rose with a shaky undertone.

He looked up then, as her last few words were followed by the beginnings of tears. He pushed away from the Jeep, trying to hug her, but she held her hands up for him to stay away.

"I need you to stay close to me, so I can protect you, Em!" he was clearly upset.

"I'm pregnant, Mark! Not incapacitated" she shot back; the restricted tears now burning the back of her throat.

He let out a frustrated breath. "I know that! I just can't have you away from me. For my own sake."

His honestly cut her to the core. Emily took a step back, looking confused, as her emotions settled. The others must have decided the couple needed some space, because they took a few steps back, and then turned to get back in their cars, leaving Mark and Emily with their Jeep.

With the limited privacy he continued. "Emily, I can't have you away from me, even if it's just in the car behind." He stopped for a few seconds searching for the right words. "Babe, I love you so much and when you were sick back there, I guess it all became too real."

She took a step closer. "What do you mean?" She was calmer now.

"We're having a baby. The last thing you should be doing is heading to a fight. You need to be resting and relaxing, not worrying about getting shot at, or killed. I need you close to me, so I can feel sane and know you're safe." Then he asked something, though he already knew the answer. "Will you stay back, tonight? Stay with the others?" She tried to protest, but he continued trying to convince her. "You could stay with Amelia and the others. If we need a healer, I can heal anyone to some degree, and then we'll bring the rest to you. Then I can really focus, and be at my best, because I'll know you'll be out of harm's way."

That one stung; the ultimate guilt-trip.

"And how will I know you're safe? Mark, you know I can't do that." His pleading eyes did nothing to shake her resolve. Pouting petulantly, he leant back against the jeep, protectively crossing his arms over his chest. One minute she wanted to rip his throat out, the next she couldn't stand his pain. Forcing their bodies against the vehicle, she pulled his face down to look at her.

"I know exactly what is going through your mind. Don't you think I feel the exact same for you?" Then she let everything go. Everything needed to be out in the open. He grabbed her hips, holding her still.

"I'm terrified, Mark. You and our baby, that's all I can think about. Do you really think I could just sit around, while you, my sister and well, my only real family, go and risk your necks while I wait? When I can help?" His brows creased as her words struck a chord. "We stick together; to the end. You cover my back and I'll cover yours. I'm not sitting out while you need a healer."

Mark let out a deep exhausted breath, shaking his head, and looking everywhere but at her. "If anything happens to you, I don't know what I'd..."

She was already shushing him before he could finish, confidently pulling his head back to face her. "Nothing is going to happen to anyone. We are going to get those people out, then the Jarly will take over. We will leave and our family will be safe!"

With nothing more to say, he pulled her shoulders close, and hugged her with more force than ever before. Letting her head drop onto his chest, he kissed her hair, still holding her close.

Amelia rudely leant over and honked the horn, making Amy think she could use a lesson in compassion.

Emily pulled her head back, awkwardly glancing at the people watching them. She wiped her cheeks; as Mark pulled open her door, "Come on. Lets go!"

She jumped in, as Mark ran around the front, yanking open the driver's door, and getting into the seat. Riley pulled out of the lot first and the formation started.

Five minutes later, Riley came on the radio, "Okay guys, in a few minutes we're gonna turn onto Arizona-90, so we need to be a bit more alert. Bring up your roofs. Mark, push the button above the clock on the dash board." They did as he directed. "The entire state is still looking for you, so we'll play it by ear. If we get split up, for any reason, meet at the Mustang Mountain Shell gas station. Does everyone know the place?"

"Yeah, that's just off of highway 82, right?" Rick quickly responded.

"That's the one," Riley agreed.

"Yeah. I know the place," Mark said, loudly.

"Got it," James added.

"Good, so that's the plan."

Just as the short conversation finished, they took the left turn and Emily picked up her husband's hand. Looking at the dashboard, she noted it was 7:47 p.m. They were ahead of schedule, even with the rest stops. Sure enough, ten minutes down the road, Rick and Amy pulled up at a red light, next to a cop cruiser.

"Emily?" Amy whispered, into the radio.

"Don't panic. Just keep looking straight." Emily spoke too quickly, her own pulse pounding in her ears.

Thankfully, the officer was preoccupied with checking the license plate of the Beetle in front of him and not paying attention. When the light turned green, Riley deliberately turned left, away from the cop squad. After a few turns and short cuts, they were back on course and everyone was relieved when they passed the Shell gas station, without any further distractions.

CHAPTER EIGHTEEN

Abel awoke abruptly, feeling the sudden bite of the coarse rope that had been used to bind his feet. His hands were also bound behind his back. His head was covered by a black bag, through which breathing was harsh and labored. His head was throbbing, with a point above his occipital bone feeling tight and tender. The only noise appeared to be coming from his own panicked senses.

Lying on his side, he felt the cold, unyielding, cement floor below. As he began to move, searching for comfort, a calloused hand grabbed his left shoulder, pulling him up into the seated position. His legs were dragged out and bent, so they supported themselves and were stable. He was pushed back, further leaning against a solid wall. Whatever they had used to cover his face released a sour odor that he hadn't previously noted. When it was ripped off with a sudden jerk, the room became bright and blinding.

His eyes were wide, as he took in his surroundings; the lighting blurred and hindered his vision. His shirtsleeve was carelessly ripped aside, and a sudden sharp pain drew his attention to a needle. It withdrew from his skin, instantly heating the immediate area and bruising the flesh. In a matter of seconds, his extremities felt heavy and drawn, his eyes drooped, and his legs sagged gracelessly. As his vision continued to blur, it was as if he could feel the thickening blood pump through his drugged veins. A wave of nausea hit, as his stomach cramped and churned. Feeling week and defeated, he struggled to raise his head to catch a glimpse of his attacker.

Before he could fully rise to see the person hovering over him, he felt the jolt of a heavy fist, smacking hard across his cheekbone. His head painfully hit the tiled wall, further cracking and cutting his skin. His head dropped, as he spat out a bloody breath. Abel blinked a few times, trying to clear his vision, as a far door cracked open. The silence was broken by the careful clap of heavy shoes.

"Enough!" a familiar voice said.

Keeping his head resting on his chest, Abel looked around. The person who had hit him was still hovering nearby. He wore black dress pants and shoes. The floor was the usual grey cement, porous and cracking, and with a drain in the center. From what Abel could see, the walls were tiled white, with molding around the edges. The man who'd spoken continued, walking casually towards Abel, before crouching down in front of him. He looked immaculate in his brown suit and dress shoes. A hand came up, lifting Abel's jaw with ease.

Abel continued to blink, his head heavy with haze, as his gaze focused. "Jacob?" he whispered, his eyes lazily rolling with sleep.

"Abel." Jacob said his name as if he was unimpressed, "You just couldn't help yourself, could you?"

Abel looked at the man who'd hit him and recognized Tom Edwards, who still had his fist clenched, at his side.

"Tom." Abel nodded by way of greeting, condescendingly.

Further scanning the room, he noted three men in white; guns strapped to their chests. "What are you doing to those people?" he asked Jacob. He was furious, even though he couldn't control his facial movements.

Jacob let out a frustrated breath and dropped Abel's head. "That's none of your concern." He stood, taking a step back, and waving over the men in white.

Tom knowingly grinned, stepping out of the way as two of the men took Abel's arms, and yanked him to his feet, so that he was at eye level with Jacob.

"What did you see?" Jacob demanded.

Abel tried, but failed. to smile. "Everything." He started to laugh, but Tom's sudden wrenching occupied his attention. Tom's grip dug into Abel's right shoulder and he punched him in the stomach. Abel released his breath, hunching back over, and gasping for air.

Jacob shook his head, clearly disappointed. "You know, I always liked you. You were a genius! Now look what you've done." Nodding at Tom, he walked out of the room, slamming the door as he left. Abel watched after Jacob, as the two men in white threw him back against the wall, holding him upright. Tom rolled up his sleeves and stepped in front of Abel, consuming the view.

*   *   *

"Abe, when you get this, call me back, right away." John left his third voice mail.

"Still no answer?" Kristine asked, as she passed him another cup of coffee.

John was getting worried now. It wasn't like Abel to not answer his phone. He hit 'End,' tossing his phone back on the dining table. Kristine came to sit next to him. It was 7:50 in the evening now, and Abel had been supposed to call and check in two hours ago. Erik and Tess were already in bed.

"No, nothing!"

Kristine reached across and covered his free hand. "Don't worry, sweetheart. I'm sure he's just busy with errands or something. He'll call back."

John nodded, staring down at the table, even though he knew Abel was always home by six o'clock for his hour-long jog. John creased his brows, tapping his fingers on the table, as he thought. Finally, he pushed away from his seat, grabbed his coat, and slung it over his back. "I think I'm just gonna go round there... Make sure everything's okay."

"You sure?"

"Yeah, it's not like him. I just want to make sure, and if I catch him... Well, then we can talk about our next move."

John had sat up with his wife half the night before, going over what had happened at the meeting, and then Abel's reaction at the office. She agreed that there was something a bit too strange about the sudden pay increase and bonuses.

Kristine stood, taking their cups to the sink, then coming back to pull on his unzipped jacket. "Okay, be safe. Don't let him talk you into anything stupid!" Her brows rose, with sincerity.

"Will do." He leant down, kissing his wife, before turning and walking into the garage.

The drive over to Abel's was short. He lived only six blocks away, in the second last house, on a dead-end street. John rushed to the door and rang the doorbell. He could hear Tess's howl, but no one came to greet him. Knocking three times, he peeked in through the adjacent window and saw Tess running to the door, tail wagging enthusiastically. Finally, John had enough; he searched his keychain for Abel's spare key, letting himself in.

Inside the main entrance, he yelled, "Abe... Abel, it's me!"

Tess rubbed all around his feet, jumping, and then running towards the kitchen and back.

"Where is he, girl?" John whispered in his doggie voice. "Where's Abel?"

Eventually, John followed the dog to an empty food bowl, and her water was only half full too. Letting Tess out to relieve herself, he looked around the house. He couldn't hear anything; the house was silent.

"Abel!" John called, opening the basement door, heading upstairs to the bedroom. The bedroom door was wide open; bed rumpled from Tess and blinds still closed. John walked slowly back downstairs where Tess returned and followed close on his heels. Returning to the kitchen, he filled her food bowl, and Tess barely gave him enough time to pull his hand free, before she attacked it. Deciding to check out the basement, he forced the door back, attempting to block an intrigued Tess, and eventually following the stairs down. Turning on the lights, as he went, he noticed one light was already lit above Abel's workbench. The only thing on it was a small black square.

Turning the box around in his hands for a few seconds, he noticed the latch on the side, and pulled it open to unveil the outline of a key. John stood there, staring at it for a minute, before the light bulb seemed to click in a sudden surge.

"Abe, what are you up to?' He spoke aloud, recognizing the key imprint.

Keeping hold of the black box, John ran back up the stairs, picking up the phone in the kitchen. One last time, he tried to phone Abel's cell but it went straight to voicemail. He listened to Abel's recording, as he stared down at the dog that had completely finished her dinner, and was now loudly guzzling down her water. John cussed aloud and hit 'End,' as Abel's recording advised, "Wait for the beep."

He searched the house for any sign of what Abel might be up to. When he saw the computer screen blinking, he stopped in Abel's office, sat down and moved the mouse. The screen came back to life to reveal that Abel had recently downloaded all of his photos onto the computer, obviously freeing up space on his camera's memory stick. He looked through a few of Abel's last pictures. They were of John's family, when they and Abel had taken Tess to the dog park for a picnic a few months back.

"Abel!" John whispered angrily to the screen, shaking his head. "You promised!"

Forcing himself into the garage, he saw it was empty. Then he knew. On the far left wall there were a few metal shelves, which Abel used for storage. A few tools and items were spread across the floor; with Abel's black backpack missing. John turned and punched the door with frustration. He stormed back into the house to see Tess lie down in the front entrance, staring at the door.

Quickly refilling her food and water, he headed for the front door. "It's okay, girl. I'm gonna find him." He rubbed her ears for a moment, and then backed out of the house, locking the door as he went. As he walked down the driveway and got into his car, he spoke to himself. "And when I find him, I'm gonna kick his fucking boney ass!"

John shifted the car into drive, heading straight home. It was coming up to nine o'clock now, and was unusually cloudy because the only form of light was coming from the street lamps above. Five minutes later, John put the key in the door and let himself in.

"Kristine!" he called, taking off his jacket and hanging it up in the closet. "Kristine!" he repeated looking around.

Heading into the TV room, he found it empty. He continued around the house until he saw her sitting alone at the large dining table they only used when guests were over. He took three steps closer to the room.

"What are you doing in..." He trailed off, when he saw the fear in her eyes. When he finally entered, he saw that she was not alone. There were eight people standing at the other end of the room; four women and four men.

"Who are you?" John ran to his wife's side, pulling her up to her feet, and placing her behind him. "What are you doing in my house?" he yelled.

CHAPTER NINETEEN

The entire group, human and Jarly, found themselves taking fewer breaths, rarely blinking, as they watched the sun go down. Their fears intensified, as they continued their journey into Sierra Vista.

"Okay guys, we have to stop for some gasoline." Caleb spoke into the radio. "Amelia should we break formation and meet at the house?"

"No. We'll stop too and refuel."

"As you wish."

James still couldn't get used to the formal use of speech the brothers tended to prefer; their conversation often feeling stiff and forced.

The first chance they got, Riley pulled into another station. There was a cold nip in the air. Now feeling completely fine, Emily jumped out to stretch her legs. They had stopped halfway between Huachuca City and the Sierra Vista Municipal Airport, Emily hated the fact that they were so close to home, but still couldn't return. She missed their king-sized bed and 'blackout' blinds. She never could sleep comfortably unless the room was pitch-black. Only now did it occur to her that the majority of her well-kept plants would be dead. The summer's sun and lack of water would have finished them off. She let out a groan of frustration.

The men pumped gas into each of the vehicles, as the women all went to the bathroom, apart from Amelia and Isobel, who stayed in the car. This gas station was larger than most, being attached to the far end of a small Wal-Mart – the bathrooms were actually in the store.

The men paid at the pump, and they all got into their vehicles to wait. After starting their cars, they quietly pulled them over, to park out of the direct light and out of view.

"Amelia, Mark!" James sharply spoke into the small radio.

"What?" Amelia blurted back, as Mark turned to the Mustang parked next to him.

James was turned around in his seat and staring out the rear window. The others followed his gaze back, to the gas pump, where two cop cars were refueling. "Seriously!" he yelled back at them, in frustration.

They didn't dare breathe, as a million of Mark's fears rushed through his head.

"What do we do? The girls are inside; they don't have their crappy-ass disguises," Rick said quickly.

Amelia watched the police officers, as their drivers continued to pump, then started thinking strategically, when one of their partners got out from the farthest car and started to head into the Wal-Mart entrance. Not waiting for orders, Mark jumped out of the jeep, his baseball cap pulled down lower than normal, and headed for the entrance. He kept his head low, and Rick and James followed shortly after.

As Mark reached the entrance, he pulled open the door just as the other police officer was leaving. Mark held his breath and kept his head low, as they bumped shoulders.

"Hey, sorry 'bout that," the officer apologized.

"No problem." Mark didn't make eye contact, as he swiftly continued into the store.

James and Rick had stopped, as if in a conversation, their heads hung low too, as the officer passed them and got back into his cruiser. Moving faster, and then pulling the doors wide open, they eventually followed after Mark. Just as they turned the corner, they looked over their shoulders and simultaneously cussed as the two other officers came in to pay.

* * *

"Em, you sure you're okay?" Amy brought up the last rest stop confrontation, while they washed their hands. The girls were the only ones in the large bathroom, which had crumbling, blue-tiled walls, with a curved entrance, rather than a door.

Emily flicked her wet hands in the sink. "Really, it was nothing. Mark's just worried about me and the baby." She walked over and grabbed a napkin. "He wants me to sit out tonight."

Amy considered it for a minute, and then moved to stand by her sister, resting her hand on her shoulder. She always did this when she had something serious to say. "Maybe Mark's right? Maybe you should sit this one out."

Emily was already shaking her head, turning to throw the brown napkin into the waste bin. "Not a chance! We're doing this together. That's the only option."

Amy wanted to protest, but Emily started to grin. "Don't make me make it an order!" She raised her brows, clearly joking.

Amy squinted at her big sister. "You know, sometime you can be really stubborn!"

"Look who's talking."

Julia laughed at the two sisters, as Mark ran around the corner.

"Mark!" Emily was surprised, and looked around, though she knew the other stalls were empty. They were still well within the boundaries of the ladies' restroom.

"We gotta go," was his only reply. He grabbed his wife's hand, and practically dragged her back into the store.

They turned the corner, running into James and Rick. Amy and Julia went to stand by them, confused and concerned. All three men were looking around, over their shoulders, and down each aisle. Of course, the bathrooms were at the opposite end of the store. In hindsight, Mark kicked himself; the women's restroom being the best hiding spot against four male officers.

"What? What is it?" Emily directed her question at her husband, but James answered for him.

"Three cops inside. One out."

"They were refueling and then they headed in. One said he had to grab some things," Mark added. For the first time in the past week, it was Julia who cussed the loudest. The group stayed together, glancing around, and then Emily gave her orders.

Spinning around to see the two couples behind her, she said, "Okay, split up. We're too obvious. Get to the cars."

They nodded and Rick pulled Amy into the first aisle, as James backtracked with Julia, heading down the previous one. Mark pulled Emily to his right side, so she was next to the wall. They continued along the main aisle, while the other customers paid no attention. Only two aisles from the exit, a tall, blond, police officer stepped right in front of James and Julia, picking up one brand of shampoo, and reading the specifications. Trying to play it cool, James rested his arm over Julia's shoulders, turning down the next aisle. Near the end of the next aisle, Amy and Rick were practically running. They took a sharp right, and Amy ran straight into another officer, falling backwards.

"I'm so sorry." He bent down, reaching for her hand, but Rick got there first, pulling her up to her feet. The cop was clearly a man who took care of himself; his uniform did nothing to disguise his broad shoulders, and V-waistline. He smiled genuinely and his heavily tanned forehead creased. "Hey, don't I know you from somewhere?"

Her face reddened as she dropped her head, letting her hair fall forward. "No, I don't think so." She tried to casually smile. Rick pulled her under his arm, tight into his ribs, making the officer look over.

"Both of you." He looked back and forth. "I'm sure I know you from somewhere."

At the other end of the aisle, with no one else in sight, Mark and the others had met back at the exit. They waited, watching nervously. Mark and James took a step towards the officer, who had his back to them, but Emily grabbed their forearms, holding them back.

Rick shook his head, trying to look indifferent. "Sorry, can't say we've met." Then he smiled, taking a casual step around him, with his wife held tightly. "Have a good night, Officer," he muttered, not turning back around, as he and Amy made their way to the end of the aisle.

The others had already backed out into the parking lot, as the officer stood there frozen, clearly still trying to remember. He watched, as they made their way out of the store and into the dark parking lot. The two police cars had moved from the pump to the opposite side of the parking lot.

Emily's team rushed back into their vehicles, as Amelia's voice sounded on the radio. "Everyone okay?"

Emily reached down and took the walkie-talkie, holding it close to her lips. "We're fine, just another close call. Let's get the hell outta here."

"I'm getting sick of these close calls," Mark muttered under his breath, as she released the talk button. "I've never seen so many cops on patrol, in my life." She dropped the radio into her lap, reaching over to take his hand, as the group pulled back onto the highway, heading closer to their destination.

CHAPTER TWENTY

Abel's eyes fluttered open with a jolt, as his pant leg snagged on a broken tile. His limp body was being dragged by the wrist, to a destination unknown. His head bobbed and fell as he discreetly took in his surroundings. He quickly recognized the outline of the office basement, but grew confused as the basement should have ended. Instead, it merely opened up into another wide hallway. The walls were caked in clay mud and the tiled floors had fallen away to reveal a dirt track. He cringed, as the odd sharp stone or jagged rock scraped along his bare lower back and the underside of his legs.

A sudden turn had them stop and his eyes closed, feigning sleep, as he listened intently. The two guards let go of his wrists, dropping him harshly to the ground below. He focused on his breathing, remaining constant and steady.

"Pass me the fucking key." One spoke to the other.

"I thought you had it," the other responded, exasperated.

With a loud huff, the first guarded muttered, "Fuck sake," under his breath, before banging loudly on the door before them.

Roughly six long seconds passed before the heavy metallic door clinked and rattled, as it opened from the inside.

"Where are your keys?" demanded a harsh woman's voice; older than the others'.

"Must have left them upstairs," the first arrogantly muttered, as the two reached down and proceeded to drag Abel into the open space.

"Who's this?"

Abel gave himself away, when he visibly winced, as a pointed toe poked at his left bruised ribs. His eyes grew wide and accusing, eventually locking with that of a middle-aged brunette. Her lab coat fell to knee-length, and he saw that it was splattered with red splotches, as she bent over, hovering, her eyes scrutinizing. Her narrow pointed nose and thick glasses only accentuated the deep creases in her forehead and the smeared red lipstick; spread halfway across her yellow teeth.

Glancing past her, Abel noticed the familiar rows of metallic tables, and reflective surfaces consuming the room. Even from the floor, he could see the odd dangling hand and blood-soaked ceiling.

"Dr. Hanby, his name's Abel. We caught him snooping around upstairs. Tom wants us to stow him here for a bit, until we figure out what to do with him." The second guard was much younger than the first, though he had a military style haircut and attitude to match.

"Fuck you," Abel managed to whisper, as he tried to steady and lift himself up onto his elbows.

"What'd you say?" The first guard stepped up. He was shorter than six foot, but what he lacked in height, he made up in severity; his shoulders were broad and hunched. His heavy boot came down hard on Abel's chest, forcing him back down, and causing his head to slam into the concrete floor. "How about you shut the fuck up, before I use my boot to further fuck up that pretty little face of yours?"

"Get him over there," Hanby ordered, not amused by the situation.

The boot lifted, allowing Abel to gasp for breath, before a

thick, black-fabric bag pulled over his head, instantly blocking his prying view. He tried to struggle, but his body was too weak and broken. As the two lifted him by the knees and shoulders, they purposefully slammed him onto a nearby exam table, quickly strapping him down with the attached leather cuffs.

As they backed away, one called back with a chuckle, "Oh, Tom wants you back upstairs within the hour; some debriefing or something. Have fun, Doc."

The door slammed, quickly followed by Dr. Hanby turning the lock and muttering under her breath. In darkness, Abel could now focus on the heavy breathing scattered around the room. The rhythmic click of Dr. Hanby's heels slapping on the concrete did nothing to calm the others. Whimpering and moaning now filled the silence. The familiar clink of metallic objects being picked up from their tray stiffened Abel's spine. He intently listened, as her shoes continued past his table, stopping near his feet; her attention clearly on another patient.

Abel pulled at his restraints and yelled, "Untie me, you bitch!" his harsh words echoing off of the near walls.

With an exasperated huff, the doctor lightly placed her tool onto the table next to his. The silence further broke, as Abel strained against his restraints; every tug tightened and cracked the leather bindings. Suddenly, he felt a cold clammy hand reach to his right sleeve, raising it up and pushing it past his elbow. He tried to pull from her reach, but a surprisingly firm grasp of long narrow fingers restricted around his upper arm, holding him still. He paused, resigned to his fate, as a pinch of a needle broke through his skin.

Within seconds, his eyelids grew heavy, as his head dropped back onto the metal below. The fabric covering his head lifted and fell, as his breath crew labored. A thick tingling took over his extremities, as each muscle grew stiff and heavy. He was unable to move an inch, and his only sense of relaxation came with her departing footsteps.

As she returned to the other poor soul, Abel heard the clinch of the metallic tool returning to the doctor's grasp. Only when the loud screams began from the young women across from him, did Abel finally allow himself to back away into the darkness and give in to the need to sleep.

CHAPTER TWENTY-ONE

"All right, guys, we're gonna keep south on Buffalo Soldier trail. Keep close with us, and we should be at the house in about thirty minutes," Amelia said over the radio.

"Where exactly is the house? In relation to the office building," James asked.

"It's about a ten-minute drive. Close enough for a quick rescue, but remote enough to be undetectable." It was Riley who chirped up, this time.

The drive seemed longer than thirty minutes, as they made their way along some back roads south of downtown Sierra Vista. Eventually, they reached a black gate that appeared to be the entrance of a large park, rather than a residence. The others waited, as Riley reached out the driver's window, punching in a combination that opened the electronic gates. Thankfully, the gate also automatically closed behind Damon and Caleb's truck.

The path continued under the shade of what appeared to be forest overgrowth. They followed the path another two minutes, before it came to a two-story, ultra-modern house, surrounded by trees; the front two floors made primarily of glass.

"It's beautiful," Emily whispered, not taking her eyes away.

Riley continued past and around the house, into a previously unseen underground parking lot. It was amazing. Directly behind the house, a ramp appeared to be automated, and the gravel track dropped in a solid form. The roof appeared to be the garden. All five vehicles made their way down, as the room lit up, and they parked in a line next to one another, with the Aston Martin at the far end. Riley got out of the car, pointing his keychain at the open ramp. With a clunk, the ramp rose, and locked into place, leaving the people under cover again.

Getting out of their cars, the members of the group made their way to the only door at the end of the garage. Riley held the door wide, as the others followed Amelia up the metal staircase, and into the new home. They entered through a door in the kitchen and saw that the house was even more beautiful inside, than it was out. The entire place was decorated in high-end fabrics, with a lighter, eye-pleasing pallet. Each room flowed into the next beautifully; open and welcoming. The entire main floor revealed an open floor plan, with no dividing walls. Added emphasis drew the nakedness to the extravagant artwork on each wall. Various primal animals, in their natural habitats, depicted a wide range of colors and awe.

Amelia cut everyone's gawking short. "Okay, there are a number of showers upstairs. I'm sure most of you won't protest about sharing," she said with a grin. "You have twenty minutes to freshen up, before we get to work."

By the time everyone had showered and returned to the main level, the atmosphere was purely businesslike. Amelia and Riley had a number of blueprints and papers scattered all over the kitchen table. Caleb and his brother were sitting watching T.V., while Isobel was surfing the Internet on a nearby computer. The group gradually collected around the dining table.

"Okay, so what's the plan?" Emily asked, while absently drying her hair with a small towel.

"All right," Amelia answered, looking down at her wristwatch. "It's almost eight o'clock. Here are the general blueprints for the building. There will be guards here and here." She spun the page around, so it was directly in front of Emily, and then she pointed to the main building exit. "The thing is, we have no idea what physical changes they have made over the years. This blueprint is from the original construction ten years ago. Now that they have our technology working in there, everything could be backwards."

"Whoa, hold up." James raised his hand dramatically. "They have your technology?"

"Well," Amelia stole a sideways glance at Riley, "I'll get to that in a minute. There are also locked doors at the end of each main hall, and a bunch of coded locks heading into the basement."

"So, what did you have in mind?" Emily asked the experts.

Amelia didn't answer straight away. She leant back, her face frustrated, seemingly having a non-verbal conversation with Riley. A few seconds later, he rolled his eyes, and nodded.

They both leant back on the table. "Okay, I think the only chance we have to be sure of the layout, is the man we were speaking about earlier. He has all the codes and he may even have a spare key. If he cooperates, more lives may be saved and our time will be used more effectively."

"But you were worried he may not cooperate," Mark said, pulling a standing Emily down, to sit on his lap.

Riley was already nodding, as Amelia went on. "Yes, he is a scientist. He has no idea about the truth." She lightly chuckled at the irony. "He, along with most others, has surely heard the news. He will assume you are all mad and might turn against you, endangering your lives."

Emily's head lowered, as she considered that fact. Running through the blueprints once more, she made her mind up. "This whole scenario is based on the fact that he doesn't know anything of the truth. He sounds like a fairly intelligent guy; if we tell him the truth..." She gestured around the table. "Or show him, maybe he will see the need to help us?"

"It is ultimately your choice." Amelia shrugged.

Emily took a moment to think. Looking around the table, she then turned back to Amelia. "I say we go meet with him."

Amelia nodded once. "Very well. Isobel?" she called over her shoulder, before turning back to continue; "Okay, so these are the keys to your new vehicles. You should stick close together." She passed Mark the keys that went to two black Lexus RX350 Sports Luxuries. He took one, and then passed the other set of keys down to James. "Okay, as Amadeus said, we are forbidden to intervene, but we have been given permission to wait nearby. When the rescue is completed, we are allowed to show ourselves."

"So can you explain now? What's this about them having your technology?" James returned to his questioning.

"It's not much. Your government has been stealing and manipulating the odd piece of technology, whenever they came across it." Riley's voice grew saddened. "Obviously, there are consequences with any attempt at contact and sharing. We've lost a lot."

"From the heat being generated from the office building, we believe the biggest thing of ours that they are utilizing, is our rapid space increaser." Amelia said.

"It's kinda cool. You set up this mini-device and it burrows its way through the immediate area, to the perimeters you pre-set." Riley was addressing their confused faces. "It creates a lot of heat, similar to what we are detecting, but you can theoretically create a space the size of the Grand Canyon, within minutes."

"What do you mean when you say you'll show yourselves? How?" Rick asked.

Riley laughed without humor. "Oh, you'll know when you see it."

"You know..." Emily started to speak and then paused. "You don't really sound like the others. You talk different."

"What do you mean?" Riley looked blank.

After a beat, Isobel actually laughed, from the far corner. "She's saying you don't sound formal like the rest of us. Emily, Riley has just spent a lot more time on Earth than the rest of us. Plus he's younger."

"And he has a horrible habit of largely preferring American action movies," Amelia added, grinning.

Riley smiled back at her, knowingly. "Nothing wrong with a few explosions and bad catch-phrases."

Rolling her eyes, Amelia continued. "Back to work. These are maps that will direct you to the building, as close as you can get, then you must go by foot. We have packed small backpacks for each of you."

Damon dropped six identical packs on the table, as Amelia passed them around. "Each has two compact .45 auto handguns, small explosives, three rounds of bonus ammunition, two smoke bombs, a hunting knife, a Swiss Army knife, and basic medical supplies, in case Emily or Mark have to wait until you leave, to assist."

All seemed to raise their brows with each addition to their supplies list. Emily and Mark remained completely focused on the outcome of tonight. Everything was going to change, hopefully for the better, and with no casualties.

"What are those?" James blurted out, reaching for one of the green, spike-like objects, no larger than a bullet, which were piled in one corner. Damon quickly took the object out of James's palm as he fed it into a gun cartridge.

"These are stunners. Similar to the darts we used to take you down when you first reached our camp." Damon smirked, clearly amused, as he looked down and continued his task.

Amelia cleared her throat, drawing back their attention. "Yes, I was just getting to that. Obviously, we didn't come to this point today to encourage the general slaughter and murder of many individuals that are following their own orders." Reaching for one of the objects, she held it out for the group to see. "Like Damon said, these are stunners." She lightly pinched the sides with a click, which shot three thin spikes forward. The spikes were almost as long as the bullet-shaped object itself. "These antennae will penetrate any armor your opponents may have. They will imbed just past their epidermis, sending a form of radio frequency that will affect their nervous system. It will not affect any major organ function, but it will render them paralyzed and unconscious for at least three hours." She placed the stunner back on the table. "The time the person is unconscious varies from individual to individual."

Emily was already nodding, deep in thought, her eyes trained on the table. "I want everyone to use the stunners as much as possible." Looking around the room, she settled her gaze on Amelia, "We've been through enough, and the last thing we need to add to the list is an unnecessary body count."

"Agreed." Amelia stood then, with Riley, causing the others to look up. "Well, now is better than any to get going, don't you think?"

Emily stood, pulling her pack into place on the center of her back. "Definitely."

"Okay, Riley and I will accompany you to the scientist's house, but then we must let you go on, alone."

"That's fine," Emily said, as the others got to their feet, heading for the door. As they walked into the entranceway, Damon, Caleb, and Isobel were waiting.

"Good luck." The brothers rested their hands on the guy's shoulders, as they hugged the women. "We will be waiting at the finish-line for you," Damon added, with a smile.

"Here." Isobel passed two sheets of paper to Emily, as Mark

opened the door and waited. "These are directions to his house from here. Good luck." She hugged Emily one more time, before walking into the other room. Even aliens get emotional.

"Pick us up from his address in one hour," Amelia ordered the brothers, as they nodded, serious now, and closed the door.

Finally, Amelia and Riley followed the group out to their cars, which were not hidden in the underground parking, but were directly out in front of the main door. The brothers must have brought them around, while the showers were occupied. Mark got into the driver's seat of one, with Emily in the passenger side. Rick and Amy had chosen to join them this time, as Amelia and Riley accompanied James and Julia.

Starting the smooth engine, Mark headed back down the long driveway. Amy leant forward, pulling on the back of Emily's seat. "So, what's this scientist's name anyway?"

Emily lifted the sheet from her lap, glancing down at the name, and holding it close to her face, as she read aloud; "Dr. Jonathan Stark," she said, smiling back at her sister, before turning back around in her seat.

CHAPTER TWENTY-TWO

"Who are you?" John repeated.

Emily raised her hands up and took a step forward. "Please don't be afraid, we mean you no harm, we're here because we need your help."

John scanned her face. "I know you. You're the woman from that hotel wedding party. Emily, right?"

She nodded slowly. Obviously, he had followed the news, meaning he would already be skeptical of what she had to say.

John glanced around the room, looking more closely at their faces. "You! You two are Rick and Amy. You were the ones getting married. And you... you must be James and Julia. Everyone is looking for you guys." He trailed off, taking a step back, and pushing his wife closer to the door.

"Please John, you need to listen to us. We need your help," Amy insisted.

"Get out of my house. Now!" he yelled, taking another step towards the door.

With a frustrated breath, Emily suggested, "Julia, show them. The chairs."

Julia nodded, thrusting her hands out. Kristine gasped, clinging tight to her husband, as Julia seemed to go up in flames, which radiating and pulsated throughout her entire body, within a heartbeat. Then the light pooled into her hand and she motioned with her fingers, Kristine let out a light scream, as John and her chairs pushed out from the table so they could sit down.

"Please sit," Amelia requested.

The intruding group had taken the seats at their end of the table, and were now staring up, waiting.

"What are you?" John glanced around the room.

"Please John, we don't have much time. Sit and we'll tell you everything we know," Emily answered.

Feeling outnumbered and with no real choice, John nodded to his wife, as they sat in their chairs, close together, staring at the others.

"We are the known as the Jarly. We don't come from Earth." Amelia stated the obvious.

"Only, she and I are. These others have been trained and are helping us with our mission," Riley interrupted.

"What mission?" Kristine asked, before John could.

"Our government has chosen this time and place to make contact with humans, and hopefully to make our existence globally known," Amelia answered.

"So, what does this have to do with us?" John asked.

"Only you, John. Your office building has recently been labeled as condemned, correct?" She waited for his confused nod. "Don't you think it's a bit strange that it's now swarming with military commanders and is under constant surveillance?"

"There was a chemical spill," John answered.

Riley shook his head. "This is a lie, John."

"What are you talking about?" John burst back, not getting the answers he really wanted.

Kristine gasped as Riley's third eyelid closed over. "Abel." Riley stared down at the table.

John and Kristine quickly turned to him. "What do you know about Abel? Where is he?" John asked, yelling the last question.

"I see him in a room. He's badly hurt." Riley's eyelid retracted. "If you want to help your friend, you have to trust us, and help us first!"

"Why should I? How do I know it isn't you that has him?"

Mark grew ever more frustrated, slamming his hands onto the table, and staring at John. "Our names and faces have been plastered across the news, saying we have be infected with chemicals, and by now should be on our death beds. Look at us." Raising his hands, he pointed to the others. "We are the victims here, just as much as you are. Half of our friends are trapped in the basement of that building, along with your friend. They are being tortured and tested, because when these guys came down," he gesturing to Riley and Amelia, "THEY saw. The military took whoever they could, and they have been hunting us ever since."

"Why?" John cowered away from Mark's intense stare.

Emily lightly brushed Mark's arm, as a reminder to stay calm.

James muttered, "Why do they do anything? They're curious. They want to know what the 'aliens' have done to us, and why we are so special. They have to be one step ahead of everyone else. Get all the info at any cost. Of course they want to cover up any trace of this stuff, so they created a ridiculous cover up and manhunt."

John waited for a minute, thinking, before something occurred to him. "Wait, you said they're in the basement of my office building?" He began to slowly shake his head, confused. "I've been down there. It's completely undeveloped, with a small room they use to store chemical supplies. Definitely not big enough for fifty-plus people, let alone a laboratory."

Amelia had already thought of her explanation. "We have technologies advanced beyond yours. Finding the right spot is easy."

Riley interrupted, absently spinning his car keys on his right index finger. "We have devices that can create deep underground tunnels and finish off rooms in a matter of minutes. It's like a shock wave moving the earth; creating solid, secure paths as it goes. If it's used efficiently, they could have other rooms, floors, and tunnels down there to hold hundreds captive, while they study them."

"So how did they get this technology?" Kristine asked.

"This is not our first visit, or first cover-up." Amelia intervened on the conversation. "Previous failed attempts, over the past century, have led to our technology being adapted; advancing your own abilities and materials."

"Okay, so why do you need me? What can I do?" John asked, doubtfully.

"You worked at that office for over a year. You know your way around much faster than we do. You have keys and security codes..." Emily answered. "We need you to guide us to the basement entrance quickly, so we can get in and out, hopefully before too many are alerted."

"Then what?" John asked.

"When these six complete this task, our leaders have given us permission to make global contact. There's more to it, obviously, but basically this is our last chance. If we... You fail, we're ordered to leave and never come back."

John thought this was ridiculous. Either they really were who they said they were, or it was a bunch of crazy people, with admittedly unearthly abilities, that had broken into his house.

Before John could answer, Kristine was speaking. "No, it's too dangerous. We have young children to think about. If you're telling the truth, it means there is going to be a lot of trained men... killers, who are going to be guarding the place."

"Kristine." John started to speak, trying to calm her down, but she couldn't stop.

"No, John. It's too risky."

"What about Abel? What if they are telling the truth? I can't just leave him there." He thought for a few seconds, and then turned back to the other end of the table, to the people that were watching silently. "What can I do?"

Kristine let out an angry breath, kicked her chair out from under her, and ran out of the room. A few seconds later, the bedroom door slammed loudly. John closed his eyes, his head dropping.

"I'm sorry, John. Believe me, if I thought we could have done this without getting you and your family involved, we would have." Emily was sympathetic.

John started to shake his head, speaking as he raised it. "I understand. With my help, hopefully we can get in and out fast and with fewer casualties."

Emily's brows creased as she thought, and then she started to shake her head, lowering her hands to her stomach. "John, I do appreciate your help because we do need it, but when it comes to actually going inside, I'd like you to stay behind." He opened his mouth to protest, but she quickly continued. "It'll give your wife peace of mind. And she's right, you do have a family to think about, just like I do."

"Emily, I understand your concern, but my best friend is in there, and we don't have enough time for me to tell you all the security codes and draw a map of the hidden hallways. I'm coming in with you, or you're on your own."

Emily gawked at him, frustrated, but eventually she shrugged. "I guess we don't have a choice then." She turned to Julia and Amy. "When we get inside, you two will need to focus on protecting John, if that's not too much to concentrate on."

"Of course not," Amy replied, turning and smiling at him.

"Okay, we have a deal, but when we are inside, I'm in charge, John. Nothing stupid – don't try and be a hero. We can protect ourselves, but I can't be worrying about you the entire time too.

But also know this, this is my family, John." She gestured around the table. Then her gaze fell back on him, so intense, he even leaned back in his seat. "If you do anything stupid, it's their lives before yours, you hear me? You follow my orders, agreed?"

John couldn't help but cringe form her gaze, and he nodded. "Agreed. Don't worry about me."

Emily relaxed back into her seat, and looked around. "Okay, let's get to work."

They discussed strategies for over forty-five minutes. John informed them that he and Abel had been moved from the building and had not been there in a week. He repeated that he had no idea what was going on, but that Abel had looked more into it. Though he had promised not to, Abel had gone to investigate.

"Do you still have your key?" Amelia asked.

John shook his head, but then something in his pocket caught his attention. "No, but I found this at Abel's." He threw the box down to their end of the table. "He must have made an imprint before he handed the keys back to Jacob." Amelia examined the imprint, and then passed it over to Riley. With an unspoken order, he quickly got up from the table and left the room, going out to the cars.

Ignoring the eyes watching after Riley, Amelia continued: "Okay, so you take the rear entrance?"

"Yeah, there will probably be no danger there. That's probably the door Abel would have used too. The door is rarely used and from what I've seen, all the security is at the front of the building. Though, if they got a hold of Abe, they might be more diligent. They might have the back covered now too," John added; his gaze distant.

"Okay, so once you're inside, then what?" Amelia asked.

"Then we have to go down a small hallway, past a door, and then we're into a main hallway. It does have rotating cameras at each end." He pointed to one of the blueprints, as he continued. "Here, every thirty minutes they rotate to face the opposite way, so either we wait, or find a way to cover them up." The group sat focused, following his every word, and watching his fingers as he continued to direct. "Then, we head for the right hall. At the end will be a locked door. Past that, straight ahead, is the staircase up and down, and then to the left is a narrow corridor with the elevator and a small security room. When we get to the elevator, we have to pray that the security code hasn't been changed."

"You need a code to work the elevator?"

"Yeah, if that's been changed, we'll have to take the staircase, but it's metal and echoes terribly. If anyone was alerted, we would be easy targets."

"Okay, so where is the power uplink for the elevator?" Emily asked.

John scanned the blueprints, quickly, and then pointed. "Here, it's right next to it, in the small security office."

"Okay, when we get inside, I want you guys..." Emily looked at James and Julia, "to set a small explosive to go off once we get down there. Hopefully, that will stop anyone from surprising us, then we can deal with the stairs on the way up."

"Good decision," Amelia agreed.

"Once we're down there, then what?" Mark prompted.

Once again, John used his finger to trace their path. "Well, the elevators open to a small room, only five meters or so wide. At the end, there is a glass window and another security door. There should be another room behind that, which we just use for storage. After that, if they have used your technology to increase the space, then I have no idea."

"Okay, well, from the sounds of it, you could probably get down into the basement within a few minutes. Once the cameras turn away, you can come up under them and spray paint the screens," Amelia suggested.

"Yeah, like I said, that's the back hallway. There are other halls that connect to the elevator, so this entrance shouldn't be monitored that much. Hopefully, anyone who is paying attention will think the camera has broken, or something."

"Good, so once inside, you head down, blow the elevator, get into the back room, and find the people. Then how will you get them out safely?" Amelia was asking Emily, this time.

Emily had to think about it for a minute, as the others waited in silence. "Well, either way, we're going to draw attention eventually. I'm guessing once those elevator doors open, the entire building will be alerted. I'm hoping we can get our way into those back rooms and somehow fight our way back up those stairs." She turned to her husband, placing her hand on his arm, which was resting on the table. "Once we're on the main floor with everyone, as long as we're close enough to an exit wall, I don't really care if we have to blow ourselves out."

She smiled at Mark, and he grinned back. To Amelia she said, "So, what about you? How will we know when it's all over?"

Amelia smiled. "We will be waiting in the front of the building, as long as you get as many of them out as you can, and immobilize the guards. When you see us, it will all be over, and we can take over from there. You'll return to the safe house with as many of the hostages as you can, and rest. We will have a bus waiting at the place where you leave the vehicles."

Emily nodded once, took a deep breath, and looked around the room. "Everyone ready?" she asked, getting up from her chair. The others joined her, as Riley came back in the room.

"Here." He passed a fresh new key into John's hand.

John was amazed and he glanced from the key to the stranger. "How did you…" But he stopped when Riley grinned and winked.

"Perfect." Emily smiled, as she and the others began walking into the main room. "Let's go."

Just as they got to the door, John began to hesitate. "Wait." They all turned to face him. "Let me just say goodbye to my wife."

"Of course, we'll be waiting outside. You have five minutes, okay?"

John was already nodding, as he made his way back into the house, turning the corner.

* * *

"Kristine?" John called, peeking his head around the door. Then he opened it wide, as he took a hesitant step in.

She was sitting on the edge of their bed, her back facing him, and her head hanging as she quietly wept. John closed the door and walked around the bed, stopping right in front of her, as he dropped to his knees. She didn't raise her head, when he placed both his hands on her knees and waited. Brushing away tears, she let out a heavy breath, and finally raised her head to stare at her apologetic husband.

"Just go, John," she whispered through defeated tears. He shuffled forward, so that his body was against the bed, with her legs spreading on either side of him. Reaching for her face, he hesitated as she clearly stiffened, and then he brushed her tear-stained, tangled hair out of her face.

John cupped her red cheeks as he spoke, not blinking. "Kristine, I love you, but I have to do this. It's Abel we're talking about. He needs me." John was almost pleading for her to understand.

"I need you!" she practically growled. "Your kids need you." Kristine's face tightened and she closed her eyes, trying to pull away from his grip. "John, they could kill you. You have no idea if these people are even telling the truth!"

"I believe them, Kristine. They know things, they have answers, and Abel IS missing," he replied, unmoving. After a beat, he leant up until their faces almost touched. "Please," he pleaded, closing his eyes. "Please, trust me on this one. I'll be fine."

More silence came, until Kristine pulled out of his grip and surprised him by trapping his face between her own clammy hands. This time, instead of a sniveling wife, she appeared controlled and commanding. "You come back to me, Jonathan Stark. You hear me? You come back to your family."

She let go of his face, almost snapping it away, as she leant back. Fresh tears ran down her cheeks, as he smiled at her. He got to his feet, but kept their eyes level. "I promise. I'll be back before you can even miss me."

Glancing over at the bedside, she said, "You've got three hours. If I don't hear from you, I'm calling the police and telling them everything."

His only response was to straighten and nod.

John could see she was on the verge of panic again, as her words came, her body shaking. "I love you."

He took her face and kissed her with force. Her tears made their kiss wet. "I love you, too." Then he walked out of the room.

Kristine let out a held breath, and her neck craned around, watching for him long after he had left.

* * *

As Emily and the others waited in the driveway, their true feelings gradually came to light.

"Can we trust him?" Rick asked, leaning against the hood of the nearest car.

"I think we can." It was Mark who had spoken, though he didn't sound confident.

"If he truly wants to get his friend back, he won't let us down,"

James suggested. "He needs us more than we need him, at this point. He already gave us a general breakdown after all..." Turning to Emily, James began to whisper. "We could just take the key and leave without him? The combination locks have probably already been changed. He'll just slow us down anyway."

Emily was already shaking her head. "No, we made an agreement and I fully intend to stick to it. He will come in handy and if we can avoid blowing the place up, trying to reach these people, I'd rather do that." She grinned at James, taking some of the sting out of his shot-down proposal.

Riley had run to one of the cars, and now returned with another backpack. He pulled it carefully off his shoulder, passing it to Amelia.

"Okay." She commanded their attention, as she pulled out some black fabric from the unzipped bag. "These are called Zats; they are basically like bulletproof vests, only light-weight and flexible. Unfortunately, we don't have the pant version available to us, but at least this will cover your chests." She began to pass them around, holding an extra in her free hand. "They will stop anything fast-moving, like a bullet, but won't protect against knives or large explosives. We know it's hard to keep a full shield up while concentrating the flow of energy on attacks. So put them on under your clothes, they will definitely help."

The men in the group didn't worry about appearances. They swiftly pulled their shirts off right there in the driveway, donning their new protective material. It felt more like sticky Spandex, than a protective shield. Pulling their t-shirts back on, the women kept hold of theirs, clearly waiting to change in the car. Just then, John rejoined the group. Amelia passed him the remaining Zat, and told him to put it on under his shirt.

Emily pulled Mark aside, and they walked to the end of the driveway, out of earshot. She felt guilty that she hadn't brought

this up before. "Mark, I feel stupid, given the timing and everything, but are you going to be able to handle this?"

"What do you mean?"

"Well, sweetie, you did swear a pretty serious oath to respect
all human life, do no harm, heal at all cost…" She spun her wrist,
spreading her fingers as if to say, *Yada Yada Yada.*

Mark surprised Emily by throwing his head back in pleasant
laughter. "Really? You ask me this now?" She shrugged, apologetically. "Baby, I also swore to guide and protect you. Right now,
that's the oath I'm sticking to." He trailed off, clearly thinking. "I'll
admit, I'm not thrilled at the prospect, but if it's my life…your
lives…" She held her breath, as he spayed his fingers across her
stomach. "…Against theirs, there's nothing I won't do to protect
my family. Nothing." His intense gaze wouldn't falter, as a cold
shiver ran down her stiffened spine. He then grinned, adding
humor where it was much needed. "Plus, they're bad guys and
doctors are allowed to blur the lines, when it comes to bad guys
trying to torture and kill their loved ones." He winked, stepping
back, and re-joining the group.

"Okay, you four take one car and follow us." Mark gestured to
the two couples, as he spoke. They nodded, splitting into their
teams. Mark took the driver's seat again, while Emily got into the
passenger side.

As John opened the rear door, Riley stopped him. "I hope
you find your friend." Then he took a step back, as John smiled
without humor, nodding as he scrambled into the rear seat, and
slammed the door.

"Good luck," Amelia loudly whispered, through Mark's
open window.

"You too!" Emily called back.

Mark turned the keys, igniting the engine, and he pulled out
onto the street. Rick was driving the car behind, and the two

women in the backseat turned in their seats, as they watched Riley and Amelia waving good-bye.

Turning the corner out of sight, Amy and Julia dragged up their backpacks, and began searching through them, pulling out random objects. Amy pulled out the gun holder, and fastened it into place around her waist and thighs; placing her two stunner-filled guns into either side. She put the extra ammunition into one of her baggy, side pockets, which could easily fit twice as much. Julia did the same, placing the bullets in one side-pocket and the smoke bombs and medical supplies in the other. She slid her hunting knife into the leather holder, on top of the right gun, leaving the small Swiss Army knife to fit snugly in her back pocket.

When they were ready, Amy lifted her husband's bag and took out his supplies, while Julia began passing James his. The drive only took twenty minutes, before Mark pulled up to the designated spot.

"That's Abel's Mustang!" John yelled, from the back seat. Without another word, he quickly yanked the door wide, running to the abandoned Mustang, where he glanced into the windows, and searched the area.

"He's really in there, isn't he?" John asked, disappointed, as Emily and Mark began to put on their gun holsters and packed their pockets with supplies.

"Yes," Emily replied, solemnly.

John nodded, turning to watch them get ready. John saw Mark place his second gun into the left holster. "Do you have another one?"

"Do you know how to shoot?" James asked, walking up with his waiting group.

"I've shot before. I used to hunt with my dad when I was younger."

The group turned questioningly to Emily, who was on the far

side of the car. She stared at John for a minute, calculating, before she turned to the group. "Can anyone spare a gun?"

"Here." Amy pulled her extra gun from the left holster. "I prefer to use a knife, anyway."

John nodded, taking the gun and extra bullets she passed him. He lifted his shirt, the Zat now in place, and tucking the gun in the small of his back under his belt. Emily walked around the car, taking Mark's hand. The night was so dark now, the air cool and crisp against their bare flesh. The only light came from the street lamp that Abel had parked under.

"Okay, follow close behind Mark and me, and stay in a line. Keep low, move fast, and stay on guard. We will stop in the bushes, just across from the front entrance. John, you follow behind us," she instructed, referring to Mark and herself. "James; you and Julia bring up the rear. We need to take out the guards in front, silently, so no one is alerted and waiting for us, when we get back out." They nodded, crowding closer together in a football-like huddle. "Then we make our way around back and get inside. John said there is a room right across from the entrance. We run in there and then... We'll figure out the rest."

"What if anyone gets captured?" Amy whispered.

The thought of being captured and held against their will hadn't occurred to Emily. She stopped abruptly, frozen, and unsure of what to say.

Before an answer came, Mark responded. "It's really up to you, but in my case, I'll be going down swinging before I let them get their hands on me."

"Plus, we can blow them to bits for the next three days, if needed," James added.

After getting into formation, they set off. Swiftly, they made their way down a few narrow alleys and deserted streets. Staying out of the street lamp's reach, they jumped and hurdled over the many cement barricades. After a few more turns, the building came into sight. With the only light coming from the main entrance, the white tent had now been removed, leaving a relatively hidden line of attack.

Keeping low, they made their way to a group of trees that bordered the left side of the building. Catching their breath, they watched as three guards patrolled the end path. John recognized one as being the security man who had stolen the photographer's camera, breaking the memory stick.

Julia and Amy flanked John's sides. They were in charge of his safety, putting his life before their own, at least until they were within the building. Emily turned to nod once, directing James and Rick as they raised their guns up, silencers already in place, and taking aim. Mark, needing no order to raise his gun, slowly took aim at the third guard.

Emily looked out at their prey, and her breath caught at the back of her throat as she raised her left hand, her fingers spread wide. Satisfied with their position and the ensuing decision, she looked back at her shooters. As they readied their aim, Emily counted to three in her head, and then closed her fist tightly. Three consecutive shots, barely audible, forced the three guards to drop abruptly and silently, where they stood. The group watched as their victims shuddered for a second or two before going completely still. Emily smiled at her husband, and then gestured with her head to follow.

Staying in the shade of trees and foliage as much as possible, they made their way around the side of the building, stopping on the opposite side of the path to the back entrance. Looking left and right up the path, Emily nodded back at her group, and then Mark and James walked out from the shade, facing opposite ends of the path, as the others quietly ran for the door.

Emily peeked through the window and gripping the handle

firmly; she was pleasantly surprised when it pulled open. In three bounds, she was in the building, and into the opposite room. She turned and waited, as the others made their way in, conscious of every move as they closed the door behind them.

Remaining low to the ground, James being the last one into the room, was closest to the doorframe. He poked his head back around the corner, getting his bearings. One end held a short dead-end, the other led to a closed door with a circular window at head height.

James pulled back into the room. "It's clear."

"Okay, can you see the cameras? Which way are they facing? If they're facing the other way, we go for it. Run to the end of the hall and huddle under the left camera." In encouragement, she nodded around the group, ensuring they all understood. "We'll block the view, and then head for the locked door. John, give me the key." Emily held her hand out, expectantly.

Reaching into his jeans pocket, his gun already in hand, he passed her the key. "Then what?"

"Then we get past the door, turn left, and head for the elevator. James, I want you and Julia to go into the security office, off to the right, and find the power for the elevator. Set one of the explosives to go off after four minutes. Then you guys get back to us. We'll head down and go from there."

"Okay, and what if there are guards in either hallway?" Amy asked.

Emily thought about it for a second, and then her light blew out of her feet and began to pulsate throughout her body. She got to her feet, as John's jaw dropped, still shocked by their abilities. "Then we take them out."

The others stood, instinctually raising their shields, as they pulled guns into their right palms; ensuring their left hands remained free for other means of attack. Julia and Amy chose to go with their hunting knives, saving the extra bullets for the expected fight for escape. One by one, they left the protection of the room, making their way to the near door.

James took lead, peeking through the circular window once again. To the left, the camera was facing down the other hallway, which aided their plans. Just as he was about to turn and look right, a single guard walked past the window, startling the others. Thankfully, the guard didn't appear to notice the flickering light emanating from their growing powers. James whipped his head back, as the others pressed against the wall and waited.

Emily's eyes grew wide with concern. "On the count of three, James, pull the door open. Take him out. Keep him quiet."

Standing up straight and taking a deep breath, James was sliding his guns back into place, when inspiration hit him. The others watched as he carefully removed one of the stunner bullets from its casing, squeezing lightly, and forcing the antenna forward. Waiting for the man to pass the window again, James silently slipped through the slight crack in the door. Coming up behind the armed guard, he quickly stood, covering the man's mouth and pinching his nostrils, as he plunged the three spikes into his chest, from behind.

James didn't miss a beat, and his hold remained stiff and unyielding. At first there was a natural struggle, though James felt little in resistance. Eventually, the racking shakes ceased, as the guard's body fell limp and appeared lifeless. James pulled his hand away, carrying the body under its armpits. Freeing one arm to turn the doorknob of the closest room, he dragged the body into the empty space, dropping him to the floor, and then re-closing the door with a click.

Turning back, he made his way into the main hall, where he reached the entrance, and held the door wide open as the others filed out. They waited under the far-left camera, until it turned to face the other direction, and then they ran to wait by the locked door. Adrenaline coursed through each of them, fiercely, and they breathed heavily, controlling their panic. Emily unlocked the door. Lightly pushing her aside, Mark entered the new hallway, followed by Rick. Immediately they were met by three guards, who were too surprised to react before Mark and Rick took action, silencing them. Taking a sharp left, the group ran for the elevators.

"James! Julia! Go!" Mark held the security door open, as they made their way in, searching for the power controls.

It took them only a minute to set the bomb and get back into formation. The others stood guard, as John punched his code into the pin pad, praying that it hadn't been changed. They could hear the elevator rise, then a 'bing' as the doors opened to an empty elevator. As the seven filed in, John let out a breath, which he hadn't realized he was holding.

Emily grabbed John by the shirt, forcing him sideways into the button-control corner, hoping he would be shielded enough when they reached the bottom. Amy stood in front of him, as Julia pushed herself into the opposite corner. Before the elevator doors had a chance to close, the members of the group took their positions. James and Rick stood in the open, along the back wall, while Emily pushed Mark into a crouched position in the center of the elevator, crouching behind him, so the boys had clear shots. Those who could see had their guns in either hand, and were armed and ready. Emily extended her arms to rest on either side of Mark's shoulders; reaching far enough forward so that the blasts wouldn't deafen him.

With the elevator doors taking longer than normal to close, the group watched as two more guards noticed the three fallen, and ran into view at the opposite end of the hallway. They turned in time to see the elevator doors start to close. One swiftly spoke into the radio strapped to his shoulder, and then both began to run, guns in hand, towards the very obvious, glowing elevator.

Wasting no time, Emily's team began to shoot. Bullets flew back and forth, before Emily and Mark managed the take-out shots, with two bullets to the guards' chests. When the doors finally closed, the men dropped awkwardly, arms and legs buckling.

Emily cussed loudly, dropping her head forward to rest on Mark's neck. The elevator slowly lowered, as she spoke. "He used his radio."

"Which means they'll be ready and waiting," Mark responded.

Emily pulled her head back up and looked around. "No one hurt?" She continued to glance around, but mainly focused on John, who shook his head, clearly stunned.

"Okay, when the doors open you guys stay put." She made eye contact with Julia, John, and her sister. "Babe, take out the room's lights. When we secure the room, then come out."

When the elevator stopped and the doors opened, the bullets were already raining through the crack. The group shot back as best they could, as the girls and John stayed tight to the walls. When the doors were wide enough, they saw the small room that John had described back at the house. It was filled with thirteen guards, in military style camouflage, with a range of guns at their disposal. As the shooting continued, Mark aimed high, taking out the two panel fluorescent lights, and covering them in darkness.

The only light came from their shields, which were taking heavy fire, causing the light to be distorted. Five seconds later, two red lights came on in the far corner of the room, lighting up the area.

Mark and Emily got up from their crouch, and ran out into the room, as James and Rick followed. When their bullets were used up, the combat training kicked in. Not wasting time reloading, with six men still standing and Emily's group unharmed; James and Mark took on two trained soldiers each, as Emily and Rick fought the remaining two.

The soldiers were good. They knew instinctively how to fight; throwing their bodies about, twisting and dodging attacks. James blocked one stab of a short blade, punching the guy square in the nose, kicking him in the gut, and dropping him instantly. Emily quickly crossed her wrists, forcing them up, as she blocked a twisted stab to the face, leaving the soldier awkwardly outstretched and vulnerable. Gripping his wrist, she twisted his fist free of the blade, and raised her knee, hitting him in the ribs and knocking him against the wall, where he slid down, heaving.

In the time it took him to attempt to stand, Emily forced more energy into her right fist, taking two quick steps until she was standing in front of him. He looked up just as she lunged, dropping her fist across his jawbone; knocking him out. His head hit the cement wall, leaving his body to slump in a pile on the floor. Turning, she let her guard down long enough to take a hit to the cheek, from one of Mark's men. She lost her step, staggering back as the man raised his fist for another swing. Before he could make contact with her reddened cheek, his fist was stopped by James' palm wrapping around it, squeezing with an audible crunch. Emily took a few more steps back, out of his way, as James finished him off.

Unconsciously rubbed her cheek, Emily turned to Rick and Mark, who simultaneously finished fighting their men. Rick went to help James, as Mark hurried to her side. "You okay?" he asked, pulling her hand away from her face.

She dropped her hand to rest at her side. "Yeah, just missed one, is all."

Mark smiled, starting to heal the inevitable bruise. "You're doing great," he whispered, triumphant.

"Thanks. You too."

When he dropped his glowing hand, she let out a sigh of relief, her face showing not even a scratch. Turning back to the elevator, she called, "Okay, we're good."

The others came out and when the group was huddled back together, they made their way to the combination-locked door. Julia used her abilities, and without physically touching them, she dragged the dead and unconscious bodies back into the elevator and closed the doors. Now they had room to work. Rick and Amy positioned themselves at the open entrance to the staircase, with their guns reloaded and ready for anything.

John punched his code into the door three times. "It's not working. They must have locked it down," he said apologetically, glancing around the room.

James cussed, punching the glass window, which was so thick that it barely even cracked.

At the same time, the backup lighting flickered, and the elevator made a loud bang.

"Bomb went off." Rick was stating the obvious.

"Okay, get back," Mark ordered, moving Emily behind him.

The others took a few steps closer to the elevator, as Mark spread his arms wide, and closed his eyes. After a few seconds, the air around them became denser and Mark's energy hummed with growing intensity. Even with their shields fully intact, and John under the staircase out of the line of fire, the others couldn't help but cringe away from what was about to happen. As he sucked in a sharp breath, Mark blew out steadily, which was followed shortly by a wall of energy. The light spread out before him, shattering the glass, and successfully breaking a two-meter hole in their path.

Before long, they were all bombarded again. The blast had created a fading wall of smoke and dust that neither side could see through. Mark quickly reacted, pulling his guns back into place, and shooting blindly. As the dust settled, they saw more men, clearly outnumbering them, and shooting with precision. As one went down, another two came from around hidden corners. Only John seemed to be surprised by the state of the architecture. As he had said before, the room on the opposite side was white, with cemented walls, but where the room should have ended, a large, dark, dirt tunnel continued farther than he was able to see.

As they shot, the entire group using everything they could now, the two groups gradually got closer and closer, until they were all fighting, spread wide, with no middle line separating them. Julia and Amy had John in a corner; to fight, they used one gun, along with their telekinetic abilities, turning the soldiers so that they aimed at each other, rather than their group. John meekly shot at those he could see. Gradually the room got quieter, as the glowing team eventually won the immediate battle.

"Okay, we gotta keep going," Emily ordered, wiping dust from her face, as she and Mark ran into the darkness.

The others caught up to them, as they reached a solid wall, which was easily fifteen feet tall, with crystallized ceilings. They looked left and right, both directions leading to more tunnels. Clearly, what once had held temporary lighting had been shattered, further hindering any attack or escape. However, at the end of each hallway, small lamps held true, halfway up the wall. To the left, the tunnel eventually turned left again. To the right, it split into two. Emily had to stop and think for a minute, calculating their next move. The others waited patiently for their orders, as they continued to look down the tunnels, and back the way they came.

"Okay, we don't have enough time – you four go that way." Emily directed Amy, Julia, James, and Rick to the right. "If you find them, get them back here where we will meet up, and leave as a group. Mark, John, and I will go this way. Okay?" she asked, already walking backwards down the left tunnel.

The others nodded, turning to run in the opposite direction. Both groups reached the end of their tunnels at the same time. With Amy's group, there was a closed door to the right. On the left, another three guards waited, hidden in the shadows. Thankfully, James had poked his shielded head around the corner, before the others could continue. The soldiers shot and gave their position away, so it was all too easy for the four to overpower them.

"Check out that one," James suggested to Rick and Amy, as he and Julia got ready outside of the door.

The couple ran to the other door. Rick held both arms ready and nodded to Amy, as she quickly turned the door handle. It was locked.

"Get back," Rick ordered, and as she did, he opted to kick the door open.

The room was pitch-back, but no one seemed to be trying to attack them. Amy quickly slid her left hand up the inside wall until she reached the light switch. Unlike the tunnels, this room was fully furnished and looked just like the rooms on the upper level. Rick lowered his guns, as they both took a step inside. The room was filled with tables covered in lab equipment and was as big as half a gymnasium. With a closer glance, Amy began to run to the far end, where people lay still, on metal tables.

Rick followed, raising his guns, as they stopped feet from the first table. Both frantically searched around for anyone breathing but no one was. Twelve tables held cadavers, with numerous cut lines across each of their brows. One, in particular, held a small boy, not much older than Matt. Tears filled Amy's eyes and she covered her mouth as she sobbed and buried her face in Rick's chest. Pain laced through both, as they recognized eight of the wedding quests. Rick held her tight, as he began backing out of the room.

"Amy!" Julia cried, from the opposite room.

Amy and Rick turned to see Julia helping wounded individuals into the hallway. The two ran to help. As they reached the other room, trying to navigate amongst the clearly confused and distraught captives, James assisted from the back of the large room. This room was exactly the same at theirs, but it had no tables, sheets, or cruel surgical devices.

Slowly, more than twenty people filed out of the room. Each had the same injuries, from one test or another. They all had large cuts down their left forearms, a blood-red dot on their temples, and pink eyes. They were also exhausted, barely able to hold their own weight up.

One woman stumbled and grasped Rick's forearm. "Please." She gasped hard for breath, the left side of her salt and pepper hair completely shaven. "Where is my husband? They took him," she mumbled, her eyes pleading. "Help me find him." Clearly in need of absent glasses, she squinted to focus.

Rick wrapped his free arm around her shoulders, ushering her towards the others crowding out of the room. "Let's worry about getting you out of here first. We'll heal you up and find your husband."

She didn't seem convinced, but her head drooped, as she let him support the majority of her weight. When they reached the others, he asked two younger men to support her.

"Sarah!" Amy recognized her friend who was cradling her forearm to her chest. Recognizing another, she said, "Trish?"

"Amy?" Trish cried out, overjoyed by the rescue, but seemingly terrified and confused by her glowing friend.

"Dan?" Rick made his way around the others, stopping to help his fallen friend, who was slouched in the far corner holding his bruised ribs.

A few more people were recognized from the wedding guests, along with the people from the news reports: Charmaine

Shannon, Lilly Andrews, and Ian Hunter. When James finally came back into the hallway, he spoke loud and clear. "Okay people, I know you're hurt and confused, but we're gonna get you out of here. You have to trust us. Just keep low and behind us. Stay together." He finished and then made his way back to Rick and Amy. "That's it," he said, speaking just to them.

"Let's get back to the meeting spot," Rick suggested, as they reached Julia.

A few hands grasped at each of them, either for support or in fascination with their glowing forms. Carefully freeing themselves, they turned towards the main tunnel, only to stop in their tracks, as two small metallic balls with flashing lights rolled towards them.

"Amy!" Rick yelled, pointing to the bombs.

Without a second thought, she flew her right hand forward, as if to brush away something in the air. The balls quickly changed direction, flying back down the dark hallway. The four waited, as the screams and yells of many more began, drowned out by two loud explosions and debris. The bombs were, thankfully, not big enough to affect the integrity of the tunnels. Amy and her group sprinted around the corner, into a cloud of smoke and falling chunks of soil.

Reaching the other side, near the entrance, they were met by a group of twenty armed guards; six of whom were lying dead on the dirt below, while four others had fallen, holding tightly to wounded limbs. The remaining ten were ready and waiting.

As the bullets began to fly, Amy tried to focus on the bullets themselves. Rick was the only one with any ammunition left, as Julia and James used their abilities to throw energy bolts and various objects. Rick shot with brilliant accuracy, as his wife used the numerous bullets coming their way, ricocheting them back with heightened speed. When the enemy was out of bullets, they utilized alternative weapons, severely hindering their attack.

Just as Julia thought they were about to gain the upper hand, another wave of men and women ran down the staircase, replacing those who had fallen. Forced into hand-to-hand combat now, the smaller group fought three or four soldiers at a time. Their ability to attack with their light was overshadowed by their need for protection. Gradually, the injuries grew in number for Amy's team, as keeping their shields intact grew harder than before.

Rick had taken a ten-inch blade to the thigh, which had gruesomely exited out the back of his leg. He had also been cut across the abdomen and left shoulder. James fought a younger man who was using pinpointed spikes on his brass knuckles, and took a few shots to the face and ribs. Blood and sweat from a cut above his left brow began to blur his vision immensely. Julia had suffered two broken knuckles, light cuts, which covered her entire body, and a bleeding nose. Blood pooled in her open mouth; the only way she could catch her breath.

One soldier's choice of weapons was two machetes. He had cornered Amy, with a sickly grin. Although she had managed to impede the majority of his attempts, she did take two hard blows to the back and left leg. Where the knife had hit and sliced her skin, the flesh pulled back, and the growing wetness warmed her skin, slowing her down. The last slash hit her directly across the face, and she couldn't help but let out a blood-curdling scream; falling backwards and grabbing the side of her face. Though the blade had been stretched to its limit, still half an inch had trailed into her sensitive tissues, distorting her features.

Refusing to let her guard down completely, she struggled to keep her attacker within sight. She rolled onto her stomach, trying to lift herself up, and onto her hands and knees. It made her sick to hear the man's laughter, taunting, getting closer and closer. Barely able to hold her head up, she raised her shield, and spat out the blood that was pooling in her mouth. Just as the soldier got within reach, she drew enough strength to twist her body; both hands and one knee still on the ground, as she raised a leg up and kicked him in the groin.

Surprised by the sudden move, he let out a high-pitched screech, before falling on the ground in a pile beside her. He tried to grab at her, but she dropped back onto her stomach, rolling out of his reach. Finally, forcing one last bolt of energy out of her fingertips, she forced him back, farther into the shadows, and out of her limited sight. Still holding the side of her face, with one eye swollen shut; she managed to get herself to her feet, shaking. The fight had stirred up even more dust and dirt, but it gradually began to fade, unveiling a wall of frightened individuals. Amy jumped; lunging behind one of the last remaining men, whom Rick was fighting. Without a second's hesitation, her hand gripped the sides of the man's face, snapping his neck in one fluid motion. The walls echoed with the almighty crack.

Rick smiled at his wife, and then froze, taking in the condition of her face and blood-soaked body. His smile faded into shock and fear. She was so weak now, practically falling into his arms, when he ran to her. They lowered to the floor, where he lightly rocked her back and forth. The group of spectators didn't move from their spots, as the fight ended and they noticed two bright lights coming from the opposite end of the hall.

∗   ∗   ∗

When Emily and the others separated from the group, running down the left hallway, it was the gunfire behind them that gave her the sudden idea. Still running, she pulled two smoke bombs from her side pocket. When they reached the end, she gestured for the others to stick against the wall, as she pulled the pins and tossed them around the open corner.

They waited and listened, as three or more men noticed what she'd thrown and began yelling and shooting at the opposite wall. Still out of the line of fire, Emily waited, as the smoke set off with two loud pops, and the men started coughing and yelling to each other with muffled voices. Obviously, they had covered their mouths with their hands or clothing, leaving them vulnerable. After a few calculated seconds, the smoke began to reach their corner, as Emily signaled to the others, and rushed out into the open hall, shooting in every direction.

John joined in as well. Keeping the majority of his body behind the wall, he shot without aiming. The enemy bullets merely hit Emily and Mark's shields, falling inoffensively, and pooling at their feet. The shooting continued for several minutes, before the couple ran out of bullets.

The guards found shelter behind makeshift metal blockades. Seamlessly, the couple dropped their guns, fluidly transitioning into their bonded energy. Focusing, they forced more light into their palms, letting off blasts of energy in one form or another.

The opposing bullets decreased in number, until it was clear that only two opponents remained. The smoke had gradually faded, allowing both sides to get a better view of their targets. As the two men focused on the couple, John took them off-guard by shooting them from the side. Both men dropped, almost simultaneously, as silence filled the air. John came out from his cover, joining Emily and Mark in the middle of the hall.

"Nice job," Mark commented to John.

"Thanks."

The exhilaration and intensity of the gunfight had left all of them out of breath. Looking down both ends of the small hallway, they saw that one held another dead end, while the other had a single door. On a closer look, two other doors appeared on the right and the left sidewalls. John took the left, Emily the center, and Mark the right. All three doors were locked, so as Rick had, they chose to kick it open. John's room held nothing but lab equipment and testing supplies. The back of the room was filled with metal tables, with black wrist and ankle restraints. He searched the room, but couldn't find anything.

When Emily kicked the door in, she quickly found the light switch. The room was smaller than John's, though it was filled with even more tables. They were lined in four rows of five tables. She covered her mouth when the smell of rotting flesh hit, her stomach flipping, as she tried to hold back her primal need to gag. On every table, a lifeless body lay, covered in hospital-grade blue sheets from head to toe. Blood covered the floors and spattered walls. She walked up and down the aisle, searching for any survivors, anger and hatred growing with every step.

When she reached the back row's second to last table, she noticed the sheet move up and down, lightly. Hope bloomed after everything she had just been though but she still couldn't stop her hands from shaking, as she grabbed the corner of the sheet. Taking a breath, she quickly pulled back the paper-thin sheet, to reveal a dark-haired male in his early thirties. His head was resting slightly to the right. Blood had dried across his face, though it still flowed from his mouth and nostrils. His left eye was badly swollen and bruised. He tried to speak, but no words escaped his lips. He was breathing, but the air came unsteadily.

Emily ripped the sheet off the remainder of his body to reveal even more torture. His hands were badly mangled and broken. His dark clothes were sticky with his blood. His arms and legs were held down by the black restraints.

"It's okay, I'm here to help you. I'm gonna get you out of here." Emily began untying his feet and hands.

Even when he was free, he couldn't move a muscle, as they fell limply to the side. He could only focus on her face and breathe. She focused, getting to work on healing, starting on his abdomen. His eyes widened, as her glowing shield pulsated throughout her body, gathering in her hands. When he began to feel the warmth under his skin, his eyes strayed from her face, staring up at the ceiling.

"Abel!" John's voice sounded from the doorway. He ran to Emily, who glanced over her shoulder at the interruption then back down at her patient. "You're Abel?"

Abel tried to answer, but he still couldn't control his voice. His tongue swollen and heavy, he merely nodded once, and then let his head drop to the left to see his best friend reach the table.

"Abel, what did they do to you?" John frantically scanned his broken body.

Abel still couldn't speak a word; the very attempt caused darkened blood to pour from his mouth and trail down his cheek.

"Don't move. This is Emily, she can fix you, just hold still!" John ordered. "I'm gonna check on Mark. I'll be right back. Just hold on!" He ran from the room, leaving Emily to work in silence.

When John ran into the last room, he found Mark trying to help thirty-odd people to their feet. They all varied in age and size, and had similar, dark circles under their eyes; the week of torture and lack of sleep showing on them. Barely keeping their eyes open, most focused and fussed over the wounds on their arms and faces.

"Come on people. You have to get up! We're gonna get you out of here," Mark ordered, as he helped individuals up, their bare feet scraping along the white tiled floor.

"Anne!" Mark recognized Emily's best friend.

She was trying to get herself off the floor. "I can't. I can't," she repeated from the back corner of the room, her body shaking. He reached her quickly, lifted her into his arms, and started back towards the open door.

"John, help me get these people out!" Mark barked, gently placing Anne on wobbly legs, and leaning her against the outside wall.

"Okay people, I know you're tired and hurt, but we need you to find the strength to get up and walk," John prompted the people who had made no attempt to move. "It's almost over. You can go home soon."

That's when John noticed two others from the news. A redhead and her husband; Elizabeth and Ryan. He couldn't remember their last names. Without another word, he and Mark continued to help the remaining injured, forcing them to their feet, and guiding them out into the hall. When the room was empty, John disappeared back into Emily's room, to check on her progress.

When he reached the table, Emily had begun work on Abel's face. Her glowing palms made seeing his features impossible. Abel lay still, gripping the sides of the table now. John waited on the opposite side as Emily continued with her eyes shut, focusing.

After a few minutes, Mark left the others in the hall to check up on his wife. No one said a word, as he came and stood at the end of the table, quietly waiting. After another two minutes, Abel took in a deep steady breath, as Emily pulled her hands away, opening her eyes.

Emily continued to examine Abel's body, as John leaned over his friend. "Abel? You okay? How do ya feel?"

Still lying down, Abel held his hands in front of his face, examining his previously broken fingers. After that, he propped himself up on his elbows, and looked around at the three people hovering over him, stopping on John.

"I feel fine." His words were clear and his eyes amazed. Turing to Emily, he said, "I was convinced I was dead and you were an angel, come for me."

Emily let out a laugh, as Mark smiled. "I'm no angel." She gently rested her hand on his forearm. "We're just here to get you and the others out of here."

Just then there was another explosion, gunshots, and screams coming from the hallway.

"No!" they all screamed, turning towards the interruption.

Abel jumped down from the table, still amazed at his near-instant recovery, as he joined the others in running into the hallway. He couldn't help glancing sideways, as Mark's light increased and began to hum.

Mark reached the doorway first, letting off a wave of energy. It passed over the people that had fallen, huddled, without added injury. Gaining force, it hit the first row of shooting guards, knocking them on their backs. Smoke and debris filled the hall, as Emily yelled backwards at the two best friends.

"Get down and stick with the others!" She ran to Mark's side, and both began to fight the remaining guards. The couple faced six men and women; this time with machine guns and fully equipped utility belts.

"Fuck this!" Mark burst out, his shield returning to its familiar hum again. Another burst left his body, knocking three more to the floor. When he joined his wife, the last two soldiers became no match for them. Within three blows, they too joined the others crumpled at Mark and Emily's feet.

"Come on." Emily ran back through the dust with Mark, signaling for the survivors to follow.

The group banded together; their escape so near and freedom within a grasp. They clung to that thought as they forced their way forward. Ignoring their physical pain, they joined the couple in a run to the meeting spot. Mark and Emily came to an abrupt stop, as they reunited with James and the others.

"Amy!" Emily cried, running to her sister, who was bleeding

out onto the floor, in Rick's arms. Mark joined and helped the healing, as Amy tried to smile up at her sister through the pain.

"We're almost there, kiddo," Emily said to distract her sister. "All we have to do is get up those stairs and onto the main floor, then we'll blow our way out of this hell hole."

Mark finished working on Amy's leg, and turned to fix Rick's thigh, as his wife healed her sister's face and back. James and Julia joined their friends, keeping their eyes open for the next attack. The fifty injured stood wide-eyed and watching against the back wall, waiting for more direction. When the rescuing group was finally healed, and getting to their feet, Emily turned to the wall. It was too dark to see many faces, so as she spoke, she looked at John, who was front and center.

"The time has come to leave this place. Stay together and keep your eyes open. We just need to get up those stairs," she said, pointing towards the exit, "and through a few more hallways, then we will be outside. Is anyone too injured to run?" No one came forward. "I know you are all injured and exhausted, so help each other. When we get outside, I promise we'll heal you all – we just need some time and shelter."

CHAPTER TWENTY-THREE

The group took the first few steps together, in a silence that indicated they were just as eager to leave as the others. Taking the opportunity while they were not under fire, Emily and Mark took the lead, heading back through the hole Mark had previously created, up the vacant, spiral staircase. John and Abel followed the couple, with the large group filing in behind them. The staircase was narrow so only two people could take a single step. Mark ran up the stairs, taking two at a time. In the middle of the group, Julia and Amy followed, with James and Rick bringing up the rear. Emily knew the growing silence and lack of attack was not a good sign. Either they really had just taken out the entire guard squad or the main floor would be their biggest problem. Like most of Emily's gut feelings, this one would prove to be right.

Just as their footsteps echoed near the top steps, another show of bullets showered around them. The couple paused, stopping before they turned the final corner into the line of fire. The fifty-plus others stopped where they were on the staircase, panic-stricken, and some even attempting to descend.

"Amy, Julia!" Emily called, leaning over the metal railing. She watched as their lights pushed past the others above them on the stairs. A minute later, they joined Emily and Mark at the top, looking expectantly at her, and waiting for orders. "Okay, this is the last stretch. When we step out, I want you to shield yourselves, but focus the fire back on them. Mark and I will attack, but I want you to focus on protecting the people. Shield them as we make our way down the hall. Amy you take our left, Julia you take the right, create a wall and throw back whatever they send our way. Okay?"

"Yep." They nodded and prepared themselves, with their arms stretched out.

"Okay. On the count of three," Mark announced.

They took their positions, getting ready to leap into the hall, as the bullets continued. "One. Two... Three!" Emily yelled, and then jumped with the others into the line of fire.

Nothing got past their shields. The girls forced their hands out, stopping the bullets dead, a meter from them. The firing stopped for a second, as the attacking soldiers saw the impossible. Then Amy glanced sideways at her friend, and together they pushed their palms out, causing the frozen bullets to shoot back, and hit the first wave of soldiers, collapsing where they stood. The shooting began again, with Emily and Mark's light hitting man after man. The short hall was filled with fifteen men. Soon, only five were left standing. Through the locked door, Emily could see the camera-patrolled hall, concealing even more men ready for action. *When is it going to end?* was all Emily could think.

Rick and James decided the only remaining threat was coming from above. They forced themselves past the frightened individuals, now sitting low on the metal staircase. When Rick and James got to the top, they ran out to help their family. Amy and Mark took out the last two men, and the six regrouped, finally turning to stare into the hardened faces of the many soldiers on the other side of the door. Neither side moved, as they waited for the other to attack. The soldiers raised their guns in preparation.

"Almost there," Emily whispered, her gaze fixated on the door, as a new wave of energy grew and passed throughout her limbs. "Not much longer."

The group stood, panting, as they waited for Emily's next move. Their shields returned to full capacity, in the meantime. Emily turned to Mark and squeezed his hand, gesturing with her chin to the locked door. He grinned back at her, walking to stand only feet from the door. The men on the other side looked confused, as he stood there alone, closing his eyes. Emily stood just behind her husband, protectively, as the others stepped back, blocking the entrance of the staircase. Mark focused on his breathing, slowly spreading his arms wide – his light grew as he concentrated. The accompanying hum brought a wicked grin to Emily's tired face. The right corner of her mouth pulled upwards.

One soldier yelled, and the others began shooting through the glass. Emily knew Mark had to focus, so she lightly placed her hand at the small of his back, sharing energy and shielding them both. Two seconds later, the energy blew from Mark's chest. The door blew off its hinges, hitting the four closest soldiers, knocking them into the second row, as the bullets began to fly.

"Stay here!" James yelled back down the stairs, as he and the others joined the fight.

The three men ran right up to the soldiers, forcing them to fight with their fists. Even Julia and Amy used their energy attack five men, running down the other end of the hall. Trying to avoid as much physical strain as possible, Emily stayed near to the doorframe, as she focused her light on the attack. When needed, she pulled her knife and threw it, commanding it back as the girls were able to, and repeated.

Retreated back down the hall, the remaining soldiers made their way back around the corner. Emily watched, confused at their cowering. Then she noticed the remaining few press their fingers to clear plastic earpieces, listen, then join the others around the corner. A blast of fire came as a surprise, bordering the right side of the hall, and shattering the wide windows.

The wave threw the group of rescuers up and back against the opposite wall, knocking them down to the floor. Scrambling to their feet, they saw that the previous windows had been replaced with new guns; pointing at them. These guns were different than anything they had seen. They completely covered the user's forearms, up to the elbow, and had a wide circular end. The guns began to make noises, growing with intensity, as if to power up.

Emily wasn't sure what to do. She turned to her group. "Push it back on them!" she yelled, holding her palms out ready.

The soldiers were only two meters away, as they aimed directly for her group. The tip of their guns began to glow, like a flame, with the same light as the rescuers' shields. There was no doubt they were another stolen adaptation. As the light turned red, the men pulled their elbows back, and the guns fired. Emily's team gritted their teeth; the blast hitting their invisible wall. Their fingers pulled back, as if the light was physically touching them, forcing them back.

With a loud grunt, the others followed Emily's lead, forcing the energy back on their attackers. A second row took aim, but before they could reload, Emily started a chain reaction of blasts; the anger pulsated throughout her group. One after another, they all managed to gain enough strength and their shields hummed with intensity. Screaming now, the building began to shake around them, and the hallway lights burst, leaving them in darkness. The heat of their abilities grew intense, the air growing thin like a smoky mirage. The humming grew louder. The opposing soldiers tried to fight back with whatever they could shoot, but the growing blaze was increasingly blinding them.

One minute the entire hall was illuminated, then next, it was pitch- black, and the firing had stopped. Emily and her group's shields had disappeared. As they stood, hands still spread wide, and breathing heavily, they stared into the room in front of them.

Where the men had stood and bombarded them, there was only a black hole now. The room was empty. The walls, ceiling, and floors were charred black, and beginning to crumble. Nothing remained, but smoke and dust, which lingered in the air.

Trying to control his breath, Mark turned to the others. "Is everyone okay?"

Amy and Julia stood, staring into the room, while the others turned to Mark and reported that they were fine. After a few more shocked moments, Emily realized they still weren't out of the woods. She turned, running back through the burned doorway to the entrance of the stairwell.

"Come on!" she yelled, to the people who cowered where they sat.

Emily rejoined her group, followed by the survivors, and they all filed into the hall, continuing towards the exit. The survivors slowed; dragging their feet, as they stared into the black, dilapidated room to their right, then back at their saviors.

The group turned the right corner into the next hall. Not worrying about the cameras anymore, Emily raised her shield again, and was followed by the others. Where the easy exit used to be, there was now a large metal plate that had somehow been welded over the door in a very short time.

"Mark?"

He was already glaring dubiously at the blockade. "I can't, Em. I…" More exhaustion filled him by the minute.

She was already shushing him, gripping his shoulder, and squeezing reassuringly. "We'll find another way."

Emily turned to John, who with Abel at his side, had caught up with her group. "How do we get out, now?"

John looked at Abel, answering for him, and pointing down the remaining corridor. "We'll have to go out the front door. We just go around the corner, through another locked door, then left.

That will open up to the main lobby."

Emily nodded as he spoke, and then turned back to the group, which was listening intently behind them. "Okay, that's the plan then. Get ready," she ordered, taking the first few steps to continue.

Mark caught up with her in two bounds, the others walking a few steps behind, as he drew on his energy again. "I can't wait till this is over!" he whispered to his wife.

Just as they turned the corner, he had enough of this lock and key business. Needing less of his light, he let out another, smaller blast, and then smirked, as he walked through the newly created doorway. Emily laughed to herself at how casual this was all getting to be. Last week, her biggest worries had been getting everything finished for her sister's wedding, finishing off some medical charts in preparation of a leave, and now this. They had spent the last few days learning what takes years to master. The conscious copying of abilities from their new friends had made the process one hundred times faster and easier. They could control energy and use it however and whenever they wished. They could fight like Jet Li or even Bruce Lee. Her mental monologue ended, when they walked past the smoking debris. They were surprised to find no one attacking them.

"Turn left," Abel called, from a few steps back.

They did. They followed another narrow corridor left for five paces, then right, and then another left. At the end of this corridor they could see the main lobby. Their corridor was extremely narrow. Barely two people could walk down it at the same time. It was obviously not a commonly used path. Emily stopped at the end, as the large group behind waited and listened. Footsteps scurried about the open lobby. She turned to face her glowing group, finding John and Abel close behind.

"Okay, when we go down there," she said, pointing down the remaining hall, "and get out into the lobby, where is the exit?"

John answered this time, as they all seemed to huddle closer together. "It's on the right. We're pretty close. It's a big open space, with the doors in the center of the far wall."

Emily nodded, turning back to look down the hall as she thought about it. "Okay. James, Rick, you two take the lead. Amy and Julia, same drill, anything that comes at us, keep it away from the people. Mark and I will follow you guys." She turned and looked up at James. "Let's take them out and get the hell out of here." With her encouraging last words, she gestured for them to proceed.

When the first four reached the end of the hall, they hesitated. Rick poked his head around the corner, pulling back almost immediately, as a volley of gunfire flew past his head. With continuous fire, the opposite side of the narrow hallway began to shatter and break off in chunks. Rick cussed loudly. Turning to the others, he had to speak loudly over the noise of the falling metal fragments.

"There are at least thirty guys blocking the exit. They've constructed little barriers that they're hiding behind," he said, abruptly stopping and cringing farther back, as two blasts of energy hit the wall near his head. "Five fuckers have those energy guns. They're on the far left."

Emily listened closely, trying to think up new strategies. She looked out into the hall, through the fire, and noticed which columns were weight- bearing throughout the main floor. The first row was only a meter away from the entrance to their hall. The others lined the far wall.

"Okay, here's what we do. James, Rick…" She gestured with her chin. "See if you guys can get across to those far columns. Take one each. Mark and I will cover you, and then take this row. Try and make your way closer to the door and take them out." Then she turned back to her sister, "When you think it's safe enough, come out, and do the same. Make sure the survivors stay here until the fire stops." Her sister quickly nodded, turning back to inform the others of their plan.

James turned to Rick. "Ready when you are."

Rick grinned back, flaming hands raised. After a few beats, they both ran out, the bullets following close behind them, as they made their way to the first column, unharmed. Emily and Mark took this opportunity to fire back. The distraction gave James and Rick the time to sprint across to the other side of the large hall, firing and blocking as they went. When they reached the other side, they both turned back to face their group, encouraging the others to follow.

Taking a few seconds to steady themselves, Emily and Mark ran out from the corridor, making it to their pillar with less opposing fire than James and Rick had faced. Now she could see, as she shot, the large group that blocked their escape. Men and women, of varying ages, created a wall across the exit. Some were wearing camouflage clothing, while others wore white. Two men stood in the center, standing out in their restrictive suits.

The firing continued for three minutes before anyone else moved. As the four had dropped the rival numbers to half as many, James and Mark began to move up the columns until they were at the first. Rick and Emily stayed close behind. The men in uniforms began to edge forward, coming closer, spreading and filling the room. The fighting continued and there were only ten opposing men left, when Amy and Julia stepped out with a few brave others. John and Abel had picked up discarded weapons from the fallen guards in the previous hallway. As they turned the corner, bullets flew past them, though the first people Abel saw were Jacob and Tom; front and center.

With a scream, he focused all his aim on them, firing everything he had. When they recognized him, they were taken back by his healthy appearance. Abel ignored everyone else as he pushed forward; it was two against one. Using the nearest pillar to shield himself, he continued to shoot, gaining attention, as John came to his aid. Now two against two, it was shot for shot. No one else seemed to matter, as Abel's vision tunneled to focus on the two men that had left him for dead. Tom's laughter was demonic; he was enjoying himself out in the open, while Jacob took shelter when available.

Amy and Julia were too preoccupied with the larger group to help in this small face-off. Not even attempting to fire back, the girls threw all the strength into their expanded shields. Utilizing the slingshot affect, the soldiers learned fast, replacing their guns with blades. The group of survivors stayed back. A few had picked up guns as well, but with no training they were no real threat to the soldiers. Those that Julia and Amy could not shield dropped rapidly. Thankfully, only five of the surviving group, three men and two women, had been lost so far.

Slowly, the remaining few edged forward. The fight was even now. Six were left opposing Emily's group, while Jacob shot at John from behind his own pillar, and Tom focused on Abel. The groups screamed at one another. Both sides eventually ran out of bullets, and dropping their guns, they calculated their next moves. Abel sprinted from his pillar, lunging at Tom, and falling backwards with him. John knocked Jacob down with a solid punch to the face. Jacob didn't stay down; he pulled John down with him, as they began to roll on the white marble tiles below. Tom had a little more physical training than Abel, but Abel was way more determined.

"Back for Round Two?" Tom mocked Abel, grabbing his shoulders and slamming their foreheads together, with force.

Partially dazed, Abel cringed back a few steps, regaining his footing. Tom pushed off the wall, punching Abel square in the jaw, and letting out a grunt. Instead of falling backwards, Abel grabbed Tom's shirt, pulling him onto the floor. Abel jumped on his chest, grabbed Tom's collar in a tight grip, and lifted his hand up to repay the favor. After three punches, Tom, being forty odd pounds heavier, hit both of Abel's sides, spinning him around, so that it was Abel pinned below him.

John and Jacob continued to fight until John managed to hit Jacob's head into the solid floor more than enough times to knock him out cold. As Jacob's body went limp in his hands, John stepped back, and dropped Jacob to the ground below. Searching the room for his best friend, John found Abel just a few meters away, with Tom sitting on his chest. John dove at Tom before he could get another blow in. Abel managed to collect himself, getting to his feet, while dodging the line of bullets fired past his head. James and Rick finished off their men, and now turned to help the women. Mark stood, defending a smaller group of people, which had broken away from the main group; as Emily was forced to fist-fight with her soldier.

Easily a foot taller than Emily, the soldier's bare arms glistened with sweat and bulging muscles. If any of the others had not been so preoccupied, they would have seen she needed some help. To begin with, she and the soldier began staring at each other, circling around, in a tight spot. The soldier lowered his fists, beginning to laugh, as he untied his utility belt, and dropped everything to the ground.

Even though Emily had the upper hand with her new abilities, this man terrified her. He was just so big. Finally, when he thought the time was right, he ran at her. She did manage to block most of his attempts, but he blocked her energy bolts, as well. Dodging and twisting, Emily found that the bolts became of little use, as she drew on her light to back up her punch, knocking him back a few steps. She kicked, hitting him in the ribs, but this only seemed to anger him; his grin faded, replaced by fury. Not paying attention, she stepped back, right into one of the black marble pillars. The sudden coldness along her back startled her, making it perfect for him to step up, and forcibly grip her throat. As she tried to struggle, he effortlessly raised her two feet up the wall; his grip tightening.

Choking, she continued to fight, but her energy and strength were rapidly fading. After twenty long seconds, her limbs were beginning to numb and run cold. She scratched at his outstretched arm and the hand that restricted her throat. She really started to panic when her vision began to tunnel, and her shield began to fade. Just before she totally lost control, she saw Abel and John come up behind the solder, and hit him square in the back.

He instantly dropped her and she fell to the ground, coughing for breath. Now, she watched the two friends take on the giant. It was easier for them, since they had the two machetes he had dropped with the utility belt. It was John's solid stab to the chest that stopped the man's heart, killing him instantly. Abel ran over to Emily first, as she finally caught her breath, clutching at her raw throat.

He helped her to her feet. "Are you okay?"

Her voice was weak, but she managed to answer him. "I'll be fine. Go protect the others."

When John joined them, and after Abel had determined she was going to be okay, they left her to continue the fight. As she built her shield up, she took a second to look around the room. With the energy blasters, Mark and the others were now finishing off the last three men, while John and Abel got in another fistfight with two other soldiers.

The electricity throughout the building had been shut down in an attempt to hinder their escape. In the darkness and lack of attack, it was only then that Emily could see the flashing red and white lights outside the main windows. They were obviously coming from police cruisers. She was exhausted and her knees began to shake so violently that she had to use the near pillar for support. When the fighting stopped, Mark and the others cheered, as they looked around at their victory.

Mark scanned the room, searching for his wife. His smile quickly faded when his gaze fell on her sliding down the pillar, barely holding her head up, as her light faded away. Her breathing was unsteady; every breath scorched. Mark sprinted to her side and dropped to the ground next to her.

He lifted her head up with one hand. Her eyelids drooped, as she tried to focus, looking as if she would lose consciousness at any moment.

"Em. Baby, are you okay? Where are you hurt?" He looked her up and down once, then went back to her face.

Her answer was lethargic, as she blinked slowly. "I can't hold myself up any more. I have no strength."

"Are you hurt?"

She shook her head, though she cringed and nodded, pointing to the red marks around her throat. He gasped; noticing the rough outline of fingers, as his illuminated hand gently caressed and healed her skin. If not for his hand, her head would have fallen, limply. Any minute now she was going to pass out. With her throat healed, Mark gently lifted her into his arms, and turned to walk back to the entrance.

"Hang on baby, we're getting the hell out of here," he whispered into her ear, holding her close,

"What's wrong?" Amy panicked, searching her sister's body.

"She's fine. She's just exhausted."

"Okay, let's go!" James called loudly, as they made their way through the main doors.

As the first twenty people made it out of the building, the group stopped abruptly, on the main path. The group stood unmoving, faced with seven police squad cars. Two men hid behind each, with guns pointed, ready to fire.

"Stay where you are!" One overweight, middle-aged officer, yelled into a microphone.

Looking past them, James saw five dark figures light up in the field across the street. Mark squinted, as he tried to focus on Amelia and her team. He couldn't make out their faces, but he could see they were clapping. The cops turned around and pointed their guns in the opposite direction.

"You there! Stop what you are doing, and put your arms up!" the office called back at them.

Emily managed to keep her eyes open long enough to see the response. Only Amelia complied with his wishes, raising one glowing hand into the night sky. Directly above, four large spotlights shone bright. The police gasped and pointed their guns straight up. Six other, even bigger, sets of lights then joined the four lights, outlining crafts of immense proportion.

James and Rick cheered, hooted, and howled, taking Amy and Julia's hands, as tears ran down the girls' faces. Emily turned and smiled up at her husband. Feeling her gaze, he turned back down; their eyes locked.

"We did it, Em! We did it!"

Emily nodded; exhaustion was coming to claim her. She let her head drop to the right again, as the five Jarly took their first steps towards them. Finally, Emily turned her head, letting it drop back. Her breathing deepened, as she smiled up at the starry night sky.

"We made it," she whispered to herself, before her eyes closed and rest came.

CHAPTER TWENTY-FOUR

One Year after the Rescue

Standing on the large wooden steps, Emily was completely silent, as she took in the room. One step below her, Julia's seventeen-year-old cousin, Jaime, wore a matching, dark-gold, strapless silk dress, with a brown ribbon under the bust. She looked up, smiling. Emily's gaze moved down to the large crowd staring back up at them. Row after row, both human and Jarly sat in silence. In the front row, Amelia and her team were grouped together. Amadeus sat at the end of the long bench, lightly bouncing baby Sophie, Mark and Emily's five-month-old daughter, in his arms, as she lightly cooed. Emily couldn't help but smile down at her daughter; so beautiful.

Sophie was the perfect baby. Already sleeping right through the night, she never cried much. Naturally, she was very attached to Emily. Mark and the others liked to joke that she was a momma's girl. As long as Emily was within sight or nearby, Sophie was completely at ease. Mark was a close runner up, though. Physically, their baby was the ideal split between the two. With thick, ash-brown hair and olive skin, like her father. Her newborn blue eyes had gradually darkened into her mother's shade of green. She even had her mother's full, pouty lips. Amy insisted she was the perfect type of chubby. As much as anyone had concluded or agreed, Sophie was the most spoiled baby of two worlds.

While Emily continued to smile, she made the mistake of making eye contact with Amadeus. He merely smiled back, undoubtedly reminded of her stage fright. Quickly looking away, back to the ground, she followed the white strip of fabric up the stairs to the first set of feet. Following the legs, she saw a young boy, no older than fifteen, dressed in a black suit. When her gaze finally reached his face, she saw that he was not looking at her, but up at the top of the stairs. Jumping from his face to the next, directly across, she saw that Mark stood staring in the same direction. Emily had always been a sucker for the suits. After a few seconds of her ogling her husband, he noticed her stare, and quickly looked across at his wife. He winked, causing the light blush to increase in her already perfect makeup.

Taking a deep breath, she decided she should probably focus. Straightening up, with both hands gripping the beautiful bouquet of white roses, Emily followed the line of men to James, who stood at the top of the steps, his smile consuming his features. Unlike most others, James did not profusely sweat or stutter as he recited his speech. He spoke his vows loud and clear with complete conviction. Across from him, Julia was grinning, but couldn't hold back the growing number of tears. When it came time for her to repeat after the minister, she had to focus on every word.

Like Amy's stunning wedding dress, Julia had designed her own and wore it with pride. White, with a sweetheart neckline, it was strapless, with a corset around the bust, and a moderate poof in the skirt. Less traditionally, her dress also featured a matching dark-gold and white pattern, alternating with satin roses that started on the right hip creating a downwards spiral around the train. The same gold bordered the top of her dress. With her blonde hair, Amy had used her expertise to intricately braid it into a full up-do, with random soft curls bouncing off her collarbone. A small diamond clip held a short veil onto the hair, and it trailed halfway down her bare back.

After the rings were exchanged, the couple was officially pronounced husband and wife. A short, but tender kiss had them turning back to the crowd of friends and family. Cheers and clapping broke the silence. All sides of the room lit up with Jarly energy. Not only were Amadeus and his team physically glowing, but at least twenty other Jarly had attended. Though most humans were nowhere near mastering such a power, Emily and her small group of heroes had mastered their own light. Only after months of practice, and one-to-one training, they too could contribute to the light show.

Julia gripped James's arm, as they made their way down the steps, and along the long aisle. On the second step, Rick and Amy came together, being best man and maid of honor. Amy took her husband's arm as they followed quickly after, then came Emily and Mark, followed by the two teens.

Awaiting the newlyweds outside, Amadeus's wedding gift was nothing but extravagant. The growing crowed waved goodbye, as James and Julia pulled away in their chauffeur-driven, black, Rolls Royce Phantom. Mark wrapped his arms around his wife's waist, resting his chin on her shoulder. Amadeus, still smiling, passed Sophie over to her mother. Sophie curled into her mother's embrace, falling fast asleep. Emily held her close to her chest, as she glanced around.

Now that the car was far out of sight, everyone around seemed to relax, and start up conversations. Mark laughed and pulled away from Emily. She saw him take two long strides before scooping Abby and Matt into each arm.

Emily, with Amy and Rick, quickly followed. "Abby! Matt!" She tried to loudly whisper, trying not to disturb the baby.

"Auntie Em!" Abby cheered, with less restraint.

Rick quickly stole Matt from his brother-in-law's arms, into a giant bear hug. Amy quickly joined her husband, as he rested his free arm over her shoulder.

"It's great to see you all!" Emily lightly twisted on the spot, rocking Sophie, who was slowly gaining awareness of the growing group around her. It was too exciting to sleep.

"I know, it's been too long." Elizabeth spoke, with Ryan at her side.

"How is everything?" Mark asked the couple, as he played with Abby. She giggled as he lightly tickled her ribs.

"We're doing great, thank you," Ryan answered, as if it was a rehearsed line, spoken too many times. He seemed to pause, then added in a hushed voice. "We have our moments. Our nightmares."

Mark solemnly nodded, knowing all too well about the stresses and continued effects of Post Traumatic Stress. Just then, Riley and Amelia made their way through the crowd, hand in hand.

"Hey guys!" Riley added, instantly lightening the mood. The others couldn't help but laugh at how human the Jarly could act, playfully swinging their interlocked hands. No wonder they could stay hidden for so many years.

"Ri-Ri," Abby cheered, as Mark passed her over.

"How are you doing, Abby?" Riley laughed, setting her on his hip.

"Good." She nodded, enthusiastically.

Next to reunite was the Stark family, along with Abel. Catching up, everyone seemed to relax within the group. Caleb and Damon came up behind Rick, quickly pulling Matt out of his arms. The entire group laughed when Rick's flame burst out around his feet, as soon as the child had been stolen; the surprise had set him off.

Rick laughed, shaking his head, and releasing his shield. "Still got it!" he said, as he mock punched Damon in the shoulder.

As the group stood together in the pebble-covered churchyard, Emily smiled to herself. Mark came back to his wife, wrapping his arms around her, holding both of his girls.

"What?" he whispered, for only her ears.

She shook her head, resting it back on his chest. "Nothing."

The last wedding she'd attended had ended with her world left upside down, followed by fear, loss, and a state hunt. After such a stressful year, Emily finally realized something. Everything she had been through, all the pain and suffering…it was for this moment. She realized she had really gained more than she had ever lost. She'd gained more than new friends, she'd gained the family she had always wanted and needed.

* * *

Later that evening, with the reception in full swing, the remaining partygoers danced under the large, white dome constructed on a plot of Jarly land. Clearly not to be outdone, the Jarly had filled the tent with immaculate ice sculptures, food to feed an army, and a never-ending flow of champagne. Julia and the two sisters, Emily and Amy, watched from one of the large, round, silk-covered tables. The men had gathered into a group on the far side, taunting James with inappropriate jokes and alcohol-fuelled banter.

Amelia and Isobel silently joined the girls. "Enjoying your party?" Isobel had two large drinks in each hand; pink and bubbly, bobbing with cherries.

Julia laughed. "Of course, when will you Jarly stop lavishing us with all this extravagance?" she mocked, lifting her chin to the nearby, six-foot-tall chocolate fountain, accompanied by a nearby table filled with exotic fruits and treats. "A simple tent and buffet would have been more than enough."

"Hush!" Amelia sluggishly swatted her away. "This is nothing. We were more than excited to do all this." Her hand popped out to direct around the room, "When will you humans realize how much you have done for our people? For your own people? Nothing will ever be good enough." She hiccupped the last word, making Emily grin.

Slowly, the attendees began to leave, until all that remained were the close few. Two long tables had now been awkwardly dragged together loudly, waking Sophie who had been peacefully sleeping next to her mother, propped up in the detached car seat. Mark hastily apologized, as he took his tearful daughter in his arms, lulling her back to sleep, before taking the seat next to his wife.

"Well," James began, raising his glass of champagne, his arm resting around his new wife's shoulders, "words can't justify how appreciative we are for everything each of you has done for us." Julia and the others raised their glasses, gesturing to their Jarly family.

"From the bottom of our hearts, we thank and love you, all," Julia clarified, and then added more light heartedly, "even though you did almost get us killed, multiple times."

Amadeus rolled his eyes and laughed. Standing, he raised his glass towards the happy couple. "Nothing gives us more pleasure than to see our new friends praised and celebrated, so freely. We wish you a lifetime of happiness." He paused then quickly added, "And less of the dramatic death chases." The entire group filled the large tent with their growing laughter.

Riley finally rose from his seat. "I would like to say something." He paused. At first the others thought he was simply choosing his words carefully, but after an extended silence, the humans noticed that all their Jarly companions now had blank stares, as if they were miles away. Amadeus and Amelia raised their hands in unison to touch their ears.

"Amadeus?" Mark eventually reached across the table, with concern.

Seconds later, the Jarly team rose to their feet, without a word. Concern crossed their features. Fresh light filled the room, as most of them departed, leaving only Amadeus, Amelia, Riley, and Isobel remaining.

Eventually, Amadeus answered. "I must apologize, our presence has been requested back on our ship."

"Is everything okay?" James interrupted, rising to his feet.

"Please." Amadeus raised both of his hands, in a calming gesture, "Don't be alarmed. It's nothing for you to worry about." The others didn't seem convinced, but he continued, resting his hand reassuringly on Mark's shoulder. "Please, enjoy the rest of your night."

Riley took Amelia's outstretched hand, as he added, "Julia, James, this was a beautiful wedding. Enjoy your honeymoon. We hope to see you soon." They both forced smiles, and then took their leave in another shot of light.

Isobel and Amadeus rushed to hug as many as they could, before waving goodbye, and joining their team. Silence filled the air, as the remaining party stared with concern, at the empty space previously occupied by Jarly.

"That was weird, right?" Rick broke the silence, scanning the room, as the group slowly nodded.

"I'm sure they would have mentioned if it was anything serious," Amy offered, trying to return everyone to a lighter mood.

Still not convinced, the group simply sat in silence, wondering what news was coming. After investing so much time and energy in this wedding, there was no way the Jarly would leave so swiftly for any small matter. Something was happening, something big.

SNEAK PEEK OF BOOK TWO

CHAPTER ONE

"You know…" Emily hesitated. "I'm starting to think none of it was real," she whispered, staring blankly at the blackened crack along the handle of her favorite coffee mug.

"What do you mean?" Mark spoke to Emily, while trying to get Sophie to swallow what was left of the pomegranate and apple puree, with which she much preferred to decorate the overly plain, vinyl kitchen floor.

It had been six weeks since the Jarly had abruptly departed from James and Julia's wedding. Though Amadeus had insisted that it was simply protocol and time for them to leave, it felt like a lie to Emily. Something else was definitely going on.

"The Jarly, the attack of that building, the rescue…" She stopped and smirked, as Sophie finally swallowed the last spoonful, with a satisfied look on her face. "Don't you think it was odd? We went through so much with them. Accomplished so much together, supposedly for a brighter future, and now all we get is interview requests from gossip magazines and the occasional paparazzi." Pointing at a large stack of white and cream-colored papers at the end of the table, currently being held down by a Sponge Bob doll, she said, "It's just starting to feel less and less real to me. Like one of these days, I'll wake up and be in our old bed. Sophie won't be born, and Amy will still be nagging me about what shoes I plan to wear to her wedding."

Mark smirked, lifting Sophie from her highchair, then walking over to a corner of the living room, which was surrounded by fluffy and brightly cultured toys. He kissed her crown, as she became enthralled by her Barbie in a rainbow dress, and swatted away her father's affection. Emily arose from the table, placing her dish and mug in the sink.

Hugging Emily from behind, Mark brushed his lips from her temple and down her neck, gently tugging the back of her robe to reveal more warm skin. Inhaling deeply, he whispered, "Baby, if none of this is real, if nothing happened, could I do this?" He reached around and grabbed the side of her mug. With a small flash of light, it reformed and rejuvenated until the angry crack began to fade, and the mug looked good as new.

Emily laughed in a single huff. "I don't think that's what Amadeus had in mind, when they gave us these abilities."

Mark rolled his eyes, slowly turning Emily around in his embrace. Gently, he brushed her cheek with the pad of his thumb. "What's this all about? A couple weeks ago you couldn't stop talking about them – what they had done for us – that we needed them."

"Yes, well the lack of news and appearances has made me question what is really going on."

Sophie's overjoyed wail turned their heads. There, standing on the edge of the living room, were Riley and Selene. Riley bent then arose with Sophie in his arms and a wide, toothy smile on his face. Mark returned their welcoming gesture.

"Ears burning?" he asked, with an accusatory, yet joking tone. "See," he whispered, so only his frowning wife could hear.

Riley and Selene glanced at each other, matching right brows raised. "Miss us?" They finally joined Mark and Emily in the kitchen.

Emily hugged Selene. "Just a little," she said with a grin.

"Would you like a drink?"

"Please, sit." Mark gestured towards the dark leather couch behind them.

"Actually, this isn't a simple visit," Riley remarked, all attention on the giggling baby in his arms.

"Oh?" Mark reached for Sophie and Riley returned her without as much as a blink.

"Amadeus has called a meeting and has asked that you be there as well." Selene lightly brushed Sophie's bare feet, before turning to Emily. "He has requested that the six of you accompany Earth's ambassadors." She paused, clearly wanting to say more, but simply added, "He trusts you."

"The six of us?" Mark emphasized the word six.

"We will explain more, soon. The meeting starts shortly, can you come now?" Riley appeared to be getting antsy, though he hid it well. He noticed Emily's accusative stare, then he let out an exasperated breath, his shoulders relaxing, as he covered his left earlobe. "Sorry, I'm getting a constant transmission from the station and the conversation is getting out of hand. Anyway..." He focused back on the couple. "Are you available?"

Before the words had even resonated, the word "sure" was out of Emily's mouth, and the scenery had changed.

"Good." Riley grabbed the back of a plush desk chair, and directed Mark to sit. Selene and Riley smirked, as they glanced around, confused at their new surroundings. A large, brightly lit room had taken over their living room. Twelve matching black chairs surrounded a large oval table. The only decoration appeared to be an overblown aerial view of the entire globe on the right side of the room, and on the left, a similar landscape. However, the landmasses were oddly shaped and much larger.

"Nona." Selene answered their unspoken questions. She took three long strides and pointed to a red patch on the top, right hand side of the map. "That's Meanip, the city where Amelia and I were born."

Mark examined the map more closely, as Emily scanned the room. Bare would be her first assessment. "This is where we are meeting?"

Selene looked as if she was about to answer, but two bright lights appeared at the other end of the room, as Damon and Caleb transported Amy and Rick. Amelia and Isobel arrived seconds later, with Julia tightly clutching the hand of James. It was only now that Emily noticed they were all wearing solid-black. Amelia wore an exquisite lace blouse, but it was still equally black. Emily loved how calm she felt when in their company.

The silent awe of the room was broken by Sophie's giggles and frequent hand clapping.

"Em?" Amy looked half asleep, as she made her way around the large table and into the arms of her sister.

"Oh right, it's only nine a.m. You must have been in bed still," Emily sarcastically stated, as she engulfed her sister is a large bear hug.

"Shut up! We had a late night." A small yawn completed her sentence.

One by one they greeted each other. It hadn't been easy to get together since the world had become so interested in their every-day lives. Emily shuddered every time she saw the latest titles on the odd magazine, usually referencing some form of conspiracy, alien heritage, or their new nicknames as, "The Chosen Ones." Sophie loved it whenever James was near, he always used his light to play and entertain.

"Please have a seat." Amelia gestured towards the table after her final embrace of Mark. "Amadeus will be joining us shortly."

"You could have given us a minute to get changed." Mark glanced around the room at the barely decent group.

Riley shrugged. "You're clothed, aren't you?" He grinned at their disheveled appearances, rolling his eyes. " Here." With a wave of his hand, the room filled with light again. A slight tugging on their clothing faded along with the light, revealing their individual clothing had been replaced with matching grey shirts and black slacks.

"How?" Rick tugged at the cotton shirt.

"Hey, I liked that camisole," Julia began to complain.

"Relax, your clothes were sent home," Riley said, now thrumming his fingers along the tabletop.

"Is there anything you guys can't do?" James asked, noting that they were all still barefoot.

"Hmm, can't hold my breath for very long." Riley mocked the question, scratching his chin with his index finger.

Selene cleared her throat. "Emily, I think it would be better if Sophie left the room. We will be covering some graphic topics and it's no place for a child." Emily glanced over Mark, as Selene reached for Sophie. He gave her a reassuring smile and quick nod.

"I won't let her out of my sight." Selene winked, as Sophie willingly went into her open arms.

A door just behind them silently swept open, as Selene whispered in her best baby voice that they had a large selection of toys on board, and took Sophie out. Emily nervously watched the door close behind them. Mark took her left hand, gently squeezing, bringing Emily's attention back to the table.

"So, why are we here?" Mark asked Amelia, directly.

"Need us to beat up some more people?" James asked, almost comically. "I'm ready for Round Two." He cracked his knuckles loudly, stretching his neck from side to side, and smirking as Julia elbowed him in the ribs.

"Thanks, but that won't be necessary this time." Isobel chimed in, with humor.

"We have asked the six of you here today, as we have agreed to your government's requests to view our space-station and report back to their leaders."

The mood in the room took a nosedive into the Arctic waters. "Are you sure that's such a good idea? Giving them access to everything?" Rick blurted, before anyone else could comment. "I mean, let's face it, they weren't very sensitive the last time you tried to show them what you're capable of."

"And that is why Amadeus has asked you to join the team. He is only allowing a few representatives on board, at a time." Amelia pointed to the table, which distracted the group.

"On board?" Rick asked, as realization hit. "Here?" He pointed down in general. "Are we..."

"Yes, this is our space-station."

Two illuminated fingers waved at the wall to Amelia's right. The map of Earth slowly faded, replaced by a starry night sky. "Please." Amelia got to her feet, encouraging the others to join her along the wall. A strange light covered the bottom, flickering majestically. As Amy reached the window and looked down, a sudden gasp escaped her lips and she covered her mouth, staring wildly.

Not so much a wall, but a solid window, kept back the invading space. Emily grasped Mark's shoulder, as the group looked down at the tranquil Earth, spinning softly below them.

"Is that..." Julia started.

"Earth," Riley interrupted, staring blankly out the window. He blinked a few times, then turned, focusing on Julia. "We're twelve thousand miles above the surface, to be exact."

Amelia made her way back to her seat at the end of the table. "As I was saying, Amadeus has asked that you accompany the teams that will be shown around the base. Just keep an eye out. Make sure that nothing goes wrong. You are fortunate to have your own light, while having the human emotions and correct reactions to the new surroundings."

"We just want to make sure everyone is comfortable, while watching for any mischief," Riley added. "There is a reason why we waited so long to allow human evaluation and review of our technology."

"We understand," Rick stated, after silent thought. " But seriously, you guys must know they're going to be up to something?"

Without another word, everyone slowly made his or her way back to the chairs, some fidgeting uncontrollably, while others seemed to stare off into space. Riley and Amelia suddenly cupped their left ears and listened to an unseen transmission, as if they were answering a call. The others simply stared in silent confusion. Eventually, Amelia nodded, and then they both lowered their hands. Apart from Amelia, the Jarly suddenly stood in a formal line along the edge of the glass, at ease with the apparent lack of protection. Emily couldn't help but feel a pinch in her stomach, as the glass could not have been thicker than an inch or two.

Amelia steepled her hands on the table in front of her, as she spoke in a low and calming voice. "The others will be joining us shortly. Please, follow our cues. We only ask that you observe the others and advise if something doesn't feel right. As part of your initial light transfer, you are able to communicate speechlessly with one another."

The seated group all looked around in shock.

Isobel wordlessly drew Emily's attention to where she was standing at the glass wall.

"How d..."

Isobel shushed her with a single finger to the lips. *It's best if we communicate this way. There's no need to create alarm.* Isobel didn't even make eye contact, as she scanned the room.

"As I was saying..." Amelia drew their attention back to the

table. The shocked and excited faces around the room, indicated that Isobel and Emily's telepathic conversation was not the
only one.

"Wait." Mark lightly smacked the table with a confused look
on his face. "If you can communicate like this, why didn't you tell
us about this before? We could have used the extra encouragement and g..." Mark stopped abruptly, as he listened to whatever
Riley was advising him.

"Mark," Amelia calmly called his attention to her. "As we had
explained, we were only allowed limited influence and assistance.
Please believe me when I say we wish there was more we could
have done, but I must repeat one of your human expressions." Her
eyes widened and her face contorted in sympathy. "Our hands
were tied. There is much more about us that you are still unaware
of, and with time you will learn much more. Beginning today, I
would imagine."

Only Emily was accustomed to the expression on Mark's face.
To everyone else, he would have appeared to be placated and
quiet, as he nodded and looked away, but under that skin there
was frustration and anger brewing. Reaching over, she returned
his reassuring squeeze, brushing her thumb over his rough skin.
Instantly, as their eyes met, his shoulders began to relax and he
took a deep breath.

Amelia touched her ear again, quickly, then gestured to the
others. Before anyone could ask, she silently stood and watched
the empty space at the end of the room. As all eyes turned, a beam
of light flashed, and within seconds Amadeus, and three large
Jarly soldiers, materialized, accompanied by at least ten humans.
Four women in military-style uniform, in various colors, were
scattered within the group of men, two of whom looked as if they
were on the verge of throwing up. Some whispers suggested a
Russian background; a few others were clearly North Korean, and

Japanese. The majority of the group appeared to speak with muttered American and British accents.

Here we go, Isobel muttered, for only Emily to hear...which made her grin and Mark look confused.

The group beamed, as Amadeus stepped forward. "Friends," he said. Previous frustration seemed to simmer, as his smile grew with sincerity. "I thank you, for joining us."

As he continued, a brooding American, with a strong Texan accent, rudely interrupted him. His long crooked nose and large bushy brows gave him a severe expression. "What are they doing here?" he spat with blatant outrage. "This is not a civilian mission; they do not have the clearance or approval."

Amadeus stopped his rant with a simple raise of his hand. "General Clay, these men and women have every right to be at this meeting. They know our kind better than any. We have a history and shared abilities. If their presence upsets you, I will be more than happy to escort you back to your base and continue our tour with them, alone." His comment, though in response to Clay, was clearly addressing the whole group. His voice appeared calm and collected, but even the broody Texan took an unsteady step back. It was easy to see why Amadeus was in charge.

Amy's girlish snicker and glance towards a smirking Amelia suggested an unspoken joke or snide remark.

Obviously chastised, the general mumbled something to his subordinates, and then grumbled directly to Amadeus, "Please, continue."

Amadeus turned towards the table. "If you'd follow me?" He gestured to the door, which was being opened by another of the unnamed Jarly guards.

Who are they? Emily glanced, one by one, at each and every official, who insisted on exiting the room before her family and friends.

Isobel was silent and Emily glanced at her from the corner of her eyes.

These are the selected representatives of your planet. You didn't think we were only contacting Americans, did you? She caught Emily's eye and gave her a knowing smirk. *After your team had successfully proven your place among our people, we called various meetings with our old contacts, much like Thomas, which led to more prominent leaders of Earth and we arranged this. A number of nations have chosen to either have the Americans research, on their behalves, or to avoid us all together. We knew the early stages of awareness of us would not be an easy one.*

She continued, as everyone filed down a long narrow corridor. Everything was extremely bright and clinically clean. Very little color covered any of the walls and high ceilings. After two rights and a left, a heavy metallic wall, easily wide enough to fit three people width-wide, at once, confronted the group.

"The first room we are going to show you is our communications." Amelia took the lead. A previously invisible line split the door in two, and with a sudden swoosh, the room was accessible.

Hundreds of blinking screens covered almost every surface of the room. Four Jarly jumped, standing, to Amadeus's attention. With a single nod, one stepped forward to describe the purpose and functionality of the room. Emily noted that only the women appeared to be writing anything down, and furiously fast at that. As the Jarly, who introduced himself as Trick, finished his speech, the room was slowly depleted of prying eyes, when everyone continued to the next room.

So far, little had truly interested Emily's group, as much as it should have. They had been guided though the information deck, the lunchrooms, sleeping quarters, and additional bathing and recreation rooms. Mark, for obvious reasons, had much more interest in their medical bay, while Rick and James couldn't contain their excitement for the fitness and rejuvenation areas.

As the group entered the next room, they found the walls were shiny and highly reflective. As a short, dark-skinned man, with a severe limp in his left leg, stepped forward to ask Amelia what this room was used for, the room itself appeared to move and descend in a slow rotating motion. It was the closest thing to an elevator the ship could command. Every once in a while, a man or woman would lazily walk onto the platform and exit out of the opening spaces, as each floor became visible. Emily watched with fascination, noting at least eight different floors before they were slowly ushered off. This floor was darker than the others; the space was all but deserted.

So, they're all scientists? Emily continued, with Isobel.

Most of them, yes. A few are men of power, who insisted that they had to see this first hand, before they would allow others to do so. General Clay, for instance, only cares about a few key components of our weaponry and defensive capabilities. Isobel clearly rolled her eyes, then was distracted by something Riley whispered.

A frisson of frustration crossed her features, as she bit down on her lip and glanced at Emily, who was clearly confused. *It would appear that a few members of this group have already tried placing a few devices along our controls and are attempting to gain access to our systems.*

Anger spiked within Emily. *Why would they even attempt such secrecy and deception, when all this information is being given up willingly?*

Don't fret, we have already scanned and immobilized their devices. This will all be addressed at the end of the tour. Isobel continued walking past Emily, to the front of the line.

They all stopped at the end of a wide hallway. Another set of doors, three times as large as the last, concealed the room ahead. The hallway was so dark, at this point, that Emily was only able to see Mark to her right and Amy to her left. The others were faint outlines.

As she engaged her inner light, Isobel's flames consumed her legs, illuminating her features. Mesmerizing the group, before clearing her throat, she spoke loudly and clearly. "Ladies and gentlemen, we are about to enter one of the most important rooms on this station." The entire group seemed to lean forward, listening more intensely. "As the medical lead on this base, I must advise, do not touch anything. Please, stay together. There will be points where we will be able to answer any questions you may have. You will notice that the room is significantly louder, and may seem unstable. Rest assured, you are in no danger, if you stick together and follow my rules." She glanced at Caleb, and he again took the lead.

With a nod to his brother, Caleb and Damon both raised their lit arms, commanding the heavy doors to open. A sudden gust of wind and heavy air shot a shiver down Emily's spine. Amy gripped her left hand, as she leant into Mark, who wrapped his arm protectively around her shoulders. Slowly, the doors slid away to reveal a blackened room, illuminated by a shimmering, blue orb. Almost everyone's jaws fell, as they took in the view. The orb was easily ten stories tall and equally as wide. It sat on a narrow metallic stand. The wind whipped violently through their hair, as Emily tucked herself more tightly under Mark's shoulder, gripping his opposite hip from behind. His lips were moving, but the noise was so overwhelming, she could only nod and continue to glance around the room.

Something small and disc-shaped fell out of the pocket of the scientist in front of Emily. Glancing down, she noticed what appeared to be a small flashing light and rotating camera. This must have been what Isobel had been telling her about. It was no accident that this is where the scanner had dropped.

"This way," Isobel summoned the group. She was not yelling, but somehow everyone was able to ear her clearly. To the left, there was a glass room and the others in front of Emily appeared to be excited, pushing forward. Instead of purposefully stepping over the device at her feet, Emily raised her bent leg high, slamming in down on it, crushing it under her heel.

Got one, for ya!

Isobel grinned at Emily's enthusiasm. Gradually, the room was filled and the doors closed behind them. The noise of the room all but disappeared, fading to a light, buzzing sound.

"This is our core." Caleb gestured to the orb behind him, "This device powers the station, and all our technologies. It can be created in a number of sizes, to manipulate the smallest of devices." As he finished, a serpent-like spiral of blue shimmerlight traveled in a wide circle at the center of the orb.

"What was that?" The question escaped the lips of a cowering Japanese scientist, before the others apparently scolded her.

"Please," Caleb encouraged her, with a toothy smile. "Now is the time for questions." He winked at the embarrassed women. "That was Calobie, an essence of our home world, Nona. A chemical reaction, with a number of living and non-living components and elements, drives to create a form of energy. Calobie is a form of living material that, in essence, sparks the other compounds and continually rejuvenates the system."

"What specific materials make up this reactor, then?" A whitehaired, pointy-nosed man, with a thick British accent, interrupted.

"Obviously, there are a number of elements only found on Nona and localized planets. Along with Sulphate, Magnesium, Calcium, Potassium..." Caleb continued naming at least thirteen different elements. "But the main Earthly equivalent would be water-diluted, Sodium Chloride."

A few of the scientists glanced nervously at one another, and even Mark stiffened.

"What?" Emily whispered.

Mark turned to Riley, who silently nodded, then looked down at his wife. "Em, everything they need to power all this technology, makes up over seventy percent of Earth's surface."

It was as if a light bulb went off, exploding uncomfortably in Emily's skull. " Ocean? Sea water, can do all this?"

Mark was clearly distracted by his own thoughts; he simply pulled her closer, kissing her temple, as they both turned to witness another passing of Calobie.

ABOUT THE AUTHOR

Lauren Somerton

Born in Southampton, England, Lauren Somerton grew up with a close-knit family, which she still cherishes and relies on, to this day. At the age of ten, her parents decided to provide Lauren and her brother with a better future and more opportunity by immigrating to Calgary, Alberta,  Canada. Her mother, Charmaine, has always encouraged Lauren to read and explore her creativity through writing.

After grade school, she chose to pursue an education in cultural studies and ancient history, which led to a Bachelors Degree from Mount Royal University, in Anthropology. Throughout her studies she got to dive into research, further fulfilling her curiosity and sparking ideas for future epics. Writing has always been a source of relaxation and intrigue for Lauren, who would provide short stories to friends and family, or spend mornings reliving every small detail of the vivid dreams of the night before.

CPSIA information can be obtained at www.ICGtesting.com
Printed in the USA
LVOW07s0301020316

477376LV00001B/44/P